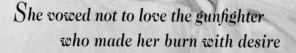

*She vowed not to love the gunfighter
who made her burn with desire*

"I THOUGHT YOU WANTED TO STAY WARM," THE STRANGER SAID.

"Taking off my clothes doesn't seem like the way to do that!" Maura replied.

He seized her then, and pulled her close. "Trust me—it works."

For a moment she was dizzy with the nearness of him. "I don't even know your name."

There was a heartbeat of silence. Then he spoke flatly. "It's Lassiter."

"Not . . . *Quinn* Lassiter?" she asked in a trembling voice.

"The same. You think I'm going to shoot you?"

"Of course not." She glanced up at him from beneath her lashes. "You wouldn't, would you?"

"No. Never." He cupped her chin in his hand and forced her to meet his eyes. "I'm going to make love to you, angel. Real nice, hot, hang-on-to-your-hat love. If you want me to, that is. I'll keep you warm all night long. Fact is, I'll make you sweat. I'll even make you burn. And you won't need clothes, and you won't need fires." He slid a hand slowly, languidly, down her bare arm and Maura shivered. "That's a promise."

Dell Books by Jill Gregory

Always You
Cherished
Cold Night, Warm Stranger
Daisies in the Wind
Forever After
Just This Once
Never Love a Cowboy
When the Heart Beckons

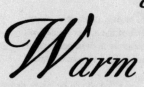

Cold Night, Warm Stranger

Jill Gregory

A Dell Book

Published by
Dell Publishing
a division of
Random House, Inc.
1540 Broadway
New York, New York 10036

ISBN: 0-440-22440-3

Printed in the United States of America
Published simultaneously in Canada
August 1999
10 9 8 7 6 5 4 3 2 1
OPM

To Maggie Crawford
Maggie, thanks for everything!
This one's for you!

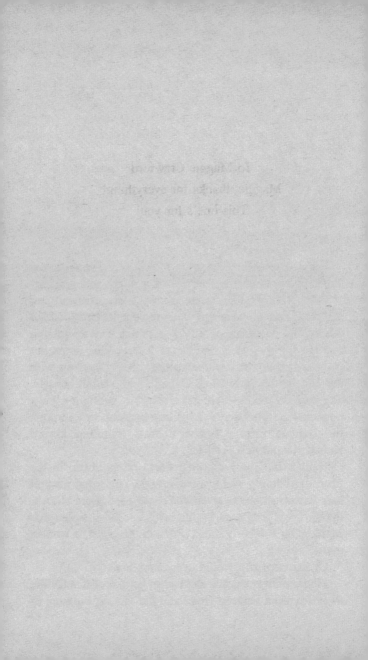

Chapter 1

ON THAT SAVAGE JANUARY NIGHT WHEN SNOW engulfed the Rockies in a raging blur of glittering white, when the wild creatures hid and shivered, and no one stirred in the tiny, dirty town of Knotsville, Montana, Maura Jane Reed had no inkling that her life was about to change forever. She drank her tea and shivered in her thick blue robe, struggling with the bone-numbing loneliness she had known all her life. She had no inkling that miles away, a gunfighter on a horse named Thunder was fighting his lone way through the blizzard, across Looper's Pass, barreling toward Knotsville and into her life.

Neither did she know that thirty miles north, in the town of Hatchett where a high-stakes poker tournament had drawn gamblers, adventurers, and fools from all over the territory, a fortune in diamonds had been stolen that same night, a killer gunned down in the street, a woman murdered.

Or that any of it would ever touch her.

Maura only knew that she had to get out of Knotsville, away from the Duncan Hotel and the vicious bullying of her adoptive brothers, and build a decent life for herself. She was twenty-four years old and had never gone to a dance, owned a new dress, spoken aloud without giving careful thought to each word, or kissed a man.

Come spring, she thought, hugging her arms around herself, trying to ward off the chill that threatened to permeate her bones, *I'll find a way to get out of here—I'll go someplace where Judd and Homer can never find me. Never hurt me—or anyone else I know or care about.*

Shivering, she peered again through the window of the hotel kitchen, mesmerized by the whirling sea of white. Even Willy Peachtree, the wizened old-timer who helped her run the place while Judd and Homer caroused, hadn't made it over from the saloon since the snow had begun in earnest.

"Maybe it will never stop," she mused as she set her cup down on the table. She tucked a strand of auburn hair behind her ear and pondered the great drifts of snow enveloping every dark, grimy inch of Knotsville's Main Street. Even wrapped in the bulky robe, with long johns and a flannel nightshirt underneath, she felt halfway frozen. The blizzard had begun three days ago and showed no signs of abating.

At this rate, it might be days before Judd and Homer returned.

The thought cheered her.

She was lonely, but not for her adoptive brothers.

A deeper, more painful loneliness assailed Maura. As she left the kitchen, hands cradling the cup of tea, padding in thick socks across the small square hotel dining room and toward the lobby stairs, she felt as if she were the only inhabitant left in Knotsville—there was no one staying in the hotel and more than half the town had gone to Hatchett just like Judd and Homer to partake in the festivities of the poker tournament, which was to draw gamblers from across the East and West. She hadn't seen another soul in days, not since the blizzard started.

But it wasn't anyone in Knotsville she was lonely for either. Thanks to Judd and Homer, no one dared befriend her or get too close. The one time someone had tried . . .

Her blood congealed at the memory of what had happened to the new young cowpoke at the Hendricks's spread who had invited her on a picnic when she was seventeen. His name had been Bobby Watson. He'd been beaten, stomped, and run off before he had a chance to collect his first week's pay.

And then there had been the young doctor passing through town on his way to Nebraska only last year. He had dared invite her to sit down at his table with him in the dining room, to talk and share a meal.

When Judd and Homer had finished with him, he'd been a bloody pulp thrown onto the morning stage.

She leaned her forehead against her palms at the memory and took deep breaths. And forced her thoughts away from the terrible images of her adoptive brothers' handiwork.

Somewhere, someplace there was a man Judd and Homer couldn't beat, stab, shoot, or hurt. Someone who couldn't be frightened off or driven away, who wouldn't be left scarred for life, or half dead because he'd dared to be nice to her.

And somewhere, someplace there was more to living than this dreary cycle of endlessly scouring the hotel, washing and pressing bed linens, sweeping floors, cooking meals for guests and for Judd and Homer.

There has to be more to life than this, Maura told herself grimly as she reached the lobby, where a single candle burned in a wall sconce.

Somewhere, there was someone who would care if she felt cold or lonely.

But she wouldn't find him—or whatever she was searching for—here in Knotsville. The Duncan boys would see to that.

She had to leave—and soon. Before she turned into the same kind of dreary, dried-up broomstick of a woman that Ma Duncan had become, especially in the months before she died, the months Maura had nursed her and had wondered if the poor, miserable woman had ever known anything of happiness in her entire life.

I'm going to be happy, Maura told herself as she reached the staircase. *Maybe I'll go to San Francisco and open a dress shop—sew dresses for rich ladies, and have my own carriage, and my own snug little house with a rug from Turkey and a Chinese vase on the mantel and shelves full of books and a hearth in every room. Or I'll go east—to Boston or New York—and I'll meet an educated man in the park, a professor or a doctor, and we'll drink tea together and discuss books and go to plays or perhaps the opera . . .*

The front door of the hotel burst open. Maura gasped and whirled back from the stairway, spilling her tea as an icy gust of snow and wind whipped at her. She gave a strangled scream as a snow-draped giant of a man hurtled across the threshold and into the lobby with the force of a norther.

He kicked the door shut behind him.

"Hell of a night."

His eyes flickered over Maura, bundled in her many layers, her hair wild and loose about her shoulders, the scream still dying on her lips.

His cold gray gaze narrowed. He advanced on her, snow dripping from the broad brim of his black Stetson and melting from his great black boots onto the floor. "Lady, I'm warning you. I'm a damn sight too tired to pick you up, so if you faint, you're going to stay right where you drop. Got that?"

Chapter 2

"I'M NOT . . . GOING TO FAINT. I NEVER FAINT."
The man's eyes flickered over her, quick as a hawk scanning a baby field mouse. "Then get moving," he said. "I want a room. But first a hot meal and a bottle of whiskey. Think you can handle that?"

She nodded. Her voice seemed to have disappeared. For a moment she could only stare at the tall, black-haired stranger who had blown in out of the night.

With eyes paler, grayer, and icier than sleet, he stared back.

He was a stranger—a dark-and-dangerous-as-the-devil kind of stranger. He wore a long black duster draped with snow. From his black hat to his black boots he dripped with snow. But something else clung to him besides snow and ice. Power and menace. It emanated from him. His face was hard and handsome, all strong planes and harsh angles, with a ruthless jaw, and those commanding ice-gray eyes beneath slashing dark brows. His mouth was a thin line, uncompromising, lacking any trace of humor or softness, as hard and no-nonsense as the rest of him.

A gunfighter, Maura guessed. Fear, mixed with a kind

of mesmerized fascination, quivered through her. They'd had gunfighters pass through before, but no one ever quite as intimidating as this man.

He looked like he could gobble her whole for dinner and casually spit out the bones.

"What's the problem, lady?" he growled, his gaze locked on her face. "Don't you have a free room?"

She found her voice, what was left of it. "Yes, sir, I've a room. Eight of them, as a matter of fact—all empty. You may have your pick—there's no one in the whole place except you and me."

His expression never changed, except for an almost imperceptible lifting of his brows.

Maura's cheeks whitened. What an idiot she was. Why on earth had she told him that she was alone? What if he . . . if he . . .

If he what? she asked herself. *If he decided to try to take advantage of you?*

She had a feeling that even if there *was* someone else there, nothing would stop him from "taking advantage of her" if he had a mind to. He had the look of a man who took what he wanted, when he wanted, and Lord help anyone who stood in his way.

It was doubtful, she reflected with a tiny shock, that even Judd and Homer would be able to stand in his way.

But she also realized something else after that first flash of alarm. For all his dangerous air, he really didn't look like the kind of man who would harm a woman. There was no cruelty in his face—only toughness, and the kind of dark, scowling handsomeness that would have women throwing themselves at him right and left. She had no doubt that he could have his pick of women, as many as he liked.

And suddenly intensely aware of her thick robe, wool-stockinged feet, long johns, and flannel nightgown, Maura was absolutely certain she looked nothing like the kind of woman he would want. Not that she would even if she were dressed up in her Sunday best. Ma Duncan had told her once that she was pretty, but she knew that couldn't be true. She was too tall, too slim, too small-breasted. Too quiet and tongue-tied. Perhaps if her eyes were vivid green instead of plain brown, if her hair weren't a simple boring red but was instead the romantic color of copper. If her lower lip wasn't so wide and was shaped more like a tiny perfect rosebud . . .

But it wasn't. She wasn't. And he was already looking past her into the gloom of the dining room. ''I'll have a steak, mashed potatoes, and pie,'' he said curtly as he strode past her.

When he reached the table in the corner, he tossed his bedroll down against the wall, pulled out a chair, and sat with his back to the wall.

Maura hurried after him. She should tell him that the kitchen was closed. Breakfast would be served at sunup. Not a moment sooner.

But she didn't. She couldn't. Beneath the hard set of his face, he looked tired. And hungry.

How had he ever made it through the blizzard? she wondered. And where had he come from?

But before she could ask him, he spoke again.

''Whiskey.'' He pushed his hat back and closed his eyes. ''Bring that first.''

''All I have in the kitchen right now is some beef stew

with carrots and potatoes. And a chocolate cake,'' Maura peeped at him nervously. ''Will that be all right?''

He did open his eyes and look at her then, a long, narrow-eyed look that had probably brought hardened outlaws to their knees. Maura's heart pounded harder in her chest, but she managed to keep her gaze steady on his.

''It'll do,'' he grunted after what seemed like an endless silence. ''Did you say you're all alone here?''

''Y-yes.''

''Who the hell would leave a girl all alone in a place like this?'' he growled in irritation.

Maura's shoulders relaxed. He wasn't going to shoot her because she didn't have any steak. He wasn't going to rape her because she was all alone. ''Actually,'' she confided quietly, with a small, shy smile, ''I don't mind at all. I like being alone sometimes.''

He leaned back in the chair, stretching his long legs out before him. His eyes closed, dismissing her. ''Whiskey. Fast.''

With as much dignity and speed as she could manage in her robe, Maura turned away and made for the kitchen.

When she brought him the bottle of whiskey and a glass, he didn't even glance at her, just took it and poured himself a good dollop of liquor. He gulped it down in one long swig.

Maura returned to the kitchen as he poured himself some more.

But as she took down plates and utensils from the shelf, and set the stew to heating on the stove, and sliced up some of the morning's corn bread, she couldn't forget the expression on the stranger's face. He looked like a man intent on getting drunk, not for fun, not with relish, but with desperation. As if he were running from something. Or someone.

Except that man out there didn't seem like the kind who would ever run from anyone. Except perhaps . . . himself.

Maura burned her fingers on the stewpot and nearly dropped it, but slid it onto the countertop just in time. She stuck her fingers in her mouth, and decided she'd best concentrate on what she was doing and forget about that stranger out there. Judd and Homer always told her she spent too much time thinking and not enough doing. Which was almost laughable since she spent every minute of her life running this hotel, working, cleaning, cooking, while they spent the better part of their days and nights in the saloon, playing either faro or poker, drinking, or getting into fights. But she knew they had always been contemptuous of her love of books and ideas, and jealous of the praise their mother, a former schoolteacher, had heaped on her for her good marks in school. The only thing Judd and Homer had ever learned in school was how to torment the teacher, poor frazzled Miss Lansdown, with dead mice in her desk drawer, snakes under her chair, spiders dropped down the back of her neck.

If the boys were here, they'd waste no time in reminding her that the stranger out there was none of her business. Running the hotel was.

The stranger seemed to be asleep in his chair when she brought out the tray of food. His hat hid his handsome face.

"Here's your dinner, sir." She set down the heavy tray and began setting out the plates. She noticed that almost half the whiskey was gone from the bottle. He tossed his hat onto an empty chair and surveyed the food.

"Much obliged." Picking up his spoon, he tasted the stew. Without comment, he began to eat.

"Is everything . . . all right?"

"Just fine. Much obliged," he repeated, continuing to take spoonful after spoonful as she continued to stand and stare at him.

She couldn't seem to take her eyes off his face. He needed a shave, Maura thought—though that wouldn't make him look any more handsome. Staring at his strong-jawed countenance, intriguingly shadowed with a dark growth of beard, she could only conclude that he was already handsomer than any man had a right to be.

He ate quickly, hungrily but not sloppily, she noted with approval. Not like Judd, who chewed with his mouth open, or Homer, who used his fingers more times than not.

The stew was gone. All of the potatoes, all of the meat, all of the carrots—gone. So was the corn bread. He reached for the plate of chocolate cake.

Then suddenly he seemed to remember that she was still there.

"You want something?"

His eyes were so cold that Maura shivered as they touched her.

"No . . . no. I was just wondering. Did you ride far?"

"Far enough."

"How did you get through? I mean, the snow . . . it must have been difficult."

"I've seen worse."

"Um . . . do you have business in Knotsville or are you just passing through?"

He set down his fork. He leaned back slightly, enough to regard her again, staring at her so intently that Maura felt a blush stealing into her cheeks. "You always talk this much?"

The blush grew hotter. "No. As a matter of fact, I hardly ever talk at all—at least not to anyone except myself." She rushed on, "But my brothers have been gone for days and I haven't really seen another soul and . . ." Her voice trailed away as she saw him give his head a shake and return his attention to the chocolate cake.

He thinks I'm a nuisance, she thought in dismay. *A silly, chattering ninny in long johns and stocking feet. A pest.*

"I beg your pardon." She scooped up the empty plates and hurried away.

At the kitchen doorway she paused and glanced back. He had finished the slice of cake, every crumb of it, and had poured more whiskey into his glass.

But it was the slump of his broad shoulders that caught her attention. And the haunted expression in his eyes. They'd lost their hard metallic gleam. Now, instead of looking cold and frightening, they just looked bleak.

He was scowling out into the distance, staring at nothing. But his features were taut, as if he was seeing an old nightmare unfolding before his eyes: something terrible, something far away yet dreadful enough to chill the soul and strike the heart with despair.

He looked alone, embittered, utterly drained.

Maura felt an almost irresistible urge sweep through her, an urge to run back to him, to lean down and wrap her arms around him, to kiss that strong bronzed jaw and tell him "there, there" as if he were a child.

It was absurd. She gave herself a shake as she forced her feet to proceed toward the kitchen.

But she couldn't erase that bleak expression from her mind.

Even as she washed up the dishes, even as she tidied the kitchen, she wondered what would make a man look so weary of life.

When she returned to the dining room for the plate of chocolate cake, that drained expression was still locked in place on the stranger's face. But the moment she approached the table where he was sitting, it vanished. His eyes hardened, his broad, powerful shoulders straightened, and the coldness was there again in every line of his implacable features.

He threw his napkin down on the empty plate and pushed back his chair.

"Is there anything else I can get for you?"

"A room. A bed. And I don't want to be disturbed before morning." His speech had become slightly slurred, and Maura guessed the liquor was taking its toll. But it wasn't affecting him as much as she would have expected, for his eyes were still as hard and piercing as ever, his movements steady as he stood up, brushed past her, and started toward his gear.

"If you'll follow me, I'll get the key and show you to your room. I thought you'd like 203. It's our best room." She gave him a tentative smile as he plopped his hat on his head and slung his bedroll over his shoulder.

"It has a fireplace. That will come in handy tonight. I

can't remember when it's been so cold. Or snowed so long. Can you?''

His only answer was a grunt.

Maura felt like a fool. Why couldn't she seem to stop chattering at the man? He was obviously not interested in making conversation. And she rarely spoke more than a few words at a time to anyone.

So why was she babbling so much tonight?

Perhaps, she thought, because she had so much bottled up inside her. Twenty-four years' worth of loneliness and it all seemed to be spilling out now.

Maybe it was the snowstorm, being cooped up almost all alone in Knotsville for days. Maybe it was something about this night that was so magically white and frosty, it made her want to warm herself with more than tea and toast—with conversation and companionship.

Well, she'd picked the worst possible person, she decided as she fumbled for the key on the peg behind the counter, and locked the money he had paid her in the metal box in the drawer. And he was obviously not at all interested in exchanging even the most basic pleasantries with her, she thought as she led the way up the narrow, uncarpeted stairs.

''There's wood in the box. I hope you'll be comfortable,'' she said primly as she fitted the key in the lock and pushed open the door.

He started past her, and Maura tried to ease out of the way of his large frame and that thick bedroll. But the liquor must have affected him, for he staggered and fell against her. She was knocked forward into the room, but he grabbed her shoulders just in time to keep her from tumbling to the floor. Strong hands held her steady.

At his touch, a blaze of heated sensations ran through her. It was so startlingly intense, Maura cried out.

He was watching her, his head bent toward her in concern. "Are you hurt?"

"No . . . no. I'm fine."

But she didn't feel fine. Something was happening to her. Something she couldn't explain. Warmth and weakness swam up from her knees. It radiated across her belly, then spread upward, enveloping her breasts in a searing heat. Then her hands began to shake.

Every nerve in her body was on fire.

This had never happened to her before.

It's the first time you've ever been this close to a man, she told herself dizzily. *That's all.*

Especially to a man like this one.

She noticed his eyes were still fastened upon her, studying her. The icy glint was gone. There was a flicker of warmth in his expression now, and suddenly his hands slid to her waist.

Their grip tightened and he stared down into her eyes.

For a moment, there was silence except for the wind roaring at the window. A deep, electric silence that sliced through the numbing cold of the night.

Then the stranger's hand lifted and he brushed a knuckle across her cheek.

"Sorry about that, angel."

She swallowed. "My name is Maura," she whispered.

"Pretty."

He touched her hair then, wrapping one of her auburn curls around his finger.

Maura Reed, you'd better get out of here right now,

she told herself, fighting panic. *Before this gunfighter gets any ideas. . . .*

But as she started to pull away, the hand still at her waist drew her against him.

"Don't go."

She stiffened.

"Stay with me, Maura."

"Wh-why?" she croaked out.

He smiled then. A slow, easy half-drunk smile that transformed his hard masculine features, softening them ever so slightly into vibrant warmth and making Maura's heart flip like a pancake on a hot griddle.

"Why?" he repeated, releasing her hair and slipping his hand around her nape with expert, practiced ease. "Honey—why not?"

She could think of a hundred reasons *why not,* but only managed to gasp out one. "I . . . have work to do. Chores. Cleaning up the k-kitchen."

"Now that sure doesn't sound like much fun."

"Life," Maura murmured, echoing what Ma Duncan had repeated many a time, "is not supposed to be fun."

The arm around her waist tightened. "Who says?"

She stared at him as her heart began to race. He was confusing her. Unsettling her. Affecting her in a way she'd never been affected before.

Heavens, why was she still here at all? If she didn't leave soon, and make it very plain that she meant what she said, he might get the wrong idea and then she'd be in real trouble. . . .

"If you'll excuse me, I'm sure you're ready to go to bed—"

"You got that right."

Hot color rushed into her cheeks and he grinned, pulling her even closer against him.

"Hell, Maura, you're even prettier when you blush."

"I'm not blushing . . . and I'm not pretty." She flushed deeper then, feeling the heat scorch her cheeks. "I think you'd best let me go right now!"

"Not pretty?" His eyes gleamed into hers, and she saw a flicker of surprise in their silver depths. She noticed with a rush of panic that instead of letting her go, he was now holding her tighter and closer than ever. The sensation left her feeling breathless. And warm. Some of the biting night cold ebbed as the strength and heat of him seemed to envelop her.

"Of course you're pretty." His voice was low and rough in the dimness of the room. "Didn't anyone ever tell you?"

"Ma Duncan told me—once. She said . . . oh, never mind! Just let me go!"

There was quiet for a moment as those hard eyes pinned her. "Is that what you really want?"

Say yes. Run away right now, lock yourself in your room and don't come out till sunup.

But Lord help her, some part of herself wanted to stay. To stay and be held like this, sweet-talked like this. To be near this fascinating, dangerous man, this rough-and-tumble stranger who was too handsome for words.

Go! a voice inside her shrieked. *Go right now before it's too late.*

"Maura," he said softly, his eyes boring into hers. "Won't you stay and keep me company for a spell?"

"That isn't possible." She shivered as the wind rattled

the windows and a frigid blast of air swept across the floorboards.

"It's going to be an awful cold night. On a night like this a man needs a little company. And so does a woman."

"N-not this woman."

"You sure about that?"

"Very sure." But staring into those gleaming silver eyes, she wasn't sure about anything. Her blood was pounding in her ears. He thought she was a woman who would stay in a hotel room, talking—no, *flirting*—with a complete stranger. Perhaps he even thought she would climb into that bed with him and let him make love to her! She had to get out of here, and fast. Why had she stayed this long with a man like him, someone dangerous, bold, and altogether too good-looking?

Maybe because most of the girls she'd gone to school with years ago were married now, with husbands and homes and babies of their own. And she'd never even been courted, never even had her hand held—much less been kissed.

Maybe because she was curious—and lonely—and cold. And nothing exciting or wonderful or the least bit romantic had ever happened to her before—until tonight when this forceful stranger had burst through her door and awakened every drowsing feminine nerve in her body.

The wind screamed again at the window like a wild thing dying and a deeper chill swept through the room. It whistled beneath the cracks of the shutters, piercing her very bones, and Maura trembled from head to toe.

"I'll build a fire," he said roughly, his mouth against

her hair. "You'll be warm. And," he added, with a short hard laugh, "I promise not to bite."

Warm. She so wanted to be warm. And held, held tight. Just this once.

"I suppose it wouldn't hurt to stay—for a little while." She took a deep breath as he began drawing her farther into the room. "But if you bite," she told him with a tentative little smile, "I'll leave at once."

"Deal," he said with a smile, then kicked the door closed behind him and dumped his bedroll on the floor, followed immediately by the long duster he'd worn all through dinner.

"Believe me, sweetheart, I'm gentle as a lamb. You're perfectly safe."

But she had never felt less safe. He looked formidably big and strong in the heavy flannel shirt, dark pants, and boots that encased his powerful body. She didn't know what to do, what to expect, and was relieved when he turned from her and hefted a log from the wood box, tossing it onto the hearth as if it weighed no more than a pin.

"Not much wood left."

"There's a little left outside in the shed. We're running low, but I can get some more . . ."

"In this cold?" His back to her, he put a match to tinder and a tiny golden flame soared. "Not on your life. You're staying right here. We'll find a way to keep warm. Somehow."

She wasn't sure about the sound of that. For a moment Maura was tempted to run. Glancing around the darkened room she had cleaned and swept and aired for years, she saw it tonight as if for the first time: the wide feather bed with its pink and yellow handmade quilt, the oil lamp and china pitcher on top of the nightstand, the rag rug on the floor, the ladder-backed chair with its embroidered cushion, and the shutters with their chipped green paint, bolted fast against the wild night.

What was she doing here, with this stranger?

She hurried to the lamp, intending to light it, hoping to dispel the intimate atmosphere, but the stranger's deep voice stopped her.

"Don't trouble yourself, angel. The firelight's enough to see by."

Golden flames the color of a summer sunset danced out behind him even as he spoke. He moved away from the hearth, advancing toward her with measured steps. She caught her breath at the imposing size of him, the lean, dark face and cool, watchful eyes.

"We don't need to see much, do we, angel? Only each other."

Panic struck then. This was madness, this crazy little game she was playing. He didn't want company—he wanted to make love with her! She wasn't actually going to let this man, this *stranger,* take her to bed!

She didn't know him, not even his name. There was nothing between them, she was a virgin, she was afraid, she was a fool, and it was wrong . . . *wrong* . . .

Maura was light and quick on her feet, but he was quicker. She darted for the door, but he blocked her path before she had gone two steps. His hands dropped onto her shoulders, heavily.

"Spooked you, didn't I?" As her eyes widened, bright with fear, he lifted one big hand and brushed it across her cheek. "Calm down, honey, there's nothing to be scared of."

"I'm not scared." But she was. And they both knew it.

He stroked her hair, his fingers winding gently through the vibrant red curls. The warmth and gentleness of the simple touch set off a wave of yearning inside her. His touch was so heartbreakingly gentle for a man of such powerful proportions—and the expression in his eyes was one of such warmth as she had never seen before.

No one—*no one*—had ever looked at her in quite that way. Before she knew what she was doing, she moved a step closer to him. "I'm cold. So cold. I just want to be warm."

"Then this is your lucky day. You see, there's three things I'm real good at, angel—shooting a gun, tracking a man—and keeping women warm."

She laughed in spite of herself, caught in the spell of hard silver eyes, in the delicious sensation of a strong hand caressing her neck. Then, as he pulled her slowly, gently into his arms, Maura's knees shook and she swayed. He caught her with one swift movement and scooped her up.

His eyes were intent on her face as he carried her toward the bed. "You don't have to be afraid."

"I'm not," she whispered, half defiantly.

But that wasn't true—her heart was thundering like a train, and her breath felt trapped in her chest. Yet she knew that she didn't want to leave—not really. She was cold. She wanted to be warm. She was lonely. She wanted to be held. For just one night, this one damned empty, wild, blizzarding night she wanted someone, something . . .

His chuckle scraped over her rough as burlap as he lowered her onto the bed.

"Reckon you won't need all these clothes, Maura."

"Don't be so sure." She sat up quickly on the mattress, brushing a stray curl back from her cheek. "Even with that fire"—she nodded toward the lovely golden-red blaze—"it's going to be awfully cold in here."

"Don't count on it, darlin'." Amusement gleamed in his eyes as he gave a tug at the tie that fastened her robe. When its folds parted and she gasped, he gave a sudden sharp laugh as he saw the red and black flannel nightshirt covering her body, the navy blue woolen long johns encasing her legs, the brown socks hiding even her feet.

"I see you like a man to work for his pleasure." He grinned. "Never figured you'd be so full of surprises."

"More than you know," Maura muttered a bit breathlessly, thinking dazedly of her virginity, of her own recklessness at being here, at letting things progress so far. She ought to warn him—no, she ought to *stop* him—but before she could say a word, he pushed her back against the pillows with a strength that shocked her, straddled her in one easy move, and with a dark grin that curled her toes, he began to peel off everything that stood in the way of what he wanted.

Chapter 3

 "WAIT—WAIT JUST A MINUTE!" MAURA PUSHED his hands away as he began to sweep her night-shirt over her head. She tugged it back down. "I never said I would let you . . ."

"You never said you wouldn't."

"You didn't give me a chance to say anything!" Breathing hard, she knew she had to decide: stay or go. Yes or no.

Once and for all.

"Well?" he growled. "What do you want to say?"

Maura had no idea. She simply stared at him, trying to think, trying to keep her mind on the decision before her, when he looked so ruggedly handsome, all she could think about was how she'd like to comb her fingers through his black hair, or touch that dark stubble along his jaw, or . . . kiss him.

"Time's up," he announced suddenly, and with one movement swept the nightshirt over her head and tossed it on the floor. Her hair cascaded down, bright as the flames of the fire, to swirl around her shoulders, and her golden-brown eyes went wide with shock.

Now she wore only her thin white camisole above the long johns and coarse brown socks. She was practically *naked.*

"Just hold on a minute," she cried. Breathing hard, she crossed her arms over her breasts. "I have to think."

"I thought you wanted to stay warm."

"Taking off my clothes doesn't seem like the way to do that!"

He seized her then, and pulled her close. "Trust me— it works."

For a moment she was dizzy with the nearness of him. Her breasts were thrust up against his chest, the rough flannel of his shirt scraped her tender flesh. His breath was warm on her cheek, and his mouth was only scant inches away from hers . . .

"I don't even know your name," she whispered desperately.

There was a heartbeat of silence. Then he spoke flatly. "It's Lassiter."

Snowflakes hurled themselves against the window as he braced himself for her reaction. He knew damn well what was coming. It was always the same.

"Lassiter?" He heard her sharp intake of breath. She jerked back, but not before he'd felt the slamming of her heart against his chest, the shudder of fear jolting through her bones.

"Not . . . *Quinn* Lassiter?" she asked in a trembling voice.

"The same." He watched her grimly. He knew what they said about him, what she would believe just by hearing his name.

Quinn Lassiter, deadliest man in the West. Fastest gun-

fighter alive. There's a lump of steel where his heart should be. He kills as casually as most men spit.

She went pale as the snow swirling outside the window. "I've heard of you," she croaked.

He shrugged. "Probably a pack of lies."

"They say you've killed more than twenty men. Is that . . . true?"

"More or less. But—"

"And they say you shot Johnny the Kid between the eyes, and captured the entire Melton gang single-handed. Is that t-true?"

"I reckon. But—"

"And last spring," Maura plunged on, her pulse racing, "you fought three gunfights in one morning and killed all three men with only two bullets . . ."

"It wasn't anything special," he growled. As her lips parted and her eyes grew glassy, he lifted a brow. "I reckon this means you *are* scared of me?"

His hands went to her bare, creamy shoulders, so narrow and vulnerable beneath his fingers. She was tense as a knot of wire. Fear, hesitation, and uncertainty vibrated through her.

"Am I right? Answer me."

"Scared? Why, no. Why in the w-world should I be scared? It's only—" Maura jerked back from beneath his hands and bolted off the bed as though she'd been shot from a cannon. She snatched up her nightshirt and held it in front of her like a shield.

"It's only that I forgot. Completely forgot. You see, I left something on the stove. Burning on the stove. So silly of me . . . careless, really. I have to go. Or we'll have a fire. I have to go . . . take it off the stove . . ."

"Maura."

He reached out, seized her wrist, and yanked her back into the bed. Whipping the nightshirt from her limp fingers, he tossed it to the floor again.

"You think I'm going to shoot you?"

"Of course not. Only . . ."

"You think I'd hurt a hair on your head?"

"N-no, never." She glanced up at him from beneath her lashes. "W-would you?"

"No. Never." He cupped her chin in his hand and forced her to meet his eyes. They were gray as slate, but somehow his expression was softer, more rueful than it had been before.

"I'm going to make love to you, angel. Real nice, hot, hang-onto-your-hat love. If you want me to, that is. I'll keep you warm all night long. Fact is, I'll make you sweat. I'll even make you burn."

"You . . . will?"

"Yep. And you won't need clothes, and you won't need fires." He slid a hand slowly, languidly down her bare arm and Maura shivered. "That's a promise."

His eyes . . . She stared into those mesmerizing silver eyes. Something inside of her was melting. Maybe it was her last lick of sense. But in that moment she knew something she hadn't realized before. Quinn Lassiter didn't want to be alone tonight any more than she did.

"Still afraid?" he asked softly.

"No. I'm not afraid," she heard herself say, and it was almost true. Before she even realized what she was doing, she lifted her arms and wrapped them around his neck. Her blood pounded at her own daring. He was all muscle. All steel and musky male scent. She could feel his strength in her fingertips. It shocked and frightened her, more than his name had. But it also excited her. She clasped him tighter.

"Hold me," she whispered, gazing up at him through wide golden-brown eyes. "Just for tonight—all night—will you hold me?"

Quinn Lassiter hauled her up against him then. One powerful arm encircled her waist, virtually imprisoning her against the steel of his body. One hand twisted itself firmly in her hair, an act of possession. "Sweet Maura, don't you worry. I'll do a hell of a lot more than that."

Then he lowered his head and slanted his mouth to hers, cutting off any more doubts, any more words.

It was a hungry kiss, demanding and needy, and yet strangely tender and warm. Maura, who had never even had the opportunity to speak more than three sentences to a man without worrying that Judd or Homer would break his jaw, and who had certainly never *ever* come close to kissing a man before, was convinced that it was the most absolutely perfect kiss there could ever be. Her mind was reeling over the fact that she was crouched half naked on a bed, in the arms of a legendary gunfighter who would no doubt ride out of her life forever in the morning. But somehow she felt she should make the most of it. Her daydreams aside, she might never have the chance to kiss any man again—unless she *did* manage to get away from Judd and Homer and Knotsville. This might be the closest she ever came to wonder, excitement—to romance. To the possibility of falling in love.

Of course she knew Quinn Lassiter didn't love her—and she couldn't possibly be in love with him, but the way he was kissing her made her *feel* loved. And needed. And wanted.

Just for tonight, she told herself dizzily as Quinn deepened the kiss, blurring her mind with dark, lovely sensations that sent pleasure streaking through her. *I won't be alone. Just for tonight, I'll have someone. And so will he . . .*

His lips were warm, firm, and strong and they knew how to brush, feather, and slant over hers in just such a way that a tingling warmth radiated through her. As he deepened the kiss and the urgency of it leapt through her, she tightened her arms instinctively around his neck, and realized faintly that his hands were stroking up and down her back, caressing her shoulders, drawing her in closer and closer under the spell of pleasure.

He was kissing her ever more deeply, urging her lips apart, each movement becoming more and more insistent, until at last she gave way, filled with pleasure but confused and unsure of what she was supposed to do. Instantly, the moment her lips parted, his tongue swept inside her mouth. She was shocked and tried to draw away, squirming in his arms, but Quinn Lassiter held her fast, his arms imprisoning her, his mouth locked on hers as his tongue boldly licked hers, flicking over it in smooth, light strokes that filled her with such heat, her senses spun. She clutched at him, a whimper in the back of her throat, her fingers digging into his strong shoulders.

Suddenly she no longer wanted to draw away. She wanted to get closer, as close as she could. To her astonishment, her own tongue shyly slid against his in a tentative caress.

Lassiter half chuckled, half groaned. His arms dragged her even closer against him, and he deepened the kiss once more, tasting her fully, exploring her, his tongue thrusting inside her mouth with hungry, deliberate parries. Hell, her lips were as sweet and soft as little pink daisies. As his tongue played with hers, he felt his own need hardening. This girl tasted even better than the whiskey had—more like wine, like pure, potent strawberry-flavored wine.

She strained against him, returning kiss for kiss, her mouth sweet and yearning. Her tongue kept meeting his tentatively, stroking it, pulling back, an intoxicatingly teasing ploy that only made him want her more. Lassiter always took what he wanted, and this time was no exception. He heard her mew like a kitten as the kiss became more insistent, deeper still, and his muscles bunched with tension as her tongue darted forward again in the timidly enticing little dance that made him groan.

"That's it. Don't be shy. You're good at this, Maura. Real good."

"So are you," she whispered, and he chuckled, drawing out the kiss, intensifying it. He began to stroke her body in smooth, gliding caresses that made her tremble provocatively against him.

Swiftly, urgently, he lowered her upon the mattress.

Snow raged outside the window, smothering the night. The Rockies loomed in the distance, fiercer, mightier even than the storm. But inside this room, the fire crackled golden in the hearth and the girl's soft arms enveloped him. And what had happened in Hatchett was misting into a dark, ugly blur as he gave himself up to the effects of the liquor and to the passionate woman beneath him.

One by one he stripped off the remainder of her ugly, bulky garments. First the long johns, then the coarse brown socks. He sent them sailing to the floor, followed by that wisp of a camisole and her dainty pantalets.

She was lovely. Small, creamy breasts, and nipples that were already hardened into taut rosy peaks—whether from the chill or arousal he couldn't be certain.

When he eased her down against the pillows and shifted his body atop hers, he could feel the heat singing through her blood. But also, even through the haze of whiskey, he could still feel her tension, especially the wild beating of her heart, and he attributed it to fear of his name and reputation, despite what she'd said earlier.

"I won't hurt you, Maura," he promised again. His lips grazed her throat. "I want to make you feel good."

He felt her tremble as his mouth trailed kisses across the wild pulse in her throat, across her shoulders, then burned a path up to the delicate shell of her ear. Her skin was warm, smooth as silk, and smelled like honeysuckle.

"Delicious," he muttered against her hair.

She moved beneath him, her body shifting, welcoming the weight of his. When his hand closed over her breast a shudder shook her, and her eyes shimmered up at him. Then, as he began to knead and tease and to rub his thumb back and forth across her taut nipple, he heard the moan of pleasure deep in her throat.

He was hungry for her. Damned hungry. When he began to strip off his own clothes, she helped him, her fingers fumbling over the buttons of his shirt, sliding down his chest, touching him cautiously at first, then with an eagerness that made his blood surge. There was a sweetness about her that penetrated the haze of whiskey and wanting, that made him sweat as his shirt, pants, and vest landed atop hers on the floor. The potency of the liquor, the need to forget, the wanting of her, all melded into a fierce desire to take her quickly.

He covered her soft body with his own muscled and battle-scarred one, nibbled at her shoulders and then her breasts, took her mouth and once more urged those silky lips apart. Hot, ravenous kisses had them rocking against each other, holding each other, demanding more and more from each other. He drank in her taste, her honeysuckle scent, the velvet texture of her hair brushing his chest and his shoulders, and was dimly aware of her responses, her squirming body, small whimpers, her fingers knotted in his hair.

She was giving herself to him, her tongue moving frantically against his, her breasts straining upward against the muscles of his chest. With ever heightening need and tension building hard and furious inside him, he stroked his hands over her, down along her thighs. With need pounding through him, he probed the warm silken depths of her.

She cried out and her entire body stiffened.

Quinn paused, his lips on her throat. "Come on, angel. What's wrong?"

"Nothing," she gasped. Her face was delectably flushed—with passion, he concluded. "I . . . I . . . just didn't expect . . ."

"Sure you did. It's not as if you've never done this before."

He chuckled, and soothed her with a long, hot kiss and

this time, when he slipped his finger inside the moist warmth of her, she received him with only a shudder, and clutched at him, her nails digging into his back.

"Hell, you smell so good. Like flowers," he muttered into her hair, and suddenly shifted, his body covering and locking upon hers as his blood surged with a red-hot need that would no longer be checked. Her long, delicate-boned body fitted to his powerful one, arching against him, welcoming him, even as her lips welcomed his mouth. He moved roughly, savagely over her, restraint giving way to a blind, scorching need as ancient as the earth.

Maura's heart pounded frantically as sensation after sensation swamped her. She clutched at Quinn Lassiter's broad back for dear life, and frantically fought the tortur-ous ache he'd been relentlessly stoking inside her.

And even as she struggled against the tormenting de-light he created, she was filled with wonder that a man so large, so strong, could be so wonderfully gentle.

Then he pushed her thighs apart and thrust inside her and the pain shattered her, rending her in two.

She cried out, her eyes flying open, her entire body going rigid. But he was on fire, heedless of her cry, per-haps drunk, perhaps only hell-bent on finishing what he'd started. She didn't know, she only knew that he filled her and began to plunge within her again and again with sin-gle-minded purpose as tears gathered in her eyes and spilled down her cheeks, and her body writhed helplessly beneath his.

He stroked her, and kissed her mouth with slow, deep kisses. Slowly, exquisitely, a miracle happened. The great, sharp pain inside her ebbed and she began to tremble all over. The ache that came from pleasure returned. His thrusts were rhythmic, relentless, drawing her up with him into a kind of thundering race.

Heat seared her and she could scarcely breathe as her hips arched upward and her legs locked on his long, solid ones. Her body sheened with sweat, she drew him in, closer, deeper.

The pain that had come before no longer mattered. Now there was only this, only him.

He wanted her, needed her, perhaps almost as much as she needed him tonight, needed him to fill her emptiness, her loneliness, to keep her warm and transport her from this dreary little town to a place where she was loved, if only for an instant, where anything was possible, if only for a night, where life wasn't gray and tedious but filled with a translucent rainbow of dreams and possibilities. . . .

She caught her breath as his glittering eyes held hers and his powerful thrusts filled her. She clutched at him and cried out as they hurtled toward an unknown spark, the edge of a white-hot frenzy. Upward and over . . . climbing, falling, soaring . . .

To a pinnacle of blinding, shattering release.

Afterward, he rolled off her as if in a stupor. Which, she realized dizzily, he most likely was, considering all the whiskey he'd drunk. He grunted, brushed a kiss across the tip of her nose, and pulled her close, nestling her against the warmth of his body.

For a while Maura lay snuggled beside him, the memories of their lovemaking drifting through her mind. She felt peaceful, warm. Shyly she draped an arm across his chest as she cuddled closer, drawing from his warmth and strength and solidness, breathing in the male scent of him, the scent of whiskey and leather and sweat, holding on to him and this moment. The fire crackled and the storm raged and the moments slipped by. As the hour of dawn edged closer, Maura sat up at last and studied Quinn by the flickering amber light of the fire.

Even asleep he was a formidable man, his muscular frame hard and powerful, his granite features and dark stubble combining to make him look both tough and impossibly handsome. Yet his black hair fell almost boyishly over his brow, and his eyes were closed, hiding the weary cynicism in their piercing depths. And there were scars on his body that hinted of past savageries endured.

She reached out without thinking, and with gentle fingers brushed a lock of midnight hair from his brow.

"Where are you headed, Quinn Lassiter?" she whispered, her voice as soft as a drifting feather. "Will you be gone at first light? Will I ever see you again?"

She nearly jumped out of her skin when he answered her.

"Helena."

"Wh-what?" she gasped, drawing her hand back, staring at him in shock. He'd appeared fast asleep!

"Going to Helena." His words were slurred and heavy, no doubt from both the liquor and his exhaustion. "First thing . . . in the morning."

"Oh." Shyly, she framed another question, though he looked to be asleep once more.

"What's in Helena?"

He grunted, shifted his weight, moved his leg against hers. "Range war. Hired my gun."

"You could be killed."

Another grunt. "I'm too mean to die," he muttered, and lowered his arm from the pillow, draping it instead across her naked thigh. Her skin burned where his bronzed muscles touched her pale flesh.

Take me with you, she thought suddenly, caught in a swift, blazing urge to ride away from here with this black-haired stranger, to escape Judd and Homer and this gray, dreary life . . . to find love and adventure at his side, to make love with him and come alive with him just like this every single night.

But she couldn't speak the words. They were absurd. He wouldn't want her . . . would he?

As if sensing the intensity of her gaze on him, he opened his eyes. They gleamed up at her in the golden embers of the firelight.

"Cold, angel?"

"N-no." She gave a shaky laugh, blushing. "I don't think I'll ever be cold again." Her heart lifted when he smiled.

"Come here."

He tugged her down atop him and his mouth found hers again. Heat and desire rushed back, intense as flame. When he rolled her over and eased his powerful body onto hers, Maura felt a surge of purely feminine triumph. She reached for him, welcomed him, met his kiss with eager, parted lips.

And it all began again. . . .

Chapter 4

WHEN MAURA AWOKE THE NEXT MORNING, THERE was no sign that Quinn Lassiter had been there at all. None. None but the indentation in the pillow where his head had rested, and the blood staining the coverlet and dried now upon her thighs.

She clutched the coverlet to her, forlorn and aghast.

What had she done? *Why?* She must have been crazy to make love to a man she didn't know, a stranger who cared no more for her than for a rabbit skittering across his path. A man who didn't even bother to say good-bye . . .

What had she been thinking?

The answer was simple—she hadn't been thinking at all. Only feeling. Not a very wise way to conduct one's life, she told herself as she wobbled out of the bed, shivering in the morning chill, and then stood staring down at the rumpled pillows and twisted coverlet, remembering.

The memories filled her with a deeply luxurious glow. And a seed of anger. Quinn Lassiter had bolted quicker than a wild mustang from a rope. Shoulders drooping, she gathered up her clothes and bundled the robe around her. She went to the window and gazed out at the morning.

It was still early, and the sky cut a wide swath of pale china-blue. The Rockies loomed to the west, their awesome gray peaks dominating tiny Knotsville like a regiment of fierce, mythical giants.

But the snow had ceased at last, the sun glimmered, and the town was blanketed in pristine white. People were stirring, a team of horses was trotting up Main Street, and children in jackets and mittens were scampering about, tossing snowballs.

The boys will be back today, Maura thought on a sigh. *And Quinn Lassiter is gone forever.*

Anger and disappointment stabbed through her. *You'd best take a bath, wash that bedding, clean this room, and forget all about Mr. Quinn Lassiter,* she told herself as she turned from the window.

He doesn't figure in your future. And it's the future that matters. Think about how best to hide your tips from the customers so Judd doesn't find them, think about how and when you can get away from here, think about your dress shop in San Francisco.

But don't think about Quinn Lassiter. He's gone—just like the blizzard. Just like the night. Gone for good.

But when she went down to the kitchen, she found a pile of freshly chopped firewood filling the wood box by the stove. Her heart lurched, at first with gratitude and pleasure, then with a twist of bitterness.

I guess that's how a gunfighter says goodbye, Maura thought, kneeling to touch the rough wood. But she knew that all of the firewood in Montana couldn't warm her the way he had.

By the time the boys arrived home, it was dinnertime. Inky shadows cloaked the Rockies, and the coming night promised to be every bit as cold as the previous one.

Maura had laundered the bedding, cleaned out the hearth, and restored the bedroom where she and the gunfighter had spent the night to its former state.

The stage had come through at last, and there were three guests in the hotel now, a husband and wife traveling to Wyoming, and an older man passing through to Butte, staying only the night.

She'd already served them all dinner, and had fifty cents in tips in the pocket of her calico dress. She'd been hoping for a chance to steal up to her room so that she might hide the coins in the toe of one of her stockings, or deep in back of the bureau, but Judd and Homer came stomping in before she had the guests' dishes cleared away.

"Hey, there, runt," Judd said, following her into the kitchen and giving her a shove, paying no heed to her armful of plates. "You'd best have plenty of grub left for us. We're halfway starved."

"There's more than enough." Maura quickly set down the dishes, picked up a fork, and began turning the chicken pieces as they sizzled in the skillet. My, Judd appeared to be in an unusually expansive mood. His eerie lashless eyes, so pale a green they were almost yellow, shone like tiny lamps in his round face. And Homer's mouth was twitching in a smug, self-satisfied smirk, the kind he wore when he'd finished throwing some greenhorn fresh off the stage into the watering trough outside the livery. In most ways the brothers looked almost identical. Of average height, they both had the same thick necks, brawny builds, round-as-a-platter faces. And the same lank brown hair. But Judd, at twenty-five the elder by a year, had a bristly handlebar mustache, and his stringy hair hung all the way to his shoulders. Homer's straggled around his ears and just past his chin. His eyes had a few sparse brown lashes, and he had more of a paunch than Judd did—and an even bigger chip on his shoulder. But Judd, with his squashed nose and freckled ears, had by far the more dangerous streak of mean.

"Did you win in the poker tournament?" Maura ventured, stirring string beans and onions in a pan beside the chicken.

Homer stuck his hands in his pockets. "You might say that."

"We done just *fine*." Judd exchanged a quick sly glance with his brother.

"We done so good, runt," Homer boasted, his nose wrinkling with pleasure at the delicious aroma of frying chicken rising from the skillet, "that one of these days we might even buy you a little present. Seeing as you're our sweet little sis and all. How'd you like a new Sunday dress?"

Maura stopped stirring the string beans and onions and stared at him in amazement. She hadn't had a new dress in years—all she'd done was let out and resew the same ones over and over, adding a bit of lace trim now and then, or a sash when Ma Duncan would slip her some money.

"You *did* win," she breathed, thinking longingly of the splendid pink velveteen fabric she'd seen in Peever's General Store last week, fresh from the East. She had a picture in her mind of the gown she could sew from it—a fit-for-a-princess gown with long full sleeves like pretty bells, and a white velvet sash and grosgrain ribbon at the bodice. . . .

"Son of a bitch. Don't get carried away, Homer." Judd glared at him, his mood shifting abruptly, as usual. "We done all right in Hatchett," he added, scowling. "But you don't need no new dresses. The ones you got now are just fine."

Maura turned away to stir butter into the bowl of mashed potatoes on the table.

Judd helped himself to a hunk of fresh-baked corn bread. Homer immediately followed suit.

"You take in any money while we were gone?" Judd demanded as he chewed the bread with gusto.

"There was only one customer until today. Because of the blizzard, you know," she added, hoping they wouldn't notice the heat stealing into her cheeks as she thought about that particular customer. "The stagecoach didn't make it through until this very afternoon."

"Well, bring some of this grub out front for us pronto." Judd sniffed approvingly at the chicken frying in the skillet. "Me and Homer have worked up a hell of an appetite trying to get back here tonight just so's we could help you out."

Help me out? Maura bit back a strangled laugh. The only thing Judd and Homer ever did to help out was to stay out of her way. They tracked mud onto the floors, broke crockery, tore and dirtied their clothes, and added all the figures wrong when they tried to check her arithmetic regarding the hotel books. And twice in the past month they'd started fights in the dining room, breaking the front windows and several of the chairs. They still owed over fifty dollars at the saloon for having shattered the mirror over the bar when they got drunk in November and took target practice at the whiskey bottles, but Big Ed, the owner, was too intimidated by them to press for payment.

Ma Duncan had been a schoolteacher before she married and had tried to teach all of them as much booklearning as she could—but her sons had refused to go to school or study after they turned twelve, and only Maura had appreciated the opportunity to gain an education. Not only had Maura paid attention to her lessons, she had been absorbed by them, and had enjoyed learning everything from geography to spelling and even elocution.

But the boys cared nothing for schooling, for chores, or any kind of work.

And why should they, when they've always had me or poor Ma Duncan to handle everything for them?

"Well, I do appreciate your desire to help me out," she said carefully, not looking into either face as she began arranging the chicken pieces on a platter. How she would love to give them a piece of her mind one day. But she knew she never would. She'd never dared speak back to either one of them. Even on the boys' best days, violence simmered just beneath the surface, and like everyone else in Knotsville, Maura was afraid of them. "We *are* running low on supplies. If you could get over to the mercantile—"

"Hell and damnation, Maura Jane! You didn't have nothin' to do while we were gone," Homer exclaimed. "Why didn't you go yourself?"

"You're getting mighty lazy, little girl," Judd added, wagging a dirty finger at her. He stuffed another piece of bread into his mouth. "What would you have done if we hadn't made it back today?"

"There's enough for today. But by tomorrow—"

"Listen here." Judd grabbed her arm and spun her around to face him. "Since when do you give us orders? If we feel like loading up on supplies, we will. You hear? And if we don't, then it's up to you. Where'd you be if our folks hadn't taken you in when you were just a little mite—too little to be of any use to anyone? Ever think about that? And why in tarnation Ma wanted a girl, I'll never understand."

"But she did—and you had it easy for years." Homer threw her a contemptuous glance. "Now you can finally earn your keep and you've got the gall to complain about it."

"You'd have been in some gutter by now if not for our pa saying you could come live with us," Judd added. "And don't you forget it!"

Suddenly his arm shot out and he seized a handful of her hair. He gave it a tug, enough to make Maura wince, then let the curls go, slowly, letting them ease through his dirt-encrusted fingers as she watched him in wide-eyed apprehension.

"You got everything you need and want right here—a warm bed, all the food you can eat, and decent clothes to wear," he growled. "Lots of women would be happy with that and not start trying to give orders to their menfolk. But not you."

"Not you," Homer repeated, jeering.

Maura's heart slammed against her rib cage. She fought the anger that rose like acid in her throat, the resentment combined with fear that tingled through her. Her voice trembled. "I only asked you to—"

"Shut up." Without warning, Judd shoved her backward. She careened into the table, slamming her hipbone against the edge, but managed to bite back the cry of pain as she caught herself and straightened.

"Stop your damned bellyaching, runt," Homer warned, taking a step forward, "and get that grub on the table now. We're likely to die of hunger listening to you whine."

He grabbed a chicken leg from the platter and bit into it as he shouldered his way out of the kitchen. Judd did the same, helping himself to a fat chicken leg and then leaving without a backward glance.

A trail of grease and crumbs was left in their wake.

Slowly, shakily, Maura eased away from the table. She dipped her hand into her pocket, thankful that over the sizzling sounds of the skillet and the boys' rumbling voices, they hadn't heard the coins jingling there.

"As soon as I have enough for a ticket on the stagecoach, I'm leaving," she whispered to herself as she set platters of chicken, string beans and onions, and mashed potatoes on a tray, then removed another loaf of bread from the oven.

"And when I have my own dress shop one day I'll have all the gowns I want and never wear the same one more than once in a week. No one will tell me what to do. And no one will lay a finger on me. And I'll never chop firewood again or wash piles of dishes every night for hours on end."

And there would be only two things she'd remember fondly about Knotsville or this damned hotel.

One was the bleary affection in Ma Duncan's faded eyes when, on her deathbed, she'd thanked Maura for caring for her and told her she could have her pink silk handbag and the pretty enamel jewel box tucked in the upper drawer of the bureau. Maura would never forget the way Ma Duncan had squeezed her hand with the last of her feeble strength and told her that she'd been a good daughter, a far better and more dutiful child than her own flesh-and-blood sons.

Ma Duncan hadn't exactly loved her—there hadn't been enough juice left in her to love anyone, Maura had realized long ago. The woman had been a dried-up mound of dead dreams and lost hope, too tired and dejected to feel much of anything. But she had cared about Maura, had tried her best to be good to her and see that she had what she needed.

She was the closest Maura had ever come to family.

The other memory she would take with her and keep always was last night—the night spent in a stranger's arms, with snow falling outside, a fire crackling within, and Quinn Lassiter's mouth and hands warming her body, holding her close and banishing for a few short hours the knowledge that she was alone in the world.

"I don't regret it," she said to herself as she placed the last slices of bread upon the plate. "The only thing I regret is that Quinn Lassiter isn't a stick-around, settle-down kind of man, instead of a sweet-talking, too-arrogant-to-say-goodbye gunfighter."

The ache that curled through her at this thought surprised her. She steeled herself. Quinn Lassiter had gone off to Helena without a backward glance. And she had her own path to travel. A path she would travel alone.

You don't need Lassiter. You don't need anyone, she told herself. *You have to concentrate on getting away from Judd and Homer and this town, and making a decent life for yourself. A life where you won't be afraid to speak your mind, where you can do as you please, earn some money of your own, and settle down someplace friendly. Perhaps even find a friend or two,* she thought wistfully— and maybe, if she was lucky, someone to love, someone who would love her back.

February brought more snow and furious winds that galloped out of the mountains and raced headlong across the Montana plains. Long bitter nights followed endless shivery days. Maura worked diligently and single-mindedly and each evening carefully counted out her precious pennies, but by the end of the month everything changed— and her tedious gray world was tilted upside down.

All of her careful plans—the treasured coins she'd gathered and secreted away to buy her a ticket to a new life, her dreams and hopes and visions of a future in San Francisco—all disintegrated into a meaningless haze.

For when the harsh winds of February began to ease toward the milder ways of March, she was struck broadside by a terrifying realization.

She was going to have a baby.

Quinn Lassiter's baby.

Chapter 5

 SHE WAS CHANGING BED LINENS ON A WEDNES-
day morning when the first wave of queasiness
washed over her. It passed shortly, and Maura
dismissed it—until the sensation returned the following
day while she washed breakfast dishes. A few moments
later came a strange dizziness, a light-headedness that
had her gripping the edge of the sink, fearful she would
keel over.

Maura had never felt anything like it before. Groping
her way to a kitchen chair, she sank down, gulping deep
breaths of air, wondering if she could have the fever or
influenza.

And it was then that she remembered with a white-hot
shock that her monthly time had come and gone, and she
was late.

Nearly three weeks late.

Perched on the chair, clinging to the sides of the seat,
Maura remembered the bouts of nausea and dizziness that
Hallie Gordon, the blacksmith's young wife, had suffered
when she was with child. And she knew with sudden
blinding clarity that this was the same thing.

How did this happen? she wailed silently, her hands flying to her throat.

But she knew how it had happened. The memories of that long snowbound night with Lassiter hadn't faded during the past weeks—if anything, they'd grown more vivid, floating through her mind with disturbing warmth each night as she tried to sleep. The gentleness of his touch, the heat of his kiss, his deep, gravelly voice saying her name, telling her—like a miracle—that she was pretty.

But she hadn't ever expected she'd get pregnant after just that one time!

She'd been a virgin for twenty-four years and the one time she decided to find out what it would be like to lie with a man, to be held in his arms . . .

It only takes one time, she reminded herself, wishing she had considered that before. But she hadn't. That night she'd thought only of how cold and how lonely she was, how hard life was, how much she needed someone, if only to share the dark hours before the dawn.

Self-pity had landed her in one fine fix.

She paced around the kitchen, returned to the sink, and stared down at the pile of still-to-be-washed dishes. A quiet dismay swept through her. She was going to be bringing a child into this world—and giving it a life. But what kind of life would that be?

The same kind she had here in Knotsville? With Judd and Homer as uncles? Stifling the baby as they stifled her, putting the child to work, no doubt, from the time she was old enough to toddle, shouting at her and bullying her as they did Maura?

No.

Maura took a deep, steadying breath, her mind filled with one thought and one thought only. No, she wouldn't let that happen. This child, her child, was going to have a better future than that.

Ma Duncan did her best for me, she thought desperately as she reached for a soiled plate. *But she couldn't love me. She couldn't protect me from Judd and Homer. I'm going to do better for my baby. My baby will know love. It will have a real home. Pretty dresses, if it's a girl,* she vowed. *And an education. If it's a boy, he'll learn manners and respect, right from wrong, as well as figuring and spelling and geography, and how to earn a living in this world.*

Things were going to be different for this baby.

So help me God, I'll give my baby a better life than the one I've had, she vowed fervently, one hand moving to her belly, lying protectively against it, as if she could shield the tiny life growing within.

She swayed at the sink as the enormity of what lay before her struck through to her soul. The first thing she had to do, the very first thing, was to get out of this town.

And once she left there would be no turning back—she must make sure the boys didn't find her and drag her back. If they did, she'd never get away again.

Shoving her auburn hair back from her eyes, Maura began washing the dishes, as if she could wash away every obstacle as she did the soiled remnants of food. She'd have to leave soon, before the boys caught any inkling that she was going to have a baby. She shuddered at how they would react to *that*. They'd demand to know who the father was, they'd shout at her, condemn her, no doubt call her a whore.

Well, they wouldn't have that chance, Maura decided grimly as she rinsed the dish in her hand and set it down, reaching for another. She had six dollars and twenty-two cents saved up. It would have to be enough.

She'd leave as soon as an opportunity came along, but . . . where would she go? To San Francisco? To follow her dream and try to get work as a seamstress in a dress shop, and then gradually learn enough and save enough to open her own shop someday?

She heard Judd hollering for her from the lobby.

"Mr. Edmunds in Room 201 says he knocked over the china pitcher in his room—there's broken china all over the damned floor. Get up there and clean it up before he gets back from the saloon," he told her when she hurried to his side. His pale green eyes glared at her. "Then bring me and Homer some pie and coffee. Go on, get a move on, girl. I swear you been loafin' in that kitchen for hours now."

She didn't bother to answer, just returned to the kitchen for a broom and dustpan, and scurried upstairs to Room 201. On the way, she glanced along the hall to Room 203, where she and Quinn Lassiter together had made this baby that was growing inside her.

He has a right to know.

The thought popped into her head. She froze in the hallway, clutching the broom and dustpan in suddenly shaky fingers.

He won't care, a small voice insisted deep inside her. *He won't even remember you. Why bother?*

Because it's right. I should tell him. A man has a right to know that a child of his is going to be brought into the world.

She could go to Helena, she thought, a tight knot in her throat. See if he was still there. But then what? What if he didn't want her—want *them*—what if he didn't care about the baby?

Then she could go on to San Francisco. Find a job, tell everyone her husband died and raise her child alone.

But it would mean living a lie for the rest of her life— and foisting that lie on the baby.

Uncertainty assailed her as she forced herself away from Room 203 and entered the room where china fragments were scattered across the floor. What if Quinn Lassiter *did* say he would do right by her and marry her? If she went ahead with it, she'd be married to a stranger—a stranger who didn't really want her. Or love her.

Her heart twisted painfully. She knew she ought to be used to that—to living with people who didn't love her. She'd done it all her life. Yet she'd always hoped for more, hoped that if she ever did marry, she'd find some- one who would care about her.

As she swept up the bits of broken china, Maura came to a solemn realization. The time for thinking about her- self was past. She needed to think about the baby. What was best for the baby was all that mattered now.

I guess first I'd better find Quinn Lassiter—and then worry about telling him, she reflected as she hurried back downstairs. *Your baby deserves a name—and a home. And some security.* Whether he liked it or not, Mr. Rides- Off-at-the-Crack-of-Dawn Quinn Lassiter owed her—and the child—that much.

On her way to the kitchen with the broom and dustpan

filled with china bits, she saw Judd and Homer straddling chairs at a corner table, talking with their heads bent close together.

They'd been doing that a great deal, the two of them, ever since they'd returned from the poker tournament. But whenever she was near, they abruptly stopped talking.

She knew they were up to something, but had an uneasy feeling she was better off not knowing. All their lives the boys had done as they pleased, caused plenty of trouble, and dared anyone to do anything about it.

With no sheriff in town, no one wanted to tangle with the Duncan boys, so no one ever did.

But something more than the usual bullying and mischief had been brewing ever since they'd come back from Hatchett. Maura was certain of it. She just couldn't imagine what it was.

And now she didn't have time to wonder about it—or to care. She had to think of the baby. And of a plan for getting out of this town without delay—and on a stage bound for Helena.

Judd Duncan leaned closer to his brother's ear. "It's all set. At sunup tomorrow, you and me are heading to Great Falls. Heard there's a feller in town who might want to buy what we got to sell."

"You mean the diamonds?" Homer's eyes had lit up, and in his excitement he spoke louder than he'd intended.

Judd grabbed his grimy plaid shirt collar and yanked it hard.

"Keep your voice down, you damned fool. You want

everyone in town to hear?'' He dropped his voice to a raspy whisper. " 'Course I mean the diamonds.''

"Well, who is this feller?''

"Rich businessman from San Francisco. Owns two of the biggest brothels in the whole town—keeps 'em stocked with the prettiest women in the West, so they say.'' Judd's grin split across his face as he tugged the tip of his mustache. "They go around all decked out in fine fancy clothes—till they take 'em off.'' He chuckled. "He's got himself a mining interest here in Montana Territory, too. Might even open a fancy brothel in Great Falls, I hear.''

"And he's lookin' to buy some diamonds?''

"Seems he's got a lady friend with fancy taste.''

"Well, it's about time.'' Homer paused as Maura came up with two plates of cherry pie and cups of coffee balanced on a tray. He waited, leaning forward, his stringy hair falling across his face, until she had disappeared into the lobby. "I mean, what's the point of having grabbed that damned necklace if we can't sell them stones and get rich? We'd best bring 'em along to show this feller, right?''

"*Are you crazy?* You want to get our throats slit while we sleep?'' Judd's fork clattered to his plate as he threw his brother a contemptuous glance. "I'm too smart for that, even if you ain't.''

Homer flushed. "So what do we do?'' he asked resentfully. "Won't he want to see 'em before he buys?''

"We'll bring one of 'em with us. One diamond. Enough for him to take a look at it and see that it's a top-quality gem.'' Judd shoved the last bit of pie in his mouth and continued talking around it. "That smarmy little gambler, Ellers, sure had good taste in jewels—and in women. Too bad he lost 'em both.''

Homer chuckled. "Reckon his bad luck is our good luck," he said slyly. "All right, then, so we take one diamond along and leave the rest hidden here safe and sound." He nodded, helped himself to a gulp of coffee. "It's a damn fine plan, Judd. Smart. Almost as smart as my idea to follow the woman that night."

"Shut up about that night!" Judd's hard lashless eyes flashed a warning. "If anyone ever finds out what happened—especially that gambler—we're dead. You could just say goodbye to that little fortune we've got coming. You could say goodbye to *living*. So keep your mouth shut about that night, about the diamonds and *everything*."

"Sure, Judd, I'll shut up. I don't want no trouble. But is Ellers really as good with a knife as everyone says? They say he can hit a bird in a tree from fifty feet and slice it clean through."

"That's what they say. And if he ever finds out what happened in that alley in Hatchett, he's gonna slice us in two just like a couple of little birds."

"How would he ever find out?" Homer scoffed. A grin started and spread from ear to ear. "No one saw what we did. He can't have any notion we've got the diamonds. Hell, there were more'n a hundred folks in Hatchett that night of the tournament. Why in hell would he ever think of us?"

Judd leaned back in his chair. "You're most likely right. Ellers could be halfway across the country by now, with a new bit of calico on his arm, cheating at cards and winning the pay of every cowboy who sits down at the table with him. If we don't let nothin' slip to no one, we'll probably never see him again.''

"But we're going to see some high times once we sell those diamonds," Homer exulted, setting his coffee cup back in its saucer with a rattle.

"They're worth a fortune," Judd growled. "More than the prize in that poker tournament. More than you or me can spend in a whole year. So listen up. We'll leave at sunup tomorrow for Great Falls. I'm going upstairs and get us one of them sparklers to bring along.''

"Judd—you sure it's safe to leave the rest of 'em here?''

"Safe enough. No one knows we got 'em, no one'll find 'em where they're hid. Not even Maura.'' Judd pushed back his chair, punching his brother in his shoulder as he went past.

He spoke roughly to Maura, who was closing the hotel guest book as he started up the stairs. "Hey, runt, me and Homer are headed to Great Falls tomorrow on a little business trip. No slackin' off while we're gone. You hear? I want all the windows washed by the time we get back. And you shine my boots tonight before I go to bed. Don't you forget now.''

She stared after him as he took the steps three at a time, his burly form nearly knocking over the slim young traveling salesman from Wichita in the brown derby who was just starting down the stairs.

Judd and Homer were going to Great Falls—tomorrow.

This was her chance.

She swallowed hard and stared around at the dingy lobby of the small hotel, at the dimly lit dining room with its peeling paint and frayed curtains, at the wedge of dull gray town beyond the windows.

This would be the last night she'd spend here, the last time she'd see Judd and Homer—if all went well.

This time tomorrow—if she didn't lose her nerve—she'd be on her way.

Chapter 6

 THE STAGECOACH RUMBLED INTO WHISPER VAL-
ley in a cloud of glittering dust that for a moment obliterated all the stores and buildings
lining the street. The passengers jostled together, clutching at the overhead straps and at each other as they
pitched forward, then back. Their stomachs, already roiling from the greasy meal they'd eaten earlier, churned
hideously as the coach at last rolled to a stop.

Maura Jane Reed gasped and fought to keep down the
biscuits and gravy that had been her lunch. She would *not*
throw up here on this stagecoach—or on the street. She
would *not*.

Waiting until all the other passengers had descended
from the coach, Maura at last stepped down into the road
and wearily shook the dust from her skirt. For a moment
she merely stood and stared along the boardwalk at the
town of Whisper Valley.

The sight, thank God, was reassuring and cheerful.

The town appeared bustling and prosperous, the main
street lined with storefronts and buildings that looked
freshly painted and maintained. Women in calico or ging-

ham hurried along, smiling and nodding to one another, their children in tow behind them. Ranchers and cowboys and miners strode along the boardwalk, horses were tethered at hitching posts all along the street, and two dogs chased a striped cat up onto the roof of the general store.

Whisper Valley wasn't as big as Helena had been, but it appeared to be much larger than Knotsville. The question was: Did it hold the one man she'd come to find?

In Helena she'd learned that Quinn Lassiter had finished his work there only three days earlier and had moved on. The clerk she questioned at the hotel had heard him speaking with the rancher who'd hired him to fight in the range war. He'd said something about heading out to Whisper Valley.

But what if he'd already been here and gone? Maura wondered uneasily.

She took a deep, steadying breath as the stagecoach driver set her satchel down in the street. She forced herself to stop thinking that Quinn Lassiter might have already moved on. She was tired, dusty, and disheveled from her travels, and the now familiar queasiness was still plaguing her, but she had to forget all that—and all of her doubts as well—and just try to find him.

The hotel seemed like the logical place to start.

"Quinn Lassiter?" The woman behind the counter of the Whisper Valley Grand Hotel peered at her in amazement from beneath a gray frizz of hair. "Now why would a sweet little thing like you be looking for a man like *him?*"

Startled by the question, and by the open astonishment and curiosity in the woman's brown eyes, Maura fought the urge to stammer out some kind of made-up explanation. Then she realized it was nobody's business but her own.

"It's a personal matter," she replied.

The woman shook her head and leaned across the counter. "Don't you know about him?" she asked confidentially. "Haven't you heard the stories? Honey, my name is Mabel Barnes and I know everything that goes on in this town, and I can tell you, we don't often get men of his ilk passing through here. No, thank the good Lord, we don't."

"Mrs. Barnes, if you could just tell me if he is still—"

"Why, I quake nearly every time I see the man, and that's the truth. People scatter when they see him coming. And you're going looking for him! Now if that doesn't beat all!"

"Are you saying Mr. Lassiter *is* in Whisper Valley?" Hope fluttered in Maura's heart. "Is he here in the hotel?"

"He's staying here, but he isn't here right now. He's over in the saloon. The Jezebel Saloon, right there across the street."

Right there across the street. Maura turned and gazed out the window, watching a young cowboy shove his way through the swinging wood doors of the Jezebel Saloon and disappear inside.

Should she go there right now, before she lost her nerve?

Her palms grew clammy at the thought. Then she glanced down at her wrinkled gingham gown, her dusty shoes. She looked like a rag someone had used to wash the floor. Who'd want to marry a woman in a dirty gown, with dust clinging to her hair and cheeks, and no doubt pale enough to be mistaken for a ghost?

"I'd like a room," she told Mabel Barnes. "And a bath."

"Well, how about Room 204?" The woman tilted her head sideways, like a bird. "That's right down the hall from Mr. Lassiter—he's in 206."

Her heart jumped, but she managed to speak calmly. "That will be just fine."

An hour later, as a lilac sunset gilded the sky beyond the window and shadows gathered over the mountains, Maura studied her reflection in the narrow mirror over the hotel bureau.

She was clean at least, but that was about all she could find to say for herself. Clean and neat.

Her gingham gown was nearly threadbare, the once vibrant blue and green colors faded from innumerable washings. Her cheeks were still pale, perhaps from weariness after having sat up on the stagecoach for so many long, jolting hours. She pinched her cheeks and ran her hand over her upswept auburn hair. After her bath she'd finger-combed it until it was dry, then tamed the wild springy curls into a topknot that she hoped looked neat and presentable. She'd had to use all of the hairpins she kept in Ma Duncan's little enameled jewel box just to make it appear smooth.

At least she looked more ladylike than she had that savage January night, with her hair loose and flowing, and her layers of thick, mismatched clothes.

But what she'd done that night with Quinn Lassiter, a stranger who'd ridden in and out of her life, was anything but ladylike. So why was she trying to convince him she was a lady?

You're just stalling, she told herself crossly, pushing away the nervousness that fluttered in her chest. *Go now before you completely lose your nerve.*

She picked up her shawl, draped it around her shoulders, and trudged downstairs, trying to ignore the pounding of her heart, trying not to think about the enormity of what she was about to do. She couldn't bear to think about Quinn Lassiter's possible reaction. She couldn't bear to think about anything but finishing what she had set out to do.

The Montana wind whipped at her face and hair as she crossed the street to the saloon, and a few stray strands flew out of the topknot she'd so carefully constructed. But it was too late to fix it now. Her knees were trembling, and she took a deep breath before she set her hand upon the wooden doors of the Jezebel Saloon.

It took all of her resolve to push them open.

For a moment, Maura couldn't make out any one person in the vast, smoke-filled room. She noticed first the stout bartender wiping glasses behind the gleaming brass-trimmed bar, then a saloon girl carrying a tray of whiskey bottles and glasses to the table near the piano, then a snoring cowboy asleep with his hat over his face in the corner, and finally, beneath a painting of a woman wearing nothing but a tangle of long gold hair, she saw the table of men playing poker with deadly seriousness.

Quinn Lassiter was among them. His chair faced her as she froze by the door. Dressed all in black, he was studying the cards in his hand, his expression cold and unreadable as stone. He was, if possible, even more handsome today than he had been that lonely bitter night. Rugged, clean-shaven, dark as a wolf and just as tough and dangerous.

As Maura hesitated, noting in one swift instant the relaxed set of his broad shoulders beneath his dark shirt and vest, the jet-black hair that brushed his collar, the cool way his eyes flicked from his hand to the cards on the table, he startled her by suddenly glancing up.

He stared straight at her.

For a moment her heart lurched into her throat and she couldn't breathe at all. She waited for some change in his expression, for some gleam of recognition in his eyes, for she had recognized him at once, would recognize him even in a room far more crowded than this one, and surely, surely he would recognize her. . . .

But he didn't. His glance touched her briefly with all the warmth of an eagle looking through and past a cloud. He returned his gaze to his cards and threw a four of spades from his hand.

It was at this moment that she became aware that everyone else in the place was staring at her—and with far more interest than Quinn Lassiter had shown. Ladies didn't much entertain themselves in a saloon, so it was only natural she would draw attention.

As she bit her lip, uncomfortable under the scrutiny, wondering if she shouldn't wait until Quinn Lassiter finished his poker game before attempting to approach him, she heard a deep voice behind her.

"Hey, lady, what say I buy you a drink?"

The sleeping cowboy had awakened. He was smiling at her blearily.

"No. Thank you."

"You sure? Come on over." He hiccuped. "I'm awful thirsty and I hate to drink all by my lonesome."

Flustered, she turned and started toward the door, deciding she would wait for the gunfighter at the hotel, but in her haste to leave the saloon she tripped over a chair leg and stumbled into a table.

The commotion drew Lassiter's gaze again. This time he frowned.

"Something you want, honey?" A saloon girl in a frilly red dress and striped silk stockings poked her in the ribs.

"Um, no. I just . . ."

The girl stared at her through curious worldly eyes the color of violets. "You just what, honey? You looking for a job?"

"No, a . . . a man."

Apparently she had spoken more loudly than she intended, for rich laughter greeted this remark from around the Jezebel Saloon.

"Then you've come to the right place, ma'am." A man dressed in a gambler's frilled shirt and fancily embroidered vest threw her the smoothest smile she'd ever seen from across the poker table. Quinn Lassiter's frown deepened.

"Not any man," Maura rushed on, feeling her cheeks grow hot, knowing they must be as bright red as the carpet and flocked wallpaper of the saloon. "I came to find Mr. Lassiter."

The laughter died away. The gunfighter's expression didn't change noticeably, but Maura saw an even more intimidating coldness flicker in his eyes. It was all she could do not to shiver.

She took a tentative step toward him, trying to shake off the nausea that clutched at her. Lord knows, this was not the way she'd wanted this discussion to begin. He was already angry. And everyone in the saloon was staring from one to the other of them. "I didn't mean to interrupt your game," she said quietly.

"Lady, you already have."

"Is it possible . . . may we . . . talk privately?"

"Business?"

"Yes," Maura lied, her stomach turning over. She knew it would only draw more speculation if she told him it was a personal matter.

He tossed his cards down and shoved back his chair.

"Hold my place, Cassidy. I'll be back," he told the balding dealer with a curt nod.

With long, smooth strides he stalked right past Maura to a table in the far corner of the saloon, then waited for her to catch up. He didn't hold the chair for her, but stood standing while she slipped into a seat, then he settled himself with his back to the wall. His frost-gray eyes pierced her.

"What kind of job do you have in mind?"

"I . . . beg your pardon?"

"Job. You know, work. You want to hire me, don't you? You must need a gunman real bad to chase me down in a saloon. In the middle of a poker game," he added darkly.

Maura clenched her hands on the table before her. "I'm afraid I . . . lied, Mr. Lassiter. This isn't about a job."

His mouth tightened. "Then what?" he said impatiently.

Shaken by the fact that even now he showed no signs of recognizing her, she forced herself to continue. "It might be better if we speak privately." Maura glanced over her shoulder at the assortment of people in the saloon. "Perhaps we could step outside—"

"Curly," Lassiter interrupted her to call to the bartender. "You got a back room I can use to conduct some business?"

The bartender jerked his head toward a door beside the stairs. Lassiter grabbed her by the elbow and hauled her toward it. He pushed her into the small, cluttered office where sunlight filtered in between the slats of brown shutters, then kicked the door shut behind him and folded his arms across his chest.

"Talk."

Maura found that her voice failed her beneath that harsh, unsympathetic stare. *Well, what did you expect?* she asked herself. Hearts and daisies? Open arms and welcoming kisses?

"This isn't easy for me," she began, then faltered. He looked as stern, unapproachable, and intimidating as a mountain.

"Spit it out." There wasn't a trace of warmth or encouragement in his tone, only an unmistakable warning.

"Mr. Lassiter—Quinn." His name tumbled awkwardly over her tongue. "Don't you remember me at all?" she asked desperately.

Those hard eyes, like splinters of ice, narrowed on her face, growing, if anything, even colder.

"Should I?"

She nodded.

"Lady, I've never seen you before in my life."

"In January. The blizzard . . . The Duncan Hotel in Knotsville . . ."

Her voice died away as he shook his head.

"Please." Maura tried again, lifting her eyes to his face, willing him to look at her, really look at her, to recall even one moment of that night which had had such a drastic impact on her life. "Take a . . . good look at me. Try to remember."

He studied her a moment, then shrugged. "What town did you say you were from?"

Her face flamed with humiliation. Nausea clutched harder at her. For one awful moment she was afraid she was going to be sick right here in front of him, that she'd lose her meager lunch all over his boots!

"This would be much easier if you remembered me," she managed to mutter.

"Well, I don't. And lady, interesting as all this is, if you don't want to hire me, and you're not going to tell me what the hell this is about, I've got a poker game to get back to."

He turned on his heel and started toward the door.

"Wait!"

Slowly, hitching his thumbs in his gunbelt, he turned back toward her, his expression distant. Perhaps even bored.

Suddenly anger burst through her, pure, white-hot, scalding anger. How *dare* he. When she thought of the days of anxiety she'd suffered, huddled on that stagecoach, alone, fighting queasiness, dizziness, and the fear that Judd and Homer would come after her, she wanted to scream at him and hit him and make him sorry he had ever set foot inside the Duncan Hotel.

"You ought to remember me, Mr. Lassiter," she snapped, advancing toward him, her hands clenched. "Because I certainly remember you. And I'm not likely to forget the time we spent together. Because the fact is, Mr. Quinn Lassiter, that whether you remember me or not—whether you like it or not—*I'm going to have your baby!*"

Oh, God, she hadn't meant to tell him like that. Never like that. Of all the scenarios she'd ever imagined, none had ever included shouting, anger, her own voice throbbing with accusations.

He didn't move. Only his jaw tensed and his mouth twisted into a razor-thin line. A dangerous glitter came into his eyes. Maura instinctively took a step backward.

"Is that so?" The words lanced through her.

"Yes." She spoke through trembling lips. "That is so!"

"Seems to me I'd remember something like that."

"One would think so." How stiff she sounded, how cold. Almost haughty. But it was time she developed some backbone. If she didn't stand up for herself—and her child—no one else would.

She gripped her skirt, glaring into Quinn Lassiter's handsome face.

"You were different that night," she said scathingly. "Maybe that's why I—" She took a breath. "Never mind. It was a mistake. A very stupid mistake."

"Not as stupid as the one you just made."

Before Maura could blink, Quinn Lassiter's brawny arm shot out. He snagged her wrist in an unbreakable grip and yanked her toward him. "Telling me that whopper just won you the big prize." Granite eyes nailed her own brown ones. "You're not going anywhere until you explain what you're up to."

"How d-dare you. Take your hands off me right now."

"Not until you've filled me in, sweetheart." His lip curled in a tight, humorless smile. "I want to know if this little scam you're trying to pull was your idea—or did somebody put you up to it?"

"Scam?" Maura tried to wrench free of his grasp but failed. Frustration swept through her. "You think I'm lying? Why would I lie about something like this?"

"That's what I'd like to know, lady."

"Lady?" A near-hysterical laugh bubbled from her lips. "My name is Maura. *Maura Jane Reed.* Don't you remember that either?"

Maura. Quinn frowned. The name triggered something . . .

He stared at the slender, auburn-haired girl more closely.

There was a delicate beauty about her. Something subtly alluring about her fine pale skin and all that bright curly hair so tidily swept up off her neck and carefully pinned. And her eyes, those soft, golden-brown eyes that were so clear, so velvety, and so enchantingly expressive. Right now they expressed fury—and a touch of apprehension. But there was something familiar about them—he seemed to recall them glowing with a different kind of passion. . . .

Maura.

A jolt hit Quinn, a flash of memory that struck him like a bolt of summer lightning. In his mind's eye he saw a girl with fiery curls entangled with him in a hotel bed. A roaring fire, hot kisses . . . a godawful blizzard . . .

"Hell and damnation!" he exclaimed. "The girl who was all bundled up in those ridiculous layers of clothes. That was you!"

Crimson color stained her cheeks. She felt ill. *The girl all bundled up in those ridiculous layers of clothes*—that was how he remembered her. She felt as though he'd struck her across the face. "Well, Mr. Lassiter, what do you know?" she managed to say in a high, tight little voice. "You *do* remember after all."

"Yep." His gaze ran over her with insulting languor. "I sure do. You were awfully cold that night—at first. Seems we managed to keep each other warm."

Maura wondered if she was going to die from humiliation or from nausea. She struggled to speak calmly, though she wanted to shriek. "So now you know. I'm telling the truth."

"Like hell." He dragged her closer, his fingers tightening around her wrist like steel bands. "All I know is that I met you before and that we had a little fun—no," he amended ruthlessly, a mocking light entering his eyes, "a lot of fun. But I sure as hell don't know that you're carrying my baby."

His taunting words, the coldness in his eyes, the cynical arrogance with which he was treating her all swirled around her in a nightmare haze. She stared up at him, no longer able to see the big, gentle man who had loved her that January night, the man who had told her she was pretty and kissed her mouth as if he were drunk with the taste of her. He'd only been drunk with whiskey, she realized. Today he was stone-cold sober and about as gentle as a grizzly.

"How dare you speak to me this way. You have no *right*."

The words poured out of her in a torrent. "I only came here because I thought you might want to know—about the child. Your child! *Our* child!" Frustration shone in her eyes as she tried without success to break his grip. "I was trying to do the right thing. I thought *you* might want to do the right thing too."

"And what might that be, sweetheart?"

"You could . . . marry me."

For an instant shock widened his eyes, then laughter burst out of him, ringing through the room. "You picked the wrong man to try to play for a sucker, angel. In case you haven't noticed, I'm not the marrying, settling-down kind."

"I know that!" Bitterness filled her. And so did a ragged, determined pride. "And what makes you think I'd want to be saddled with you for a husband the rest of my life? I'd rather jump into a rattlesnake pit."

"Then what's this all about?"

"It's about my giving you a chance—a chance to do the right thing by me—and by our baby. I thought you might want to marry me so that you could give this child your name. So it wouldn't be . . . a bastard." She choked a little over the word, then mustered her composure and rushed on. "That's it. Just your name, nothing more. I thought you owed it to him, or her"—she drew a deep breath, fighting back the tears scalding her eyelids— "and to me," she finished quietly. "I thought you owed both of us that much."

A muscle twitched in his jaw. She saw cynicism in his

eyes, and a fierce scorn that seared her to the core. "So I'm supposed to marry you and then light out?"

Her chin inched up a notch. "You could go your way and I'd go mine. I wouldn't ask anything else of you—unless you wanted to help me get settled somewhere with a little bit of money until I can get started on my own—"

Harsh laughter cut her off, chilling her to the bone. "Nice try. But you're not getting one red cent, sweetheart." He hauled her closer, hard against his rock-solid, muscled frame, and his eyes bored down into her face. She could smell the cigar in his vest pocket, the musky male scent of his skin, the danger of his anger. The heat of his temper scorched her, radiating from every inch of his powerful frame. "I don't believe for a minute that there even *is* a baby, and if by some chance there is, it sure as hell isn't mine."

"Why would I—"

"Good question." He studied her upturned face with cold, measuring eyes. "I don't know why the hell you're lying to me, or who put you up to it, but I've got to hand it to you, it takes guts to come in here and try to pull this off." His voice was low, like the menacing growl of a wolf. "Trouble is, it's not working. You picked the wrong man when you laid this trap."

Just as suddenly as he had grabbed her, he flung her away. Maura stumbled back, nearly falling over a chair. She grabbed it and steadied herself just in time, clutching it as her knees shook beneath her gingham gown.

"Now get out and stay out." Quinn Lassiter's voice whipped at her in that cluttered office where sunlight illuminated the hard planes of his face. "I'd better not lay eyes on you again while I'm in Whisper Valley. It wouldn't be healthy. You understand?''

Maura didn't trust herself to speak. Her mouth opened, but no sound came out.

''You understand?'' he demanded again, and took one threatening step forward.

She immediately jumped back. ''Yes, yes—I understand!'' Infuriated tears stung Maura's eyes. One slipped down her cheek before she could blink it away. But her voice came out low and strong, shaking with fury.

''I can't imagine what made me ever think that a man like you, a man who hired out his gun for a living, who kills for a living, would care about the birth of a new life.'' She drew a deep, shuddering breath. ''Just forget I was ever here. Forget I ever mentioned it. Just like you forgot me.''

She whirled around and bolted for the door. The next thing she knew she was running through the saloon, abandoning dignity with the greater need to get away from Quinn Lassiter, far far away.

Quinn followed her back to the main room and watched her flee as if pursued by a mountain cat. Even when the double doors stopped swinging behind her, he continued to stare after her.

Pretty little thing, he admitted, returning to the poker table. Too bad she was a liar and a con artist and nothing but a pack of trouble. He remembered her body being warm, soft, and kissable. Her eyes, that snow-swept night, had hypnotized him deeper than the flames of any fire. And she'd been hot and lush as a rose beneath all those thick ugly clothes.

He grimaced and mentally shook himself. It wasn't

like him to go on about a woman's charms. There were many women in the world and each of them had their charms—and he'd never met one yet who could make him forget about all the others—or the ones yet to come.

And this one, lovely as she might be, was obviously a conniving liar, not to be trusted. If she knew what was good for her, she'd steer clear of him—or better yet, hightail it out of Whisper Valley.

Curly the bartender was clearing away old bottles and replacing them with new ones as Quinn took his seat. Lassiter nodded to the dealer, picked up his freshly dealt cards, and put the girl in the faded gingham gown out of his mind.

Chapter 7

MAURA DIDN'T STOP RUNNING UNTIL SHE reached the privacy of her room. There she bolted the lock, pressed her hands to her burning cheeks, and leaned against the door.

"He's a terrible man," she gasped to herself, taking in deep, powerful gulps of air. "I hate him. And we don't need him," she whispered to the baby, her hands touching her belly, as if she could somehow reassure the tiny child growing within her. "I was so wrong about him. He seemed different that night—I didn't know what he was really like. But don't worry, we'll never have to see him again."

She stumbled to the bed and sank down. Then she spilled out the contents of her handbag and began counting her money. Three dollars, seventy-five cents. It wouldn't last long, but she had enough for a small dinner tonight, breakfast in the morning, and another day's travel on the stagecoach. After that, she'd have to find work and earn some more money for her journey. She'd need train fare to San Francisco, and the sooner the better. She couldn't shake the fear that Judd and Homer would come after her, so the sooner she was clear out of Montana, the safer she'd be.

Closing her eyes, Maura tried to rest. Exhaustion dragged at her, the weariness pulling not only at the limbs of her body but at her mind, her heart. Everything looming before her seemed huge and formidable. Nearly impossible.

You can do it, she told herself. *You can do whatever you have to do. You must. The child has no one else.*

The thought filled her with anxiety, but also with a profound determination. Curling on her side upon the bed, she forced herself to relax enough to drift into sleep.

It was dark in the room when she awoke. The sun had long since slipped behind the mountains and a velvet blackness cloaked the sky, broken only by a handful of stars and a glimmering silver half-moon hanging low among the treetops at the edge of Whisper Valley.

With her muscles still aching from the hours spent in the cramped stagecoach, Maura rose and lit the kerosene lamp on the bureau. She washed her face and brushed out her hair. Carefully, she pinned it all up once more, this time allowing no strands to escape.

Then she went down to the dining room, determined to eat something to keep up her strength, even though she had little appetite and the smell of grease drifting through the hotel lobby and hall made her queasy.

Maura scarcely noticed the other people dining, she barely tasted the chicken fricassee and dumplings placed before her on the pretty blue-and-white china plates. The coffee tasted bitter, and the dark-crusted wedge of apple pie remained uneaten.

She wondered if Judd and Homer were pursuing her

yet. She wondered how far she might get before they caught up with her, what they would do if they did. She wondered if anyone in San Francisco would hire her as a seamstress. And if this awful queasiness would ever go away. . . .

The room seemed to be closing in on her. No longer able to sit still, Maura hastily paid for her dinner and hurried outside. Her thin gray shawl did little to protect her from the bitter cold of the night wind, but for a moment, just a moment, the chill felt good. She lifted her face to the wind, and breathed deep, as if trying to draw strength from the cold, crystal night.

Quickly she began to walk, consumed by restlessness. She had nearly reached the end of the boardwalk before she realized how violently she was shivering. If she caught a chill, that wouldn't be good for the baby. She started back.

She was passing the saloon when a man suddenly lurched out the doors. He stumbled into the wall, clung to it, belched, and then turned and squinted through the darkness at Maura, who had paused, startled, at the sight of him. As she started to edge past in the darkness, he reached out and grabbed her.

"Hey, lady, can I have this dance?" he bellowed drunkenly.

It was the same cowboy who'd spoken to her this afternoon. He must have been drinking all day and all night, Maura realized, repulsed by his red eyes, whiskey breath, and leering, slack-jawed grin. He was scarcely able to stand without swaying, yet his grip on her was surprisingly strong.

"I don't wish to dance, and you don't look as if you're

in much shape for it," she retorted breathlessly. "Let me
go."

She tried to yank her arm free, but he only dug his
fingers into her flesh that much tighter, and laughed
again.

"I jest wan' one little dancy. C'mon," he pleaded.

He dragged her against him and started to spin her
around as if they were dancing, but he lost his balance,
tottering sideways suddenly, dragging her along with him.

Together they fell against the side of the saloon, and
Maura winced in pain as she struck the wall.

The cowboy didn't seem to feel anything. He twisted
suddenly, chuckling, and pinned her against the saloon's
wooden exterior with his body. "Whee, now that was
kinda fun, wasn't it, honey?"

"Let me go this instant!" Maura struggled, gasping at
the sweat and whiskey stink of him, intensified by his
proximity. Her panicked efforts to break free mounted as
he pawed at her breasts.

"Stop that! Stop, you're hurting me—"

Suddenly an unseen figure hurled the cowboy away
from her and into the street. As Maura clutched her shawl
around her, the cowboy tried to rise to his knees, but
instead groaned and collapsed back into the dust.

A wave of dizziness assailed her. She tried to clear her
head and swallow down the fear as she turned to thank
whoever had come to her aid. "I don't know how to thank
you. I'm so grateful—"

She broke off in shock.

Quinn Lassiter loomed over her.

"What the hell are you doing wandering around outdoors at this hour? Coming back to the saloon to try and bamboozle me again?''

''Of course not! This has nothing to do with you,'' she cried, then bit her lip. In truth, it did. Everything she'd done for weeks now had to do with him—planning her escape from Knotsville, searching for him in Helena, traveling here to Whisper Valley. Everything.

''Just leave me alone,'' she gasped. She pushed away from the wall in despair. She whirled abruptly—too abruptly—and started back toward the hotel, but the damned dizziness returned at that unfortunate moment, and she swayed dangerously. She tried to clutch at the wall to keep from falling, but before her fingers could brush the whitewashed wood, Lassiter's arm snaked around her waist.

''Hold on a minute,'' he said quickly. ''Are you all right?'' Then his tone sharpened. ''This better not be an act.''

Maura closed her eyes and waited for the dizziness to pass.

It didn't. Once more she swayed, this time against him, and his other arm slipped around her to steady her.

Her cheeks were pale but with a slightly greenish hue. For one wild moment he wondered if she really might be pregnant.

''Leave me . . . alone.'' Her voice sounded weak, distant. She drew in a deep unsteady breath. ''I d-don't need you. I don't need anything . . . from you.''

And then she fainted. Straight into his arms.

Quinn swept her up, his face tight. He felt a bit green himself. ''Like hell you don't, sweetheart,'' he muttered, and stalked through the darkness toward the hotel.

Chapter 8

 "Land sakes, what in heaven's name did you do to that poor little thing?"

Mabel Barnes rushed out from behind the counter of the Whisper Valley Grand Hotel, her brown eyes bulging with shock. "You didn't shoot her, did you?" she breathed in horror.

"Get out of my way." Quinn started toward the stairs.

At that moment, Maura's eyes fluttered and she moaned.

"Honey, you all right?" Mabel scurried over for a closer look as the gunfighter paused, frowning down at the girl in his arms. "Don't you worry about a thing, I won't let anyone hurt you—not even *him*." She threw a nervous glance at the tall, dark-haired gunman who glared at her as though he'd like to chop her up into little pieces and throw her off the nearest cliff.

"Do what you will to me," the woman exclaimed, straightening her shoulders with fierce determination, "but I'm going to look out for this young lady. She's a guest in *my* hotel, the finest hotel in Montana, and my husband and I didn't work our fingers to the bone to let just any old scum and outlaws and gunfighters come in and molest our innocent paying guests . . . *not* that I'm calling you scum, Mr. Lassiter,'' she added hastily, growing almost as pale as the young woman cradled against the gunfighter's chest. "That's not what I meant at all. I only meant that—''

"Please, Mrs. Barnes," the girl whispered desperately, her golden-brown eyes fixed pleadingly on the other woman's face. "I think . . . I'm going to be sick."

The gunfighter stared uneasily down at her. "Now just hold on—''

"Get her upstairs—Room 204—quick!" Mabel was already scurrying down the hallway, her broad hips swaying from side to side. "I'll get a bucket!''

Moments later Quinn found himself out in the hallway, alone, pacing. His gut twisted as he stared at the closed door.

Could it be that the damned girl really was pregnant?

But not with his baby, he told himself. It couldn't be his baby.

Why not? The question sprang into his mind and wouldn't disappear. *You did sleep with her. Even if it was only one night* . . .

"To hell with this," he muttered suddenly, and charged down the stairs two at a time. He had to get out of here. Maura what's-her-name wasn't his responsibility. And he needed a drink.

But he'd no sooner pushed out the hotel door and headed toward the saloon than he spun around and went back. He'd never run from trouble in his life and he wasn't about to start now.

He'd stay and get to the bottom of this once and for all.

He rapped hard on the door of Room 204 and frowned when Mrs. Barnes called out, "Come in."

The woman was propping pillows behind the girl's head, fussing over her as she lay pale and silent on the yellow coverlet spread over the bed. Pale lamplight shone on the auburn-haired girl's waxen complexion, making her look even more fragile than she had before.

Mrs. Barnes threw him a swift glance over her shoulder. "So it's you," she hmmphed. "Well, the young lady told me you didn't shoot her or anything, that she just fainted, so I suppose I shouldn't have been so hard on you, Mr. Lassiter. You did a good turn by bringing her here. And the good news is, she didn't actually need the bucket after all," she rattled on, patting the girl's arm.

"That's a mercy, anyway. When I was in the family way, I felt sick every single day for months but never once actually—" She broke off, seeing Maura flush. "Pardon me, honey," she said kindly. "I certainly didn't mean to embarrass you, but it's plain as day that you're in a delicate condition and why you're traveling in these parts all alone like this I just can't understand. Not that I haven't seen it before—goodness knows, running a hotel like this my husband and I have seen all kinds of things, but I'll never for the life of me figure out what kind of a man leaves a woman to fend for herself at a time like this—"

"Mrs. Barnes. *Please.*"

"What's wrong, dear?" Mabel Barnes peered into her face. "You think you're going to be sick?" She grabbed the bucket she'd set down beside the bed, and held it level with Maura's chest.

"No . . . it's not that." Maura sat up, swung her legs

to the floor, and set the bucket down alongside the bedside table. She didn't trust her strength enough yet to try to stand, but she forced herself to glance squarely first at Mrs. Barnes, then at Quinn Lassiter, lounging with his shoulders against the mantel.

"I do appreciate all your kindness." She shifted her gaze back to Mrs. Barnes and kept it there with rigid determination. "But I'd like to be left alone now—to rest."

"Don't you fret, honey. I understand. Women in your conditon do need their rest." Mrs. Barnes nodded vigorously. "You lie here a spell and take it easy while I go downstairs and fetch you a nice hot cup of tea."

"Please don't trouble yourself."

"Why, it's no trouble. None at all. Matter of fact, I—"

"You heard the lady." Quinn pushed away from the mantel and strode forward. He grasped Mrs. Barnes by the arm and propelled her toward the door. "She wants to be left alone."

"But—but—aren't you leaving too?" Mabel Barnes sputtered as the gunfighter pushed her through the door. "It wouldn't be proper for me to go and leave you here alone with her!"

"Afraid I'm going to shoot her?" he asked dryly. "Reckon I haven't shot any ladies who were in a delicate condition since last month."

"That's not what I meant, Mr. Lassiter! My word! I'm thinking of her reputation!"

"Seems a little late to be worried about that." Before she could say another word, or do more than stare at him in openmouthed astonishment, Quinn closed the door in her face.

"Alone at last," he growled, stalking over to where Maura perched on the edge of the bed.

Maura half expected to hear Mrs. Barnes banging on the door, but when that didn't happen, she knew the woman's awe of the gunfighter had gotten the better of her.

She swallowed. She'd have to get rid of Quinn Lassiter herself.

"Our business is finished." Firmly, she pushed herself up from the bed. If only this awful light-headedness would ease. Facing Lassiter was a formidable enough challenge without feeling dizzy and weak. "You made that clear enough in the saloon."

"Could be I was wrong."

"What would make you think so?" she asked tightly, regarding him through wary eyes.

Instead of answering, he studied her in turn, taking his time, his gaze hard and appraising, his eyes unreadable. The silence lengthened and Maura felt her tension increasing, stretching her nerves taut. She fought the urge to fidget beneath that relentless hawk's gaze, to smooth her hair or straighten her skirt.

"I'm waiting, Mr. Lassiter," she said at last.

"I need to ask you a few questions."

"What sort of questions?"

He took a step closer, not touching her, but near enough that Maura felt panic coil in the pit of her stomach. This powerful nearness threatened her—it threatened her composure, her ability to think clearly, to keep her emotions in check. It would be so much easier if she could just forget everything that had happened between them that night.

But she couldn't. Each time she looked into his face she remembered how that grim mouth had felt scraping over her throat, she remembered the warmth and gentleness of his touch, the way his thumbs had tormented the peaks of her breasts, and the thick texture of his dark hair sliding between her fingers as that superbly muscled body fitted itself against hers.

"If you're really carrying a child," he began, but he got no further for Maura gasped.

"You think I'm lying? *Still?*"

The black brows drew together. "I didn't say that."

"What *are* you saying?"

"If it's true—how do you know it's mine?"

Her cheeks blazed crimson. Sparks burned golden in the depths of her eyes as she struggled for words.

"How *dare* you." Her voice was low, nearly a whisper, but it shook with outrage.

He seemed neither to notice nor to care. "How many men have you been with in the past month?"

"How many . . ."

Maura couldn't speak another word. Without thinking, she lifted her hand and drew back to slap him.

He grasped her wrist before the blow could connect and he held it firmly.

"Just tell me how many."

"Goodness, who knows? A dozen. Two dozen. Perhaps even a *hundred*," she replied, meeting his eyes with a blazing defiance she hadn't even known she possessed, a defiance she'd never dared show her adoptive brothers but that seemed to be kindled effortlessly by this far more dangerous gunfighter. "A girl can hardly keep track of such things. After all, we get so many fascinating, irresistible men passing through Knotsville, what's a girl to—ohhhh!''

She gasped as he hauled her against him, one hand cupping her chin, forcing her head up so that she had no choice but to meet his eyes.

"How many?" Something deadly in his tone made her gulp and then moisten her lips. "I'll ask you once more."

"And if I refuse to answer—what are you going to do? Shoot me?" But she felt far less confident than she sounded as she fought for calm.

"Trust me, sweetheart, you don't want to find out."

Maura wrenched free. "No one else," she muttered, whirling away from him, sweeping toward the window. "Only you."

She stared out at the night, listening to the pounding of her own heartbeat.

Quinn stared at her rigid back, the soft curves of her hips and buttocks beneath that faded gown. He suddenly wondered . . .

No. She wasn't. That hadn't been her first time—had it? Alarmed, he struggled to remember something beyond the heat and the pleasure.

"Only me?" he demanded. "Is that the truth?"

"Who would lie about something like that?" Maura turned from the window, her hands clenched in the folds of her skirt.

"You'd be surprised what people will lie about."

She shook her head. "Don't you trust *anyone?*"

"Yeah. I trust myself. What about you, lady, who do you trust?"

"No one," she whispered back, realizing that it was true.

"Not even yourself?"

"I thought I did. But not after that night. When I . . . when we . . . I've never done anything that rash and stupid and ill-thought-out before."

"Must've been my charm," he commented dryly.

"No, it wasn't that." Maura spoke bitterly. "It was me. Being silly and foolish and not looking before I leaped. And now . . ."

He frowned as her voice trailed off dejectedly. She looked so lost that he had to fight a sudden urge to wrap an arm around her shoulders and tell her everything would be all right. There was something sweet about her that wrenched at him—but he fought the protective instinct. Lassiter knew better than to take anything or anyone on appearances. This girl could be a master con artist, an actress of the first order. She probably was.

Except that he *had* slept with her. And enjoyed it too. He remembered that soft, lush body, the bright velvety curls—and those lustrous eyes that had penetrated even his whiskey haze.

And from what he'd seen tonight—and heard from Mrs. Barnes—it looked a hell of a lot like she was in that so-called delicate condition.

Hell. Scowling, he took a turn around the room. He needed to think, needed to figure all this out.

"Get some rest," he ordered at last, yanking open the door. "We'll talk again in the morning."

"There's nothing to talk about."

"If there's a baby—if it's mine . . ."

She held her breath. "You'd be willing to do the right thing? To give the baby your name?"

Quinn Lassiter spoke tightly. "Don't go jumping to any conclusions. Just get some shut-eye."

He stalked out, slamming the door behind him.

Silence filled the air around her.

Maura didn't know whether to feel hopeful—or afraid.

She fought the urge to sneak out of town on the first stagecoach and raise the child alone, without any help from the all too reluctant Quinn Lassiter. But she owed her baby a chance at a good start in life—and the gunfighter owed her baby a name.

When morning comes, she thought, sinking wearily down on the bed, *we'll see.*

It was going to be a long night.

Chapter 9

SLEEP ELUDED QUINN LASSITER THAT NIGHT.

He emerged from the hotel after downing three cups of coffee and a plate of eggs and immediately spotted Maura standing before Kent's Mercantile. She was clutching her shawl around her shoulders against the March wind while she gazed into the window of the store.

His mouth tightened as he watched her.

He remembered how she'd fainted, the green tinge of her skin, the concerned, knowing words of Mabel Barnes.

And everything Maura had told him in the saloon flooded back.

I'm going to have your baby. I thought you might want to do the right thing.

Fury and resignation struggled within him. He wanted to believe she was lying. But the events of last night—and his gut—told him she wasn't.

Damn it all to hell.

Some ready-made ribbon-trimmed dresses were displayed in the general store's front window, along with several hats and bonnets, several barrels of potatoes, a stack of pots and pans, and an assortment of tins brimming with peppermint candy. As Quinn approached Maura, watching her from beneath the brim of his hat, he noticed that she seemed fascinated by the lot of it.

"Come on." He placed a hand on her elbow to draw her away. He had no way of knowing she was seeing nothing but the yawning uncertainty of her own future.

"Where . . ." she began warily, lifting her gaze to his face.

"To the church. You want to get hitched, we'll get hitched."

"I beg your pardon." Maura wrenched her elbow free. "You can't just walk up to me and tell me we're getting married."

"Why not?" he countered, his face hard as a tombstone. "Because it isn't romantic? Well, neither is going to bed with a man who comes into your hotel only to get out of a blizzard."

She gasped and turned ten shades of red. Too overcome to speak, she backed away from him but he advanced on her and seized her arm.

"You wanted me to marry you, didn't you? You wanted me to give the kid a name."

"I *don't* want to have this discussion in the street," she hissed. A woman in gray gingham passing by with two children clinging to her skirts stared for a moment and then continued briskly on her way.

"Fine, then we'll have it in the alley."

Without giving her a chance to protest, he dragged her off the boardwalk and behind the mercantile. The alley was narrow with patches of ice remaining from the last snow. It was also deserted. When Quinn backed her against the cold frame of the building, Maura knew she wasn't going to get out of here until he was good and ready.

She braced her hands against the wall behind her. Her shawl fluttered in the wind, and a wayward curl wisped from her chignon to blow across her eyes. "This isn't a very romantic place for a proposal."

"I've already told you, this has nothing to do with romance."

Of course not. Romance was not for Maura Reed. She stared at him hollowly, trying to keep her lips pursed in a semblance of defiance even though the wind whipping through the alley was making her shiver. She wished she were sitting before a fire, snug and warm and drinking tea. Or even crowded on a stagecoach, crammed between other sore bodies, weary from traveling but sheltered from the mountain wind—and from the deadly chill in his eyes. She wished she were anywhere, anywhere but here—with him.

"Then what does it have to do with, Mr. Lassiter?" she asked with as much verve as she could muster.

"Responsibility, Miss Reed. Yours—and mine."

"For the baby?" She stared at him, then shook her head. "You surprise me. I'd just about decided men like you didn't possess a sense of responsibility."

He edged even closer, hemming her in. It was all Maura could do not to run. She knew he would only grab her.

"You don't know a damned thing about men like me."

"I know that you kill people for a living. That you pride yourself on how many men you kill—"

"And women? How do you know I don't kill women

too?'' he demanded, then suddenly some emotion she couldn't decipher flashed across his eyes, and Quinn Lassiter actually turned ashen. As she searched his face, wondering at the terrible grim stillness that had come over him, Maura could only draw one conclusion and it filled her with fear.

''You . . . *have* killed a woman, haven't you?''

''Only one,'' he grated so harshly she recoiled, squeezing against the wall of the mercantile as if trying to sink into it and escape. ''But don't push me, lady, or I swear it could be two.''

Her knees sagged. She felt them giving out on her and reached blindly out, but before she could fall, Lassiter had snaked an arm around her waist, supporting her. She wanted to resist his help, but her legs were too weak and she found herself leaning against him, allowing him to hold her up.

For a moment they stared at each other, with the wind rushing around them in the icy little alley, carrying with it the distant barking of a dog, the slamming of a door from some shop on the main street, the muffled sound of a wagon rolling through the town.

She's just an itty bit of a thing, Quinn thought as his hand tightened around the girl's waist. He could break her in two as easily as snapping a twig. They both knew it.

And they both knew he'd been bullying her unconscionably from the moment she'd sought him out in the saloon.

Yet she'd stood up to him, stood up to him as few other people he'd known ever had dared to do. This girl with the fiery curls and gentle eyes had the most infuriating temperament he'd ever seen in a woman—and she was made of far stronger stuff than she appeared to be.

"Listen. I didn't drag you back here to fight with you," he said shortly. "I wanted to explain something."

"Fine." Maura swallowed. "Explain."

"I reckon I believe you about that baby you're carrying. If you say it's mine—"

"It is."

She spoke with an utter simplicity that could only come from the truth, and Quinn felt his heart sinking like a stone. "Then I'll take care of it," he said grimly. "I take care of what's mine."

Stunned, she could only gape at him. "G-go on," she managed at last.

"I'll marry you just like you wanted—and do what's right by the baby. I'll give it my name, and set you up someplace safe where you can raise the kid."

"Set me up?" Maura fought against the relief and hope rising in her. She saw only harsh determination in his face. He'd sooner be shot through with arrows, she guessed, than be making this little speech. But he was making it, and that was something. "What do you mean?" she asked quietly. "Where?"

"There's some land I own in Wyoming—a ranch. It was payment for a job I did. You can have it."

He sounded so cold. So impersonal. But he'd obviously given this a lot of thought. "What about you?" she asked a bit dazedly.

"I'm not sticking around," he told her, eyes narrowed. "And you sure as hell aren't coming with me."

"You're going to continue to be a gunfighter?"

"Damned right. It's what I do—it's what I'll always

do. Till the day I die. And that reminds me—I've got enemies, sweetheart. Lots of 'em. Believe me, you don't want me anywhere around you and the kid. So if you think you're getting a conventional, stick-around husband, you're wrong.'' His tone was rough. ''That's not part of this deal. I get you started on the ranch, hire some men to work it, and then I'm gone.''

Gone. Maura read the determination in his face. ''Fine,'' she responded as coolly as she could, but even to her own ears, her voice sounded shaky.

''You accept that? You're not going to start nagging me to stick around?''

Pride shot through her and her chin lifted. ''Don't be silly, Mr. Lassiter. I'm certain both the baby and I will be much better off without you.''

''You got that right, lady.''

His hand dropped from her waist. As if realizing for the first time just how close he'd been standing, just how tightly he'd been holding her, he stepped back and cleared his throat. ''So it's all understood between us then?'' He still sounded wary and suspicious, as if he thought she was setting a trap. ''You know that this won't be a real marriage—that I'm not sticking around?''

''I understand perfectly. It's going to be a kind of . . .'' She searched for the right words. ''Business arrangement.''

''Right. Nothing more,'' he warned. ''And nothing less. A business arrangement.''

Absurdly, Maura found herself fighting back tears. What was wrong with her? This was what she'd wanted, after all. He was going to give the baby a name and help her get started. She'd have a place to live—her very own place, with no one else telling her what to do. And she'd have her child. Someone to love.

It was more than she'd ever had before. It should be enough.

It *is* enough, she told herself firmly, thinking of the tiny beautiful life growing inside her. *I don't need or want Quinn Lassiter to stick around. My baby and I will be just fine on our own.*

There was no threat in Quinn's eyes now, no fury. He was watching her steadily, perhaps even with a flicker of sympathy.

Well, she didn't want his pity!

But she could almost . . . almost . . . see once again that strong, tender man who had held her against the winter chill, whose lips had captured hers with such heat and power. A tremor of longing shook her.

But she quickly took command of herself and drew in a deep breath. Those kisses, that cold, splendid night, were gone forever. She was in an alley with a hardened gunfighter, making a business arrangement, plain and simple. *Take it or leave it, Maura,* she told herself desperately. *Do what's best for your baby.*

"Yes," she heard herself saying in a faint voice. "I'll marry you."

Quinn Lassiter nodded. He didn't even smile. Just took her arm and started steering her back toward the street.

"Fine. Put on your prettiest dress and we'll get this thing over with."

She faltered and stopped in her tracks. "I'm afraid this *is* my prettiest dress."

He glanced down in surprise at the threadbare gingham she'd worn the day before as well. The fabric was faded and dull, and frayed at the cuffs. It looked like something she'd worn for years while scrubbing floors and washing dishes.

"Hell, I thought every woman owned at least *one* fancy Sunday dress," he muttered without thinking.

Suddenly, he saw the sparkle of tears in her eyes. Tears! Something clenched in his gut. She averted her head, but it was too late. He'd seen those ominous glistening droplets.

Shit.

"But this one's not so bad," he said quickly. "I mean, it's a hell of a lot better than those godawful long johns you had on that night we met. I mean, it's a *dress,* isn't it—hell, don't *do* that," he ordered tersely as more tears began to stream down her cheeks. "Don't cry!"

"I'm n-not c-crying!"

"You sure as hell are." He stared at her. Wasn't that just like a woman to sob because she was getting married in an old rag of a dress?

"You want a new dress?" he growled. "For the wedding?"

"Of course not. That would be s-silly."

"Why would it be silly?"

"Because this isn't a special occasion. It's a b-business arrangement."

"It damn sure is." He tugged her over to the boardwalk as a wagon rolled down the street. The wind whipped at the skirt of her gingham as they continued toward the hotel. They hadn't gone ten more steps before he heard a sniffle. A definite sniffle.

Quinn stopped short and grasped her by the shoulders.

He turned her in the direction of the mercantile. "Go buy one of those fancy gowns."

"Buy one?" Maura shook her head. "No. I can't do that."

"Why not?"

She'd never bought a dress in her life. She'd sewn the few that she owned. "I—can't afford it," she stammered.

"I can." He yanked a pouch from his pocket and pushed some greenbacks into her palm, even as she shook her head once more.

"I don't take charity."

His brows lifted. "It's not charity, Maura. We're going to be married. I'm going to be your husband."

Maura's eyes flew to his. All thoughts of a dress vanished from her mind. Did he mean he would expect all of his husbandly privileges?

"Get yourself a bonnet too," Quinn went on, as if he hadn't just said something significant enough to rattle all that was left of her wits. "And whatever else you might need for a journey. We'll be leaving Whisper Valley tomorrow."

"So soon?"

"Could be a job waiting for me, hunting down some rustlers. The sooner I get you settled on the ranch, the better. Now do you want to get yourself a dress and get this wedding over with or do you want to stand here jawing all day?"

She swallowed and pushed the greenbacks into her pocket. "I'll meet you at the church then."

"No, you won't. I'll call for you at the hotel after you've changed your clothes. We'll go to the church together."

There was no tenderness in his tone. Only taut command.

And suddenly she couldn't keep still a moment longer. "Since this is our wedding day," she said, her eyes still sparkling with the glitter of tears, "we'll do as you wish. But only today. After this . . ." She gathered her courage. "Don't expect me to go along with everything you want. I'm marrying you for the sake of the baby, but I *won't* be your doormat. I've played that role all my life and I'm telling you right now, that is *not* part of our arrangement."

"I don't remember ever saying it was."

"Well, in case you thought so—"

"Sweetheart, I won't be around long enough to try to make you a doormat—or anything else for that matter. Got it?"

She forced herself to meet his cold glance without flinching. "Oh, yes, Mr. Lassiter." Her voice was a low quiver. "I've got it."

She whirled around and headed nearly at a run toward the mercantile.

Quinn watched her go, enjoying the sight of her gently rolling hips beneath that plain, worn gown, the determined set of her narrow shoulders, the way the sun set fire to her carefully coiled hair, nearly blinding him with its brilliance.

If he wasn't so disgusted with himself for landing in this pickle, he might almost look forward to pulling the pins from that spiraling mass of curls, to watching them tumble down past her shoulders, all wild and free. He might even have looked forward to tangling with that unexpected temper of hers. And certainly he would have looked forward to taking her to his bed, to freshening his memory of that fateful damnable night by exploring every naked inch of her.

But right now he wasn't looking forward to anything.

He wasn't about to lose his freedom, the only good thing he'd had in his life for the past fourteen years. The only thing he cherished more than his gun, his horse, and his aim.

And that woman marching across the street to buy a wedding gown had better not expect him to trade in his liberty for a home, a hearth, and a baby.

Because he'd rather eat every cow pie in the territory than suffer a fate as horrible as that.

Chapter 10

 "IT'S THE MOST GORGEOUS DRESS I'VE EVER seen," Maura exclaimed.

She reached out one finger and touched the pale blue satin gown with the puffed sleeves, yellow sash, and pearl buttons, caressing the fabric tentatively, as though fearing it might disappear in a puff of smoke. "But so is this one."

Her gaze shifted to the ivory silk gown with its billowing beaded train and scalloped neckline.

Both dresses were stunning, far lovelier than anything she had ever hoped to own, or needed to own. Even for her wedding.

"I don't think either one is quite right for me, though."

Reluctantly, she dropped her hand and stepped back from the counter where the balding little clerk had draped them for her perusal.

With a grunt the clerk began to whisk them away, but a light, cool, feminine voice stopped him.

"Not so fast, Jimmy. I think those dresses are perfect for her. Why don't you try them on?" the voice asked her, and Maura turned, startled, to gaze into the wide-set turquoise eyes of the most beautiful young woman she'd ever seen.

"Forgive me for meddling." The girl flashed her a smile so warm and beguiling and sympathetic, Maura couldn't help but smile back. "But with your coloring and your figure, these would be lovely. You ought to buy them both."

At this, the baby in the young woman's arms gave a squeal, and the girl in the blue-checked shirt and trim blue riding skirt lifted the tiny girl up to her shoulder. "Oh, there, now Tory, you'll have all the pretty dresses you like when you're old enough. Surely you can share these two with this nice lady."

And turning back to Maura, she grinned. "I'm Emma Garrettson," she said. "Don't mind me, I tend to speak my mind. It's a habit I have. My husband tells me it's one of my more annoying habits. But then according to him, I have so many that—"

She broke off with a laugh that sounded like chiming bells. "Sorry. This is none of my business. But you looked so . . . so taken with the dresses. I had a feeling that there's a special occasion."

Maura's natural reserve vanished beneath the warmth of Emma's smile. "My wedding," she blurted out, then blushed.

How strange to say those words.

Emma Garrettson's face lit up like a candle. "How wonderful. When are you getting married?"

"Today." Maura's blush deepened.

"Today!"

"In a few moments. We're just passing through town

and decided . . . that is . . . I have to pick something out and meet Mr. Quinn . . . that is, my fiancé''—she stumbled over the words, positive by now her cheeks must be as bright as berries—''at the hotel as soon as I'm ready. I was going to get married in this,'' she rushed on, aware that she was babbling, but unable to stop as Emma Garrettson watched her with rounded, fascinated eyes, ''but it's so old and drab and my . . . er . . . fiancé insisted that I have a new dress.'' She finished and took a deep breath. ''I'm Maura Reed,'' she added, amazed that she'd been having such a long and intimate conversation with someone she'd only just met and hadn't yet told her name.

The clerk, Jimmy, was listening too, and appeared just as transfixed as Emma.

''Well, goodness. That was very thoughtful of him. Your fiancé, I mean. The least you can do is pick out something that will dazzle him,'' the dark-haired girl pointed out. ''The blue one. That will do it.''

Maura turned and gazed longingly once more at the pale blue gown, shimmering almost silver in the light.

''Do you think so?''

''Trust me. It's perfect for you. Why don't you slip into the back room and try it on? If it needs any adjustments I can do it for you in a trice.''

Maura found herself swept along by Emma Garrettson's enthusiasm. She allowed herself to be escorted into the small neat office behind the long counter, and was soon stepping into the magical blue gown.

''It's beautiful.'' Emma stroked the baby's cheek. ''See the pretty lady, Victoria? Tell her she must be married in this dress.''

The baby cooed, and Maura laughed. Turning to survey herself in the long mirror that hung behind the office door, she gave a gasp of pleasure.

The delicate blue color was striking with her auburn hair. The puffed sleeves made her look and feel like a fairy-tale princess, and the gown, cinched gracefully at her waist, fell to the floor in a graceful sweep of diaphonous fabric.

"It needs to be taken in just a bit at the waist since you're so slender," Emma said. "Here, slip it off and hold Tory for me, and I'll have it ready in no time."

Maura changed quickly back into her gingham and found herself sitting on the floor playing with little Victoria Garrettson while Emma worked deftly with a needle and thread.

"If I wasn't so nervous about getting married today, I could do that myself," she said by way of apology. "I'm quite good with a needle and thread. I was planning to go to San Francisco to find a job as a seamstress in a lady's dress shop when—"

She broke off, biting her lip.

"When you met Mr. Quinn and decided to marry him?" Emma finished easily for her, glancing up from her task.

"Something like that. Actually his name is not Mr. Quinn, it's Mr. Lassiter. Quinn Lassiter."

"The gunfighter!" the girl exclaimed, then gave a cry as she stuck herself with the needle. "Damn. Lost my concentration. Tucker told me Quinn Lassiter was in town. Tucker is my husband," she explained as she deftly pulled the needle through once more. "I seem to remember him mentioning that they played cards together a day or so ago. Tucker lost twenty dollars to him—so he must be a good card player. But . . . how strange! One wouldn't think a famous gunfighter like him would settle down. . . . Oh, pardon me!'' she added with a sheepish laugh. ''I'm babbling. I hope you'll be very happy.''

''You're very kind,'' Maura said softly. The baby nodded at her shoulder, her small, pudgy body going slack. Tory was falling asleep, her tiny bow of a mouth pursed, her eyes closed daintily against rounded cheeks. ''You haven't even asked me a single question about why I'm getting married in a strange town in the middle of the day, in a store-bought dress I'm selecting only moments before the ceremony.''

''It's none of my business—unless you want to tell me.''

Maura shook her head. ''It's a long story,'' she murmured, then her voice trailed off as another bout of queasiness returned. ''Perhaps you'd best take the baby,'' she managed, light-headed enough that she feared she might drop the precious bundle in her arms. ''I'm not feeling well all of a sudden . . .''

''I know that look.'' Emma set the dress aside and hurried to her side, scooping Tory into her arms. She gazed down at the auburn-haired girl seated upon the floor, one hand to her brow.

''You're positively green,'' she murmured sympathetically. Her hand gently rubbed her baby's back. ''I felt ill when I was expecting my child too.''

Maura said nothing for a moment.

''The dress is ready,'' Emma continued, easing the uncomfortable silence in her brisk, breezy way. Maura glanced up at her gratefully.

"Why don't I go along to the hotel and help you dress? There are a lot of little buttons here that need fastening and you don't want to keep Mr. Lassiter waiting."

Keep him waiting? Maura surged to her feet so quickly her head spun and she had to grasp the edge of the desk.

"How long have I been here?" she gasped. "I told him I'd buy a dress and come back right away—"

"Oh, let him wait for you," Emma advised. "He'll be that much more eager. I'm a firm believer in training a man right from the beginning so he understands that a woman cannot be rushed while getting dressed, baking a cake, or making love. Not that I had to teach Tucker much when it came to *that*. He has always known just how to . . . Goodness, listen to me rattling on." It was her turn to blush, and to laugh.

"You don't know Quinn. He's not a patient man—or a trainable one—" She broke off, cursing her own loose tongue. "I must get back," she finished, suddenly eager for Emma to accompany her. She could use a friend at this moment. She was about to take the most important step of her life, and to face a man who was as unpredictable as a mountain lion. It wouldn't hurt to have a friendly face at her side.

"I'd appreciate your help, Emma—if you can spare the time."

Emma Garrettson assured her that she could, and Maura hastily returned to Kent's main room to pay for the dress and watch impatiently as Jimmy folded it into a box. But as she lifted her parcel the door to the mercantile opened and a tall, handsome, gold-haired man in a buckskin jacket and wide-brimmed Stetson strode in.

"Thought you were only buying flour and hairpins."
He walked right up to Emma, lifted the awakening baby
from her arms, and gave the tiny cheek a kiss. Then he
turned, tucking Tory comfortably in the crook of his arm,
and leaned down to give Emma a quite different kind of
kiss, long, deep, and possessive. "I missed you, Malloy,"
he growled.

If Emma had looked beautiful before, now she positively glowed. "Hold on to your horses, Garrettson," she
told him, but there was a soft breathlessness in her casual
tone. "There's someone I'd like you to meet. This is
Maura Reed."

"Pleasure, Miss Reed."

Maura smiled into razor-sharp blue eyes. She couldn't
help but notice how Emma and Tucker Garrettson looked
at each other. As if they couldn't get enough.

A twinge of envy raced through her at their obvious
happiness.

"So . . ." Emma concluded her explanation of
Maura's situation as Maura focused her thoughts. "I'm
going to help her dress for the wedding. Would you mind
taking Tory for a little while?"

"No problem. My father and yours are making a bet
about her right now in the saloon. They've bet ten dollars
over who gets the bigger smile when I bring her in and
she sees them both together."

Emma snatched the baby back from him and kissed the
top of her head. "You're *not* taking my daughter into a
saloon," she began with mock indignation, but suddenly,
the door opened yet again and this time Quinn Lassiter
stalked in.

The mercantile fell silent.

The gunfighter paused just inside the doorway, his hard gaze riveted on Maura.

He paid no attention to anyone else, his eyes locked on hers as if no one else in Whisper Valley existed.

Slowly, he came toward her and took the parcel. "Reckon you forgot the preacher's waiting."

"I didn't forget."

"Having second thoughts? This whole thing was your idea."

"Of course not!" Indignation swept over her. "We have an arrangement and I'm prepared to stick to it."

She felt Emma Garrettson's eyes on her, and forced herself to glance at the other woman. Staring back and forth between Maura and Quinn, Emma looked both puzzled and concerned.

"Then we'd best get a move on." Quinn took her arm. "The day's not getting any younger," he added grimly.

"I still have to change—"

"Forget it. You look fine." With the parcel tucked under his arm, he began steering her toward the door, pausing only long enough to nod coolly at Tucker Garrettson.

"Oh, no, Mr. Lassiter—you can't do that!"

Emma Garrettson stepped into his path before Tucker could stop her.

"Malloy," her husband growled, but she ignored him.

"Maura has bought the loveliest dress—she *must* be married in it. I insist."

Quinn stared at her and the gurgling baby girl in her arms. He wasn't sure he'd heard right. "You insist?" he repeated, sounding somewhat dazed.

"I do." Though the winning smile she bestowed on the gunfighter did nothing to soften his granite features,

Emma nevertheless ignored her husband's warning look and continued with airy determination, jiggling the baby as she spoke. "Every woman ought to be married in a beautiful gown. I do believe it's a law in Montana, isn't it, Tucker?" She breezed on, unperturbed when her husband rolled his eyes. "Besides, I promised Maura I would help her dress for the wedding and so I will. It won't take long at all, I give you my word. Besides, you two will need witnesses, right? Tucker and I would be happy to help out. Wouldn't we, darling?"

"Emma, I reckon these folks wouldn't welcome two strangers horning in on—" He broke off as he caught the urgent light in Emma's eye. Quickly, he glanced over at the auburn-haired woman his wife had befriended. She looked tense and pale and none too eager to go off with Lassiter.

Something was going on here, something that his wife had picked up on with female intuitiveness but that left him baffled. Nevertheless he trusted Emma's judgment in such things. Maybe the girl needed help. Maybe she was being forced into this marriage? She sure didn't look happy.

For that matter, neither did Lassiter. But then, who would ever imagine a man like him getting married?

"We'd be glad to oblige," he said steadily, and gave Maura a reassuring smile before turning to the gunfighter.

"How about if I buy you a drink over at the Jezebel while the ladies get ready?" he suggested lazily.

Quinn's jaw tightened and he started to refuse, then something made him look at the girl who was going to become his wife.

She was watching him, her chin angled forward in that

defiant way of hers, but there was a wariness in her eyes. Mixed with something that could only be hope. Hope that she'd have a chance to wear that new dress?

Hell, what was wrong with him? He was going to rush her off to the wedding without giving her a chance to get all gussied up—all because she'd kept him waiting?

"Reckon I could use a drink." It took every effort of will he possessed to hide the agitation churning through him. This marriage business was turning out to be damned difficult. And he had a suspicion it would only get worse. Already he couldn't wait to get away.

"Maybe two drinks," he told Tucker grimly, then forced himself to smile at Maura.

"Take your time, angel. I'll come fetch you when you're ready. The preacher will keep. After all," he added dryly, "last thing I'd want to do is break any of Montana's sacred laws."

He tipped his hat to Emma and held the door for them to pass through.

The moment Maura reached her hotel room, she sank down on the bed.

"Dear Lord, what am I doing?" she moaned, burying her face in her hands.

This was wrong, the entire situation was wrong. How could she marry a man she didn't love, a man who didn't love her?

The sweet sparks and easy accord she'd seen between Emma and her husband only served to emphasize just how much was lacking between her and Quinn Lassiter. Their business arrangement of a marriage would be a disaster. But she had to endure it for a while. For the sake of her baby . . .

"Why don't you tell me the whole story?" Emma Garrettson spoke softly, sitting down on the edge of the bed. Peering into her lovely, earnest face, Maura saw something she'd never seen in her entire life.

Caring. Concern. Friendship.

"Perhaps I can help," Emma murmured encouragingly. "I'd like to try."

The story poured out of Maura. She held nothing back. Drained and exhausted, she ended on a note of despair. "I want to do what's best for my baby. But I don't even know how long Quinn will stay. He's trying to do what's honorable, but he doesn't care for me. Maybe this whole temporary marriage idea is a horrible mistake!"

"No, no, don't think that." Emma put her arms around Maura's shoulders and hugged her. To Emma's surprise, the fragile young woman hadn't begun to cry. She was upset, but not overwrought.

She's stronger than she looks, Emma thought. Which was good. She'd need to be if she was going to marry that handsomer-than-sin flint-eyed gunman Emma'd met in Kent's Mercantile.

And yet . . . Emma had sensed something more beneath the surface of Quinn Lassiter's hard exterior. It *was* honorable of him to want to marry Maura and take care of the child. And he *had* backed down about the wedding gown. It took a strong man to change his mind. Many men were too stubborn to give in to a woman, fearing they'd appear weak, but Lassiter had done the right thing as soon as he saw the hopeful look on Maura's face.

Perhaps Lassiter was like Tucker, mule-headed on the

outside, and gentle as a lamb underneath that ornery exterior.

"I happen to think there might be hope for you two yet," she said slowly, easing back and smiling into Maura's eyes. "Believe it or not, Tucker and I hated each other for years. So did our fathers. If we could become a family—a wonderful, happy, united family—*anything* is possible."

"It's not like that with us." There was a lump in Maura's throat. "Quinn has made it plain—he's leaving as soon as he has me settled on his land. This is only a temporary marriage—so that the baby will have a name, and a home. And that's for the best," she said quickly, trying not to sound as miserable as she felt. "It was my idea. I . . . wouldn't want a man who felt trapped, like he'd been roped into something he only wanted to get out of. It's not as if we . . . love each other."

"No, that's true. Right now. But in time . . . well, you never know what might happen between two people," Emma suggested gently.

For a moment Maura felt a stirring of hope, a wild, ridiculous hope. Then she remembered Quinn's words, the grim purpose in his eyes. *I get you started on the ranch, hire some men to work it, and then I'm gone.*

She shook her head. "No. Quinn isn't the kind of man to . . ." She sighed. "There will never be love between us," she finished quietly.

A small silence fell.

"Maura, if you've changed your mind about this arrangement you've made, if you want to back out of it, you're welcome to stay with Tucker and me until you figure out what to do. You don't *have* to marry Lassiter if you think this agreement between you won't work or if you simply don't want to go through with it.''

Maura stared at her gratefully. Emma looked so determined there was no doubt she meant what she said. A weight lifted from Maura's shoulders.

She had a choice after all.

But she knew what she was going to do. Her momentary panic had passed. She had made this bargain in the first place because it was good for the baby—and that hadn't changed. Nothing had changed. It was still her best course of action. If only . . .

What? she asked herself bitterly. *If only Quinn Lassiter wasn't a gunfighter, wasn't a roaming, no-ties kind of man?*

If only he wanted to try to make a real home for her and the baby, to see if they could find a way to stay together, to find some tiny thread of love to bind them?

She knew better.

He didn't want love. Or a home, or a family. He never would.

And the sooner she accepted that and stopped wasting time with such idiotic dreaming, the better.

''It's all right.'' She heard her own voice as if from a great distance. How calm she sounded. How sure. ''I'm going to marry him,'' she said softly.

''Maura, you're certain?''

She opened the box and, with a rustle, lifted out the pale blue gown. It drifted like a cloud as she laid it across the bed.

''Yes, I'm certain. I want my baby to have a name.'' Determination swept through her as she gazed at the other woman. For as long as she lived, she would never forget the kindness of Emma Garrettson. Just as she would never forget her duty to her child.

"Please." She touched Emma's hand. She'd delayed long enough. It was time to see this through. "Will you help me to get ready now?"

Chapter 11

 THE WEDDING WAS OVER IN NEARLY LESS TIME than it had taken Maura to don her dress.

A few words from the preacher about the holiness of matrimony and the power of love, a mumble of prayers, and then Maura Jane Reed had taken Quinn Lassiter to be her lawful wedded husband, and Quinn Lassiter had taken her to be his lawful wedded wife. In sickness and in health, forsaking all others, and not till death would they part.

Emma and Tucker Garrettson were the sole witnesses. They'd left Tory in the Jezebel Saloon with her two grandfathers, and Emma had even given Maura her pretty opal earbobs to wear with her new gown, since Maura had precious little jewelry of her own—only the ivory cameo necklace in the shape of a rose, which her mother had left her. She'd brought along Ma Duncan's enamel jewel box, but aside from the cameo necklace tucked inside, there were no other jewels in it—only hairpins and buttons. Ma Duncan had been buried in what little jewelry she possessed, and when Maura explained this to Emma, the other woman had instantly removed her own dangling earbobs and insisted that Maura have them as a wedding gift.

Then there was the matter of the ring. When it came time for that part of the ceremony, Quinn Lassiter had frozen.

He'd turned toward Tucker Garrettson, his expression that of a man who has gone out to face an enemy in a gunfight without either his holster or six-shooter.

But bless Tucker. He'd tugged a cigar out of his pocket, slipped the paper ring off it, and handed it to Quinn without blinking an eye.

Maura's hand trembled when Quinn took her slender fingers in his and slipped that paper ring into place. It didn't matter that it was poor paper—it might have been an emerald for the way her heart slammed against her chest as Quinn pushed it past her knuckle and settled it into place.

Then the preacher had told Quinn he could kiss the bride.

Maura had lifted her face to his and closed her eyes. But the kiss he'd brushed across her lips had been quick, cool, and abrupt, a stranger's kiss. When she opened her eyes as he pulled away, his expression had been grim.

The last fragments of her silly hopes faded.

This was a marriage of convenience and she'd better not forget that. Quinn Lassiter obviously hadn't. She was expecting far too much, even now.

Stop being an idiot, she told herself after a wedding supper served in the Whisper Valley Grand Hotel, with Emma and Tucker as their guests.

The Garrettsons had sent the baby home with her grandfathers and had done their best to make the meal seem like a celebration. The only awkward moment had come when Tucker had inquired about their plans.

"I'm taking Maura to Hope, Wyoming. Starting up a little ranch there. Then I've got a job lined up in Laramie." Quinn had tossed back a swig of whiskey.

"A gunfighting job?" Tucker had looked startled. "You're . . . staying in the same line of work even after getting married?"

"That's the idea," Quinn said evenly.

Tucker had glanced swiftly back and forth between Maura and the gunfighter, then leaned back in his chair with a frown. Under the table, Emma had reached over to give Maura's hand a reassuring squeeze.

A little while later the Garrettsons had departed for their ranch—but not before Emma had taken Maura aside and said fervently, "Try not to worry. I'm sure everything will work out for the best."

Maura's eyes had shone with tears as she hugged Emma goodbye.

"Write to me when the baby is born!" Emma whispered just before she and Tucker took their leave and went home to their ranch and family.

Which had left Maura and Quinn all alone in the lobby of the hotel.

"We ought to turn in early." Quinn had pulled a pocket watch from his black vest and frowned at it. "We'll be making an early start."

With Mabel Barnes watching in openmouthed fascination, he'd taken her arm and escorted her up the stairs.

So it was that with the crimson shadows of a magnificent sunset streaking the sky beyond the window, and silence settling over the town, Maura sat on the edge of her bed and faced this man, this stranger, who was now her husband. Her breath caught in her throat as she gazed at him. He was so handsome in his dark shirt, vest, and fitted trousers, all of which set off to perfection his broad-shouldered, muscular physique. The fading sunset threw rich glints of light across the splendid hard planes of his face and illuminated the cool silver depths of his eyes.

But there was no warmth in him, she noted with a shiver. Only tension, and reserve, and a cool aloofness, which had been there ever since they'd spoken their vows.

"We're going to leave at first light for Wyoming," he told her shortly, pulling up a chair and straddling it, his long legs stretched out to either side of him.

She nodded. "The town is called Hope?"

"That's right. Last time I rode through to check on my land, Hope was a nice, pleasant little town. I reckon you'll like it well enough. And there's about a hundred acres of land—as I said, it was payment for a job. The man who hired me already had a spread in Kansas—he'd been intending to sell this land that was left to him by an uncle, but he signed the deed over to me after I wiped out the rustlers who'd been bleeding him dry."

She smoothed her skirt. "I see. And you accepted it as payment. So did you plan to start a cattle ranch some-day?"

Quinn bit back a laugh.

"No, I never planned to start a cattle ranch. Not in a million years," he snorted.

He'd never planned to be married, either, even a marriage like this one. The last thing he'd expected was to have to worry about a wife and child.

He wanted to be riding over the plains, sleeping under

the stars, following the scent of water, gold, money, or blood.

He wanted freedom, open skies, with no one he had to talk to, no one he had to listen to. He wanted his horse, his saddlebag, and a whiskey flask in his pocket. He wanted to cook his own dinner over a campfire at night, to pick out any whore he wanted from whatever saloon was handy and bed her and walk away in the morning. He wanted to keep every human being he encountered a stranger.

He didn't want to be responsible for the thin, delicate, red-haired beauty sitting opposite him in a pale blue wedding dress, watching him as if what he had to say was the most important thing to her in the world.

But he *was* responsible for her. For now.

He stood up and stalked to the window. "But I will start a ranch," he said in a low tone. "For you. And I'll hire some good men to run it. Then you can take over, make a go of it. Just like we talked about. You game, angel?"

Though she nodded, her gaze was bleak. Sad.

What the hell did she want from him? He was doing right by her, he would make sure she and the kid had a place of their own and a steady income.

So why did he feel like the walls were closing in on him?

There was something about her, Quinn thought, his gut clenching. Something that tore at him like nothing else ever had. This girl with her freckles and her wide mouth, her deep, soft eyes, she made him sweat. She made him want to kiss her again, and that was something he wouldn't do. Ever.

They had a business arrangement and business partners didn't kiss.

Her next words startled him.

"I'm sorry. I really am." To his amazement, she sounded sincere. "I know this is going to take time away from your business—from all the other plans you have for your life. I wish there was another way."

"I've never been one to make plans, angel. Don't worry about it. I just like to stay on the move." He came back toward her, studying her closely as she bent her head and stared at the floor.

"You're not going to start bawling again, are you?" he asked, suddenly uneasy.

"No, of course not. Why should I cry? Everything is going to be fine," she said softly, but she didn't look at him.

Quinn took his seat opposite her and raked a hand through his hair. "What about you?" he asked, trying to distract her from starting up with a fresh bout of tears. "Reckon you must have had other plans, Maura."

At that she did look up. Golden-brown eyes met his. A rueful smile touched her lips. "I was intending to leave Knotsville one way or another," she said slowly. "But I thought I'd go to San Francisco and work in a dress shop. I'd hoped that one day I might open my own—" She broke off suddenly, shaking her head. "You don't want to hear this."

"Sure I do." Surprisingly, against his will, he was interested. She was going to do all that, go so far, all on her own—this itty-bitty thing? "Didn't you have ties in Knotsville—family?" he asked.

"No family. Not really. I do have two adoptive brothers.'' A shadow flickered across her face. "And you probably should know—they *may* come looking for me."

"Sounds like you're not too pleased at the idea."

"They're violent men," she said quietly, meeting his gaze hesitantly. "I'm sorry. I should have warned you before. If they do come after me, if they find me . . . us . . . there could be trouble."

His eyes narrowed. "Are you saying they might try to force you to go back with them?"

She moistened her lips. "Yes. If they come after me, if they find me . . . I should have told you—"

"You're afraid of them."

"Everyone in Knotsville is afraid of Judd and Homer."

"Don't be."

"You don't know them—"

"I know them." For a man who'd just been told that trouble in the form of two angry, violent men might be following them, he looked remarkably at ease.

"You know Judd and Homer?" Maura asked, confused.

"I know men like them. I've come across them nearly every day of my life, in one town or another. They're nothing. Nothing for you to worry about ever again. I may not be able to give you much as my wife, Maura, but I can give you that."

He sounded so cool, so confident. Maura drew in a breath as he stood up.

"You'd best get some shut-eye."

She stared as he started toward the door.

"Quinn." She came off the edge of the bed in one swift motion. "What about you? Where are you going?"

"I've got a room down the hall."

"Oh. Oh, yes. Room 206."

Quinn's gaze settled on her pretty, composed face, trying to find some clue as to what she must be feeling.

"Do you want me to stay here?" He turned and took a step back toward her then. Only one step, but he saw her entire slender body go rigid. "Somehow I thought you'd rest easier," he drawled, "if I gave you some breathing room."

"Yes. Yes, I would. I mean, I will. That's very considerate of you."

He came toward her then, slowly, lazily, but with a deliberation that made her heart squeeze into her throat.

His hand came up suddenly and pushed into her hair. His other hand gripped her hip firmly. "Don't think I don't know my rights, Maura. I'm not likely to forget 'em."

"But . . . we have a . . . business arrangement—"

His rough laugh cut off her words. For one heart-stopping moment she thought he was going to kiss her. His head dipped down toward hers, lower, lower still, his eyes gleamed into hers with an intense light that had her blood sizzling. She drew in her breath, inhaling the pleasant tobacco-and-pine scent of him, absorbing the nearness of him, and her hands rose like fluttering butterflies and encircled his neck. But at that precise moment he released her, sucked in his breath, and stepped back.

"So we do." He forced himself to clamp down on the desire jolting through him. Damn if he wasn't distracted by the wide-eyed confusion with which she was watching him, by the alluring way that blue gown fit her curves, by the sweet feminine scent of her skin and the way her upswept curls tantalized him. *Don't get drawn in any further,* he warned himself. *Get away from her.*

"For your sake and the baby's, get some sleep," he said tersely. "I'm putting you on the stage at eight o'clock sharp. So rest while you can. Tomorrow's going to be a long day."

And with that, he turned and left her standing in a pool of golden lamplight on her wedding night.

Chapter 12

MAURA'S FIRST GLIMPSE OF THE TOWN THAT WAS to be her new home came on an unusually mild March afternoon, when the light gleamed like pewter in the huge, endless sky and the air blowing down from the mountains smelled of rain.

Quinn, who'd ridden his bay horse, Thunder, alongside the stagecoach during their six-day journey from Whisper Valley, was there when the steps were let down. He helped her to alight and led her a little away from the commotion of horses, disembarking passengers, and trunks being tossed unceremoniously into the mud.

"Hope, Wyoming!" the stagecoach driver had boomed as they'd galloped into town.

Hope. She'd been encouraged that her new home was in a town called Hope.

But as she scanned her surroundings that afternoon, she felt only doubt. The place looked decidedly un-hopeful.

Smaller than Whisper Valley and more desolate, the town boasted only one real street, a dusty, narrow avenue flanked on both sides by a row of storefronts badly in need of paint. *Forlorn* was the way she would describe it, every bit as dull and gray and unpromising as Knotsville.

Her heart sank, but she tried to smile at Quinn as she moved up the street a few paces, scanning this way and that, looking for something about which she could make a cheerful comment.

The distant mountain peaks, the clear, luminous air, the cotton-puff clouds? The latter were huge, translucent, glorious to behold above the dreariness of huddled buildings squatting on treeless land. And in every direction, as far and deep as the eye could see, stretched beautiful purple sage, or golden prairie, or mountains glistening with snow. But mostly the town was dominated by a sky so rich and majestic a blue, it would put the sea to shame.

"What beautiful country," she murmured. Quinn didn't answer.

He was staring along the street, his face shadowed by the gray brim of his Stetson. There were few people about, few horses or wagons. But the passersby who were walking along the street or scurrying in or out of stores appeared tense and almost furtive.

Several glanced worriedly at Quinn, Maura noticed, as he turned back toward the coach and lifted her satchel, which the driver had set down at the edge of the boardwalk.

He did make an imposing figure, dressed all in black, with his commanding height and tight-lipped expression, but when a woman in a bonnet sashayed out of Hicks Mercantile, saw him, shrieked, and dashed back inside, Maura felt her throat tighten.

"What was that about?" she asked, glancing uneasily toward the store.

Quinn frowned, obviously at a loss. "Something's spooked this town," he muttered. "I wonder what."

At that moment there was a blur of movement and a shout.

"Hold it right there, mister! State your name and your business!"

A man stood at the open second-story window above the general store, cradling a shotgun that was leveled straight at Quinn.

"Get out of here, Maura," Quinn said softly. "Take cover on that porch down the street. Now."

"I'm not leaving you."

"You damn well are—"

"Answer me, mister, pretty darn quick or you'll be pushin' up daisies before the sun goes down!" the man with the shotgun yelled, but there was a decided quaver in his voice.

Quinn swore under his breath and squinted against the glare of the sun as all around them the other stagecoach passengers and the driver scattered in different directions, leaving the coach, horses, and trunks in the street.

"You the sheriff?" Quinn asked in a tone so clear and cold, it could have frozen a dish of warm butter.

He sounded so calm that Maura couldn't help staring at him. Her hands were trembling, but Quinn looked every bit as steady and solid as those mountains framing the horizon. Yet she sensed the tension humming in him and knew it was on her behalf.

"I'm asking the questions, mister," the man hollered back. "Who are you and what do you want with us?"

"I'm a stranger in town," Quinn called out evenly.

"And I'm not looking too kindly on Wyoming hospitality."

"Quinn, just tell him who you are," Maura urged, her heart pounding.

No one and nothing moved on the street.

"I reckon someone had better start explaining." Quinn's deep, hard voice carried along the deserted boardwalk. Hope might have been a ghost town for all the response his words brought. In a softer but deadly serious tone he said, "Maura, don't argue. Go down the street until you reach that porch with the rocker. Sit down in the shade and keep quiet. Do it. Now."

She followed the direction of his glance. The rocker was on the front porch of a small neat frame house near the end of the street. The small sign hanging over the door proclaimed WALSH BOARDINGHOUSE.

It was well out of range of any gunfire that might take place here in the street.

"I'm not going anywhere and leaving you all alone." Fear clawed at her, but she hooked her arm through Quinn's, never mind that her hands were shaking. "Not a very hospitable place you've picked for our new home, Mr. Lassiter," she whispered.

Amusement sparked for a moment in his ice-gray eyes, then disappeared. "I told you twice now to scoot."

"I told you twice now to forget it. They might think twice about shooting you if there's a woman in the way."

"I damn well don't need you to protect me."

"And I don't need you getting yourself killed before the baby and I are set up on our ranch. Why don't you just answer the man and explain that we're about to become upstanding members of the community—"

She was interrupted by a woman's cool, clear voice tinged with a southern accent. Her words rang across the open street. "You can put that gun down, John Hicks!" she said commandingly. "This isn't the leader of the Campbell gang. It's someone a hell of a lot more dangerous!"

"Who?" the man yelped, and as Maura jerked her head to locate the woman who had spoken, she heard the faint clicks of doors and windows opening and saw, here and there, curious faces peeking out.

The woman who'd spoken had apparently just emerged from Eliza Peabody's Millinery Shop across the street. There was a package tied with purple ribbon under her arm.

"He's someone who could blow your fool head off before you even think about pulling that trigger!" she responded, and started toward Quinn and Maura with unhurried, graceful steps.

"Who in tarnation is it?" the man on the landing croaked out, but the shotgun remained steady.

The woman laughed. "Don't panic now. He's not going to shoot you unless you force him to. Just come down and say hello to Quinn Lassiter."

"Son of a bitch." The man jerked the shotgun down. The woman chuckled again and kept walking.

"Come along and say howdy properly, John," she invited, and there was just a tinge of mocking humor in her tone.

Maura glanced at Quinn and saw that he, too, was watching the woman approach. A handful of other people appeared on the boardwalk and in doorways now as well, following discreetly behind her, wary, uncertain, yet obviously reassured that Quinn was not who they had feared he might be.

The leader of the Campbell gang.

What in heaven's name is going on here in Hope? Maura wondered, but she had no more time to ponder their strange welcome for she was caught up in studying the woman who sidled up to them.

She was of medium height, but there was nothing else ordinary about her. Her face was exceptionally beautiful—oval-shaped with porcelain-white skin and vibrant even features. Her eyes were a darker, more intense shade of blue than the sky, her nose long and sculpted, her lips rosy red and shaped like a perfect bow.

Maura felt dowdy as a dandelion beside her. The woman wore a smart lavender hat perched atop glistening gold hair that was swept into a sophisticated knot—a knot so impeccable that Maura knew not a single strand of hair would dare to stray from it. The hat matched the lavender dress that rustled as she walked, and around her shoulders was a lovely and stylish crimson cape. She looked to be in her middle to late twenties—and gave off a strong impression of boldness, beauty, and sophistication.

"Well, Quinn Lassiter, as I live and breathe. It *is* you, isn't it? I'm sure I'd know that handsome profile anywhere." Her voice was husky, tinged with southern charm, intimacy, and a trace of amusement. But her eyes were not amused as she paused before Quinn and Maura and stared into the gunfighter's face.

No, her eyes were intent, alert, and eager. As if she were drinking in the sight of him, Maura realized.

Her heart skipped a beat. When he told her they'd be settling in Hope, Wyoming, he hadn't mentioned being acquainted with any of the town's inhabitants. She glanced hesitantly at Quinn, waiting to be introduced to this woman.

"Serena." Quinn's voice was as easy as always. He might have been speaking to a shop clerk about purchasing a can of beans. "I'd like you to meet my wife. Maura Lassiter."

He showed no emotion as Serena physically flinched at the word *wife*.

"Maura, this is Serena Walsh. An old friend."

Now the woman's lustrous blue eyes swept over Maura like a cool breeze. In her gingham gown, simple bonnet, and threadbare shawl, Maura felt decidedly frumpy. But she managed to muster up a tentative smile, telling herself that the sensations of jealousy rising in her were just plain ridiculous.

Serena Walsh is an old friend. You're his wife.

For whatever that was worth. He'd barely spoken to her and hadn't once touched her during the journey across Wyoming. When they'd stayed overnight at way stations or hotels along the route, he'd shared her room, even the bed, but had remained downstairs until she was asleep and then had taken up space on the mattress without once brushing against her.

Not that she'd wanted him to. After all, that's how she'd gotten herself into this situation in the first place.

"How do you do, Miss Walsh?"

"That's *missus*. I'm a widow, dear. Twice widowed, to be plain." Serena nodded, but didn't smile. Her gaze shifted sharply back to Quinn.

"You've surprised me. And that's not easy to do."

"You're surprised because we're married?" Maura

piped up. "Now why is that?" she asked as calmly and pleasantly as she could manage.

The woman's brows rose, and she shot Quinn a quick look. His face remained impassive.

"Why, only because I never thought Quinn Lassiter would take himself a wife. Seems to me you said that same thing yourself once, honey, didn't you?"

He answered dryly, "Reckon you can see I've changed my mind."

"Oh, I do see that all right. But what brings you two to Hope? Oh, that land." Serena smiled knowingly. "Don't tell me you're finally planning to settle down at last—on that pretty little parcel on Sage Creek."

"Looks like you've got it all figured out, Serena." Quinn met her gaze evenly. "Now you tell me something. What's wrong here? Hope looks a hell of a lot worse off than the last time I passed through. And what's all this about the Campbell gang?"

"Well, if you're looking to tangle with those boys again, you've come to the right place."

A deadly glitter entered Quinn's eyes. "Go on."

"Because of them, the whole town's going to hell in a handbasket." Serena gestured toward the nearly deserted street, the crumbling storefronts. From the corner of her eye Maura saw the man with the shotgun approaching, his thin, sallow face wary, and behind him, a slim young girl striding in a blue-checked shirt and denim pants. Behind them bustled a stout woman with a basket of eggs on one arm and a hopeful gleam in her deep-set eyes, and farther back still, a tall man who looked to be a rancher accompanied by a petite, sunbonneted woman. All approached cautiously, all eyeing the gunfighter in black with an odd mixture of curiosity, fear, and hope.

"A dozen families have packed up and moved in the past few months," Serena continued as the others joined them. "Most folks are afraid to go out and about these days. You never know when the Campbell gang will be back."

"And we heard that Luke Campbell, their cousin— he's the leader of 'em and the worst of the lot—escaped from prison not too long ago." The shopkeeper, Hicks, spoke quickly as he drew up before Quinn. In his nervousness, his words all ran together. "We think he's headed here to join up with the rest of those sons of bitches. They're hiding out somewhere in the mountains between here and Casper." He waved a hand vaguely, then suddenly stuck it out toward Quinn.

"My apologies, Mr. Lassiter. When Hattie Phipps ran into my store plumb hysterical, she thought you was him. Luke Campbell, that is. And so did I. Last time those Campbell boys came to town, they shot up my store and near ran off with my daughter Nell here."

"He's telling the truth, mister." The young girl nodded vigorously, sending the black braid down her back swinging. She hooked her arm through her father's. "I spat in Lee Campbell's eye when he tried to rob our store. He knocked me down and dragged me out to his horse. I got away thanks to Sheriff Owen. But he said he'd be back for me." Her lime-green eyes darkened with both anger and a trace of fear. "Pa said they'd get me over his dead body."

"It's true, Mr. Lassiter. John Hicks was just trying to protect his family. We've been expectin' Luke Campbell to show up any day—like the devil himself." The stout woman carrying the basket blew out a sigh.

"In that case, no hard feelings." Quinn's gaze scanned the street. "Where's your sheriff? You'd expect all the ruckus to bring him running."

"Ray Owen's dead," the tall man answered, shaking his head. "The Campbells killed him as they hightailed it out of town, right after he stopped 'em from running off with Nell."

"Deputy?"

"Resigned. Took himself off to Dodge. Guess he reckoned it was safer there."

"Oh dear." Maura uttered the words without thinking, and everyone turned to stare at her.

"My wife," Quinn said curtly. "Maura."

"How do you do, honey." The woman smiled broadly, at the same time surveying Maura up and down. "I'm Edna Weaver. My husband, Seth, owns the bank. This here is Alice and Jim Tyler of the Crooked T Ranch. And you already met John Hicks, who owns the mercantile— and his daughter, Nell."

"I'm very pleased to meet you, all of you."

Maura smiled at each of them, relieved to see that after that initial inhospitable greeting, the inhabitants of Hope appeared friendly and decent after all. Edna Weaver, robust and well-dressed, with her bushy steel-gray bun and matronly olive-colored gown and shawl, had a smile that seemed to come straight from the heart. Her deep-set brown eyes were keen but also kind, and she sounded sincere in her welcome.

John Hicks and the husky fair-haired rancher, Jim Tyler, both doffed their hats and nodded respectfully to her, while Alice Tyler, who looked to be no more than ten years older than Maura, offered her a quiet smile.

"Are you only visiting Hope or will you be staying awhile, Mrs. Lassiter?" she asked in a soft voice. She was petite, with soft black curls that fell to her shoulders and wisped around her face, which seemed almost too small for her large yellow sunbonnet. She was pretty in the way of a simple, homespun doll.

Maura opened her mouth to reply, but Serena Walsh cut in before she could utter a word. "They're settling here. On a parcel of land out by Sage Creek."

John Hicks, Mrs. Weaver, and the Tylers all exchanged glances at this. For one awful moment Maura wondered if they were going to say the Lassiters weren't welcome. Perhaps the town was afraid of any man as proficient with a gun as Quinn was known to be.

But before anyone could speak, Serena gave a taut laugh.

"Yes sirree, folks, the great gunfighter Quinn Lassiter is going to become a family man and a rancher!"

Quinn's eyes narrowed. He'd had enough of aimless chatter with the inhabitants of Hope, none of whom interested him very much. And Maura, despite the eager way she'd smiled at her new acquaintances, was looking decidedly peaked as they stood in the street.

He'd noticed that his new wife never complained, no matter how long and wearying the journey, but he'd come to recognize a certain pinched look about her lips and a pallor to her skin that signaled her fatigue.

"Time for us to be moving along." He shifted the satchel to his other hand, took Maura's arm, and nodded curtly at the little group of citizens. "Thanks for the welcome, folks."

But as he steered her toward the livery at the end of the street, Serena followed. "Wait, Quinn."

When they stopped and turned, she placed a hand on his arm. "If you two need a place to stay the night, I've got a fine room in my boardinghouse. It's yours, if you like. I'm not sure you'll find the cabin down at Sage Creek fit just yet," she added. "Last time when you rode down there, Quinn, you said it was in bad shape. Remember?"

"We'll manage," Quinn said curtly. "But thanks for the offer, Serena."

Maura barely had time to murmur hasty goodbyes before he was once more leading her toward the opposite end of town.

"My land's only a little over an hour's ride from here. But if you're worn out we can stay overnight in the hotel." He paused as they reached a ramshackle building with shot-out windows, a charred roof, and a lopsided sign that read in faded black letters: GLORY HOTEL.

"If it's all right with you, I've had enough of hotels to last me a lifetime. I'd much prefer to spend the night at Sage Creek."

"You heard what she said? It might be in pretty bad shape."

"I don't mind. I want to see it. I want to start settling in."

They continued toward the livery in silence, but it felt to Maura like a companionable silence. She appreciated his not even suggesting they stay at the boardinghouse. She wanted to ask him how he knew Serena, for how long, and other questions about the Campbell gang, with whom he was obviously familiar, but this wasn't the time.

She forced her thoughts forward—toward her new home.

Quinn had arrived in Hope a short time before the stagecoach rolled in and had already corralled Thunder at the livery, paid the owner to see to his feed, and arranged to purchase a wagon and a team of good sturdy horses.

While Maura waited on a bench inside the barn, he finished paying the man, a hulking red-haired fellow named Jethro Plum. Then he tied Thunder behind the wagon, set her valise and his bedroll and saddlebags inside, and came to fetch her.

Another silence fell as they left Hope behind and headed north toward rolling sage-colored hills. The horses clip-clopped along through tall grama grass while sunshine dappled the ground and the March wind blustered down from the mountains, still smelling of rain. The land was vast, intimidating, yet beautiful with its dark buttes and golden-green prairie. Rangeland glistened beneath the rich golden sunshine, stretching as far as the eye could see, some of it flat, some winding through hills and mountains. She saw a herd of antelope on a gray bluff, but they disappeared in the blink of an eye. A russet fox slithered through the tall grass to her right, and high above, a meadow lark circled and chattered, seeming to lead the way.

Wild, spacious country, Maura thought in awe—country not for the timid or the weak—country as wide and grand as the great soaring blue sky that dominated everything below.

"How long has it been since you've seen your land—

and the cabin?'' Maura ventured at last, breaking the silence that had fallen over them.

"Nearly two years." He held the horses steady as a jackrabbit scooted across the trail. "I looked the place over after Sam Gable gave me the deed." He glanced at her. "The cabin had already been abandoned for some time, but it was built sturdy enough. I reckon we can clean it up and make do for now. And I'll add on some by fall."

Possibilities twirled through her mind. A small, tidy house. Curtains at the windows. She'd embroider some samplers to hang on the walls, and perhaps some bright, pretty pillows to make the sofa and chairs more comfortable. She'd plant a garden as soon as the weather warmed. And if there were wildflowers growing nearby, she'd set some in a bowl every night on the table as a centerpiece.

By the time the baby came, she'd have sewn yellow curtains for the nursery, and a soft baby quilt—and perhaps there'd be a rocker so she could sit with her child, hold him or her, sing songs as the night stars popped into the Wyoming sky. . . .

Her fanciful daydreams ended when the wagon rolled over a rise and started down the slope toward a long, tree-sheltered valley.

It was a lovely spot. For miles in every direction there were open fields of grass and Indian paintbrush. The cabin was a tiny speck in the center of the wide, deep land. Enchanted, she held her breath as they drew nearer and the wagon jolted over rocks and brush. What could only be a creek—Sage Creek—glittered beyond the cabin, sheltered by a long creekbank studded with newly budding cottonwoods and quaking aspens.

"How beautiful . . ." she murmured, but her voice died away as the wagon rolled closer and she saw more clearly. There were only two other small buildings besides the cabin—a crumbling shed and an unpainted barn. No corrals, no outbuildings. And she'd seen no sign of cattle.

Desolation in the midst of open, gorgeous country, with blissful quiet enveloping everything—save for the chirping of the birds. The Laramie Mountains towered protectively in the distance, dwarfing the lonely wood structures nearly hidden in the midst of rugged, rolling land.

She hadn't expected much, but as they approached the cabin disappointment trickled through her. The place couldn't have appeared more unwelcoming. Its two small windows were both boarded up. The chimney was crumbling. Old dead weeds choked the exterior, and nearly blocked the door. It looked more like a shanty than a ranch house.

A cave would have been more inviting, Maura thought, her eyes taking in the sad unpainted wood, the missing plank across the slanted roof.

The prospect of sleeping within that bleak little building filled her with misgiving.

But she steeled herself as Quinn halted the team and climbed down from the wagon. It might be crude, it might be filthy, it might appear uninviting right now, but it was hers. Hers and Quinn's, however long he might stay. With a good scrubbing, some repairs, some paint . . .

"Doesn't look like much, does it?" Quinn helped her

down, his hand lingering for a moment at her waist as he set her upon the hard, weed-strewn ground.

"It looks . . . very nice."

"Yeah, if you're a raccoon or a snake, maybe."

Maura couldn't help but smile. The gunfighter's hand was still cupped at her waist. He seemed to have forgotten that as he stared down at her, his eyes glinting beneath the brim of his hat.

"You look tired."

Maura shook her head. "Only a little."

"Maybe we should have stayed in town. Gotten a fresh start on this place in the morning."

"No." Without thinking, she touched his sleeve. "I'm glad we came here tonight," she said impulsively. "Something feels right about this spot."

He released her then, pushed his hat back, stared around at the open beauty surrounding them. "Yeah, it's pretty enough, I reckon—if you don't count the cabin," he agreed dryly.

"Once it's cleaned up and painted and the weeds are pulled, it won't be so bad. And I can already imagine it with lace curtains at the windows, and a garden right over there, and perhaps we could have a porch here in the front where we could sit outside at night with the baby and watch the fireflies in the summertime . . ."

His face changed. It tightened, and the easy smile left his eyes. Her portrait of domesticity made him feel like he was choking. He'd rather face ten outlaws in a show-down than . . . curtains.

"Yeah, sure. A porch. And a garden. Whatever you want, sweetheart. Just don't expect me to stick around to watch anything grow." He scowled. "Or to sit on your porch and gaze at the stars. I'll be coming and going as I please, once I've got the ranch going.''

"That's just fine. Fine by me." Maura tugged her shawl tighter around her shoulders. "Make yourself scarce as you like. It'll mean more peace and quiet for me.''

Instead of lightening, his scowl deepened. He turned abruptly and stalked toward the cabin door. "Might as well see how the old place—''

Then he froze. "Someone's been here. Recently.''

"What?" Maura stared as he knelt down, studied the ground, the crushed weeds.

He straightened and shot her a warning look. "Wait here.'' It was a command, a command that made her heart jolt into her throat.

"Don't follow me. Don't *move*.''

His gun glinted suddenly in his hand—she'd never even seen him draw it—and then he eased open the door and disappeared inside.

Chapter 13

 IT WAS INCREDIBLE HOW SUDDENLY THE AIR HAD changed, had become charged with danger, the wild, peaceful beauty shattered as if by a cannon blast. Maura's heart thudded as the seconds ticked by and Quinn made no sound and did not reappear at the door.

What if there was someone inside, and they shot him? Or stabbed him? What if at this very moment he was lying on the floor, bleeding to death . . .

"It's all right." He slipped out of the cabin, a thoughtful light glinting in his eyes. "No one's here now, but someone's obviously been here within the past day or so. Looks like they cooked a can of beans on the stove. Come on."

"But where are we going?" She tried to sound as calm as he did. "I thought we were staying here tonight." The thought of journeying all the way back to Hope made her shoulders sag with disappointment, not to mention exhaustion.

"Until I find out who's going to show up here, I want you out of the way."

"Can't we just start getting the cabin cleaned up and when he comes back, tell him that he'll have to find another place to bed down?"

Quinn's lip curled. "He might be the kind of hombre to shoot first and discuss property ownership later. Get in."

He hoisted her into the wagon with no wasted motion and came around the other side. "Once you're settled in a safe place, I'll keep a lookout for him."

"And then?" she asked warily as he flicked the reins and sent the horses trotting briskly toward the cottonwoods that bordered the creek.

"Then I'll run him off."

"You won't shoot him or anything, will you? I mean, it might be someone harmless, someone who thinks the place is abandoned—which it was—and that no one will mind if he spends a few nights there."

"He's going to find out differently."

She didn't like the sound of that. "Promise me you'll give him a chance to explain before you . . . before you—"

"Blow his head off?" he supplied helpfully.

"Exactly." Maura gulped. "There will be enough to do in the cabin from what I can see without having to mop up blood and bury a corpse as well!"

He laughed at this, but it was a harsh laugh. "You're too softhearted for the West, Maura Jane," he said as he halted the horses beneath a cottonwood, well hidden from the cabin by a stand of trees and rock. "You'll have to toughen up some."

"I'm plenty tough," she assured him. "Living in

Knotsville with Judd and Homer Duncan wasn't exactly a tea party.''

"Then why are you so damned worried about a stranger? Strangers spell trouble. That's lesson number one. Remember it.''

Her eyes flashed as he helped her down from the wagon for the second time. "You were a stranger when you showed up in Knotsville.''

His silver eyes shone in the fading afternoon sunlight. "See what I mean? If you'd steered clear of me then, we wouldn't be in this fix right now.''

She averted her face, pretending to look out over the creekbed, hoping he couldn't see that he'd hurt her feelings.

"Hold on. Guess I didn't mean that the way it sounded.'' He cleared his throat. "It came out wrong. Just . . . forget I said it.''

"No. You're right.'' She turned slowly back toward him, lifted her eyes to his face. "I should have steered clear of you. I made a terrible mistake.''

"I've made worse.''

"Worse? What could be worse? We're married and there's a baby coming and you—''

He scowled. "Go on. I what?''

He was watching her face, his eyes intent, fastened upon hers as if he were trying to see into her mind clear down to her soul.

"You don't want to be here with me any more than you'd want to be in a rattlesnake pit!'' she burst out.

"That's not exactly true.'' He reached out a big hand and smoothed a wayward strand of hair back from her cheek. He found himself staring into those soft, dark, troubled eyes of hers, unable to look away.

"You're a lot nicer to look at than a rattlesnake. And you don't bite. Right now," he went on, and for some reason his hand stroked down her cheek, an infinitely gentle caress, "I don't much mind being here at all."

"You don't?"

Before he could answer, they both heard the sharp snap of a twig.

Quinn released her in a flash and spun around, shielding Maura with his body even as he drew his Colt and aimed.

"Freeze!" he ordered.

The buckskin-clad figure on horseback ten feet away gave a startled yelp and gaped at him.

"Get down off that horse—real slow," Quinn barked. Behind him, he heard Maura's fearful whisper.

"Don't shoot him—he's only a boy."

The youth on the horse swung out of the saddle a bit too hastily for Quinn's taste, but he made no move for the six-shooter slung in the holster on his hip. He looked all of seventeen, tall and stringy, with dark chestnut hair cut raggedly beneath his hat, narrow rebellious blue eyes, and a square, clean-shaven jaw that jutted out with both pride and stubbornness.

A kid all right, Quinn thought, taking his measure— lean, gawky, and out to prove something to the world— and probably to himself, he thought, remembering a time when he had needed to do the same.

Matter of fact, the look he threw Quinn was sullen and angry enough to curdle milk, but there was wariness beneath it, and an edge of painful bravado beneath the cockiness of his voice.

"If the woman wasn't here, I'd have shot you dead!" the boy thundered. "The only reason you're still breathing, mister, is because I didn't want to take a chance of hitting her."

"The only reason you're still breathing is because she told me not to shoot you." Quinn shifted his Colt a notch so it was pointed at the boy's shoulder instead of his heart. "Toss your gun on the ground nice and easy."

"I won't." The boy gritted his teeth. "If I do that, what's to stop you from shooting me down? I'd sooner throw myself off a cliff than give you my gun, mister, so forget about it."

Quinn fired into the dirt. The bullet pinged an inch from the youth's booted foot. He jumped back.

"Drop your gun," Quinn ordered again.

"No, Quinn—don't shoot at him again!" Maura pushed around Quinn to get a better look at the boy. "What if you miss and accidentally hit him? Anyone can see he's not an outlaw."

"Maura, get back and stay out of this—"

"No, I won't. Why don't you just talk to him before someone gets hurt?"

"Better listen to the pretty lady, mister," the boy advised with a cocky grin, "if you know what's good for you."

Quinn snorted contemptuously, half inclined to nick the kid, just to teach him to be so damned cocky. Especially when he was the one facing the business end of a gun.

"I'm waiting."

Beneath Quinn's ominous stare, the boy's grin slowly faded, replaced by a grimace. If the expression in the youth's eyes could have killed, Quinn knew he'd be six feet under. But just the same, the boy at last heaved a sigh and tossed his gun down on the ground.

"Now what?" He hooked his thumbs in his pockets and glared.

"Supposing you tell me who you are and why you've been trespassing on my property."

"*Your* property?" The boy stared and gave a contemptuous laugh. "To hell with you, mister. You're a liar. This ain't your property."

The bullet whizzed an inch past his knee.

"Hey!" The youth's voice cracked in sudden panic as he yelled and leaped back. "Damn it, what the hell are you doing?"

"I'd be obliged if you wouldn't cuss in front of my wife," Quinn told him coldly.

Maura marched forward again. "Quinn, that's enough. You're scaring this boy and I won't have it—"

"Scared? Who the hell are you calling scared— Er, pardon me, ma'am," the kid amended hastily as Quinn's face hardened and he raised the Colt again.

"All right, all right," the boy muttered. He eyed the revolver warily now, and some of the cockiness had faded from his face. "Maybe it is your land. Maybe not. I've been here for a couple of weeks now. Before that, the place looked like no one'd touched it for years. How was I s'posed to know it wasn't just an old abandoned shack? I didn't hurt nothing—hell, there's nothing in there worth enough to hurt—or steal. But anyway, you got a deed that says it's yours?"

Quinn's smile could have frozen a sunbeam. "This gun says it's mine."

"Oh, Quinn, really." Maura spoke in a low tone. "Can't we be civilized about this? Obviously this is a misunderstanding. Anyone can see he means us no harm. There's no danger here, so why don't you just—"

Without warning, the creekbank exploded with shots. Quinn dove for Maura and knocked her to the ground, taking her weight on him as they rolled to the earth. He was shielding her with his body even as he raised the gun and fired at the black-bearded giant on a pinto horse charging toward them through the trees.

The kid had dropped, too, then grabbed his six-shooter and rolled over. He fired at the giant as well, and plumes of acrid gunsmoke thickened the air.

But the rider kept coming and Quinn saw that the giant's shotgun was aimed at the youth sprawled in the dirt.

Quinn squeezed the trigger again. This time the giant reeled backward over the hindquarters of his mount, and toppled to the ground with a crash. The horse neighed, swerved, and came to a shuddering halt near the wagon.

"You got him!" Quinn heard the kid shout.

He shifted his weight and peered down at the woman lying beneath him. Dirt and weeds and brush clung to her hair and around the collar of her dress, but though she looked shaken, she wasn't shot. "Maura. Are you all right? Did I hurt you?"

"N-no. What . . . happened?"

"That's what I'm going to find out," he told her grimly. "Stay here. Stay *down*. I'll be back."

He was gone before she could try to stop him, and as she turned gingerly over and lifted her head to survey the scene, she saw that the boy was following right behind Quinn, both of them edging forward with their guns drawn, moving at a half crouch toward the fallen man.

They stood over him. The kid nudged him with his boot.

"He's dead," the youth said with satisfaction. He glanced up at Quinn, and this time his eyes were bright with appreciation. "Nice shooting. Do you know who this is?"

"No, but I've got a feeling you're going to tell me," Quinn growled.

"Ox Morgan. The bounty hunter. The *famous* bounty hunter."

"I know the name," Quinn said dryly. Ox Morgan was one of the West's more brutal thugs, a bounty hunter who brought nearly every prisoner in dead—or close to it. He was rumored to have captured and killed more than thirty men in the past three years.

"What I want to know, kid, is what did he want with you?"

At that moment Maura made a small sound behind him and Quinn turned to see her standing only a few feet away, staring aghast at the dead man sprawled in his own blood.

"I told you to stay put."

"Who is he?"

"A bounty hunter who was after your friend here, the innocent kid you wanted me to let—"

Quinn broke off as the boy sagged to the ground.

"He's hurt," Maura cried, and rushed forward.

The youth closed his eyes a moment and then opened

them with a yelp as Maura touched his arm, where a bullet had nicked him. Blood soaked his shirt.

"I'm sorry," she gasped. "Lie still and I'll help you."

"It's nothing, ma'am," he began to babble. "Nothing at all. Doesn't hurt . . . a bit." A shudder racked his thin shoulders, and he clamped down on his lips and tried to smile at her. "Matter of fact, I wouldn't mind dying, and going to heaven . . . if all the angels were as . . . pretty as you."

"That's quite charming," she said with a shaky laugh, ignoring Quinn's snort. The boy was white as parchment. "But I think we'd better tend to that arm before you lose any more blood."

She glanced up at her husband. "Quinn, I'll need some bandages and boiled water. And the blanket. Judd was shot once and I helped Doc Lindsay patch him up. I think I know what to do."

"Leave him here to rot, that's what you can do."

"Please." The urgent look she threw him was so full of soft appeal that he sighed and stalked off toward the wagon for his saddlebags.

"Alone . . . at last." The kid managed a wan, wavery grin. And promptly fainted.

Chapter 14

"SO WHAT DID YOU DO WITH OLD OX?"

Seated at the square pine table in the cabin's kitchen, Quinn didn't bother answering the boy's question, asked between mouthfuls of mashed potatoes. It seemed that the bullet that nicked him in the arm hadn't affected his ability to shovel in huge quantities of food.

"Quinn, um, took care of him," Maura said. "You don't have to worry about him anymore." She scooped the last of the canned beans she'd heated into a bowl and carried them to the table, then at last slipped into the rickety three-legged chair beside Quinn's.

She flushed as she felt his gaze on her and tucked a strand of hair behind her ear. She knew she must look dreadful, but she couldn't understand why Quinn Lassiter kept staring at her all the while she cooked, and as she brewed coffee and browned biscuits and set plates out around the table—in fact he'd been staring at her ever since he'd finished washing up after burying that bounty hunter.

He'd let her tend to the injured young man, brought

him back to the cabin in the wagon bed, and then had dragged Ox Morgan off to be buried. She didn't care where—as long as she didn't have to see him again.

In a very short space of time, she and Quinn had brought all of their possessions inside the cabin and done what they could to make it habitable, at least for the night.

She was bone tired, but elated somehow to be snugly ensconced in the cabin, which turned out, thankfully, to be in better shape than its ramshackle exterior had led her to imagine. She was surprisingly pleased with the swept-out, aired-out rooms, the pleasant meal she'd managed to toss together with some of the flour, cured ham, canned goods, and potatoes the youth had bought and stored in the cabin's pantry, and amazed that on her first night in her new home, she and Quinn already had company.

Not that her husband was any too pleased with their guest. But Maura found him endearing, and rather sad. He was so young, and so obviously alone. So full of pride and bluster. There was no doubt that Ox Morgan would have killed him if not for Quinn. Yet the boy couldn't humble himself enough to thank him. At least not yet.

"So you buried him?" the kid asked eagerly. "Where?"

Quinn watched, frowning, as the young man grabbed the platter of ham with his good hand and began to help himself to more. There were only three thin slices left.

"That ham is for Maura. Touch any of it and I'll shoot you in the other arm."

At this the young man had the grace to flush. "Sorry." He pushed the platter toward her. "Here, you go ahead— Maura." He grinned. "That's sure a pretty name."

"She's Mrs. Lassiter to you."

"Quinn," Maura murmured reprovingly, but her eyes were dancing. She'd spent all of her twenty-four years sheltered from male attention and companionship—except for the unwelcome and unfriendly presence of Judd and Homer—and it was quite amusing to have two such different male specimens sitting down to her dinner table.

Quinn, dark, sleek, and deadly as a panther, was being so protective of her that she wanted to whoop with laughter, even as it touched her heart. The tall, chestnut-haired young man, who had not yet favored them with his name, was full of pluck and rough boyish charm.

"Eat something," Quinn ordered. "Before this scavenger pecks up every crumb on the table."

She ate. And listened as Quinn leaned back in his chair, shot the boy a flint-eyed look that would have intimidated much more seasoned men, and grilled him with a series of questions.

"Let's get to the important matters. Who the hell are you? And why was that jackal Morgan after you?"

"It was all a mistake. I swear it didn't mean nothing, and I didn't do nothing." He popped the last of a biscuit into his mouth and chewed quickly, then swallowed. "Honest, Mr. Lassiter, there were witnesses. It was a frame-up!"

"Your name," Quinn grated. "Start with that and we'll get to the rest later."

"Lucky. Lucky Johnson. From Topeka."

"And just what have you been doing on my property, Lucky Johnson?"

"Hiding out." The boy tossed down his napkin and pushed back his chair. He began to pace around the cabin. Though he held his one arm stiffly, bound up in a sling

Maura had fashioned from her oldest petticoat, he otherwise seemed unaffected by the wound Maura had also cleansed, daubed with salve, and bandaged. He was now wearing a clean green plaid shirt that hung a bit loosely on his lanky frame. His cheeks were a bit sunken, too, as if he hadn't been eating well.

"Ox Morgan's been chasing me clear across the territory! Son of a bitch damn near caught me half a dozen places—oops—sorry, ma'am. I mean, Maura." He gave her a wolfish grin, ignoring Quinn's frown.

"And all I did was kiss one mighty pretty lady. Now I ask you, since when is that a crime?"

"If you forced her to kiss you, I'd damn well say it could be," Quinn said evenly. "And if you forced her to do anything else . . ."

"Force? Hell, no. I'd never force a lady to do anything. Why would I have to? They're only too eager to—" He broke off hastily as Quinn's mouth thinned warningly, and he threw a quick glance at Maura. "What I mean is, the lady invited me. Really nice and polite, too." He chuckled and threw himself back down into the chair, as if greatly pleased with himself.

While Maura set about clearing the plates, Quinn finally got the story out of him. It seemed that Lucky Johnson had done slightly more than kiss a lady. He'd swept her off her feet and taken her to bed.

Unfortunately, it wasn't his own bed he was caught in—it was her husband's. One Rufus Lummock, who owned the biggest freight company in Denver.

"When he burst in on us, instead of going after me, he came after Tess," Lucky exclaimed indignantly. "That was her name, Tess," he added. A frown settled over his boyish features. "Before I knew what was happening, he dragged her out of bed by her hair and knocked her clear across the room. I grabbed him before he could hit her again, and we lit into one another. Tess was crying and screaming to raise the dead, but I didn't have time to see how she was doing, because suddenly Rufus went for his gun. I wasn't wearing one," he said, then added matter-of-factly, "Wasn't wearing nothin' at all."

"Oh, my." At the sink, Maura put a hand to her throat. "He tried to shoot you? That would have been cold-blooded murder!"

"Nobody ever accused Rufus of being a decent sort," Lucky replied darkly.

"Keep talking." Quinn poured himself more coffee, frowning over the story of Rufus Lummock's striking his wife. The boy's description of that brought back memories. Ugly memories. He pushed them away and forced himself to concentrate on the rest of the story.

"So we fought over the gun and I was trying to get it away from him when it went off. Rufus, he up and died on me, and then the sheriff arrested me and charged me with murder—no mind about what Tess tried to explain to him—so me and old Ben broke out of jail—"

"Old Ben?" Soapy plate in hand, Maura paused at the sink and stared at him.

"Yep, Ben Baskin, the bank robber, was locked up with me. So anyways, we escaped, and the sheriff put out a five-hundred-dollar bounty on both of us, and Ox caught up with Ben in Virginia City, and brung him in dead, and ever since then he's been hot on my trail."

"Then I guess you owe Quinn a debt of gratitude." Maura set the last plate on the counter and reached for a dry rag. "He saved you from being killed by that terrible man just as old Ben was."

Quinn shrugged and drained the last of his coffee, but Lucky began to gnaw at his lower lip.

The boy leaned back in his chair, in much the same casual pose as Quinn had assumed. He stuck out his jaw and met the other man's eyes. Rebellion flickered in Lucky's lightning-blue eyes, but it died out beneath the hard silver glint directed at him. He glanced down, and spoke in a mumble.

"I reckon I do owe you. Ox must've spotted me over by Goose Canyon today and followed me back. So, much obliged, mister. Uh, wait a minute." Lucky peered up quickly, and jerked forward in the chair. His suddenly sharp gaze darted from Maura to Quinn and back again.

"Did you say to call her Mrs. *Lassiter?* It didn't really sink in till now, but you're not . . ." He moistened his lips, then scanned the tall, dark-visaged man before him in a quick assessment that made his eyes open wider. He swallowed hard. "You're not *the* Quinn Lassiter, are you?"

"Seems I was the last time I looked."

"But you—you're . . . I've heard of you. Hell, *everyone's* heard of you. You're famous."

Quinn stood up from the table, grabbed his coffee cup and Lucky's, and carried them to the sink. "Thanks for supper," he told Maura.

"Where are you going?"

"To check on the horses. And to see if there's anything worthwhile in the barn or the shed. Haven't had a chance to look until now. I won't be long." He turned and eyed Lucky. "You ready?"

"Ready for what?" The boy stood up too.

"To ride. You've got a long road back to town and it's getting late."

"You're not thinking of sending him back to town tonight?" Maura protested. "He's wounded!"

"Way too softhearted," Quinn muttered, shaking his head. Then he gave her a level glance. "He's not staying here. He can find himself a cave, or make camp somewhere, or ride to town—whatever the hell he wants, but he's clearing out of here right now."

"Never you mind, ma'am." Lucky grabbed his hat off a peg and started toward the door. His cheeks were flushed, but he struggled to appear indifferent. "Don't let no one ever accuse Lucky Johnson of staying where he isn't wanted. I've imposed myself on you enough, I reckon. Thanks for the fine supper," he told her grandly. "And don't you worry none about me. I can take care of myself."

"But your arm . . ."

"Doesn't hurt a bit."

"But where will you go? How will you manage?"

"He doesn't need you to mollycoddle him," Quinn said curtly. "If he's old enough to get into trouble with a jealous husband and the law, he's old enough to take care of himself." He strode to the door, yanked it open, and eyed Lucky Johnson expectantly until the young man grimaced, set his hat on his head, picked up his gear with his good arm, and marched out into the night.

Dismayed, Maura stared at the door Quinn slammed shut behind them. Annoyance and irritation vied with the exhaustion that pulled at her. She was *not* going to put up with Quinn Lassiter's highhandedness. If he thought differently, he was in for quite a shock. All she'd wanted to do was extend basic hospitality to a young man with nowhere to go, someone who needed a roof over his head for this one night, and Quinn had instead almost literally kicked him out the door.

The more she thought about it, the angrier she became.

And when Quinn came back inside just as she finished sweeping the cabin floor, she swung toward him with the broom clenched in her hand and her eyes flashing golden fire.

To her fury, he pretended not to notice.

"You look all tuckered out," he said over his shoulder as he tossed a log inside the blackened hearth. "Why don't you turn in now and we can get a fresh start on this place in the morning."

"I'll turn in when I'm ready to turn in," Maura said tightly.

"Suit yourself." He turned to regard her, his glance surveying her in a long, slow appraisal that made her bones quiver. His silver eyes darkened to smoke in the leaping firelight. "But I'd say you're ready now."

"And I say I'm not."

Quinn stalked toward her. "Maura, if this is about that Johnson kid—"

"It's about you. Thinking you can tell me—tell everybody—what to do. I won't have it."

"It has nothing to do with telling you what to do. I only said I didn't want him staying here another—"

"But it was unkind and inhospitable . . . and . . ."

Her voice shook, and Quinn saw in alarm that she was close to tears.

"Now hold on," he said hastily. "No need to get all

excited. I didn't know you cared so much about some kid who's been squatting on our property and who damn near got us both killed."

"It's not just Lucky," Maura cried. "It's—" She broke off in frustration, struggling to find words to express what she was feeling. Quinn was regarding her as if she were crazy.

"I've lived my whole life with two brothers who pushed everyone away," she choked out. "Everyone who might have been a friend. Everyone who might have tried to be nice to me, whom I might have wanted to get to know. I don't want that kind of life anymore. I want things to be different here. To get to know people in this town. I want to care about them, maybe eventually feel that I . . . oh, Quinn, I don't know—that they care about me, that I belong here. That *we* belong here. I want that for the baby."

He went rigid.

"Didn't you ever want that? Want to feel connected to a place, to people? A sense of belonging?"

He didn't step back from her, but he might as well have. He might as well have retreated a hundred miles away.

"No."

His tone was cool, indifferent, but hard as steel. "I don't like ties."

She felt as though he'd struck her. "That's right. How could I have forgotten?" She turned away and plunked the broom down in the corner.

"Maura—"

"I suggest you hurry up and get this ranch running

then so you can get 'untied' from me and the baby as
soon as possible.''

''That's just what I intend to do.''

''Yes, you've made that clear enough.'' She picked up
a damp rag and began to scrub at a coffee spill she'd
missed on the table. Her hands were trembling. ''But
you'll hate it, won't you? Every moment you're stuck
here with me, in this house, on this land, you'll hate it.
You'll hate *me*.''

He reached her in one stride and took the rag from her
fingers, tossing it on the table. He grasped her by the
shoulders and shook. ''I could never hate you,'' he told
her roughly. ''Or blame you. I blame myself.'' His mouth
twisted. ''I couldn't live with myself if I didn't take responsibility and marry you. But I can't stay, Maura. I'm
just not the type to stick around in one place for long. I
wasn't cut out to be anybody's husband—''

She nodded blindly and yanked free.

But he wasn't ready to let her go and grasped her arm,
gently pulling her back so that she had no choice but to
face him. Her mouth trembled, but she lifted her chin to
meet his gaze, searching his eyes with quiet intensity.

Quinn fought the urge to brush his fingers across those
trembling lips. God help him, he wanted to taste them, to
feel their texture, their sweetness beneath his. But he
forced himself to concentrate on what he had to say. This
was no time to get distracted. What she'd said to him
about her brothers was important and made him see
things in a way he hadn't before. He needed to set things
right.

''In the meantime . . . what you said . . . about belonging.''

"Yes?"

"You go ahead. Make friends. I don't mean with that worthless Johnson pup, but with whoever in town you take a liking to. And I won't get in your way."

"What about you?"

"I can't change who I am, Maura. I'm a loner. I don't trust people. I don't want much to do with 'em. Never have. But you go right ahead."

"I will."

He nodded. There was a silence. "Now will you go to bed? You look like you're about ready to fall down in a heap and that can't be good for the baby."

She knew he was right.

Silently she turned toward the bedroom off the parlor, aware of his gaze following her, but she didn't glance back.

The bedroom was fairly large with a sloping ceiling, but it was dark and sparsely furnished. Quinn's gear had been tossed down in one corner near an old scarred pine bureau. Her satchel sat atop the lumpy straw-filled mattress against the opposite wall. The bedroom furnishings consisted of nothing more than the bureau, with a kerosene lamp, washstand, and chipped crockery pitcher atop it, a dented metal chest on the floor near the door that contained some old moth-eaten blankets, linens, and a wicker sewing basket. And one ladder-back chair pushed against the bare wooden wall.

There was a cracked mirror but no rug, and no curtains at the one shuttered window, where part of the shutter had broken off and starlight drifted in. There wasn't even a quilt on the bed.

Nevertheless, it beckoned irresistibly. Maura was so

weary she barely had the strength to draw the bed linens from the chest, tuck them around the bed, smooth and straighten the dark gray blanket. Her knees shook weakly as she performed her toilette and dragged on an old white nightgown that had been washed so many times, it was paper-thin and frayed at the hemline.

How she wished she could look beautiful for Quinn. That she had a lovely lavender lace nightgown with silken ribbons, that her hair would fall in neat shining curls, that he would see her and . . . and what?

Come to her, take her in his arms, kiss her?

Maura's heart skipped a beat. Was she really wishing—hoping—that somehow there could be more between them than this "business arrangement" they had both agreed to?

Idiot, she whispered to herself. He's a stranger who walked into your life, and will walk out just as abruptly. To want more from him—anything more than he had agreed to in their arrangement—would be foolhardy.

Yet for some reason tears slipped down her cheeks as she at last sank into bed and turned her face on the pillow.

What's wrong with me? Maura wondered as she tugged the blanket across her shoulders. Why do I keep thinking about Quinn, wondering what it would be like to kiss him again, to be held in his arms, to share his bed?

He's no good for you. Heat coiled through her as she pictured his lean, dangerous face. *He's trouble,* she thought desperately. She fought against the memory of broad shoulders, lean hips, and muscles rippling across a dark-furred chest.

Maura pressed her eyes shut. But Quinn's powerful

body and darkly handsome face were engraved upon her mind.

The sooner he gets the ranch started and clears out, the better.

Perhaps if she listed his faults, it would help her to fall asleep. After all, he had so many, she could go on forever.

He was infuriating, dominating, exasperating, and stubborn, not to mention rude, insufferable, set in his ways . . .

That was as far as she got before she drifted off to sleep, but not before wondering when in the world he was going to come to bed.

She never heard Quinn enter the bedroom.

He crossed to the bed and stared down at the girl who lay there fast asleep. She was still slender as a flower despite her pregnancy. The high, modest neckline of a frayed nightgown peeked out above the ugly blanket she'd drawn across her shoulders. She'd left the lamp aglow, and in its weak yellow light her hair gleamed rich as amber, a mass of wild, riotous curls that spilled about her cheekbones and shoulders.

Something twisted painfully inside him. She looked so vulnerable, and beautiful, and wildly sexy. Without quite being aware of what he was doing, he reached out and stroked one of those long, luscious red curls.

He fought the urge to slide his hands through her hair, to lie down beside her and pull her against him. As if sensing his thoughts, his presence, she stirred in her sleep, murmuring, and he reluctantly drew his hand away.

But not before she turned over, and the blanket slipped down. He found himself staring down at her beautiful breasts, clearly outlined beneath the flimsy gown. He couldn't forget the luscious softness of them beneath his hands, or the musky rose-petal taste of her skin. He wanted to toss off the ugly gray blanket and tear that nightgown from her body, to explore once again each tantalizing curve and hollow of her.

But he couldn't. He wouldn't. He had to stay away from her.

Strange, she was the gentlest creature he'd ever encountered, yet her temper could flare red-hot, and her courage seemed limitless. She could look so damned sweet—and at the same time wildly sexy, with that full, kissable mouth and all that tumbling red hair. She was a bundle of contradictions. Quinn didn't understand any woman, but especially not her.

A hot tension rippled through him and he fought the ever-growing urge to climb into that bed, yank her up against him, and take her right here, here in this rough old cabin, on their first night on the land he would give her for her own.

He couldn't do that. He couldn't so much as kiss her again, not if he knew what was good for him. He wanted her too much.

That was a sure sign that he had to stay away.

As if he'd spoken the words aloud, she stirred again and her eyelashes fluttered. Slowly, her eyes opened.

She peered through the darkness at him a moment, looking adorably sleep-tousled and slightly dazed, then suddenly she pushed herself up on one elbow, her eyes going wide.

"Quinn—what is it? What . . . what do you want?"

Chapter 15

"WHAT DO I WANT?" QUINN REPEATED THE
words in a low, deep voice. "You tell me,
Maura. What do you think I want?"

Maura drew in her breath as she saw the silver fire
flickering deep within his eyes. He looked tough and dangerous, with his dark hair falling over his brow, his
thumbs hooked into his gunbelt. Why did he have to be so
damned handsome?

"I—I think you want to c-claim your husbandly
rights," she whispered, and heaven help her, the reckless
traitorous part of her wanted it to be true.

A cold tremor shot through Quinn at her words. She
was right. He did want that, damn it—which was exactly
why he wouldn't do it. He wouldn't so much as touch her,
even if it killed him.

"Try again, sweetheart." Every muscle in his body
tightened with self-control.

"Why don't you just tell me?" There was both confusion and wariness in her huge honey-brown eyes.

Quinn knew he had to get out of there. And fast. Frustration knotted inside him, and his voice came out

rougher than he'd planned. ''I want to get a good night's sleep, angel. That's all. Thought there might be extra blankets and a pillow in here. If that's all right with you?''

''You're not going to share . . . this bed?''

''Is that an invitation?''

''No! No, of course not.'' In the lamplight, her cheeks burned like rubies. ''Take what you want then and . . . and go. There's bedding in that chest by the wall.'' She snatched up the pillow beside hers and threw it at him. He caught it easily.

''Much obliged.''

''You're welcome. But in the future, I'd thank you not to sneak up on me like that. You nearly scared me half to death!''

''You look mighty alive to me,'' he said softly, and Maura's fingers clenched around the blanket, drawing it slowly up to her shoulders, covering her breasts as she met his warm, glinting gaze.

''We should get a few things straight,'' she said in a voice that shook a little. ''What exactly are we going to do about . . . sleeping arrangements? If you want the bed while you're here, I'd be happy to sleep on the sofa. Or if you want to take turns . . .''

''You can keep the damned bed.'' Quinn couldn't look one more minute at that luscious mouth, or those big brown eyes, or he'd find himself grabbing that blanket from her and tearing off that nightgown and—

He stopped this train of thought, turned on his heel, and stalked to the chest on the floor. He grabbed a blanket and headed for the door. ''You're sleeping for two,'' he said over his shoulder. ''Make yourself comfortable.''

"I intend to. But please don't come in here again without knocking first."

He wheeled back. "Afraid you might talk in your sleep?"

"I'm not afraid of anything."

"Nothing?"

"Nothing at all," she flung at him, and jumped out of the bed. She rushed barefoot to the light and extinguished it. "I'm not afraid of the dark, I'm not afraid of thunder, and I'm not afraid of you."

She faced him, hands on her hips, completely oblivious of the sight she made with the starlight gliding over her lovely face and streaming hair, and softly illuminating every curve beneath that flimsy nightgown.

"Then I reckon you won't mind living here all alone once I clear out?" Quinn asked slowly.

"Mind? I told you—the more peace and quiet the better."

"Good. Because I'll be leaving soon for that gunfighting job and I'm not sure when I'll be back."

"Just don't leave before you've hired some men to work this ranch. Which reminds me, do we have any cattle?"

His brows lifted. "Not yet."

"What kind of a cattle ranch doesn't have cattle?"

"The kind that's just getting started. Since when did you get so bossy?"

"Since I got startled awake in the middle of the night by a stranger standing over my bed."

"I'm not exactly a stranger, Maura. Not anymore."

"Don't remind me." Suddenly Maura shivered, and she glanced down, realizing for the first time that she was standing before him in a patch of starlight in her thin nightgown—and nothing else.

She dove back into the bed, and yanked up both the sheets and the blanket.

"Kindly close the door as you leave."

He took one ominous step forward. "Are you kicking me out?"

"You said you weren't planning to stay."

He dropped the bedding at his feet, stepped over it, and reached the bed before she could do more than gasp.

"And what if I am?" he asked, crouching down beside her. With one smooth movement he tore the blanket from her clutching fingers, and yanked her forward toward his chest with an easy strength that made her dizzy.

"I—I thought we agreed—"

"We did."

"Then why are you in this bed . . . with me?"

"I'm not in the bed. Yet. I'm on the bed." His hands were tight around her wrists, his face only inches from hers. Maura felt the heat and strength of him filling the room, the air. Sending every delicate nerve ending in her body into crazy spasms.

"This isn't a good idea," she managed to say, but her lips were trembling.

He was staring at her mouth. If he kissed her again, stroked her hair or skin again, she'd be lost. . . .

For one moment she thought he was going to. She saw the hunger in his eyes, sensed the desire hotter than the setting sun, felt the violent need burning clear through that sleek, powerful body. She felt a surge of triumph. And wonder. And trepidation . . .

But then he drew back as quickly as he had sprung

forward. He released her, eased off the bed, stared down at her while taking quick, rapid breaths.

"You're right. It's not a good idea. If you think you can seduce me into sticking around—"

"Seduce you! When did I ever try to seduce *you?* You were the one who sweet-talked me into staying in your room that night and going to bed with you—"

"Yeah, well, I won't make that mistake again," he interrupted her ruthlessly.

"That makes two of us!"

He turned and scooped up the bedding he'd flung down. His boots thumped across the floor. "Fine. Good night."

"Good night!"

The instant the door slammed closed behind him, Maura flung her own pillow at it. *Damn you, Quinn Lassiter.*

The bed felt cold and lonely and empty. So did her heart.

She felt like weeping, but resolutely fought back the tears, every single one of them.

Quinn had wanted her. In that heart-stopping moment when they were so close they could have kissed, when his eyes had burned into hers, she had known to the bottom of her soul that if only for that night, he wanted her. But he didn't want to get trapped. He didn't want to have to stay here. He wanted to keep her at arm's length. So he could remain free.

Don't you dare even think about falling in love with him, she admonished herself as she retrieved her pillow and sank back into the bed. *Or about letting him into your heart. Even a tiny bit. That's the worst thing you could do. He doesn't love you, he never will.*

So don't start getting ideas. Don't start counting on him, wishing things could be different . . . hoping for the impossible . . .

She tried to stay awake, steeling herself against him, but exhaustion pulled at her and the weariness that dragged at every bone in her body would not be denied. She slept, deeply and heavily.

In the morning when she awoke to pale, gauzy sunlight, Quinn was not in the cabin. Her gunfighter husband was nowhere to be found.

Chapter 16

 MAURA BRAVED THE MARCH CHILL TO TREK TO the creek to wash, then dashed back to the cabin and pulled on her oldest calico dress. Today would be a day of work—hard, ceaseless work. There was so much to do in the cabin and all around it, not to mention the drive to town to purchase food and supplies. From what she had seen last night, plates, pots and pans, utensils—even furnishings—were few, and she would need to buy a great many items to make the cabin a comfortable dwelling. Not to mention the sadly lacking provisions—she must buy flour, sugar, potatoes, onions, beef, cheese . . .

The list seemed endless.

So did the minutes as they ticked past and there was still no sign of Quinn.

She added this to the long list of things she didn't know about her husband. Now that included his whereabouts.

You've only been married a scant number of days and already you've driven him off, she thought wryly. But in her heart she knew that however much Quinn might detest the thought of being tied down in a marriage, he would be back to set up the ranch for her and their baby.

She searched the meager stores in the kitchen, found coffee, hardtack, a can of peaches, four eggs. She broke the eggs into a bowl and began to heat the frying pan, in between going to the door and scanning the horizon for some sign of her husband. She was starved, but she was loath to prepare what little there would be for breakfast until he came home. It wouldn't do to serve him cold eggs the first morning in their new home.

After all, the poor man was having a hard enough time accepting his new status as a married man—cold eggs might push him right over the edge. She giggled suddenly at her own absurdity.

The very idea of trying to tame a hard roving man into a state of docile wedded bliss by serving him warm, fresh scrambled eggs struck her as so funny she began to laugh helplessly.

"I hope you appreciate this because I'm doing all this for you, baby," she told the new life inside her.

"Doing what for who?" Quinn's deep voice behind her made her spin around, her hip nearly knocking the fry pan off the stove. She grabbed the handle and straightened it, gasping as the heat burned her hand.

"What the hell?" Quinn was at her side in an instant, holding up her wrist, his eyes narrowed on the reddened skin of her palm.

"It was only a little hot," Maura protested. "I didn't actually burn it."

"Pure luck," he muttered, his fingers closing possessively around her wrist.

"You startled me." She tried not to be distracted by

the warmth of his fingers, but it was suddenly difficult to breathe. A meadowlark warbled from the tree outside the cabin window, but she heard it as if from a long way off. She was caught in the pull of Quinn's intent gray eyes.

She hoped he wouldn't notice how her pulse was racing at his touch. She took a deep breath and fixed him with a steely gaze. "Don't you get any ideas about making a habit of sneaking up on me," she warned, and slipped free of his grip.

"Wouldn't think of it." He shook his head. "You, lady, are *way* too jumpy for these parts. What am I going to do with you?"

Maura could think of a few things he'd already done with her, all of which she'd very much like him to do again, but she was too embarrassed to bring them up here in the kitchen in the clear light of day. *He* was the one who was jumpy, who'd disappeared without a trace this morning, she reminded herself, and resolved not to do anything to frighten him off again—at least not until they'd eaten breakfast.

"It's only that I don't like surprises," she murmured, and resisted the impulse to knock his hat off his handsome head, raise up on her tiptoes, and kiss him.

She turned back to the stove and busied herself beating a fork into the eggs, refusing to show him how truly happy she was that he was back. "Where have you been? I've been waiting breakfast," she said casually.

"Paid a visit to the neighbors."

"Neighbors? We have neighbors?"

"Downright neighborly ones," he drawled. "And they were more than happy to do a little business."

"What sort of business?"

"I bought us—*you*—some cattle. Two-hundred-fifty head. And I've hired a foreman to help me get things rolling."

"My goodness, you don't waste any time, do you?"

"I told you I wouldn't."

She felt his gaze on her as she poured the eggs into the sizzling fry pan, and did a little sizzling of her own. He'd been talking cattle, but his expression was warm, lingering. She couldn't help but remember how closely he'd held her last night. Self-conscious, she brushed a stray wisp of hair behind her ears, and then pushed the can of peaches toward him.

"Would you mind opening this can and emptying the peaches into a bowl?" Maura asked, feeling herself blush beneath the intentness of his gaze. She wondered if he was remembering too.

The heat pulsed through her cheeks and she was glad when she saw he was no longer watching her. He had taken out his knife and was digging into the lid of the can.

"Tell me something about our neighbors," she said to fill the silence between them.

"You met the Tylers yesterday in town. Their Crooked T runs about twenty miles north of the creek."

Maura nodded, pleased, remembering the tall man, the small, sunbonneted woman with the quiet smile and dark curls.

"When I first came to check out the property a few years back," Quinn continued, "I made it my business to find out just how much land there was and who had adjoining property, if anyone. The Tylers' spread runs pretty evenly alongside the north end of ours, and there's also the Westman place—just over ten miles to the east, near White Canyon.''

''You remember all this from over two years ago? So you recognized the Tyler name when we met them yesterday?''

''I never met them before, but yeah, I recognized the name. I make it my business to remember people.''

''Except me,'' Maura said without thinking. Then she gave a gasp. It had just slipped out.

She glanced at Quinn. His gray eyes pierced her. Quickly she turned, scooped the eggs from the fry pan, and split them between two plates.

''I remember you now, Maura,'' he said evenly. ''It was only at first—''

''It doesn't matter.''

''I think you're lying.''

''What?'' Maura set the plates on the table with a crack and faced him, her hands on her hips. ''I don't lie.''

Her voice quavered a little. She was remembering how he had accused her of lying when she'd come to him in the Jezebel Saloon in Whisper Valley. When she'd told him about the baby. The memory of it still hurt.

He seemed to guess at her thoughts.

''I don't mean lying, exactly. I mean, you're not admitting—even to yourself—that it does matter to you. It matters to you that at first I didn't recall what happened that night or even that I'd ever met you.''

He was right. It did matter. It made her feel so insignificant. A night that had held such importance for her had been only a vague memory for him, something easily forgotten.

''It's not important now.''

"If it hurt you, then it damn well is important." Quinn frowned, and the next thing she knew he was leading her to a chair.

"Sit down. And listen up."

She stared up at him, surprised by how seriously he was taking this. "I'm listening."

"I don't know much about women."

Remembering all the ways he had teased and tormented—and pleasured—her that night, her brows rose, and he had the grace to grin. "Well, I know *some* things," he admitted, and there was a hint of amusement in his eyes.

"I noticed," Maura said, again without thinking, and this time her face flushed a vivid pink. He reached out and stroked a finger down one cheek, then let his hand drop, as if mentally recalling himself to the business at hand.

"I meant that I don't know much about courting or wooing—how to talk to a woman, say the right things, smooth her feelings. I've never stuck around with anyone long enough to give things like that much thought. Unless you count Serena."

Serena. She waited, watching his face, glad he couldn't know that her heart had twisted inside her chest.

"Oh?" she prodded.

But instead of explaining, he merely gave another shrug and raked a hand through his hair. "Serena doesn't matter."

She wondered if that was really true. Had they been lovers? Or just friends? She couldn't forget the expression on the blond woman's face when he'd introduced her as his wife.

"The point is," Quinn continued, "not only don't I know much about the fancy ways of wooing a woman, I know even less about marriage. Even a marriage like this one. But—"

Quinn abruptly walked to the counter and carried the bowl of peaches to the table, then sat down in the chair opposite hers. In the silence that followed, all they heard was the meadowlark singing outside the window.

"Someday I'll tell you a story," he said, "about a man who didn't know how to treat his wife. Who beat her, neglected her, eventually got her killed."

"Who was he?" Maura asked softly. His face had turned ashen as he spoke the words, and she could see the painful memories searing him.

"My father."

Maura couldn't think what to say. There were a dozen questions she wanted to ask, but the haunted expression had returned to Quinn's eyes—the same expression she'd seen that night in the Duncan Hotel, and all she could think about was easing his pain, soothing that strange, terrible loneliness that lurked beneath the surface of this hardened man.

"I'm sorry." She reached across the table, touched his hand.

He started, looked into her face a moment, and then pulled his hand away as if she'd burned it.

"It was a long time ago," he said coolly, and the spell was broken. He stood up and brought the coffeepot to the table, and poured them each a cup. The meadowlark must have fled, for there was now only a deep and lonesome silence.

"My point is, I never wanted to turn out like him. I've

no use for bullies, or for men who don't take care of their families, especially their women. So, like I told you in Whisper Valley, I'm going to take care of you. You and the baby both. But don't expect . . . more.''

By more, he meant love. Permanence. Staying with her and sharing a life. Her heart wrenched. She wasn't sure why. She didn't love him. She barely knew him.

''I understand,'' she replied, and swallowed a forkful of the eggs, tasting nothing.

''Do you?'' His voice roughened. ''Because if you want something from me that I can't give you, Maura, you'll only be hurt.''

''Don't worry,'' she said quickly. ''I want the same thing you do. A good home for our baby. That's it. And . . . independence. My own independence. Believe me, after years of living with Judd and Homer, the last thing I want is any man interfering in my daily life, telling me what to do.''

She met his gaze, her chin lifting. ''Perhaps we could just be . . . partners.''

''Partners?''

''As part of our business arrangement.'' She leaned forward. ''Partners in building the ranch—and partners in raising our child. Do you think you could manage that, Quinn?''

''I've never been partners with a woman before.''

''Well, if it's any comfort to you, I've never been part-ners—or even friends—with *anyone* before. My adoptive brothers wouldn't permit it.''

''I'd like to meet these brothers someday,'' he said in a low tone, and Maura quickly shook her head.

"No, you wouldn't," she said fervently. "Besides, they don't matter either."

He couldn't argue with that. He nodded at her. "Partners, then. But this partner comes and goes as he pleases—no questions asked. Just like we agreed."

"Of course. I wouldn't want it any other way."

She saw his shoulders relax. He took a long drink of coffee.

Maura carried her plate to the sink.

Once upon a time she had dreamed of finding love, love that would fill her heart and last forever. But that had been foolish and unrealistic, she told herself. She had to face that now. She was going to have a child, and she had no choice but to put aside the silly romantic daydreams of her girlhood.

The sound of horses' hooves broke into her thoughts and had Quinn out of his chair in one swift motion. Maura followed him to the door. A buggy was approaching. Edna Weaver waved to them, the feathers on her gray hat blowing in the breeze. Seated beside her, holding the reins of a handsome white team, was a portly, gray-mustached man in a dark suit and bowler.

The banker.

Beside Quinn, Maura wiped her hands on her apron.

"It's a bit early for company, but how nice that they've come to call."

"Let's see what they want, Maura, before we decide if it's nice."

Throwing him a bemused look, Maura brushed past him, and waved in greeting as the buggy pulled up amidst the weeds and scrub brush surrounding the cabin.

Chapter 17

 "GOOD MORNING, MRS. LASSITER! AND MR. LASSITER!" Edna's booming voice sent a squirrel racing from the brush toward the creek.

Maura answered warmly. "It's Maura and Quinn, please."

The woman beamed. "Then call me Edna, honey. Everyone does."

As the portly man clambered out of the buggy and came around to help her alight, she said, "This is my husband, Seth. We're sorry to intrude when you're just getting settled in and all, but we have something important to discuss and it can't wait."

Maura had no idea what this could be, but pleasure raced through her. Humble as the cabin might be, it was still home, and far better than the Duncan Hotel, where only three small bedrooms upstairs had been allotted for the family, and no place except the hotel dining room to entertain—not that Ma Duncan had ever found herself in a position to do that.

But now Maura's very first guests (if she didn't count

Lucky) had arrived, and she smiled at them as they made their way across the weed-strewn clearing.

"You're more than welcome," she said. "It's nice to see friendly faces. Please, won't you come in?"

To Maura's relief, Edna Weaver, once again holding a basket over one arm, breezed into the cabin giving only a cursory glance at the spare furnishings and puncheon floor. Quinn shook Seth Weaver's pudgy hand, but said nothing, though he did bring a kitchen chair into the parlor so that everyone could sit down. He stood, tall and silent by the mantel as the Weavers seated themselves on the horsehair sofa and Maura slipped into a chair.

"First, a little welcome gift, dear." Edna held out the basket. "Our way of apologizing for that little misunderstanding yesterday."

To Maura's delight, when she lifted the embroidered white napkin, she saw that the basket contained a loaf of sourdough, two thick wedges of cheese, and a jar of blueberry preserves—nestled beside a dozen oatmeal cookies.

"Mrs. Weaver—Edna—how generous of you." True pleasure sparkled across her face. She'd so rarely received any kind of gift, and this woman whom she scarcely knew was bestowing such a thoughtful one upon her. Upon them.

"Thank you so much. Quinn, isn't this lovely?"

"Lovely," he echoed dryly. Maura tried to gloss over his lack of enthusiasm and the cynical gleam in his eyes as he glanced first at Mrs. Weaver and then at her ruddy-skinned husband.

"May I get you some coffee?" she asked quickly.

"No, thank you, but I think we'd best get down to business and then let you folks get on with settling in,"

Seth Weaver replied. His voice was as thin as his hairline. He was a neat, almost dapper man in his immaculately pressed pinstriped suit. His nut-brown eyes were close-set and shrewder than his wife's, but his face was kindly. He had a soft mouth that smiled easily, and his ears stuck out a bit on his gray head.

"Go on." Quinn watched the banker from the mantel, his own face unreadable.

But Maura knew he didn't trust these people. She remembered him telling her that he didn't trust anyone.

What kind of life had he led, she wondered, to be so wary of everyone, so cold and distant?

She shivered, then concentrated on what the banker had to say.

"As you heard yesterday in town, the Campbell gang has been causing considerable trouble in Hope." He cleared his throat. "The plain truth is, folks are scared. My bank has been robbed twice. We lost over a thousand dollars. If it happens again, I might have to close our doors." He sighed. "And if folks are too afraid to settle in Hope and stay here, the town will die."

His face tightened. He looked at Quinn. "The missus and I have lived in these parts for more than thirty years. Since we were newlyweds, not so different from you two. We met here, married here, raised our family here."

"What does this have to do with us, Weaver?" Quinn broke in.

Edna pursed her lips, but Seth Weaver went on calmly, meeting the gunfighter's direct gray gaze with solemn patience.

"Sheriff Owen was a good man, Mr. Lassiter, but he was no match for those Campbells. And now we hear their cousin Luke, the real ringleader, is joining up with them. Well, we need someone who can stand up to them, all of them, Luke included.''

Maura had a sinking feeling where this was headed. One glance at Quinn's coldly set face told her he knew too. Edna's large, knobby hands were folded in her lap, but she was studying Quinn intently. His expression gave nothing away.

Fear clutched at Maura. The last thing she wanted was for Quinn, the father of her child, to go up against a dangerous gang of outlaws.

Yet he'd earned his living for a long time doing just such dangerous work. This would be exactly the sort of challenge that would appeal to him. But—the danger. If something happened to him . . .

Knots twisted in her stomach. She couldn't begin to guess what he would say when the inevitable question came.

''Last night in town, some of us had a little meeting. We care about our town, Mr. Lassiter. We're not willing to stand by and let it be overrun by outlaws.''

''Tell him what we decided, Seth,'' Edna urged, touching her husband's arm.

Seth Weaver patted her hand, then turned his attention back to the man who waited silently by the mantel. Maura detected a hopeful gleam in his eyes as he studied the gunfighter. ''It was agreed unanimously that I should offer you the position of sheriff. We can't afford much, but—''

''No thanks. Not interested.''

Maura was startled by the steely coldness of Quinn's voice.

"But Mr. Lassiter"—the banker held up a hand— "You haven't heard what we have to offer. Please consider—you're the only one who can—"

"Sorry you wasted your time."

Quinn swung away from the mantel and came to stand beside the old horsehair sofa where the Weavers sat side by side. He loomed over Seth Weaver, his features hard as stone. His anger was palpable in the air, and equally apparent was the rigid control he was exercising over it.

"I'll see you out," he said coolly.

Edna's mouth worked, but no words emerged. Her husband swallowed hard, confusion and disappointment flickering across his ruddy face.

"If you'll only hear me out," he began desperately.

"I've heard all I need to hear. Now I've got work to do. This meeting is over."

Maura jumped up and began speaking in a rush. "My husband is planning to start a ranch, you see. And to build us a home. We're going to be enlarging the cabin and adding corrals and such and . . . and starting a family and I don't think he really would have the time—"

"I can speak for myself." Quinn stalked to the door, opened it, and said, "What you don't understand, Mr. Weaver, is that the day I put on a lawman's badge is the day I'd just as soon put a bullet in my own head. So there's nothing left to talk about."

"Please, Mr. Lassiter." Edna stood up and threw him a quick, earnest glance as she moved toward him. "Hope needs you!" she declared. "We need someone of your skill and courage and—"

"Your husband said what he came to say, and I gave

him my answer, ma'am." His eyes were splinters of ice. "I'm no lawman, Mrs. Weaver. I never will be."

"But—"

"Edna, that's enough." Her husband struggled up wearily from the sofa and with heavy steps crossed the floor. He took her arm. "The man's given us his answer. We'd best be going."

Edna Weaver sucked in her breath, but ventured nothing more. She threw a quick glance at her husband, whose eyes had lost their hopeful gleam. He led her out into the sun.

"I'm sorry." Maura followed them through the door, the wind whipping her calico skirt around her.

"We understand, Mrs. Lassiter." The banker gave her a bleak, watery smile.

"No need to explain." But Edna's tone was stiff with disappointment.

Maura fought down the urge to invite them to come back again when she had the place fixed up. After this, she couldn't blame them if they never wanted to set foot near Sage Creek again. And once they told everyone else in town . . .

As she watched the buggy drive off, all her dreams of belonging, of having friends and neighbors who visited and gossiped and supported one another, wisped into the blue Wyoming sky, disappearing like smoke.

The buggy was just clearing the rise when Quinn strode outside and walked right past her toward the shed and the horses.

She followed him, trying to keep up with his long strides.

"Quinn. Please wait a moment. I don't understand."

He spoke without looking back. "You don't have to."

"I *want* to."

"Go back inside, Maura. I've got work to—"

"I'm not going anywhere until you tell me what the hell is going on!"

At this, he stopped dead, then spun around to face her. That redhead's temper again, he thought grimly. Her eyes were flashing in the golden glare of the sun, her hands plopped on her hips as she strode toward him, that glorious hair flying about her. She was magnificent, but he was far from being in a mood to explain himself.

Eyes narrowed, he waited until she caught up to him and then spoke as evenly as he could. "It's cold out here, Maura. You should have your shawl."

"I don't care a fig about my shawl. I want to understand."

"Understand what?"

"For heaven's sake, Quinn, I never wanted you to accept that sheriff's job, but just tell me why you're so angry that they offered it to you. It's not an insult, it's an honor. . . ."

"Honor!" He snorted. "It's no honor to be a lawman, Maura. I told you last night you were too softhearted for your own good and it's true."

"What do you have against lawmen?" she demanded. "Something pretty strong, to have treated our guests that way! They'll never come back!"

"Fine with me. We don't need them." But he saw immediately the bewilderment and disappointment that filled her eyes, and a pang shot through him. It suddenly sank in to him that his harsh reaction might have cost her any chance of being accepted in Hope, of having those friends and neighbors she wanted so badly.

He should have handled things differently.

Without thinking, he reached for her, grasped her arm and pulled her closer. All he knew was that the frustration in her pale face tore at his heart.

"Look," he said roughly, "I'm sorry I lost my temper with those folks. You want to make friends with them, fine, go right ahead. But I reckon I'm not used to trying to get along with people."

"I can see that," she murmured.

He subdued a crack of laughter, and hauled her closer yet, wrapping his arms around her to shield her from the morning chill. "Just remember it's me they're sore at, Maura, not you. No one could be sore at you."

"You are."

"Who says?" He grinned suddenly, and it transformed his face, warming the sharp angles, warming Maura clear through like a red-hot sunbeam.

"Tell you what." Quinn brushed a hand through her wind-tossed curls, smoothing them. Hell, how he wanted to kiss her. She had the most delectable lips, and the sauciest way of tilting her head to one side, and he suddenly wanted to drag her over to the creekbank and take her on the ground beneath one of those spreading cottonwoods. . . .

Alarmed at his own runaway thoughts, he loosened his grip on her and stepped back, forcing himself to regain control.

"How about if we go to town this afternoon and load up the wagon?" he asked gruffly, knowing the idea would please her. "I reckon the larder's pretty empty and you'd

probably like to get some things for the cabin—and for
yourself. You didn't bring much along in that satchel of
yours."

"That would be nice, but I thought you had work to
do."

"Not so much that I can't spare a few hours for my
wife. Besides, I've got to hire on a few more hands to
help out around here. Cattle need branding, and there's a
corral to build. Thought I'd check in town and see if
anyone's looking for work."

She nodded. He was trying to apologize, trying to
cheer her. What a strange, contradictory, impossible man.

Yet even as she took heart in his attempt to smooth
things over with her, disappointment tugged at her because he'd let her go quite so quickly.

Heaven help me, Maura thought in despair. Quinn was
too handsome for comfort, too gentle when he wanted to
be. He turned her insides to a puddle of jelly. She'd actually reveled in the hard strength of his arms around her,
and could have stood all day basking in the devastating
warmth of his smile. But that was dangerous. *He* was
dangerous.

Partnership, she reminded herself. *That's what he
wants—and what you want too. Don't start getting any
other ideas or this gunfighter will break your heart.*

She turned back toward the cabin, making an effort to
appear as casual as he, when what she really wanted was
to throw herself like a fool into his arms. "Guess I'd
better see to the dishes."

"Guess I'll see you later."

Oh, yes, he certainly would. But until then, Maura told
herself, clutching her windblown skirts as she headed

back to the cabin, she was going to put Quinn Lassiter out of her mind. She had enough to think about without day-dreaming over a black-haired devil with eyes that pierced right into her soul. Enough to worry about without wondering what Quinn Lassiter had against lawmen—and why his slightest touch made her forget to breathe.

There was so much she didn't know about this gun-fighter she'd married. She wondered if he'd ever trust her enough to let her get close, to share his past and his secrets with her. He'd told her about his father—she supposed that was something. Pity for the small boy who had lived with such a man flooded her.

And so did questions about what had become of his mother.

At noon, Quinn hitched up the team and they left for town.

Hope was just as quiet and tense as it had been the day before. Despite the glowing blue sky and crystal air, the storefronts appeared drab and gloomy. Few people appeared on the boardwalk and only a few horses were tethered on the street, most of them near the saloon.

Behind the counter in the mercantile, John Hicks nodded at her. "Afternoon, Mrs. Lassiter." He sounded wary.

Maura offered him a smile. "It's very nice to see you again, Mr. Hicks."

He cleared his throat, a dull flush climbing up his neck. "Reckon I ought to apologize again for that welcome I gave you and your husband yesterday. Folks are spooked in Hope, that's all. Didn't mean to scare you."

"I understand. And so does my husband. It's a shame about all the trouble."

Nell Hicks strode from the back room just then, carrying a box overflowing with an assortment of colored hair ribbons. "Papa, I thought I'd set these in the window so that—"

She broke off when she caught sight of Maura. "Sorry—didn't mean to interrupt while you were waiting on a customer," she said quickly. "We don't get too many these days—customers, that is," she added with a little grimace.

"You didn't interrupt—we were just about to get started." Maura returned the girl's friendly smile. Like yesterday, Nell wore a plaid shirt and denim pants and boy's boots. But despite her direct, no-nonsense air and tomboyish clothes, Nell Hicks was as young, fresh, and pretty as a spring day. The thought of how close she'd come to being carried off by the Campbells sent a shudder down Maura's back. The girl was no more than sixteen.

"If you're setting up housekeeping down by Sage Creek, I reckon you need half the supplies we've got in this store," Nell declared, setting the hair ribbons down on a shelf in the window and hurrying back to the counter. "Papa and I had better both wait on you or you'll be here all day. What do you need to start? Five pounds of flour? Sugar? We've got raisins, and molasses and eggs aplenty. Chase and Sanborn coffee. There's pots and pans on that shelf back there, and we sell whiskey and beer from those barrels right up front. And I bet you need soap and candles. We've got a fine selection, Mrs. Lassiter, better than anything you'll find between here and Denver."

Maura listened in awe as she rattled off dozens of

goods available in the store. John Hicks scratched his head and fumbled around for a pencil and ledger sheet to write down all the purchases as his daughter took charge.

"Nell here will have you set up in no time," he told Maura encouragingly. "She's been working side by side with me since her ma died when she was nine, and she knows our stock better than I do. Whatever you need, chances are she'll find it."

"I can see that." Maura was gazing eagerly at the barrels of pickles, canned goods, spices, and salted fish. Quinn had told her to buy whatever she needed.

"I need some of everything," she said simply, and Nell grinned, her lime-green eyes lighting up.

"Then you've come to the right place."

While Maura was buying flour, potatoes, lard, sugar, cheese, a side of beef, canned goods, ham, coffee, eating utensils, candles, another kerosene lamp, pots and pans, curtain fabric, and even some embroidered pillows to decorate the sofa, Quinn had stopped in at the saloon to let the bartender know he was looking to hire two ranch hands, asking the man to send anyone looking for work out to Sage Creek to see him.

Then he went to Mason's Hardware Store to buy tools and lumber for the building that would need to be done.

But as he was loading his purchases into the wagon, the sound of horses' hooves thundering in the distance made him pause, an armful of lumber in hand.

Four horses galloped over the ridge at the edge of town and charged toward Main Street. Their riders fired into the air, whooping and shouting. By the time they reached the first of Hope's false-fronted stores, they were firing at windows, doors, posts, and porches, their rough yells mingling with the crashing roar of ironclad hooves.

Quinn knew it was the Campbells even before they were close enough for him to see their faces. Lee, Hoss, Marv, and Ned Campbell were four of the meanest, ugliest, greediest outlaws he'd ever encountered. Only their cousin Luke was crueler—and even more homely.

He didn't know where the hell Luke was, but the other four were rampaging through the street, and as Quinn dumped the lumber into the wagon he heard a cry. He glanced aside and saw that Alice Tyler of the Crooked T ranch had just stepped out of the millinery shop and had been crossing the street when the ruckus began. She started to jump back as she saw the horses bearing down on her, but in her haste and fear she stumbled and fell.

Lee's mustang was in the lead, and was bearing down straight toward the woman.

Chapter 18

QUINN LUNGED AT THE WOMAN AND DRAGGED her back onto the boardwalk just as the mustang charged past. The other horses thundered close behind, and it was then that Marv and Hoss spotted him, both at the same time.

They both aimed their pistols at him and fired.

He'd managed to shove the woman through the doorway of the hardware store before the first bullets flew. He dove behind a post and fired almost simultaneously with their shots. First Marv and then Hoss toppled from his saddle.

As Lee and Ned reached the end of the street they whipped their horses around and started back. No longer were they firing into the air—they now had their six-shooters pointed right at Quinn as they came on at a full gallop, fury replacing their whoops of laughter. They'd seen their fallen brothers.

"Damn you to hell, Lassiter, you're finally gonna die!" Lee yelled, and a bullet exploded through the post only inches from Quinn's head.

He dodged to the next post, aimed, and fired.

There was a scream and Lee fell over, still in the saddle, but drooping low across his horse's mane and leaving a blood trail in the street.

Quinn fired again, but missed Ned, and this time the two remaining Campbell brothers continued straight for the ridge and out of town, leaving Hoss and Marv lying in the street.

Silence descended over the town once more as the last of the hoofbeats faded away.

Slowly, doors and windows swung open. Taut, fearful faces appeared, figures emerged with caution.

Stepping down into the dusty street, Quinn saw Serena Walsh framed in her doorway. She hurried toward him as he moved to check on the bloodied bodies in the road.

"Quinn, that was the fanciest shooting I've ever seen!"

"Stay back," he ordered, and she froze, watching as he studied the outlaw with the stringy straw-colored hair lying facedown beside the horse trough.

"This one's dead." Quinn moved past Hoss to the other brother, Marv. Lying on his side, Marv Campbell was still gasping, his chest heaving. Blood ran from his mouth and puddled beneath his head. There was a black gaping hole in his shirt from which blood ran bright and hot.

"They're . . . gonna git you, Lassiter. If it's the last thing . . . my brothers ever do . . ."

"It will be, you son of a bitch."

"Luke's outta jail. He's been huntin' for you. He'll come . . . and Ned . . . and Lee. They're gonna—"

He coughed, and a shudder racked his body. "They're gonna plug you full of . . ."

"Then I'll see you in hell." Quinn watched, his face hard as stone as the outlaw twisted and writhed and choked on his own blood. He twitched once, then again, and finally lay still.

"I suppose now . . . the rest of them are really going to go on the warpath," Serena said softly behind him, and he turned to look at her. She was pale, and appeared shaken—unusual for her.

He shrugged. "Next time it'll be their turn."

He felt a hand on his arm and spun around.

"Thank you, Mr. Lassiter," Alice Tyler whispered. Fear was still etched starkly across her small, delicate face. Her eyes were glazed with shock.

"You saved my life."

"Glad to help, ma'am." Quinn doffed his hat and started walking away. All he could think was that Maura could have been the one in the street. She was in the mercantile. If the Campbells had gone there first, instead of riding like savages through the street, who knew what the hell might have happened?

Scowling with concern, he started toward the general store. Serena fell into step beside him. "You haven't changed."

"What?" He glanced at her, for the first time noticing her scurrying to keep up with his long strides. He'd forgotten all about her, all about everyone but Maura.

"Whenever a woman needs you—you're always right there to protect her. You never hesitate."

He stopped and faced her, studying her beautiful face, those lustrous blue eyes, the wide, sensuous mouth he remembered so well. Serena Walsh was every bit as alluring as ever. "Why are you staying here, Serena? Hope

has more than its share of trouble and is mighty dangerous these days from what I can see. It's not like you to
stick out a bad situation when you can just as easily move
on. Why don't you find yourself a safer town?''

Her smile was rueful. She tilted her head and studied
him. ''That's just what I would have done a few years
ago, when you met me, Quinn, honey. But the funny
thing is, I'm tired of that kind of life. Tired of running—
running away from things, running toward other things.
I've settled here in Hope. I just got my boardinghouse
fixed up the way I like it—and the folks here are no worse
than anyplace else. One day,'' she said dryly, ''they
might even come to accept me. Oh, I'm not good enough
for most of the ladies who fancy themselves richer, or
more educated, or more proper than me—and they let me
know it.'' She gave a short, contemptuous laugh. ''But I
don't give a damn about that. The fact is, I'm just plain
tired of moving on all the time. So are you, apparently.''

The streets were filling up suddenly. People began running toward the other end of Main Street, crowding
around the fallen Campbell brothers.

''This town still got an undertaker?'' Quinn asked as
he continued toward Hicks Mercantile.

''Yes, indeed. Rufus Tweedy. That's him over there.''
Serena nodded toward a black-coated man who was lop-
ing up the street, right behind a red-faced, huffing Seth
Weaver.

''Tweedy won't be the only one celebrating tonight,''
Serena commented. ''Everyone in town will be happy
that two of the Campbells are going to be six feet under in
Boot Hill, but pretty soon they're going to realize that the

trouble is only going to get worse. The others will want revenge.''

"Don't you worry about the others," Quinn said shortly, then he saw Maura hurrying up the street, her face white as chalk, her skirts clenched in one hand. The dark-haired girl, Nell, ran along beside her, and just behind them was John Hicks, his shotgun in hand.

"Well, well, here comes your sweet little wife," Serena murmured.

He scarcely heard her. He was watching Maura's face, watching the fear lift and the rush of relief settle over her lovely features as she caught sight of him.

Then she slowed her steps as she came closer and saw Serena alongside him. Instead of throwing herself into his arms, Maura grasped his hands as she reached him and gazed into his eyes.

"I heard there was shooting—the Campbell gang. Someone said they shot at you—"

"Those boys never could hit much of anything they shot at."

"Quinn, how can you joke about it?" Her voice broke. "I thought . . . I thought . . ."

She caught herself, struggling to compose her churning emotions. Her chest felt as though a bison was sitting on it, but she managed to summon up a quavery smile. "Is there anything left of them?" she asked, trying to match his offhand tone.

"Just a little bit," Serena answered for him. "Two of those vermin are dead in the street. Quinn wounded another one, but he and his brother got away."

"Will they be back? Won't they come looking for

you?'' Maura asked, her voice hitching, and he saw the fear shining in her eyes.

Fear. For him. No one ever felt fear for him. He was the one everyone looked to as a shield, the one to stand between them and the bullets. The one hired to face the danger, the first line of defense against the enemy. But Maura had terror in her face and it wasn't for herself—it was for him.

''No need to worry, angel. I'm going to find them first.''

''What do you mean?''

''Soon as I get you back to the cabin and settled, I'm going to hunt them down. Don't worry,'' he told her as he saw the flash of panic across her face. He reached up to cup her chin, holding it gently.

She looked so distraught that he did it without thinking, forgetting even that Serena was right there, watching him, watching both of them. ''I've had some practice at this,'' he told Maura dryly. ''I put Luke Campbell in prison a while back, and I'll bring the rest of them in, too.''

Serena, glancing back and forth from one to the other, drew in a breath.

And at that moment, a man's voice spoke directly behind Quinn.

''Lassiter.''

He released Maura's chin and turned around to find Jim Tyler standing before him, feet planted apart. Alice stood beside her husband, clutching his arm.

''Yeah?''

''I owe you, Lassiter.'' Deep emotion threaded the rancher's low voice. His eyes glistened in the sunlight that angled down on the street. "My wife says you saved her life—and risked yours. I don't know how to thank you."

"You don't have to thank me. I just happened to be there at the right time."

Tyler held out his hand. He seemed to be struggling for words. "What can I do to show my appreciation? I'm not much good at making speeches, but . . . I'll never forget this. And neither will my four young sons." He spoke forcefully. "If there's anything you need, anytime, just say so."

Quinn started to shake his head, then changed his mind. "Matter of fact, there is something."

Other people were gathering around. Not the undertaker, he was still kneeling over the fallen men, but Seth Weaver, John Hicks, Nell, and several other townspeople were now clustered around Jim Tyler.

From the corner of his eye, Quinn saw Lucky Johnson shouldering his way through the crowd. He came to stand behind the Hicks girl.

"Name it, Lassiter." The tall rancher met his gaze squarely, and beside him Alice smiled at Maura. "Whatever I can do."

"I'm planning to ride out after Lee and Ned Campbell soon as I get my wife safely home. Can you spare a couple of ranch hands to camp out near our cabin and keep an eye on things while I'm gone? Maybe a man or two to start rounding up some of those steers I bought from you? Good men," he said grimly, "men you trust."

"There's several I'd swear on with my life. I'll send them over right away. But I'm coming with you to track those outlaws." Tyler's face was set. Alice made a small sound of protest, but he just patted her hand and kept his gaze on Quinn's.

"I'll send two of my top hands over pronto."

Quinn nodded. "Much obliged."

"But Quinn—you're not going after them tonight?" Maura asked, staring at him in dismay.

"The sooner I head out, the better. The trail will be fresh."

"Hold on." Lucky Johnson pushed his way forward. He bumped into Nell, knocking her off-balance, but was so intent on the discussion between Lassiter and the rancher, he didn't even notice. "I'm coming with you," he exclaimed.

"The hell you are." Quinn turned away from the youth and took Maura's arm. "Let's get your purchases and—"

"I said I'm coming with you and you can't stop me!" Lucky shouted, stepping directly into Quinn's path.

A hush fell over the throng. Maura felt her heart sink as Quinn released her arm and turned those cold, deadly gray eyes on the boy.

"I owe you, too, Lassiter!" the boy exclaimed. "And like it or not, I'm going to help bring those varmints in!"

Tyler gave him a long, steady look. "Son, we want seasoned men, men who know what they're doing."

"Young man, whoever you are, your intentions are admirable, but you're still wet behind the ears," Seth Weaver added. "Now men like Mr. Lassiter and Mr. Tyler have got the experience to go after a gang like the Campbells and come back alive. They don't have time to keep an eye on you *and* smoke out those scoundrels."

Lucky Johnson's flush deepened and a muscle jumped in his cheek. He took one swift belligerent step forward.

"I don't need no one to keep an eye on me! I can take care of myself and I can shoot just as straight, just as fast as anyone—well, maybe not as fast as Quinn Lassiter, not yet—but as any other man in this town—"

"That's enough!" Tyler frowned at him. "You're wasting our time."

Nell Hicks stared at Lucky Johnson, taking in every aspect of his handsome face, red and angry as it was. Her green eyes shone—no doubt with sympathy, Maura reflected. She felt sorry for him, too—not only was his help being refused, but he was being publicly embarrassed by the very men whose respect he obviously craved.

Then Quinn spoke and she held her breath, bracing herself for the next stinging comment Lucky would have to bear.

"Let him come."

"What?" Tyler stared at him.

"Mr. Lassiter," the banker said, "I thought you didn't want—"

"Changed my mind. He can come." Quinn flicked a glance at Lucky. "Get your gear packed and your horse saddled. Pronto."

Ignoring the flash of joy on the boy's face, and hoping he wasn't making a big mistake, Quinn took Maura's arm. "Ready?"

She nodded, her throat dry. It was difficult to absorb both his sudden turnaround with Lucky and the fact that he was leaving her, going after the Campbells on a deadly hunt from which he might not return.

"I was nearly finished at the mercantile," she said quietly, her eyes meeting his. She wanted to cry, *Don't go! Something terrible might happen to you! Stay with me.*

But instead she turned to Mr. Hicks and said with far more calm than she felt, "I don't believe I settled the bill yet. Shall we go back and finish our business?"

"My pleasure, Mrs. Lassiter. Nell, come along, girl." To Maura he explained, "She's quicker than me at adding up all those figures." Then he threw a sharp glance at his daughter, still staring at Lucky Johnson. "Nell? Nell, what's got into you? I said *come along*."

The girl startled and tore her attention from Lucky to meet her father's glance distractedly. "Oh, coming, Papa. In a minute."

Lucky Johnson hadn't once noticed her. Even as the Lassiters and Nell's father moved away, he continued to peer after Quinn Lassiter with a mixture of gratitude and amazement, as if scarcely able to believe his good fortune in being allowed to join the posse.

Nell lingered another moment, gathering her courage. She smoothed her long black braid. "Mr. Johnson." She moistened her lips. "Be careful."

Lucky did notice her then. He spun about, glaring at her. Anger flared in his thick-lashed eyes as he took in Nell's tomboyish garb and worried green gaze. "Huh? How do you know my name?"

"I've . . . seen you around town. You bought some eggs and tobacco and things in the store."

"Oh, yeah. You're that Hicks girl." Lucky hunched a shoulder. He stuck out his jaw. "Why'd you tell me to be careful?" he demanded. "You think I can't handle being part of that posse?"

"I didn't say that," Nell exclaimed.

He studied her closely. She was a kid, no more than sixteen. Last night he'd spent the whole night in bed with Orchid, the prettiest, most buxom, and most *experienced* saloon girl in town, and here was this skinny, bossy female *kid* in denim pants and a man's boots horning in on his business!

"Get lost," Lucky scowled. "You can't tell me what to do."

"Well, *somebody* ought to." Answering anger sparked in Nell's face, turning her eyes to twin green flames.

Her hands plopped onto her hips. "It's true what they said—you *are* too young and . . . and *green* to be riding with men like Quinn Lassiter. If you had the brains of a—a prairie dog you'd stay behind and let them handle this."

Lucky took a step forward and towered over her, pleased when those flashing eyes of hers widened just a little. "Seems to me what I do is none of your business, little girl. Matter of fact, if I were you, I'd go on back to that store with my daddy and leave the *men* to their work. I heard Lee Campbell almost ran off with you last time he came to town. Maybe by the time I'm done with him, you'll be thanking me for being able to sleep a little better!"

"It happens that I sleep just fine!" Nell shot back, but it was her turn to flush, her cheeks turning a deep shade of rose. "Don't you worry about me, Lucky Johnson. You're the one who needs a lick of sense if you're going to stay alive."

Lucky hooked his thumbs in his gunbelt and regarded her in amusement. "Why are you so all-fired interested anyway? Don't tell me you'd weep big sad tears if I got myself shot."

"I'd sing a song and do a two-step over your grave!" Nell called over her shoulder as she walked away. "Go on, get yourself killed for all I care. See if I even *come* to your funeral!"

Lucky laughed as he watched her march off after her father and the Lassiters, that black braid swinging behind her, her hips encased in those denim pants rolling in a haughty, feminine way that served to amuse him even more.

While Quinn loaded the wagon and conferred with Jim Tyler, Alice Tyler approached Maura outside of the general store.

"Your husband never hesitated," she said softly, giving her dainty head a slight shake. "He risked his own life to save mine. I have four young boys at home, none of them older than twelve. They need me. I'll never forget what your husband did for me today—and for them."

"I just thank God he was there to help." Maura shuddered. She glanced around the gray little town, where people were beginning to scatter and once again disappear indoors. "When we decided to come here, we thought Hope would be a safe, quiet place to settle down and raise a family. But now—"

"A family? Do you mean to say . . . is there a little one on the way?" Alice asked.

Maura nodded, her lips curving in a happy smile. "Yes, there is." She heard Serena Walsh suck in her breath. Her face wore a frozen expression. The woman had remained nearby ever since the shooting, even accompanying them to the mercantile. She hadn't said much to anyone other than Quinn, but she was listening to everything that went on. And apparently she was stunned by what she'd just heard.

"Not for some months yet," Maura added, refusing to glance again at Serena. "But soon, yes, we'll be expanding our family."

"That's wonderful. And all the more reason to rid the town of the gang!" Alice exclaimed.

"But it's so dangerous." Maura's dark eyes moved to Quinn, his face set with purpose as he spoke with Jim Tyler and put the last of the supplies in the wagon.

A knot of fear twisted inside her. "Alice, aren't you afraid for your husband?"

"With all my heart. But it's even more dangerous not knowing when the gang is going to return, or what they're going to do next. If no one stands up to them, they'll just get bolder and more vicious. That's what's been happening for months. Jim and Sheriff Owen tried tracking them before, but couldn't find a trace. But now that your husband has wounded one of them, perhaps the blood will leave a trail."

Maura swallowed hard and nodded. "Let's hope so. And let's hope the wounded man and his brother don't get the chance to put up much of a fight."

"Your husband may not have wanted to wear a sheriff's badge," Alice Tyler said softly, her eyes meeting Maura's, "but right now he's our best hope for ridding the town of those animals."

Turning to look at Quinn again, Maura knew she was right. From the first moment she'd set eyes on him back in the Duncan Hotel, she'd known that he was a man who could handle whatever peril or challenge life threw his way. There was no braggadocio about him as there was in young Lucky Johnson—only the quiet steel of a man who knows his own abilities, has honed them keenly, and is prepared to pit them and his own nerves against anything that stands in his way. If Quinn had made up his mind to end the Campbell gang's reign of terror over Hope, she knew he wouldn't rest until he'd done it.

And neither would she.

An hour later she stored the last of her purchases in the pantry and tried to calm her uneasy heart. When Quinn came inside after giving instructions to Bill Saunders, the new foreman he'd hired, and Tex and Grady, the two hands Jim Tyler had sent over, she showed him the two canteens on the table freshly filled with water.

"I've put sandwiches, a can of beans, hardtack, and a package of Arbuckle's coffee in your saddlebag." Biting her lip, she glanced out the window at the dark stallion, Thunder, who pawed the ground as if restless to be off. "Are you leaving now?"

"Yes." He drew her over to the corner where shelves held dishes and pots and pans. Beneath the shelves, a rifle was propped against the wall.

"It's loaded and ready. You know how to use it?"

"A little." She studied the gun warily. "Judd showed me once when I was twelve. I haven't had much practice."

"We'll fix that when I get back," he told her grimly. "Saunders and Tyler's men will keep an eye on things and start work on the corral while I'm gone. I've left orders for one of them to be here at all times. You won't be alone."

"I'm not afraid, Quinn." *Not for myself.*

"Good. The Campbells don't know about you or about this place. They'd have no notion I'm married now or settled here on Sage Creek, so it's not as if they'll come here looking for me—or for you. But while men like them are on the loose, you shouldn't be here alone."

She whirled away from him and paced to the table, gripping the back of a chair. "Don't worry about me. You're the one who's riding into danger."

"It's what I do, Maura," he said curtly. He studied her, brows raised. "What I'm going to continue to do. This is no more dangerous than that gun-for-hire job coming up in Laramie."

"How reassuring."

His jaw clenched. "What's wrong? Afraid I'm going to get myself killed and leave you stranded?"

A lump rose in her throat, making it difficult to breathe, even to swallow. *Let him think that,* she told herself desperately. *Let him think it's only that.*

"Don't worry, angel. I won't kick the bucket before I get this place up and running for you."

"F-fine." She picked up the canteens and thrust them at him. "Because my having to get this ranch going alone is *not* part of our arrangement." Maura forced out the words, then gave a gasp as Quinn dropped the canteens back onto the table and took her by the arms.

His eyes were dark as smoke as he pulled her toward him. "Maybe you'd like a little something to remember me by."

"I already have a little something to remember you by." In vain she tried to wrench away. He was too near, too strong, too compelling.

"Something more." Roughly he hauled her up against him, one muscular arm encircling her waist. "Don't miss me too much, angel," he said huskily, and then his mouth came down on hers in a hard, hungry kiss that jolted her like a sweep of fire. Her knees wobbled, and with a growl in his throat Quinn clasped her tighter and deepened the kiss further yet, his mouth hot and fierce upon hers, exploring, commanding, possessing.

When he lifted his head, they were both breathless. His eyes gleamed into hers, intense as flame, and he had a grin on his face. "That ought to do it."

He released her so suddenly, she gasped. Hefting the canteens, he swung toward the door.

"Keep the doors and windows locked and the rifle handy," he ordered over his shoulder just before the door slammed behind him.

Shaken, Maura sank into a chair. The bruising intensity of Quinn's kiss had left her dazed and dizzy, her lips hot, aching for more. For a moment she could only sit in a kind of fevered shock. Then she heard Thunder's hoofbeats fading away, and she flew across the room to the window.

Her hands clasped to her throat, she stared out at the sight of her husband riding toward the rise, the sky glowing turquoise and pink before him, the valley still as death.

Quinn never looked back. He sat straight and tall in the saddle, and hard competence radiated from his broad-shouldered frame as he spurred the horse over the plateau.

Maura knew the moment he disappeared that she was

truly in trouble now. But the danger did not come from without. It came from within.

She knew that somehow, against all wisdom and good intentions, she had made a terrible mistake. She had fallen in love with her husband.

Chapter 19

 "WHATTAYA MEAN SHE'S *GONE?* GONE WHERE?" Judd Duncan slammed Willy Peachtree up against the hotel's front counter and stared with disbelief into the old man's thin, frightened face.

There was no one else in the lobby of the Duncan Hotel, but if there had been, they'd have gone running after one glance at the murderous expression upon Judd's face.

"S-sorry, Judd—she didn't tell me nothin'. I thought she'd be back in a day or so. She jest said to watch the place till you or her came back!"

"How long ago was this, you worthless bag of bones?"

"W-weeks. I didn't know what to do. You didn't come back, she didn't come back . . . I tried to keep up with everythin' myself but I didn't know what to do . . ."

His voice trailed off fearfully. Judd released the old-timer, his breath rasping in his throat. Before Willy could escape, Homer grabbed him by his dirty shirt collar and clenched his fist to punch the hapless man until he saw Judd had already bounded away toward the stairs and was pounding up them two at a time. At that moment Homer remembered why.

All that really mattered was the diamonds! Homer let go of Willy, who slunk away behind the counter, breathing hard.

"Son of a bitch! They'd better be there!" Homer yelled after Judd, and then he, too, charged up the stairs.

Sweat poured down both of their faces as they raced to Maura's narrow little room at the rear of the hall. Neither of them had counted on being away from Knotsville and the hotel for this long. They hadn't counted on that damned sheriff in Great Falls locking them up just because they'd gotten drunk and shot up both saloons, the barbershop, and the whorehouse. They'd been rotting in that stinking jail for weeks—and all this time, they'd thought Maura and the diamonds were safely back here in Knotsville.

Their customer had paid handsomely for just one of those little diamonds and was willing to pay a whole lot more for the rest of them and now . . . now . . .

Judd tore through the bureau where Maura had stored her belongings. The few things she'd left behind were hurled to the floor as Homer watched, white-faced.

"Well?"

"That jewel box ain't here!"

They turned to the bed, hefted the mattress, tossed it on the floor. Next they looked under the bed, behind the bureau, knocking the washstand over, as well as the chair. They tore the room apart, refusing to give up hope.

But after everything had been turned upside down and inside out, it was clear the jewelry box and the diamonds were gone.

"She took 'em, all right." Judd thumped a ham-sized fist down on the bureau, purple color suffusing his cheeks. "Maura Jane stole 'em. Stole our diamonds!" he muttered incredulously. He shook his head. "That damned sneaky little bitch. When I get my hands on her—"

"She didn't know she had 'em, Judd." Homer leaned against the wall, feeling sick with disappointment. "She just thought she was takin' Ma's jewelry box. Ma did leave it to her."

"She had no right to run out on us! After all we done for her, she left this hotel to rot! She left, Homer! When are you going to stop sticking up for that no-good little bitch?"

"Reckon you're right." Anger flitted into Homer's pale eyes. He ran a hand through his lank brown hair, scraping it back from his face. "We took care of her all her life and the minute our backs is turned she runs off."

"We gotta find her." Judd's mouth set in an ominous line.

"Hell, we surely will. We'll get those diamonds back if we have to wring her scrawny neck to do it."

Judd headed for the door. Homer followed him down the stairs, thinking of all that money they'd never see if they didn't find Maura and the diamonds. That San Francisco businessman wouldn't wait forever. He might make a deal with someone else to buy diamonds for his pretty lady friend.

Downstairs, they were so preoccupied with their own frustration that they didn't notice the fresh footprints in the layer of dust on the floor, nor did they sense the man hiding still as death in the shadows on the opposite side of the staircase. They only saw that Willy had disappeared. The lobby was deserted, thick with dust, silent as a coffin. And from the looks of the guest book, there were no paying customers. Sure enough, Willy couldn't have been able to run this place for long all by himself.

"She's been gone weeks already." Homer gritted his teeth. "The trail will be stone-cold."

"Don't you worry none, little brother. Ain't no man nor woman been born that I can't track if I set my mind to it." Judd stroked his mustache, his round face lit with determination. " 'Specially if there's a damned fortune at stake. You mark my words—that good-for-nothing slut is as good as caught. We'll get her *and* those diamonds back. And when I get my hands on little Maura Jane, there won't be enough of her left worth dragging back. That's a promise."

Chapter 20

THREE INTERMINABLE DAYS PASSED WITH NO word of Quinn or the posse. Though Maura found much to occupy her time—what with sprucing up the cabin, clearing away the weeds and brush, sewing curtains, and organizing the pantry, it was never very long before she would stop her work, shade her eyes, and peer into the horizon to wonder where he was and if he was safe.

The days seemed endless. The nights dragged by, longer still. Silence and loneliness gripped the valley, casting a pallor even over the bright spring colors of wildflowers and new grass.

The bow-legged new foreman, Bill Saunders, and the two hands from the Crooked T ranch went about their business efficiently and didn't speak to her much other than to say "yes, ma'am," or "no, ma'am," or "thank you, ma'am" when she served them their meals or brought them mugs of coffee. But she had other company—much more effusive company—and all of it at the same time.

On the third evening, shortly after supper, the Weaver

buggy pulled up before the cabin. Mrs. Weaver held the reins, and beside her sat Alice Tyler, while in the back were perched two other women whom Maura didn't know.

She had just finished sweeping the kitchen floor and came out the door with the broom in her hand.

"Howdy!" Mrs. Weaver called in her booming voice. "Feel like a spot of company, Maura?"

Her heart gladdened at the sight of these tidy women in their bonnets and best smiles. She welcomed them into the cabin, and was glad that everything was at least neat and dusted. She had discovered a rolled-up crimson rag rug in the shed, and this now warmed the plain puncheon floor. And she'd stuck wildflowers in a metal mug on the kitchen table, and had put up the first of her white lace curtains at the front windows.

With sweeping gestures, Edna introduced her to Carolyn Mason, a tall, austere stick of a woman whose husband owned Mason's Hardware Store, as well as to Miss Grace Ellis, a prim, pale woman from Boston who taught school for the children of Hope.

"We've come to invite you to join our sewing circle." Edna Weaver came immediately to the point in her blunt way as the ladies all found seats on the old sofa, lined up in a row, while Maura slipped into a chair.

"That's very kind of you." Maura gazed at Edna in surprise. After the last visit, she hadn't expected any further hospitality. "I'd be honored to join," she said quickly.

Edna beamed and Alice Tyler threw her a delighted smile. "We meet once a week, weather permitting—we rotate houses each week," Alice explained. "Except for

Grace, since she lives in Serena Walsh's boardinghouse. And though we could meet in Serena's front parlor, I suppose . . . well, we just don't.''

"It would be awkward," Carolyn explained, picking up the thread of conversation as Alice took a breath, "since Serena isn't a member of our little group.''

"She isn't? Why not?" Maura spoke without thinking, then gave her head a little shake. "Forgive me, that was a thoughtless question.''

"Oh, no dear, not at all." Carolyn Mason waved a gaunt hand dismissively, and leaned forward on the sofa. "Serena just doesn't fit in. She's not the sewing circle type, if you know what I mean. All of us are women of education and culture. In fact, our future goal is to expand this sewing circle, once the trouble with the Campbell gang is resolved, and more decent people settle in Hope. We eventually want to form a library committee, as well, and raise funds to build a public library right here in Hope!''

"A most worthy endeavor," Maura murmured, her heart gladdening at the thought. A town that encouraged cultural activities and boasted a library would be a fine place to raise her child. "I'd be happy to be part of that committee as well," she offered eagerly.

"I knew you would, dear." Edna smiled approvingly and glanced at each of the others in turn as if to say, *I told you so.*

"Edna and I noticed immediately that you possessed an air of refinement—and that you were well-spoken," Alice put in softly. "That's why we hoped you would join us.''

"Serena Walsh, on the other hand . . ." Carolyn Mason's voice trailed off deliberately, and her mouth curled down at the corners.

Alice sighed and gave her head a tiny shake.

"From what we've heard," Edna went on, folding her large, knobby hands in her lap, "she's the kind of woman who'd rather spend her evenings playing cards with her gentleman boarders and drinking spirits and even smoking cigars, rather than engaging in polite society with . . . with . . ."

"More respectable women," Miss Grace Ellis finished quietly, then blushed.

Maura looked at each of them. "I see. You're saying that she's not respectable?"

Miss Ellis blushed deeper, and nervously patted the chestnut bun tightly coiled behind her ears. "Oh, that sounds so unkind. And we don't mean to be unkind, but—"

"She doesn't want to be part of our group any more than we want her to," Carolyn Mason stated flatly.

"It's true." Edna nodded. "But mercy me, we didn't come here to talk about Serena, now did we? Let me explain about our sewing circle and then we can get started."

The sewing circle met weekly, giving the women a chance to talk, work, and relax all at the same time, to exchange news and gossip and have a welcome respite from the loneliness and sameness of their task-filled days. Sometimes they worked together on a joint project, such as a quilt, meant as a gift for one of them or someone in town, and at other times they each worked on individual items, such as their current project: Each lady was sewing herself a new gown for the May Day dance to be held at the Tyler ranch.

"And this is our gift to you, as a new member of the circle," Edna declared. Reaching into her basket, she pulled out a length of pale yellow silk, lustrous as the sun. "Grace brought some pattern books—you can pick out whichever style you like and we'll do all the measuring for you."

Speechless, Maura gazed at each of them, touched beyond anything she could express. In Knotsville no one had ever approached her socially—everyone was too frightened of Judd and Homer, and she was shunned whenever she ventured out, except by the merchants, who handled her purchases with careful, businesslike decorum, always keeping her at a distance.

"The fabric is lovely," she said at last. "And so is the offer of friendship—and companionship. I can't begin to thank you enough."

"We're all delighted you'll be joining us," Edna assured her, her broad smile as warm and comforting as lantern light in a lonely cave.

As Grace handed her one of the pattern books, and Alice came to stand beside her and study it in the glow of the setting amber sun, Maura could only think how fortunate it was that she had baked a peach pie that afternoon, just in case Quinn came home. Though he hadn't, Bill Saunders and the ranch hands, Tex and Grady, had enjoyed it, and she was certain the ladies of the Hope Sewing Circle would too.

It was while they were seated at the kitchen table drinking sugared coffee and chatting over warm slices of peach pie that Alice Tyler brought up the subject of the hunt for the Campbells, speaking in her quiet way.

"I think the men must return soon. Either they're close to finding the outlaws, or they've lost them by now." She met Maura's eyes and gave a small, almost inaudible sigh. "I'll just be happy when they're safely home."

"All I have to say is that it's a blessing that none other than Quinn Lassiter has become part of our little community," Carolyn Mason exclaimed. She threw Maura a brilliant smile. "At first when I heard, I wondered if a gunfighter settling in Hope would mean more trouble, but then he saved Alice's life, and Edna and Alice both told me how sweet and ladylike and respectable *you* are, and I said to myself, 'Well, if a gunfighter loves a woman enough to give up his wild ways to marry her, then he's more than welcome in Hope.' " She took a sip of coffee. "Lord knows we can use all the help we can get right now. Though I *do* wish he had consented to be our sheriff—"

"Carolyn," Alice interrupted hastily, throwing Maura an apologetic glance. "It is not anyone's place to judge or to—"

"It's all right, Alice. I don't mind." Maura smiled reassuringly at her, wondering how respectable Carolyn Mason would think her if she only knew the real reason Quinn Lassiter had married her. She turned to the tall woman, who was regarding her with raised black brows. "You'll never meet a man more dedicated to doing what's right than my husband," she said firmly. "He can always be counted on to help those in need. I don't believe it matters if he chooses to wear a badge or not."

"But why would he object, Maura? I simply don't un-

derstand." Carolyn set down her cup and pursed her lips.
"There would be a salary involved and though not a fortune, I fail to see how any practical man wouldn't be
enticed by the possibility of earning money for performing a service, rather than doing it for nothing. And particularly a gunfighter, for goodness' sake—a man who hires
out his gun to anyone who has the fee!"

Maura rose, struggling to control her anger and to keep
her voice level. "I'm afraid that my husband's decisions
and his integrity are something I cannot allow to be called
into question," she said softly, and ignoring Carolyn Mason, turned to address Edna Weaver, who had frozen with
her fork in midair. "Much as I regret it, Edna, I have no
choice but to decline your kind invitation to join the Hope
Sewing Circle."

"Now, now, dear, don't be so hasty," Edna cried,
blinking rapidly up at Maura. She set her fork down with
a clatter. "I'm sure Carolyn didn't mean anything. Did
you, Carolyn?"

"Well, I only . . . I just . . . I don't see what is
wrong with . . ."

"Carolyn!" Alice Tyler spoke between clenched teeth
and for once there was steel beneath the softness in her
eyes.

"Yes, indeed, Carolyn," Grace added. If anything she
had grown even more pale, and her hazel eyes glistened
as she fixed them upon the other woman. "It is the true
sign of a lady to behave graciously at all times and it is
most *ungracious* to insult a woman's husband, wittingly
or *not*. And to do it in her own home . . ."

"Very well, you don't have to make such a fuss about
it!" Carolyn snapped. She turned to Maura. "If I said

something I oughtn't, I'm sorry. I'd be much obliged if you'd forgive me.''

Met only by silence, she glanced around the table, took a deep breath, and plunged on. ''I never meant to say a word against your husband. I'm sure he's a fine man. Lord knows, I heard he's handsome as the devil, and that he shoots a gun every bit as good as he looks—''

''Maura,'' Alice interrupted hastily as Edna Weaver threw up her hands. ''Will you please reconsider? We so want you to be a part of the Hope Sewing Circle. There are several other ladies who join us, too, all fine, upstanding members of the community—but they couldn't leave their families tonight. You'll meet them next time when we gather at the Crooked T. Say you'll come.''

Maura looked around the circle of faces. Alice nodded encouragingly at her, and Edna reached over to pat her hand. Grace Ellis even managed a thin, hopeful smile. Carolyn Mason swallowed hard and hung her head.

''Well, now that we've cleared up all our misunderstandings,'' Maura said quietly, ''I should be delighted to join—and to come to the next meeting.''

Everyone began talking at once, exclaiming with relief and pleasure. But as Maura rose to fetch the coffeepot, she caught sight of a dark figure framed in the door that led from the cabin's parlor.

Quinn!

With a cry, her hands flew to her throat. His clothes and boots were caked with dust, his lean face shadowed with dark stubble. His silver eyes glinted at her beneath the brim of his hat.

He was alive, so alive. She'd never seen such a wonderful sight.

"Ladies." His glance flicked from his wife's startled face to the astonished expressions of each woman in turn, then returned to rest once more upon Maura.

"Didn't mean to scare you," he said, and came slowly into the kitchen.

For a moment Maura could have sworn she'd seen a blaze of warmth in his expression, and a flicker of something else—pleasure? But it quickly vanished and she knew it must have been her imagination. She wanted to throw her arms around his neck, but she was remembering the rough way he had kissed her and then walked out on her, and she stood rooted to the spot, not knowing what to say or do, how to hide her true feelings. But as she became aware of the audience watching her, she knew this frozen silence would never do and forced herself to walk quickly forward.

"I'm so thankful you're back safely," she murmured stiffly, and reached up tentatively to put her arms around his neck.

Quinn embraced her, mindful of the group of women closely watching them. His own emotions were in upheaval, but he managed to hide them as he savored the feel of her softly curving body against his, inhaled the sweet woman's scent of her. Alarmed at just how good it felt to hold her, he quickly released her and stepped back.

"Don't sound so surprised." His voice was even. "I told you I'd be back, angel."

"Yes. So you did."

But he was thinking about the remarkable scene he'd come upon without warning. She'd been defending him. Defending *him*. That was his role—protector. She shouldn't have had to do that with this stuffy biddy who thought a man should jump through hoops just to prove he was civilized.

It surprised him that she had.

"Everything all right, Maura?" It was an effort to keep his tone offhand and level. "No trouble while I was gone? And the—"

He wanted to ask her about the baby, if she'd felt sick or anything like that—but not in front of this damned audience of women, all gaping at him, watching his every move. He scowled.

"I'm fine. Everything's fine," she replied quietly, but her eyes looked searchingly into his.

"Sorry to interrupt your party." As all of the ladies continued to watch with rabid interest and curiosity, he headed toward the bedroom, his bedroll slung over his shoulder.

Alice Tyler's quiet voice stopped him. "Did you find the Campbells? Was anyone . . . . hurt?"

He turned toward her, shaking his head. "No casualties. The only thing we lost was their trail. They gave us the slip somewhere in Eagle's Pass."

Alice nearly sagged with relief, but Edna Weaver's voice held apprehension. "So they could come back?"

"They most likely will, Mrs. Weaver. But not for a while, I'd wager. Lee seems to have lost a lot of blood. He won't be spoiling for a fight anytime soon. And Ned doesn't have the guts to face anything alone."

He didn't mention Luke, or what Hoss had told him before he died. If Luke was really on his way to join up with his cousins, they'd find out soon enough. No need to alarm the women at this point. He meant to search again for the Campbells when the furor had died down and they weren't expecting it—and he'd do his damnedest to rid the world of their whole greedy, lying, murdering clan once and for all before anyone else got hurt.

After dumping his bedroll in a corner of the bedroom, he headed back out to the kitchen and poured himself coffee while the ladies took their leave—nearly scrambling out the door in their haste. They seemed to think that the Lassiters would like to be alone. This irritated Quinn. Those women couldn't see through him, could they? They couldn't tell how glad he was to see Maura, that he wanted to take her into the bedroom and make love to her all night long? He'd always been able to hide what he was thinking so well.

No, it was impossible, he told himself, taking a long gulp of the hot brew. They were just being thoughtful.

"Won't you sit down, Quinn, and have some pie with your coffee?" Maura spoke almost formally when the rig had driven off. Beyond the window, the twilight sky deepened over the valley as the final rose and amber rays of the sun glimmered at the brink of the horizon. Some of the glimmer streamed in, rippling like fire across her hair.

"You don't have to fuss over me, Maura."

"I wouldn't dream of it. But you just arrived home and you're probably hungry. Have you eaten dinner?"

"Yeah. I don't need a thing."

Except you in my arms, in my bed, he thought as he felt his gut clench.

He was falling. Falling fast and hard. This had to stop.

While he was gone, he'd found himself thinking about her every time he stared into a campfire, remembering the heart-tugging beauty of her face, the way she'd responded to his kiss right here in this cabin, as if they were the only two people on earth.

Now that he was back, he was amazed to find that she looked even more irresistible than he remembered.

Fresh and sweet as a ripening peach, there for the taking.

A man could get used to coming home to a wife like this. A man could get downright . . . comfortable.

He hated comfortable.

He had to put the brakes on all this foolishness before it was too late.

He turned on his heel and stalked to the door.

"Where are you going, Quinn?" Dismay showed plainly in those wide velvet-brown eyes.

"To the creek."

"The *creek?*"

"I need to wash up. I'm filthy with trail dust."

"But . . . it's *cold* out there now. Why don't you . . ."

"I like the cold, angel. Hell, I *love* the cold. Don't bother waiting up for me. You need your shut-eye."

"But—"

The door slammed before she could finish the sentence.

She stared at it. Long seconds ticked past as fury swept through her. How many times was he going to walk out on her, slam a door on her, and simply walk away?

As many times as you let him, a voice inside of her challenged.

Maura ran to the door and wrenched it open. "Oh no you don't, Quinn Lassiter," she called, but the wind rose at that moment and tore her words away.

She ran out into the night, heedless of the chill, heedless of the darkness that shrouded the land in a cloak of blackness.

She hurried toward the creek, tripping over rocks and ruts in the earth, but never slowing. She couldn't see Quinn, despite the crescent moon glittering overhead. But in the faint light, she could make out the pewter glimmer of the creek about twenty yards ahead, glimpsed through swaying tree branches.

"Quinn Lassiter, you wait a minute," she called again. "I've got something to say to you—"

She broke off as she crested the bank and saw him. He had already stripped off his boots and his shirt. His broad, muscular chest was bare and gleamed like bronze in the moonlight. He was just tossing his gunbelt on the ground when he heard her and spun around.

"What the hell?"

Maura ran toward him. "You'll catch your death of cold out here— Ohhhh!"

An unseen tree root tripped her and she went flying, straight toward Quinn. He caught her, but the force of her stumble sent them both skittering down the slope of the bank and straight into the creek.

They landed with a resounding splash in the frigid water.

"What the hell are you doing? Are you *crazy?*" Quinn shouted.

Gasping and shivering, Maura clung to him as the icy water washed over her shoulders, soaking her gown, plastering it to her body. Her hair streamed in her face and her lips trembled with cold.

"If you're going to catch your death of . . . c-cold,

Quinn Lassiter, then so will I. I will *not* have you w-walking out on me again, without even giving me a ch—ch—chance to s-say one . . . Ohhh!'' she cried again as he seized her and pulled her into his arms and kissed her thoroughly.

''Oh . . . hhh,'' Maura gasped when he lifted his head and she could breathe again.

''You are the damndest woman!'' Gray eyes pierced hers. Scooping her up into his arms, he held her close as water streamed from her body, dripping back into the dark, swirling creek. ''Why am I always having to warm you up?''

Without waiting for an answer, he splashed out of the creek with her and onto the bank as Maura sought to quell the trembling in her heart.

''Put me down, Quinn, I can walk.'' She spoke through chattering teeth as he paused only long enough to grab up his gunbelt before stalking back toward the cabin, cradling her against his wet chest.

''Shut up and stop squirming,'' he ordered. ''Any pregnant woman crazy enough to go jumping into an ice-cold creek at night hasn't got a lick of sense anyway, so why should I listen to her?''

''*You* were g-going to jump into the c-creek!''

''That's different!''

''It is n-not!''

''I was going to wash off the trail dust. That makes sense.''

''You just w-wanted to get away from me!''

Quinn halted. They were ten yards from the cabin's front door and the moon glittered like a shard of ice in the sky.

"Now why would I want to do that?" he asked in a low, husky voice.

"You tell me," she whispered, staring up at him, shivering all over and not only from the cold.

Quinn said nothing. He carried her inside, kicked the door shut, and took her straight into the bedroom, where he dumped her on the bed.

"Take off these damn soaking-wet clothes!" He was staring down at her, at her soaked gingham gown, which clung all too revealingly to her breasts and hips.

"I'm trying." Maura's frozen fingers fumbled over the buttons of her gown. Quinn swore and reached out to help her, and the next thing she knew they were tumbling down together on the bed, sinking into the mattress, and they were clinging to one another, her mouth seeking his, seeking its warmth, its roughness, and the strange tenderness that drove the fire of his kisses.

His hands roved over her shivering body. They were warm and strong, and she gasped at the blessed heat they brought, at the sheer pleasure of his touch, and at the almost frightening need that tingled, singing, through her blood.

"This doesn't change anything between us," he panted as his hands freed her of the sodden gown and flung it to the floor.

"Not a thing." Maura tugged off her camisole and reached for him, burying her fingers in the wet thickness of his hair.

Quinn's soaked pants landed with a thud atop her camisole and then he landed on her, and they clung entwined across the bed.

"Warm yet?" he groaned against her lips, and then he

was lost as she kissed him with eagerness and ardor, and everything inside of him caught fire.

"Not . . . yet. Can you try a little harder?" She snuggled desperately against him. The writhing of her body triggered a need so violent, it jolted through him like dynamite.

For answer, he deepened the kiss with a naked intensity that blew them both way past the edge of decorum. Their mouths met, held, locked. Quinn had never wanted any woman so much in his life.

Maura filled his thoughts, his senses. Her velvety red curls held the fragrance of roses and her skin was soft as petals, and never before had he seen a face so lovely, that tugged so strongly at his heart. His powerful body moved over hers, claiming her, even as she pulled him down and pressed her lips with sweet urgency to his. He couldn't have stopped now for all the gold in the world.

"Hang on, sweetheart," he muttered, his breath warming her skin as his muscled thighs covered hers. "We're just getting started."

"Hold me, Quinn. Hold me," Maura begged. She was drowning in joyful pleasure so intense, it bordered on pain. He *had* missed her while he'd been gone, he *had* thought of her. That kiss before he left had meant something.

She wrapped her arms around him, feeling power and passion rise within her. Her slender form twisted and writhed against his in an ancient glorious dance. Soft, needy moans slid from her throat as her arms tightened around his neck and she arched her hips against his warm, strong body.

This time as he entered her, there was no pain. There was only pleasure.

"It doesn't hurt this time," she gasped mindlessly as he plunged deeper inside her, his mouth scorching down her neck, then branding the pulse at her throat. An aching need throbbed enticingly between her thighs. "Not at all . . ."

"Hurt?" Quinn went still inside her, and stared down into her flushed face. "It *hurt* the last time?"

"Yes . . . my first time. But—"

"My God."

"It only hurt at first," she said quickly, her eyes glowing into his hard, impossibly handsome face. "And only a little." Breathless, yearning, she tangled her legs around him tighter and hung on for dear life. "But don't you dare stop now, Quinn Lassiter," she whispered. "Don't stop or I'll die."

"Not a chance of that, sweetheart." Quinn buried his lips against her throat, then began to thrust again, filling her, drowning himself in her. "Sweet Maura. Beautiful Maura."

The cabin and the night and the very air dissolved as he took her then, lifting her along with him into a dark, tearing storm, thrusting them both into a world lit by thunder and lightning and hot shooting stars.

It was beautiful and shattering and endless, and when at last they shuddered together and found release, they clung to each other in the darkness that remained and gasped for air and calm and sanity.

And slowly, dizzily floated back down into the world of sound and substance, back into the cabin on Sage Creek where a gunfighter and his bride lay entwined beneath starlight, bound together by vows and by passion amidst the damp, twisted sheets.

It took a while for Maura's heartbeat to slow. She nestled in Quinn's arms, her head upon his broad chest, and felt the first true contentment she'd ever known.

This felt so right. To be here, with this man in this small, spare cabin, with the beautiful valley surrounding them, and not another soul for miles around. To be held like this, to feel his lips brush the top of her head, to feel his strong heartbeat against her ear, this was the way it should be.

This doesn't change anything between us. That's what he'd said. But he couldn't still mean that now, could he? After what they'd experienced together, the desire, the love? Surely he must be feeling something akin to what she was feeling—this awakening, this sense of possibility.

"Quinn." She whispered his name against the dark matted hair of his chest, and felt the roughness tickle her lips.

"Yeah."

"I think we've christened our new house."

"Guess you could say that."

"It was . . . quite a ceremony."

"Sure as hell was, angel." He chuckled and kissed the top of her head.

"I believe I like it here in Wyoming," she said dreamily. "This land, this little cabin, feels special, doesn't it? It feels like it will be a real home."

Her words fell into a dark well of silence. Beside her, Quinn seemed to have turned to stone.

Maura felt a lump of apprehension in her throat. "Quinn?"

He sat up, pulling away from her. She felt him staring at her through the dimness, and a chill brushed down her spine.

"Yeah, it will be, Maura," he said in a low, cautious tone. "For you and the baby. Just like we planned."

Her heart froze. "But not . . . for you?" she whispered.

"I told you." His gray eyes fixed steadily upon hers through the faint silver light, and she saw in dismay that they held warmth but also firmness. He touched her hand, his fingers just grazing hers. "I can't stay here. I can't stay anywhere. The thought of settling down . . ." His voice hardened. "It makes me want to choke."

"I know. But I thought . . ." Her words trailed off. Misery settled over her. Nothing had changed. Just as he'd warned. Why had she thought he'd feel differently?

Because you're a fool. You're a fool to love him, to want more than he can ever give you, she thought helplessly, her heart breaking. *He was and always will be a man who doesn't want to be loved, who doesn't seek what you do: the comfort of a home, a family, a life built together. Days and nights filled with laughter and love . . .*

"It's all right," she managed to say without her voice quivering at all. But inside she was shattering. "Our . . . agreement still stands," she said quietly. "You'll come and go as you please. I wouldn't ever try to tie you down."

He took her hand in his, and stroked her fingers. She

heard both the gruffness and the relief in his voice. "Glad there's no misunderstandings."

"N-none. None at all."

"If you ever need me, you or the kid, I'll come. You have my word."

His word. But not his love. Not *him.*

Maura turned her head away, fighting back the tears, desperate to hide her pain. Wearily, she rested her cheek upon the pillow.

"Get some sleep, angel. It's almost morning."

Beside her, Quinn frowned and drew the blanket up across her bare, beautiful shoulders. He cursed himself for having made love to her again, for having lost control and charged straight into trouble.

This had to be the last time. The very last time. She'd be out of his blood now, after tonight. He was sure of it— almost.

If only she hadn't chased him down to the creek and gotten them both soaking wet. This never would have happened.

Well, it wouldn't happen again. No way in hell. She was too sweet, too saucy, too beautiful. If he didn't want to find himself lassoed and hog-tied, he'd ride out of here fast and make himself scarce at Sage Creek for some time to come.

Well, hell. Soon as the ranch was running smooth, and soon as he was sure the Campbells wouldn't be back, that's exactly what he'd do.

Chapter 21

APRIL BLOSSOMED OVER WYOMING TERRITORY IN the weeks that followed. And so did the cabin and the barn and the shed—all of which Quinn decided to call Sage Creek Ranch. The buildings, which had looked so forlorn and dilapidated at first, were repaired, painted, and enlarged, and began to take on the appearance of a working ranch. By the third week of the month, the corral was almost finished and land was cleared for a bunkhouse to be built next to the barn.

Quinn worked tirelessly from sunup to sundown. He hired two ranch hands, Slim Riley and Orville Boggs, to work full-time—as well as Lucky Johnson.

Lucky, it seemed, had grown up the son of a cattle ranch foreman in Kansas, and he knew almost as much about horses and cattle and ranching as Quinn knew about gunfighting.

Though he continued to brag and bluster and spout off hotheadedly, it became apparent to everyone that he idolized Quinn Lassiter. Quinn was the only one who appeared not to see it. When Maura pointed this out after Lucky was seen imitating the angle at which Quinn wore his hat and bought himself a silver belt buckle almost identical to the one Quinn wore, and even began narrowing his eyes the same way, Quinn shrugged it off.

"Who cares what the kid does? So long as he does his work. If he starts slacking, I'll run him off quick as a wink and a holler."

But Maura was beginning to suspect that her husband had a reluctant soft spot for the brash young cowboy. He dished out to Lucky the same curt commands he gave the other men, but he had allowed Lucky to salvage his pride by letting him ride in the posse—and he had given him a job, a paycheck, and three steady meals a day.

One afternoon about a week before the May Day dance, it was Lucky who drove her into town so she could stock up on more canned goods and flour and eggs—and also to see if she could find a pair of shoes to complement her fine silk party dress.

Nell had shown her two pairs: pale cream slippers with lacy yellow ribbons that exactly matched the dress, and simple black ones with pointed toes and jet buttons. The black shoes were by far more practical, she knew, and wouldn't show dirt—but the cream ones were so beautiful that she held them up wistfully, imagining how perfect they would look with the dress.

"Look at that," Nell Hicks said in disgust. She had gone to the window to rearrange the stock displayed there, and now peered out, frowning. "That good-for-nothing cowhand of yours is wasting his time, as usual. I'm sure you had errands for him to do, Mrs. Lassiter— surely he didn't come to town just to diddle-daddle with the likes of Orchid Cody."

Maura glanced over in surprise. Nell was usually so

pleasant—efficient, direct, and no-nonsense, yes, but always agreeable. Today she sounded downright waspish. Why in the world was she so annoyed with Lucky Johnson?

Maura joined her at the window, peering over Nell's shoulder. Lucky was engaged in laughing conversation with the sleek, buxom Orchid, a titian-haired, cat-eyed saloon girl who was probably twice his age. He had snatched the pink feather boa that she'd draped around her shoulders, and was holding it behind his back, no doubt bartering for its return.

Sure enough, Orchid stretched up on tiptoe, kissed him full on the mouth, and Lucky, grinning, made a gallant show of winding the boa across her daringly bared shoulders once more.

"A few moments ago, he escorted Serena Walsh across the street *and* stood smoking with her on the porch of her boardinghouse!" Nell exclaimed. "Shouldn't he be loading the wagon, or buying lumber, or something?"

Maura's delicate brows lifted. "He probably finished purchasing what we needed and now he's simply waiting for me. Do you have a beef with Lucky, Nell?"

"I don't care about him one way or another." The girl shrugged and stalked back behind the counter. "I just don't like the fact that he's a lazy loafer with nothing better to do than make a fool of himself over women old enough to be his—his—his older sister!"

Maura laughed, then sobered as Nell threw her a hurt look.

"I don't see what's funny." The girl snatched away the black shoes and said, "You may as well take the cream-colored pair. They're the ones you like the best."

"And you'd like Lucky Johnson to like *you* the best, wouldn't you?" Maura asked softly.

Nell's eyes flew to hers. She turned as pink as Orchid's boa. "I never said any such thing!" she gasped.

"Of course not," Maura soothed her, suddenly sorry she'd been so frank. The girl's feelings were raw and as transparent as glass. "I'm just guessing." She touched Nell's arm. "Am I right?" she asked gently.

Nell bit her lip. She didn't say anything for a moment, then lifted her lime-green eyes to Maura's face. "He's never once noticed me. Except to get angry when I told him to be careful going after the Campbells!"

"I see."

"He'd come in here now and then, buying this or that—before you and Mr. Lassiter moved to town. I didn't know who he was, if he was hired on to one of the ranches, new in town, or just passing through, and I wanted to make conversation with him, but I just couldn't." She drew in a deep breath. "That day, the day Lee Campbell grabbed me right here in the store and tried to run off with me, I'd been thinking about him. About Lucky. But I didn't know his name then. I'd been picturing him coming into the store, and that I'd start a conversation and he'd notice me—that he'd like me—and maybe even start coming by just so he could talk to me. But instead, the door opened and *he* walked in. Lee. He was drunk—they all were. And he . . . grabbed me . . ."

"Don't think about it," Maura said quickly, as Nell's voice trailed off. She gave the girl a firm hug.

"I don't. Except now and then. I wish they'd find them and come back and tell us the whole gang is dead!" she burst out. Angrily, she began pacing up and down beside the counter. "But that day Lucky wanted to go with them? Much as I hate the Campbells, I didn't want him to go. I was afraid for him." She shook her head, sending her braid swinging, and tried to laugh, but all that came out was a low, gasping quaver.

"Now why should I care about a no-good loafer who never even looked at me once, much less twice, and who wastes time flirting with loose women and pretending he's as tough and handy with a gun as a real gunfighter, someone like your husband? He's going to get himself killed!"

"Not if he grows up fast and settles down with a nice sensible girl." Maura smiled.

"You mean someone like me?" Nell looked hopeful for a moment, then she sighed. "He'll never pay attention to me. I'm not . . . the type of woman he prefers."

"Then he's just plain crazy. You're smart and you're pretty, and you have a caring heart." Maura suddenly marched to the door. "Just a moment."

"Wait—what are you doing?" Nell gasped, and one hand flew to her throat.

But Maura was already calling across the street. "Lucky, could you come here a moment, please?"

When he stomped into the store, hat in hand, he scarcely glanced at the black-haired girl busily counting eggs into a basket. "Something I can do for you, Miz Lassiter?"

"Yes, I'd like you to carry some boxes to the wagon for me. This one, to start"—she indicated the carton containing the canned goods and a sack of flour. Then she thrust the cream-colored slippers across the counter toward Nell. "And, excuse me, Nell dear, I'll need a box for these shoes."

Before Lucky could reach the carton of goods, Maura stepped in front of it, blocking his path. She gave him a brilliant smile.

"Lucky, have you met Nell Hicks? Her father is the owner of this establishment."

"We've met. Sorta." Lucky flicked a cool glance at Nell, then turned back to Maura. "If you'll just step out of the way, Miz Lassiter—"

"Well, the problem is, I'm not quite finished yet. I think I'll wait for Mr. Hicks—he can help me with the rest of my purchases. Nell here was just going to have a glass of lemonade and when I saw you outside, I realized that you must be dreadfully thirsty, standing there in the sun and all. So why don't you have a glass of lemonade with her—would that be all right, Nell?"

She rushed on when Nell threw her a blank, frozen look.

"Of course it will—and you two can just go ahead and get to know one another."

Nell's cheeks were now two shades brighter than the boa. She threw Maura a panicked glance and stared mutely at the rangy young ranch hand. "W-would you like some lemonade?"

"Nope. But you go right ahead."

"I—I don't want any either. I changed my mind," she added quickly, when Lucky shot her a puzzled glance. "Is there . . . anything else I can help you with?"

Lucky ambled along the counter, eyeing the goods stacked on shelves, refusing to let his glance rest on the dark-haired girl. "Could use a pack of cards and some tobacco while I'm here," he muttered.

"Oh. Do you enjoy playing cards?" Nell asked as she reached up to a shelf for the items he'd mentioned. Maura began studying yards of sateen, then strolled along to the candy jars.

"I reckon."

"I do too." Nell tried out a smile, small dimples showing in her flushed cheeks. "I play gin rummy with my father nearly every night. Perhaps you'd like to . . . to join us sometime?"

"Not likely, little girl." Lucky shoved his hat back on his head. "I only play poker—and for pretty high stakes."

"Oh, pardon me!" Nell's eyes took on a glittery sparkle. "I didn't realize I was speaking to such a fancy-pants, big-time gambler."

"I never said I was a big-time gambler." Lucky's eyes narrowed—much like Quinn Lassiter's when he was irked. "I said I don't play gin rummy."

"Maybe you're afraid of losing," Nell went on sweetly, as if he hadn't spoken. "Maybe you're afraid of losing to a *girl.*"

"The day a girl beats me at any card game is the day I eat my spurs!" He glared at her. "Reckon those Campbells would've been mighty sorry if they *had* run off with you—you'd have talked 'em to death with that sharp tongue of yours. And if that didn't work, you'd have stomped 'em at gin rummy!"

Lucky slapped his hand against his thigh, chortling at his own humor, while Nell went pale as snow.

The girl turned away, knocking into a jar of penny

candy, grabbing it before it crashed to the floor. As Maura threw her a distraught glance, wishing she could box Lucky's ears, the young cowhand seemed to sense that he'd exceeded the bounds of civility.

"Hey—reckon you know I was just foolin' with you," he said gruffly, stepping sideways, trying to see Nell's averted face.

She didn't answer, but busied herself with moving the jar of penny candy to a shelf.

"I know it's nothing to joke about," he tried again. "I mean, I'm sure you were plenty scared. I mean, it would be only natural—"

"Will there be anything else?" Nell interrupted frigidly, whirling back to face him with lifted chin and set mouth.

He met her icy stare and a frown spread across his face.

"No, ma'am, there won't be." He slapped down some coins, scooped up the pack of cards and tobacco, dumped them in his vest pocket. Then he lifted the carton of goods from the counter.

"Miz Lassiter, I'll wait for you outside." He threw Nell a black look over his shoulder, but she'd already flounced away.

The moment the door swung shut behind him, Maura rushed over to Nell.

"I'm so sorry. He's not usually so rude! I can't imagine what got into him."

"He hates me!" Nell stared out the window at the young cowhand, who had spotted yet another saloon girl in the street and was striding toward her. "And I hate him!"

"Hmm, I can see that." Maura stifled a sigh.

She saw no such thing. She saw Nell's eyes glistening as she watched Lucky plunge into playful conversation with the saloon girl.

"The May Day dance is coming up shortly," she murmured as Nell set the shoes into a paper-lined box and handed them to her. "Perhaps you two can patch things up there."

"I'd sooner eat a cow pie." Nell straightened her shoulders and marched back behind the counter, but Maura saw her glance once more out the window at Lucky and the saloon girl, whose high-pitched laughter echoed clear into the store.

Her heart went out to the girl. She understood just how she felt. It hurt to care for someone who didn't care for you in return.

Care for someone? Who are you trying to fool, she asked herself ruefully. You love Quinn. And even if he wasn't nearly as rude to her as Lucky had been to Nell, he was equally indifferent.

And though it didn't seem to be wildly experienced saloon women he pined for, he certainly wasn't pining for her. She couldn't begin to compete with his yearnings for freedom.

When Serena Walsh entered the general store just as she was about to depart, she had to struggle to keep from staring at the woman. Serena certainly knew how to fix herself up. Today she wore a green taffeta gown, bustled, a matching hat and light peach-colored shawl.

"Good day, Mrs. Lassiter."

"Good day."

Remembering what the ladies of the Hope Sewing Circle had said about Serena, Maura forced herself to smile and appear friendly. She knew all too well how it felt to be an outsider, and she didn't have it in her heart to shun anyone. But she couldn't stop herself from wondering exactly how Serena Walsh felt about her husband. If this dashing, self-assured creature hadn't been able to win Quinn's heart, how could she—plain old Maura Jane Reed—hope to do so?

What makes you think she hasn't won his heart? a small voice inside her asked. *Maybe she has, maybe she will always own it, and you're only the girl he married because you're going to bear his child. He came here to Hope, didn't he? And she just happened to be here?*

He came because of his land, she told herself. *You're being ridiculous.* But as she met Serena Walsh's frank smiling glance, uncertainty churned inside her.

"What pretty shoes." Serena's eyes barely skimmed the cream-colored slippers inside the box. "Are they for the dance?"

"Yes, they are." Maura tried to speak warmly. "They match the new dress I've been sewing for the occasion."

"Oh, yes, you and all the other ladies of the famous Hope Sewing Circle. I'd heard you were invited to join." It was said with a faint sneer, but Maura saw that Serena's hands clenched around her reticule. "Such an upstanding group of proper ladies."

"They've all been very kind to me." Obviously, Serena was disturbed at her exclusion, but she hid it well beneath a veneer of contempt. Uncertain what to say next, Maura latched eagerly onto another topic.

"Will you be attending the May Day dance, Mrs. Walsh?"

''Why, yes, matter of fact, I will,'' the woman drawled with that faint tinge of the South honeying her tone. ''The Tylers have kindly invited the entire town—even the scandalous widow Walsh.'' The smile on her full lips didn't even begin to soften the sarcasm in her voice.

''I'm surprised that Quinn agreed to go—he never cared much for dances, as I recall. Oh, he attended them occasionally, but didn't stay long. He's a loner, you know.''

''I do know. But he's a family man now and we're both looking forward to joining in the festivities.''

It wasn't quite true, Maura reflected with a slight twinge of guilt, but Serena with her smug air needn't know that Quinn wasn't exactly counting the hours until the dance. In fact, he'd only agreed to accompany her because she'd pointed out how odd it would look if Mrs. Quinn Lassiter came to a town dance alone.

And Maura had absolutely refused to stay away.

Serena's eyes held a knowing gleam as she studied Maura a moment.

''Hmm, we'll see.'' She actually laughed. Then abruptly she turned toward Nell, who had been silently witnessing the exchange.

''Two dozen eggs, five pounds of sugar, and a pound each of potatoes and turnips,'' she said crisply.

Maura fled.

''Something wrong, Miz Lassiter?'' Lucky asked when he loped over to her.

''No, Lucky, everything's fine.''

But everything wasn't fine. She was jealous of Serena Walsh, a woman who kept implying that she knew Quinn better than his own wife did. She found she was trembling as she rode in the wagon beside Lucky. She wanted to ask Quinn about the woman, but didn't dare. She couldn't bear to have him know how deeply she cared, how much she wanted things to be different between them. If he thought she was worried about his feelings for Serena or jealous of her, he would suspect the truth.

I'd rather die than have him know, Maura thought, staring sightlessly ahead at the delicate spring landscape rolling past. *I might not ever have his love, but I certainly don't want his pity.*

So she turned her thoughts to the May Day dance—her very first dance—and tried not to think about Serena Walsh or anything else. Her dress was nearly finished—she had only to finish the sleeves and sew a row of buttons down the back. That was something she could do this very evening.

Before starting supper she fetched the sewing basket she'd found in the metal chest upon arriving at the cabin, and plunked Ma Duncan's jewelry box inside it. There were ten tiny, exquisite pearl buttons in the enamel box, buttons that would perfectly accent her gown. She set the basket beside the sofa to cheer her as she began peeling potatoes to go with the fried chicken she'd discovered was one of Quinn's favorite dishes.

She was humming, thinking ahead to the dance, and to the pleasant dinner she would have ready when Quinn came home from the range, so she didn't see the shadow cross the front window, or the dark slim figure peer inside and around the cabin, then slip around to the back and show himself briefly at the kitchen window before ducking back.

She never heard footsteps, and didn't see the man slip

away into the trees when Quinn and the ranch hands approached from the south.

Maura only knew that she felt a prickling of fear for a moment when she heard the sound of horses' hooves. But when she saw that it was Quinn and the men returning, she laughed at her own foolishness.

Ma Duncan would have said someone had walked over her grave. But it was only that she was tired, and a bit queasy at the end of the day from the smell of frying, and she wanted her dress to be completed—and Quinn to admire it.

She set the table as the men washed up at the pump, and thought no more about it.

Chapter 22

 AFTER SUPPER MAURA FETCHED HER DRESS FROM the bedroom and settled, with the sewing basket beside her, into the comfortable armchair with the flowered cushion that Quinn had bought for her in town.

"It'll be a good place for you to sit and feed the baby," he'd told her when he brought it home last week.

Touched, she'd tried to thank him, but he'd brushed it off. "We'll need a cradle too. I'll start carving one, soon as I find the time."

The armchair felt so comfortable that she took a deep breath and relaxed for a moment in the glow of the lantern before picking up the dress, and digging out needle and thread.

Tomorrow was the next meeting of the Hope Sewing Circle, but with any luck, the dress would be finished tonight and she could get started next on a nice soft little quilt for the baby.

She looked forward more than she could say to the meetings of the Hope Sewing Circle. The everyday gossip about the weather, who was sick and who was with child, which children were the brightest in Grace's classroom, and which caused trouble, the newest items one could order from the Sears, Roebuck catalog, and, of course, the plans for the May Day dance filled her with a quiet pleasure unlike any she'd ever known. She felt that Edna and Alice were on their way to becoming real friends. Friends. She, Maura Reed Lassiter, was, for the first time in her life, making friends.

And with all her heart she was looking forward to the May Day dance. Though still plagued nearly every day by queasiness and light-headedness, even that didn't stop her from anticipating ahead to the party at the Crooked T Ranch, wondering what it would be like, imagining how it would feel to dress up in the pretty yellow silk gown, to mingle with all the people from miles around, to laugh and perhaps even dance.

The idea of dancing with Quinn nearly took her breath away, until she remembered one thing.

She didn't know how to dance.

She was going to make a fool of herself in front of the entire town.

"Something wrong?"

Quinn saw Maura start and drop the needle and thread into her lap.

"There you go, startling me again!" she scolded, but there was a soft chuckle in her throat. "I thought you were going into town with Lucky to play cards."

"Changed my mind. But you didn't answer my question." He didn't tell her that he'd had a strange feeling all day, that for some reason he wanted to stick close to home tonight. Especially since not just Lucky but all the ranch hands had decided to go to town. He didn't want to leave her out here all alone.

Coming closer to the armchair, he studied her. He liked looking at her. Her hair had such a pretty sheen in the lamplight, and even in a worn old dress she always looked so fresh and neat. Usually her eyes were warm and smiling, but tonight when he'd come in, they'd looked sad. And her mouth had drooped.

"Feeling sick again?"

"No. I'm fine."

Scooping up what she'd dropped, she tried once more to thread the needle, but only succeeded in pricking her finger.

She gave a yelp, and stuck her finger in her mouth.

"Fine, eh? I don't believe it. Tell me what's wrong."

Maura drew a breath. He was so close, she could have reached out and touched his hand, clasped hers around it—but she didn't. She'd agreed to the kind of marriage he wanted, and she could never let him know that she wanted so much more, a closeness, a bond that, for his part, just wasn't there. If she touched him, he might see in her eyes how she yearned to touch not only his hand, but every part of him, including his heart.

She gripped the needle instead.

"Out with it, angel." Quinn suddenly scooped the yellow gown from her lap and tossed it onto the old sofa. He took the needle and thread and dropped them into the sewing basket, then yanked her from the chair. "I know that look. Something's bothering you."

It amazed her that he knew her so well. And scared her. If he could guess that she was upset, could he also guess her innermost feelings, thoughts, wishes?

Please, no, she prayed.

"I was thinking about the May Day dance."

"What about it?"

"I think I told you that I've never been to a dance before. Or any kind of a party." She rushed on because she didn't want him thinking she was trying to make him feel sorry for her, or worse, feeling sorry for herself. "So I'm greatly looking forward to this one—except for one thing. Oh, Quinn," she finished in despair, "the whole town is going to laugh at me!"

"Why the hell should anyone laugh at you?"

"It's so foolish, I hate to mention it, but . . . I don't know how to dance," she confessed, her lips trembling.

He groaned and let go of her. "Is that all?" He raked a hand through his hair. "Woman, you had me worried."

"It's silly. I know that." Maura lifted her chin, a gesture of defiance and strength, yet he heard the slight quaver in her voice. "But when the fiddlers start to play and everyone takes to the center of the floor, I'm going to wish like anything I could join in."

"And what makes you think there will be fiddlers and dancing if you've never been to a party before?"

"Alice told me, of course. She said that John Hicks and Jethro Plum play the fiddle better than anyone in the whole territory, and Harvey Ludstone, the barber, is a wonder on the harmonica, and that every year they roll up the rugs in the parlor and push back all the furniture and everyone dances till their boots fall off. And also," she added confidentially, innocent, excited eyes turned up to his, "I know about parties because I spied on one in Knotsville once."

"Is that so?" He was enjoying the flush that had come

into her cheeks and the sparkle in her eyes. "And what did those brothers of yours have to say to that?"

"Oh, they never knew. Ma Duncan didn't know either. I was only about twelve at the time, but that was old enough to want to see what it was all about. It was a Fourth of July dance and was held in the schoolhouse, and nearly the whole town turned out for it. Ma Duncan didn't go because Pa Duncan had died only a month earlier and she didn't think it was proper, but Judd and Homer were there." She frowned. "Everyone steered clear of them, and though they got drunk they didn't hurt anyone that night."

"And you?"

"I walked all the way to the schoolhouse by the light of the moon." A dreamy note entered her voice and her eyes grew rapt as the memory enveloped her. "Everyone was inside and I could hear the music. It made my heart . . ." She searched for the right word.

"Leap." Her lips curved. "When I stole up to the window and peeked in, I was sure I'd never seen anything so beautiful. Colored lanterns were strung, and the women's dresses were like a rainbow, and then there were the men in fancy shirts and neckerchiefs, and the music so lively, and the sound of boots stomping on the floor, and couples were promenading and waltzing, and everyone was clapping and laughing and talking at once—"

She broke off suddenly, her color deepening. "How silly it must sound to you. You must have gone to a hundred dances."

"I'm not much for dancing, but I've been to my share."

She nodded.

A silence fell. Maura plucked her gown from the sofa and returned to the armchair with it. She picked up the needle and this time threaded it. She made a stitch at the sleeve.

Quinn thought of the dances he'd attended, where he'd felt so apart from all the festivities. Once in a while he'd invited a woman to dance, but not usually, because though he sensed their pleasure when he approached them, he also sensed their trepidation. They were afraid of him—fascinated, attracted, yes, he could sense that much in the way they looked at him and spoke to him and slipped eagerly into his arms—but at the same time, they were afraid.

Only Maura wasn't afraid. He wondered what it would be like to dance with her.

Dangerous, he decided. She stirred up too many feelings in him as it was—no telling what would happen if they started in dancing. "Reckon then we should just stay home." He spoke curtly. "Then you won't have to dance and I won't have to stand around listening to a bunch of jabbering folks all duded up in fancy duds."

"All right. If you don't wish to go," Maura said, regarding him sweetly from the armchair, "there's no need to trouble yourself."

"Good." Pleased, Quinn walked to the mantel and leaned a shoulder against it. "Then it's settled. We'll both just . . ."

"Both? Oh, no, Quinn, I didn't mean *I* wouldn't go. Is that what you thought?" She smiled at him, and gave her head a tiny shake, sending her auburn curls flying. "I am going to that dance," she said softly. "According to our arrangement, you are free to come and go as you please and, of course, so am I.''

His face tightened. ''I don't recall we ever agreed that you would go gallivanting off alone to—''

''Well, when you're off gunfighting and roaming and sleeping under the stars, you don't expect me to stay at home doing chores and knitting every moment, do you?''

''You'll do as you damn well please.'' He scowled. ''But . . .''

''Lucky already mentioned he'd like a dance with me.'' She made a careful stitch. ''And Bill Saunders, come to think of it, asked me to save him a waltz. And I ran into Tex in town the other day and he most particularly wondered if he might claim my hand for a do-si-do, so you needn't worry that I'll lack for partners.''

''Hell and damnation, woman, are you going to dance with every man in town?''

She laughed up at him from beneath her lashes. ''Don't be silly, Quinn. Only the ones who ask me.''

He strode to her and stared down at her innocently upturned face. ''The hell you are.''

''Quinn.'' The needle stilled. ''Why shouldn't I?''

Glaring down into her expressive golden-brown eyes, he could think of a dozen reasons, but none that he wanted to say out loud. ''Because you don't know how to dance,'' he grated at last.

''I know,'' she murmured sadly. ''That's why I was wondering—''

''Yeah?''

''Will you teach me?''

Every muscle clenched. ''I'm no teacher.''

"But you do know how?" She studied him hopefully, and Quinn felt desire clench in his gut.

"I've been to enough dances over the years that I've picked up the basics. But—"

"Then please? Teach me how."

"I told you—I'm no teacher!"

She held his gaze a moment, then glanced back down at the fabric in her lap. Her shoulders lifted in a shrug. "I suppose then I'll just have to ask Lucky to teach me."

"Like hell!" he exploded. "Come on."

"You mean . . . you *will* teach me?"

"Can't have the whole damn town laughing at my wife," he growled. "And that includes that mongrel pup Lucky Johnson."

He gritted his teeth, stalked to the center of the room, and held out his arms. Maura laid the sewing aside and rose. Slowly, she walked toward him, her heart pounding with both triumph and trepidation.

She hadn't been touched by him, held by him, since that night when passion had overcome good sense. Since then they'd scrupulously kept to the sleeping arrangements they'd agreed upon: Quinn stayed on the sofa, she slept in the bed.

The very thought of having his arms around her again made her tremble. But she wouldn't let him see how he affected her—she mustn't! *Concentrate only on learning the steps,* she told herself, yet as she went into his arms a thrilling excitement shot through her, and it was a struggle to keep her breathing even and her face composed.

Quinn fought the urge to turn and run. He, Quinn Lassiter, who'd tracked down as many cold-blooded killers and outlaws as any man this side of the Missouri, who'd faced mountain lions and snakes and grizzlies, Apache and Sioux, rustlers and gunmen far more fond of killing than he was, wanted to run from this slender red-haired girl who placed her hand in his with the light touch of an angel, and tilted her head up to study him with a seriousness that made him ache.

"I'm ready, Quinn. How do we begin?"

He wanted to sweep her into his arms then and there and carry her off to their bed as he had that other time, but he fought down the urge and instead cupped his hand at her waist. With the other he clasped her slender fingers, holding them carefully. An electricity seemed to flow between them, burning his callused palm. Her hair smelled of lilac soap and her eyes, fixed on his with eager attention, were the most beautiful sight he'd ever seen, beating the sunset all to shame.

"There's no music." He tensed as she inched closer and her breasts brushed softly against his chest. He felt himself start to sweat.

"Oh, but there is. Don't you hear it, Quinn?" She tilted her head back and smiled at him, a delicious, enticing, and wholly entrancing smile that made him burn with the longing to taste that ripe mouth of hers.

Instead he listened as she began to hum, her voice soft and melodic and pleasing. When he could no longer hold back a reluctant grin, she stopped.

"Let's start with the two-step. Show me, Quinn, please."

He wanted to show her how damned irresistible he found her, but instead he forced himself to show her the rudiments of the country two-step, then a jig, a do-si-do, and finally a waltz.

For a graceful woman, she was a remarkably clumsy dancer. She stepped on his feet. She tripped over her own. She giggled, she hummed, she counted. And she sparkled like the sun.

She was light as gossamer in his arms.

"Ouch," he grunted when she trod on his toe once again. "I quit."

"Quinn Lassiter quitting? I'd have thought better of you."

"Then you'd be wrong." He'd noticed with concern that she was out of breath. Her hair tumbled carelessly across her cheeks, her eyes were overbright. Enough was enough—he didn't need her dancing till she dropped. "You know enough to get by. I can't take any more pain."

Her smile faded and she sighed. "You just think it's hopeless. I'll never learn."

"Sounds like you're the one giving up."

"Me?" Maura tossed her head and met his gaze squarely, looking more delectable than ever. "I never give up."

He swung her around into his arms again, and held her close for a moment. "Let's go then, sweetheart. Nice and easy, one more time."

Sweetheart. Her feet might have seemed glued to the floor, but her heart soared. *He called me sweetheart.*

It didn't mean anything. She knew that. But her spirits lifted and she hummed louder.

They whirled across the cabin floor, bumping the arm of the sofa, kicking over the sewing basket, nearly toppling into the fireplace. Her laughter rang out from every gleaming, spotless corner. She was dancing with her husband and she heard music. Even if he couldn't hear it, if no one else could, she did. It sang in her heart and echoed in her soul every time she gazed into Quinn's eyes.

Suddenly her concentration faltered just as Quinn whirled her around. Taken by surprise, her feet twisted up in each other and she tumbled. He caught her, but they both swerved off-balance and fell against the arm of the sofa. Quinn toppled over, and she was dragged over on top of him.

"My goodness—I'm sorry!" she gasped as she landed with a thump and a jolt across him. They lay across the cushions and she could feel the washboard-hard length of him beneath her.

Her heart racing, she started to squirm off him, but his arms locked around her and held her fast.

"I'm not." He should have released her at once, but he didn't.

"I suppose you're cursing the day you married such a clumsy woman," she said breathlessly, but he shook his head.

"You're not clumsy. You just can't dance worth a plug nickel. Now stop squirming and hold still. I want to look at you."

But he did more than look. As she gazed into his eyes he swept a hand to her nape and drew her downward. His lips closed over hers. Warmth and pleasure stole through her, then a sizzling heat as he slipped an arm around her waist and the curves of her body were pressed even more intimately against his.

"Maura." The single word seemed to her to hold a tenderness and a yearning welling up from deep inside him. Yet even as her heart lurched with hope, she felt him draw back, muttering a half curse.

He shifted and settled her on the sofa, even as he came off it. "We're not going to do this again."

"Do . . . what?"

His eyes glinted at her. "Make any more mistakes."

"Maybe . . . it isn't as much of a mistake as you think," she said softly, trying to sound light, offhand, even though her heart was filled with longing.

He didn't answer for a moment, just continued to stare at her as if he would see clear through to her soul.

He wheeled away from the heart-rending temptation of that soft, beautiful face and stalked toward the mantel. "There's something you should know. I'm leaving tomorrow."

"L-leaving?" She pushed herself to a sitting position on the sofa and smoothed her hair with an unsteady hand. All the happiness she'd felt only a few moments ago vanished. "Don't tell me—the gunfighting job."

He nodded and turned back to face her, steeling himself. "I'm riding to Laramie to find out the particulars. That's it. I'll be back in a day or so—in plenty of time for the dance."

"I see. Then I guess I'd better finish my dress." Slowly she rose from the sofa and went to the armchair. She knelt down and began putting back the scraps of fabric and thread that had spilled out of the sewing basket.

"Maura," he said warily, as if concerned that she was going to weep or beg or plead. "You've known all along about this job. We have an agreement—"

"I know all about our agreement, Quinn." She spoke

wearily. Pain filled her heart as she stood, clasping the basket in one hand and scooping the dress into the other. "I know every limitation and condition we've negotiated into this marriage. I know exactly what it is—and what it isn't. There's no need to remind me again."

Heaviness settled in his chest. The flushed, happy glow was gone from her face. Maura was pale now—composed, yes—but there was no mistaking the pain in her eyes. It cut through him to the core, but there wasn't a damn thing he could do about it. Things were the way they were—the way they had to be—and it would only make things worse if he led her to think it could be any different between them.

"Just so you know." He cleared his throat. Why did she have to look so damned beautiful, as touchable as a flower, as delicate as glass? "I'm leaving at first light."

She nodded and went to the door of the bedroom, pausing at the threshold, her hair atumble, a small, sad smile on her lips. "Just so you know," she said softly. "I'll miss you."

Without another word, she went into the bedroom and closed the door, leaving him as stunned as if she'd picked up a poker and hit him over the head.

Chapter 23

 FOR MAURA, THE NEXT FEW DAYS CRAWLED BY. The dance at the Crooked T ranch house was supposed to be held the following evening, but she'd had no word from Quinn, and as the hours passed she began to wonder if he would return from Laramie in time.

If anything had happened to him . . .

"Please, no," she whispered to herself late in the afternoon as she gathered berries near the glimmering silver-green creek. She missed Quinn more than she could have imagined. And she feared for him.

Maybe tonight he'll be back, she thought as she tossed the last handful of berries into her basket and started toward the cabin. He had promised he'd be here for the dance—and she'd never known him to break a promise.

A strange silence enveloped the clearing where the cabin stood amidst cottonwoods and waving grasses. Bill Saunders and Lucky had gone to town for supplies, and Slim and Orville had begun rounding up cattle for branding. But it wasn't only that none of the men were around—the air had changed. The golden April sun had whisked behind a bank of clouds, and as she glanced up at the sky, which had darkened to an ominous shade of blue, she realized that rain threatened. It hung in the still, heavy air, even as the wind picked up, blowing tumbleweed toward the barn and moaning through the branches.

She quickened her pace toward the cabin, thinking of the fire she would build in the hearth, the pie she would bake, the stew she would prepare for Quinn in case he should return sometime this evening. Somehow the little cabin with the old, creaky furniture, the narrow bed covered by a simple quilt, the plain dishes, and the lace curtains that she herself had sewn with such care had become more of a home to her than the Duncan Hotel had ever been. Not that she wasn't grateful to Ma Duncan for all she had done—or tried to do—for her. If not for her schooling, and her insistence on manners and well-bred behavior, the women of Hope might not have accepted her as cordially as they had. She owed Ma Duncan for that, and for giving her a roof over her head, and whatever kindness she could.

But this cabin on Sage Creek was the place where she belonged. If only she and Quinn could both belong here—together.

She was rounding the back of the cabin when she heard the sound of horses' hooves. Startled, Maura hurried forward. The first raindrops struck her cheeks as she made out two riders in the distance, coming fast.

Had Quinn taken the rifle with him—or was it still in the cabin? She hadn't paid attention before now. But with the Campbells still on the loose, it wouldn't do to take chances.

She pushed open the cabin door and raced inside. Relief swept her when she found the rifle propped against the wall in the kitchen, and she grabbed it thankfully.

Her heart hammering, she hurried back outside and lifted the rifle to her shoulder as Judd had taught her so many years ago.

"Hold it right there . . ."

The words died away on her lips.

Homer and Judd reined in among the weeds and sat their mounts, staring at her.

"If it ain't our own little sister." Judd leaned back in the saddle, his eyes colder than the rain that had begun to pelt her cheeks. "Stickin' a rifle in our faces after all we've done for you, Maura Jane? Now, that just ain't polite."

"Judd. Homer . . ."

"Hey, she remembers our names." Homer swung out of the saddle and loped toward her. "That's something, ain't it?"

"Don't come any closer." Maura found her voice after the first shock of seeing them. "Stop right there."

"Aw, Maura Jane, ain't you happy to see us? We come all this way looking for you."

"Why?"

"Can't we come in out of the rain to talk? We're tired, and wet, and awful hungry. How's about you fix us some coffee and we'll have us a chat."

Her knees were shaking but the rifle remained remarkably steady. She looked from Judd to Homer, studying their round, leering faces, and she felt only fear. They meant no good.

Did they intend to drag her back to Knotsville? Or to beat her to punish her for running away?

She couldn't believe that after all this time they'd shown up, that they would have put so much effort and time into finding her. Why?

"Maura Jane, it's mighty damp out here." There was an ominous rumble beneath Judd's patient tone.

But she was the one holding the rifle. They were waiting for her.

"You can come in," she said. "But I'm warning you right now that I'll be watching you. If you make one move to get this rifle away from me, I'll fire it."

"Anything you say, runt."

"We just want to talk to you," Homer put in, spreading his hands expansively.

"Then step inside."

If they felt surprise that the docile girl they'd known now spoke with a crisp, no-nonsense air, they didn't show it. She edged aside and made room for them to precede her into the cabin as the first rumble of thunder shook the sky.

"Now, Maura Jane, what's got into you? You don't seem the least bit glad to see us." Homer regarded her reproachfully, and something in his smirk made Maura's skin crawl.

Even though he and Judd were lounging on the sofa, their hands in clear view at their sides, she still stood a good few feet back, and still kept the rifle leveled at them.

"You're not angry that I ran off?" Of course they were, but she wanted to see if they'd admit to it. She had no idea what to expect from them—the fact that they'd actually tracked her all the way to Sage Creek was still sinking in.

"We was hurt, Maura, that's all," Judd said. "If you wanted to leave, well, fine. But you could have waited to say goodbye."

"You'd have let me go?"

"When did we ever stop you from doing anything you wanted to do?"

She snorted at that, and Judd glared at her. "You've changed, girl."

"Maybe I have. I'm married now and no matter what you say, I'm not going back with you."

"Married, huh? That's what we heard. So where is this husband of yours?" Homer demanded. "Why are you here in the middle of nowhere all alone? Don't he care about you?"

"Just tell me what you want. I have work to do."

"Well, that's fine and dandy, girl." Judd tugged at the corners of his lank brown mustache, giving her a half smile. "Could you make us some coffee first? We're awful parched and tuckered out and gettin' kind of a chill from that there rain."

"Make it yourself." Maura gestured toward the kitchen. She tightened her grip on the rifle, growing more and more uneasy. "Then you can leave."

As Judd heaved himself off the sofa and started to move toward the kitchen, Maura tensed and took a step back. But he didn't come toward her at all. He was glancing toward the armchair, where her sewing basket sat on the floor and the enamel jewel box peeked out from a bed of fabric scraps, thimbles, and thread.

"What are you doing?" she cried sharply as he bent down and scooped up the box.

"This belonged to Ma."

"Well, she gave it to me!" Anger throbbed through her. "You know that."

"I reckon I'm taking it back." Maura couldn't understand the crafty, triumphant smile that crossed his face as he slid the box into the pocket of his dirty gray flannel shirt. Since when did Judd care about a jewel box? He wasn't the sentimental type, and Homer certainly wasn't either—but Homer, watching him, smiled too.

"What's going on? What are you two up to?" she demanded, staring warily from one to the other.

Suddenly lightning split the sky in a flashing bolt and for one instant, Maura glanced instinctively toward the window. Homer lunged at her, knocking her sideways as he wrenched the rifle from her grasp.

With a cry, Maura fell against the wall. Before she could recover, Judd bounded forward.

"I'll teach you to point a rifle at me!" he snarled. He shoved her backward again, and Maura felt a jolt this time as her head struck the wall. Dizzily, she slumped to her knees, pain and fear swirling through her.

"All right, let's get out of here." Homer's voice sounded thin and wavery and a long way above her. "We got what we come for. Let's ride."

"Not so fast." Judd still towered over her. Through blinking pinpoints of hot red light she saw his boots. They were huge, caked with dried mud and grass. "We're not leaving till we've taught this good-for-nothing bitch a lesson."

"I don't know, Judd. Remember, I told you I promised Ma—"

"Ma's dead, you idiot! And Maura Jane's gonna wish she was when I'm through with her."

Maura tried desperately to stand, bracing herself as Judd unexpectedly reached down a hand to help her. But when he yanked her up, he grabbed her by the hair and forced her head to tilt backward until she was staring dazedly into his eyes.

"No . . . let me go, Judd," she gasped, but he sneered at her.

"You've never been nothin' but trouble."

Something vicious in his expression and the way he spoke those words ignited her fear into panic.

The baby. Nothing must happen to the baby.

"Judd . . . there's something you should know. I'm going to have a child. You don't want to . . . hurt the baby. . . ."

"Baby!" Judd looked stunned. But his grip on her hair never lessened.

"Please . . . Homer. You promised Ma. No matter what I did, this baby inside me is innocent . . ."

"Is that the reason you up and left, you dirty little slut?" Judd shouted. "Because you had a bun in the oven? Whose is it? The man you're married to—or is he just some dumb fool you talked into raising your bastard—"

He never finished the sentence.

The butt of a gun slammed down over Judd's head and he dropped like a rock to the floor, his fingers sliding through Maura's hair and releasing it as his eyes rolled back. In the next instant Homer went for his gun, but Quinn Lassiter drew first, cocking the trigger before Homer even pulled his pistol from the holster.

"Go on," Quinn invited, cold fury in his eyes. "I want to watch you die."

Homer froze. As Maura watched, every drop of color faded from his face as he stared at the tall, dark man whose gray eyes glittered with the promise of death.

"Who in hell . . . *are* you?" he croaked.

Quinn's glance flitted to Maura for an instant. "Go into the other room," he said, "while I deal with these scum."

Homer shuddered.

Quinn's gut clenched as Maura touched a shaking hand to her head. She looked as though a feather could knock her over. He wanted to scoop her into his arms and soothe her hurts, but he didn't dare take his eyes off the two buzzards stinking up his parlor.

"Sit down and take it easy until I'm finished here."

"No . . . let them go, Quinn. Please. They're my brothers. Judd and Homer. I told you about them."

"I know who they are." He stared with contempt at the two hulking men who looked far from dangerous at the moment. One was slumped on the floor, the other stood mute and motionless, watching him in silent terror.

"Please, just let them go. I owe Ma Duncan that."

"Damn straight, Maura, you do, you owe Ma plenty," Homer began to blabber. "After all she did for you. And Pa too. He didn't have to let her take you in. And think of how Judd and me always looked after you—"

"Say one more word and I'll drop you where you stand," Quinn snarled.

Judd moaned and lifted his head. At that moment, Maura swayed.

"Maura!"

The pain behind her eyes was excruciating. She

couldn't keep her balance. She felt herself falling and reached out blindly.

"Quinn—" she gasped, just before the world went black.

Springing forward, Quinn grabbed her as she tumbled sideways.

It was all the opening Homer needed. He seized Judd by the collar, yanked him up and shoved him toward the door.

"Run!" he shouted.

Quinn cradled Maura in his arms as she lost consciousness. Terror pummeled through him. He heard the Duncan brothers scrambling out the door, but gave them only a cursory glance through the window before setting down his gun and scooping Maura up against his chest.

He could have shot both of them as they ran—he could have winged them—but he swore under his breath and let them go.

Fear for Maura overrode everything else.

He carried her to the sofa and loosened the collar of her dress, then stroked his hand lightly over her cheek.

"Maura," he whispered, his voice hoarse.

But she didn't respond. The only sound was the drum of rain and the dull thud of retreating hoofbeats.

"Maura, wake up!"

This time her eyelids fluttered, and as Quinn took her hands in his and began to rub them gently, she gave a moan.

"My head."

"Where does it hurt?"

She put a hand near her temple, behind her ear, and

Quinn gingerly touched there, drawing his fingers away with a frown when she winced.

"You're going to have a fair-sized goose egg," he said grimly. Then his voice roughened. "Where the hell are Saunders and the hands? I gave specific orders that someone always be here when I'm away."

"Saunders had to go to town and Lucky . . ." Maura's voice faded as she struggled to sit up.

Quinn pushed her back down upon the cushions. "Don't even think about getting up until I say so." He waited long enough to be certain she wasn't going to make another attempt, then stalked into the kitchen, returning a moment later with a glass of water.

"Drink this. Don't argue."

His gut churned at the sight of her so weak, so pale and dizzy. He held the cup for her, but she accepted only a sip before sinking back on the pillow he shoved under her head. He wanted to give her a good piece of his mind for not having let him shoot the Duncan brothers—and at the same time he wanted to draw her close, hold her against him, somehow absorb her pain into himself.

But he did neither. He studied her in concern, met her wan gaze with a scowl, and somehow kept a lid on his temper.

"Did you . . . take that job in Laramie?"

"No. It would have meant starting right away, being tied up for weeks. I told you I wouldn't leave until you were set."

"Thank you," she murmured.

He met her gaze. "There will be other jobs," he said. "But meantime, it's a damn good thing I got back when I did. What did those sons of bitches want with you?"

"I have no idea." Maura struggled to sit up again, one hand to her head. This time he didn't try to stop her, though when she peeped up she saw him studying her through narrowed eyes.

"They took my jewel box. The one Ma Duncan left to me. I can't imagine why." She moistened her lips, distressed by the anger on his face. She knew that look.

"Quinn," she whispered, "please don't go after them. Stay with me."

The worry and pain in her eyes tugged at his heart more than any tears or pleading ever could.

He turned away, paced to the mantel just so he wouldn't have to look into those beautiful eyes another moment. "I've seen them somewhere before. Wish I could remember where. But don't worry, it'll come back to me."

"They were in Hatchett the night of the blizzard. At the poker tournament. Perhaps that's where."

He stiffened suddenly. And nodded. "That's it." He'd seen them in the Ruby Rose Casino just before he and Black Jack Gannon had stepped outside to conduct their deadly business. He'd recognized the brothers' type: ruffians who liked to make noise, drink themselves mean, browbeat anyone in their path who didn't look like they could fight back.

As his mind shifted through the events of that night, he remembered something else. They'd been lurking outside in the shadows as well, he'd glimpsed them right after the woman screamed and went down. . . .

Maura saw the pain flicker through his eyes and then saw him banish it in the space of a heartbeat. The man who looked back at her the next instant was pure gunfighter—controlled, hardened, cold as December sleet.

"I don't want them coming near you again. They never should have gotten this close in the first place." He returned to her side, looming over her as she lay upon the cushions, a muscle working in his jaw. "I ought to pack you off to Hope—to the Glory Hotel—until the Campbells are rounded up and I've made sure those brothers of yours have hightailed it out of town. And I just might."

"No." She swung her legs off the sofa. A wave of shakiness swept over her, but she fought it down. "I belong here. This cabin is my home. I won't leave it."

It's your home, too, she wanted to say, but she left the thought dangling between them. Yet he may have sensed what she was thinking, because he suddenly turned away and strode to the mantel, shoving his hands into his pockets. He spun around again at the sound of approaching horses.

Bill Saunders and Lucky Johnson were galloping fast through the rain. From the other direction came the ranch hands.

"It's only our men," he told her. "Don't worry."

"I'm not worried, Quinn—now that you're home."

His lean jaw tightened. He strode to the door, but not before she saw that the coldness that sent shivers through her had returned to his eyes. "Reckon I'd better have a few words with them about obeying orders."

Without another glance in her direction, he went outside into the rain.

Chapter 24

HE DREAMED OF THE WOMAN.

She was lying in the snow, blood soaking the strands of her curling blond hair, streaking across her ivory skin and the necklace glittering at her throat, seeping into the chill white pillow of Death upon which she lay.

He walked toward her. Exactly as he had that fierce January night, only this time when he knelt beside her and touched his hand to her pulse, he froze in shock, overcome with a terrifying, shattering horror.

Her face wasn't the face of the woman who had fallen that night, struck by a stray bullet from the gun duel with Black Jack Gannon. The face of the woman lying dead in the snow belonged to his mother.

"No!"

Quinn's agonized shout awakened Maura, and she sat up with a jolt in her bed. She rushed to him in the main room of the cabin, touched his arm, his bare chest, then shook his shoulder, all the while softly speaking his name.

"Quinn. Quinn, it's only a dream, a bad dream.'' Her

arms reached out for him, closed around his neck. His bare muscled chest was sheened with sweat in the halo of starlight that glittered in through the window. "Shhh. It's all right," she whispered.

His glazed eyes swung to her face, but his breathing remained quick and ragged.

"A dream." It was a croak, sounding so shaken and unlike him that Maura tightened her arms around his neck.

"Yes, a dream."

"But it was her—the woman in Hatchett. The one with the blond hair . . ." A tremor shook through him. "The . . . necklace."

"Necklace?"

"She was dead," he muttered vacantly. "Just the way she looked that night. Blood . . . everywhere."

A chill ran down Maura's spine.

"Except it wasn't her," Quinn rasped. "When I looked at her face, it wasn't her. . . ."

"Shhh. It's over now. All over."

Quinn closed his eyes, grasping for control, shoving the images of the nightmare away. Maura was wrong. It would never be over. The memories of Hatchett, and of the terrible events that had occurred on his family farm when he was nine years old were engraved upon his mind and his heart.

He hadn't had the dreams of his boyhood for a long time now—but he'd always known they'd return. Just as he'd known that the only way to protect himself from that kind of agony ever again was to keep his distance. Keep himself strong, in control, and invulnerable to the emotions that had rent apart that nine-year-old boy—the boy he had once been.

He'd left that boy behind twenty-two years ago and had done his best to become hard as a rock, with nothing soft on the inside, nothing that could be cracked, or hurt or broken.

But this time . . . Maura was stroking his chest, her touch tender, so feminine and gentle, that a very different kind of pain seared through him each place her fluttering fingers touched.

He flung himself from the sofa, yanked on his pants and boots, ignored her questions, and slammed out of the cabin like a man pursued.

He needed fresh air, open space. He needed to be away from that auburn-haired woman in there, to feel the cold breeze brushing his flesh, not those slender fingers.

Why couldn't she be like Serena, a warm body, a hard heart, no questions asked. Why couldn't she stop battering at that wall he'd erected around himself—battering it with kindness, sweetness, gentle touches, kisses of honey.

He was proof against everything but that—that and the quiet yearning he found of late whenever he gazed into her eyes.

He reached the crooked tree that stood in front of the corral and paused, leaning against it. From his pocket he dug a cigarillo, and he lit up as his breathing slowed and the night settled cool and bitter around him. Unseen creatures stirred in the brush, a hawk swooped past the glint of the moon, casting a swift shadow that was there and then gone in a blink, and then he sensed that he was no longer alone.

"Go back inside." He spoke without turning around.

The scent of lilacs filled his nostrils. He longed to bury his face in her soft, fragrant neck, to twine his hands in her hair. She could help him forget—forget what had happened on the farm all those years ago—and what had happened in Hatchett the night that woman was killed. . . .

But he wouldn't let her. She was already too much in his blood.

"Go back, Quinn? I don't think so." Her voice, for once, was anything but soft, anything but sweet. She stamped forward until she faced him. And he was forced to face her.

Her chin lifted as he ran his eyes over her in the moonlight. Lord, she was a sight in that sheer white nightgown, which the wind blew tantalizingly around every single one of her curves. Her hair spilled like fire over her shoulders and whipped across her cheeks. But it was her eyes that held him. They blazed like molten copper, hot with indignation and a fiery determination that made her burn like a candle in the empty night.

"I won't let you shut me out tonight, Quinn Lassiter."

"You don't have a choice."

"Oh, yes, I do. This one night, it's going to be different. You're going to talk to me, tell me what's bothering you. Tell me about that dream."

"You think so?"

"I certainly do think so."

"Well, think again. And while you're at it, go back inside—you'll catch a chill out here."

"So what if I do? I don't care. It can't be worse than the chill I have inside—because I'm living with a stranger. A stranger who holds me at arm's length, who shuts me out as if I were one of those weeds growing over there, trying to get in the door. I'm not a weed, a pesky weed to be ignored and stomped over. I'm your wife, Quinn! Your . . . partner. And I want more. I want to know you—just a little. I want to know what you feel, who you are, the hopes and dreams inside you!"

He threw down the cigarillo and crushed it under his boot as he grabbed her, yanked her close, his fingers biting into her skin. "I don't have hopes and dreams, Maura! That's the difference between you and me. That's what you don't understand."

"Everyone has hopes and dreams."

"Not me," he told her coldly. "You want to know what's inside? Nothing. There's nothing inside—does that make you feel any better? You married a man who wants nothing, feels nothing, hopes for nothing. Except maybe to rid the world of some scum before he joins that same scum six feet under."

"I don't believe you." It came out in a whisper. The wind tore at her hair, set her shoulders shivering, and whisked away the words, but not before Quinn heard them and saw the wrenching agony in her eyes. She was no longer fiery, determined, fierce. Now she was a bright-haired angel who gazed at him with such intensity that his hollow soul ached.

"Believe me," he grated back at her. His lip curled in a well-practiced sneer.

But it didn't fool her. She reached up and touched his cheek. "You're lying. To yourself as well as to me."

"Lying, eh?" Her very trust and innocence unleashed fury inside him. The moon floated behind a bank of clouds and the night dimmed into murky shadow, but the glimmer of her fair skin and her questioning eyes remained steadfast in his sight, torturing him.

"Maybe it's time I made you understand," he bit out. Savage emotions churned like acid inside him, and suddenly he could no longer hold the words back. "I told you about my father. He was a drunk and a bully. Like those damned brothers of yours. He used to beat my mother and me, and why she didn't leave him I'll never know. But she stayed and worked the farm, a dirt-poor Missouri farm high up in the Ozarks, and scraped out enough for us to get by—barely."

"I'm sorry." Maura tried to reach out, to touch his taut face once more, but he jerked back, his eyes warning her not to do that again.

"He gambled as well as drank, and one day he gambled away everything—the deed to the farm, the livestock—even my mother's wedding ring. But that's not the worst of it. He tried to get it all back on one last hand—and was caught cheating."

Maura watched his face, trembled at the pain and rage there. It was shocking to see such raw emotion in a man who personified control—and she was frightened of what she had unleashed. Ferocious anger burned in his gray eyes—his mouth was a vicious slash, and he looked as though he could tear that crooked tree right out of the ground and toss it into the wind like a stick, so great seemed the force of his fury.

"What happened?" she whispered, knowing there was no stopping him now, knowing that nothing would ease the agony of these memories until they'd spilled out, every one, like drops of blood from a wound.

"What happened? A damned sheriff named Lester Peabody happened. Seems Peabody is the one who beat my father at that poker hand, the one he tried to cheat. If that's what really happened. Peabody was crooked—as crooked as they come. Everyone in town knew it, but no one had the courage to confront him, or to run against him. He owned that town. And when he accused my father of cheating and locked him up, there was no one to say different. Then Peabody came out to the ranch first thing in the morning. Sunup. Woke my mother and me, told us we had to clear out that day. Hand over the deed, leave everything behind. He demanded my mother give him her ring then and there."

She was stunned. She could only stare at him wordlessly, and dread what was coming next.

"I'll never forget the expression on her face, as if she'd been punched in the stomach, again and again and again."

Quinn took a breath. "She said she'd have to see my father first, hear from him what he'd done. Peabody didn't like that. He demanded she give him her ring right then and there."

"How could anyone be so cruel?" Maura breathed.

Quinn's eyes glazed with remembering. He spoke softly now. "That ring had belonged to her mother, and before that to her mother. Katharine Lassiter didn't get mad often—she took what life dealt her—but she didn't want to give up that ring. So there she was, in her wrapper, a woman all alone with her child on a godforsaken farm, miles from everywhere. And she defied him. Ordered him off her land until she heard from her husband that it was no longer theirs. And that's when Peabody suddenly got other ideas about what he wanted from her.''

"No. Oh, no, Quinn."

"I tried to stop him." Moonlight stabbed the dark mask of his face. "I ran for the rifle but he got to it first. Broke it in two. Then he went after her. She fought him and so did I. But neither of us were a match for him. My mother grabbed up a knife. I'll never forget the terror in her face. But she yelled at him to let me go. The bastard threw me against a wall and I must have hit my head, because I went out cold. I was too small, too damn young and weak to fight back. And she was too frail.''

Maura's fingers shook as she pressed them to her throat. Pain knotted inside her, pain for him now as he relived those terrible moments, for the little boy who had tried so valiantly to rescue his mother.

She no longer wanted to know what happened next. But she knew he was going to tell her.

"When I came to, the place was a shambles. My mother still had her wedding ring on, but not much else. The clothes left on her body were in tatters. And covered in blood. He'd stabbed her after he raped her. She bled all over the kitchen floor she always fretted about keeping so clean. She must have put up a hell of a fight. Not that it did her any good.''

"Oh, Quinn . . ."

"I never had a chance to say goodbye. To tell her—" He broke off. There was no pain in his eyes anymore. No rage. They were empty. Colder than stone, colder than marble. His face looked gaunt and impossibly harsh beneath the shadows of the crooked tree.

"At that moment, in that house filled with blood and

the echo of her screams, I thought I'd die too from the pain of losing her, of knowing how she'd fought, how she'd suffered. I howled like an animal. Then I buried her myself, with her wedding ring, behind the garden she'd loved. It wasn't until later that I remembered that Peabody was going to get the land.'' He sighed and closed his eyes. ''You don't need all the details. I went to town, stole a gun and bullets from the general store. Went to the sheriff's office gunning for Peabody. And for my father. But the deputy tackled me first and they locked me in a cell next to my father's. They held us both for a week, then they let us go—on the condition that he leave town and take me with him.''

Quinn suddenly turned and leaned against the tree, his shoulders hunched as if bearing some incredible weight. ''That sniveling cowardly bastard crawled out of town with me and a bottle of red-eye in tow,'' he said slowly. ''I never knew if he really believed Peabody's story that my mother went crazy and tried to kill him when he went to claim the land, and that her death was an accident that came about while he was defending himself. There was no one to question him or prove otherwise—except me, and no one listened to a kid—especially when the whole town was scared of Peabody, way too scared to question his version of things. My pa included. So we left. And I ran off the first chance I got—hid in the back of a wagon traveling west, rolled out at the next town, and from there, lived off my wits and whatever pennies I could earn from doing odd jobs.'' He pushed away from the tree then, and his eyes bored into hers.

''So now you know. You know why I'd sooner drink spit than wear a lawman's badge. And why I can't feel, can't care. I lost something that day, Maura. Something was ripped out of me and it can never be put back. So quit trying." He shook his head. "Quit trying to make something of our marriage that it isn't. Quit trying to creep into my soul—I don't have one anymore. We had a bargain when we agreed to marry and I'm keeping my end of it. You need to keep yours."

"No, Quinn, I still don't believe you!" she cried as he started to walk past her, toward the house. He spun back.

"Believe it, sweetheart."

"It's not that you can't care—or hope or dream. It's that you're afraid to."

"Maybe I am." His lip curled and he shrugged, a dismissive gesture that was like a blow straight to her heart. "Think what you want, Maura, I don't give a damn. I'm in this marriage to do my duty by you and the baby. We both made a mistake that night and we're both paying for it. I can't give you more than that."

Pain tore through her, blinding her for a moment. She blinked it away, tried not to let her knees tremble too much lest he hear them knocking together over the breeze. "What makes you . . . think I want more?"

"You're a woman. Women always want more."

Cool as his voice was, there was sympathy in it now. Sympathy! His eyes searched hers almost warily. Did he expect her to cry? To break down and beg him to love her right then and there with the moon and the clouds and the night to witness?

Her heart cracked. She wanted to throw her arms around him, heal his hurts, tell him that love was the answer, not distance, but she couldn't. She couldn't. He was too far away, too hard and disciplined and unreachable for her. He didn't love her. He never would.

And why should he? She was only a silly lonely girl from Knotsville, a girl who had made a terrible mistake and given not only her virginity but her heart, to a man who had none. A man who would never love her back.

She wanted to cry. But she held the tears back with fierce effort and summoned what little remained of her dignity.

"I'd have to be a fool to want more from a man like you, Quinn Lassiter. And I was never anybody's fool."

This time she was the one who walked away. Head up, she swept past him in a ghostly swirl of white lawn and lilac scent that drifted in the crystal air.

She was chilled to the bone. And her heart ached with a pain that surpassed anything she'd ever known.

She got into bed and wrapped herself in all the blankets she could find, but it was hours before she slept, and she never knew if Quinn came inside or not. She tossed and turned and shivered and wept bitter silent tears, and told herself she should be grateful because she'd escaped Knotsville and Judd and Homer—if not for anything else.

But the cold despair blew through her and seeped deep inside her soul and drained her of everything except the heartache of a love she would never know.

Chapter 25

"YOU COMING?"

Maura frowned into the old mirror, wondering if it was too late to climb out the bedroom window and hide on the far side of the creek.

"In a moment," she answered Quinn, raising her voice so he could hear her in the parlor. She wanted to rip off the gown and her rose-shaped cameo necklace and crawl into bed, to hide from the world. But Alice was expecting her and so were the other ladies of the Hope Sewing Circle. She couldn't back out now.

But she knew Quinn wasn't looking forward to the dance this evening, that he was only going for her sake, and she had now come to dread the evening herself. Since her brothers had shown up, everything had gone wrong between them, everything had gone wrong in her life.

Even the buttons on her gown were not what she had wanted.

Why in the world had Judd and Homer stolen the jewel box? she wondered for the dozenth time since she'd had to borrow buttons from Alice. The ones she'd sewn onto the gown were plain round blue buttons, perfectly serviceable, but not the delicate glistening white pearl ones that would have complemented the dress so perfectly.

Yet there was no help for it—the pearl buttons were gone—and so, apparently, were Judd and Homer. There'd been no sign of them since yesterday, neither in the valley, along Sage Creek, or in town.

"Good riddance," she whispered, then dragged her hairbrush through her curls one last time.

Maura Jane, I guess you're ready as you'll ever be, she told herself as she turned away from the mirror. She supposed her appearance was passable, but the excitement of the evening was gone.

She and Quinn had barely spoken three words to one another since last night. He said nothing as she walked through the bedroom door, only watched her from beneath those slashing black brows. He stood at the mantel, enjoying a glass of whiskey, but the moment she saw him her feet faltered to a halt and her heart did a crazy dance in her chest. Good heavens, it wasn't fair. It just wasn't fair. The man looked devastatingly handsome in black pants, gray silk shirt, and a black string tie, his boots polished to a high gloss, his night-black hair gleaming in the lantern light. Never had he looked so sleekly, powerfully handsome, Maura thought, her breath catching in her throat. She couldn't tear her eyes from him, and searched his lean face in vain for some sign of approval or appreciation or even the faintest hint of pleasure at the sight of her.

She found none. But she thought she heard a choking sound, then heard him give a sputter, and he swallowed hard. The whiskey went down, and he turned suddenly and set his glass on the mantel with a thump.

"You look nice," he said curtly, then quickly took one more swallow of the liquor. "Let's go."

Any faint hopes Maura still cherished for the evening wilted at his cool tone.

What did you expect? she asked herself mockingly as they left the cabin in silence and walked together through the star-frosted night. *You look beautiful, Maura Jane. You're the most fetching woman I've ever seen. I'm in danger of losing my heart to you.*

The absurdity of it made her give a woeful chuckle, and Quinn glanced at her as he helped her into the wagon.

"Something funny?"

"Just the idea of me going to a party," she said quickly. She took a deep breath. "I never thought I would so this is a red-letter day for me. And now I only hope I remember how to do even one of the dances you taught me."

"All that work and sore feet better not have been for nothing." But a lighter note had entered his voice, and the furrow between his brows smoothed out when he vaulted into the seat beside her and took up the reins.

Encouraged, Maura tried a small smile. "Now you're making me even more nervous."

"What's there to be nervous about?"

"So many things," she exclaimed. "I'm likely to forget my own name, and what if I spill something on my dress? And how do I know if I look all right and—"

"You look fine."

"Fine." She folded her hands in her lap and considered. "I suppose that's good enough. Fine."

"You look beautiful," he said quickly. He threw her another glance, and this time Maura thought she saw hunger in his eyes. He quickly dragged his gaze forward again, back to the trail and the horses' bobbing heads. "But you know that."

"How should I know that?"

"You looked in the mirror, didn't you?"

Something lifted in her heart, but Maura kept her tone even. "I don't know what that has to do with anything."

"Because then you saw." His jaw jutted out. His voice grated even lower, rougher, sending intimate chills curling along her spine. "You damn near made me choke on my whiskey."

So it was true. Delight danced in her eyes, making them sparkle. "Really?"

"You don't have to sound so happy about it."

"I'm not happy. I'm sorry. I'd have hated for you to choke on your whiskey."

"Yeah, well, I could use about another pint of it right now," he muttered, and loosened his shirt collar with a finger.

She stared at the sky, aware suddenly that the stars above shone just like diamonds tossed upon a velvet sea. She'd never seen stars so brilliant, so fiery, and her heart swelled with the joy of it.

After a moment, she said softly, "Thank you."

"What for?"

"For the compliment. I've never had a real compliment before. From a man, I mean. Sometimes Ma Duncan would tell me that my hair looked nice when I pinned it up a certain way, or she'd tell me that I carried myself well, just like well-brought-up young ladies she'd known back east—which is what Ma Duncan was herself many years ago, before her father lost all his money and she married Pa Duncan and her life grew harder."

She cleared her throat. "But your compliment was much nicer. I feel much better now about going to the dance."

"Glad to hear it." His voice sounded amused.

They rode the rest of the way in silence, but Maura somehow felt it was a companionable silence. The tension inside her eased. The night beckoned her, and when they passed through the gate leading up to the Tyler ranch house and the sounds of gaiety and laughter and fiddle music echoed through the shadowy trees, she forgot about Judd and Homer and the Campbell gang, she forgot that she had blue buttons instead of pearl ones on her dress. Her heart leapt with excitement and her pulse began to race in time to the music.

Tonight she wasn't going to watch the dance with her face pressed against a windowpane. Tonight she would be a part of it, laughing, chatting—and dancing in her husband's arms.

Quinn helped her down from the wagon. His strong hands lingered at her waist after he set her down upon the grass.

For a moment, gazing up into his eyes, she thought he was going to kiss her. She held her breath. His lean, sun-bronzed face, illuminated by moon and stars, was as solid and forbidding as rock, but there was a warmth in his eyes that softened the effect, and made her want to stretch up on tiptoe and slant her mouth to his.

But she did no such thing. It must already be plain as

pudding that she was crazy in love with him, and she wasn't about to make it any plainer.

Fortunately, he released her before she had time to do anything foolish. Disappointment twinged through her as his hands fell away, but then he took her arm and escorted her toward the lights and the laughter.

"Time to face the music."

As he led her through the front doors of the big split-log house, a thrill of pleasure shot through her. The large and spacious parlor was festooned with colored lanterns and so crowded that at first Maura couldn't make out a single person she knew. But then she spotted Carolyn Mason at the long linen-draped refreshment table against the wall, and Edna and Seth Weaver spun by doing a do-si-do—Edna beaming and waving frantically to her—and before she and Quinn had worked their way around the edge of the throng more than ten steps, Alice Tyler was at her side, hugging her.

"Maura, you look gorgeous! The dress is perfect. Even the buttons," she added with a wide smile. She beamed up at Quinn. "Thank you for coming."

Jim Tyler clapped him on the shoulder. "Quite a gathering, eh, Lassiter? Wait till you taste Alice's apple pie. None better in the whole territory!"

Then another rancher sauntered up and the three men drifted off in a huddle, talking cattle and weather and stock prices, and suddenly Lucky Johnson loomed before her.

"Miz Lassiter, ma'am, before your husband notices and decides to plug me full of holes, may I have this dance?"

She laughed. With his slicked-back fair hair and stub-

born cowlick, his red-and-blue-plaid shirt and red bandanna, Lucky was quite a dashing sight. His grin was
infectious as he grabbed her hand without waiting for an
answer and pulled her toward the center of the floor,
which had been cleared of all furniture and was crowded
with dancers.

Glancing back, she saw that Quinn's gaze followed
her. His polite smile had turned into a frown.

"Lucky, are you sure you wouldn't rather wait for
Orchid or . . . or Miss Grace Ellis or Serena Walsh?"
she teased, her stomach fluttering nervously at the
prospect of dancing, even though she was eager to try.
The music filled her ears and made her long to twirl and
glide.

"They're right nice and even passable ladies, Miz
Lassiter, ma'am, but you're the woman I want, need, and
must have as my partner for this very dance!" he declared.

She laughed and swung willingly into his arms for a
country dance. Lucky whisked her across the floor so
easily that her feet flew. But when she caught sight of
Nell in a pretty store-bought gown of pink and white
gingham, trimmed in white ribbons and white satin sash,
she suddenly tripped.

"I'm so sorry," she cried as she trod on Lucky's
booted foot.

"Think nothing of it." He grinned as he noticed that
Quinn had turned to stare at them. "Aw shucks, your
husband's got his eye on us. Promise you'll put flowers
on my grave."

"Don't be silly. Quinn won't care who I dance with."

He gave a burst of laughter. "Sure he will. He hates it

when another man so much as looks at you, much less talks to you, or makes you smile. He's not really afraid of me doing it, because he knows I respect a married woman," he explained smugly, "and besides, I'm more naturally drawn toward, uh, certain other kinds of women, but you just watch what happens if Slim or Grady or Jethro Plum asks you for a dance."

"Don't be silly," she said again, stunned by what he was saying and totally at a loss. With an effort she forced herself to turn the conversation back in the direction she had decided upon.

"My, doesn't Nell Hicks look pretty tonight."

"She here?"

But his voice was too casual. Maura would have bet money that he'd already spotted Nell and seen for himself.

"There she is, in that pink-and-white-gingham dress. Oh, her hair is curled so prettily, don't you think?"

"I can't tell from here."

"Perhaps you should go closer then," Maura suggested a bit breathlessly. The exertion of dancing was wearing on her, making her long suddenly for a cool glass of lemonade. "Perhaps you'd like to invite her to dance?"

"Not likely!" he snorted. "She's the last girl I'd ask. The very last girl," he added darkly.

"Now why is that, Lucky?"

"Because she's got a viper's tongue on her. And she's bossy. Just because her father owns the general store she thinks she knows everything. And she didn't want me going with the posse that day—told me to be careful. Me!

She thinks I'm a kid! Orchid doesn't. And neither does the widow Walsh . . ."

"Why don't you give her a chance? You hardly know her."

"I know all I need to know." He suddenly frowned at her. "Hey, Miz Lassiter, why should you care if I ask her to dance? She doesn't exactly look lonely to me."

Maura turned her head and saw that Tex, one of the young ranch hands the Crooked T had sent to help Quinn, was leading Nell toward the dance floor.

"Well, no, perhaps she's not lonely. But I think you hurt her feelings the other day."

"How?" he asked suspiciously.

"I overheard you make a . . . a joke about the Campbell gang trying to steal her. And I know you meant it in fun, but that's not the kind of thing a young lady can ever laugh at. And neither should you, Lucky," she said simply.

He had the grace to flush to the roots of his hair. "I know that. Soon as I said it, I knew it was all wrong. I didn't mean it either. Not the way it sounded."

"Why don't you tell her that?"

"Because we just don't get along. And that's the end of it." But he was watching Nell dance while he said it, and a muscle twitched in the corner of his jaw.

Maura dared not push him any further. But she was satisfied that she'd planted a few seeds in his mind and given him something to think about.

As the music came to a halt, Lucky bowed to her. "I'm surprised the boss hasn't cut in on me yet," he confided. "I bet Slim two dollars he would before the end of the dance."

"Lucky! You didn't!" But Maura burst out laughing. "You obviously don't know Quinn Lassiter as well as you—"

She spotted Quinn at that moment. He was lounging in the corner with Serena Walsh, their heads close together, talking.

"—think you do," she finished quietly.

"Hey, there, Miz Lassiter, you all right?"

"I could use a glass of lemonade, Lucky."

But the smile she pasted on her face was forced and stiff as Lucky led her toward the refreshment table, poured her a glass of lemonade, found her a chair. He didn't leave her side until she'd been joined by Carolyn and Grace and Edna, all of whom were showing off their new dresses and admiring each other's.

"Next we'll start on a baby quilt for that little one of yours," Grace told her, patting her arm.

Maura nodded mechanically.

"I think we should use squares of pale blue and white and yellow so it will be fitting for either a boy or a girl," Edna declared. "That's what we did for Alice before her youngest, Jared, was born."

Maura tried to look interested, but she couldn't really concentrate. After a few moments, John Hicks ambled up and asked her to dance, and then so did Grady, the other ranch hand who'd helped out at Sage Creek while Quinn was after the Campbells.

But Maura discovered that dancing wasn't nearly as much fun as she'd thought it would be. Even the bright gowns, festively glowing parlor, rich smells of perfumes and elderberry wine and roasting meats didn't seem quite so wonderful and gay as they had when she'd first entered on Quinn's arm.

Quinn won't leave you for Serena, she told herself as she returned to her seat. And she knew it to be the truth. She didn't know all that much about the man she'd married, but she knew that he lived by a strict code of honor, the same code of honor that had compelled him to marry her, and she knew he would never abandon her or the partnership they'd agreed upon.

But if Serena was the woman he truly felt closest to . . .

That thought hurt more than she could bear.

Suddenly she couldn't sit another moment listening to the chatter surrounding her.

"If you'll excuse me," she told Carolyn and Edna, jerking to her feet, "I need a breath of air."

She fled before anyone could offer to accompany her, but not before she saw Edna watching her through worried eyes. She slipped out the front door onto the porch, walked to the farthest corner, placed her hands upon the railing and lifted her hot face to the open, starry skies.

She took deep, long breaths and with all of her will, pushed back the dangerously threatening tears.

When the sound of voices intruded into her misery, it took a moment for her to realize to whom they belonged. But only a moment. She snapped her head to the right, toward the cluster of trees whose canopy of dark leaves swayed rhythmically with the wind, as if they were dancing to the music, and saw two faint outlines. She made out the exquisite profile of Serena, recognized the dramatic upsweep of her pale clustered curls, and saw the wide set of Quinn's shoulders, the slant of his hat.

Quinn and Serena. Huddled in the shadows beneath those shiny, swaying leaves, together in the musky spring darkness.

Chapter 26

 "RECKON YOU SHOULD TELL ME WHAT EXACTLY you want from me, Serena."

Keeping his voice low, Quinn studied the woman in the shockingly low-cut violet dress. Serena hadn't changed much from the bold young woman who'd once traveled from town to town with the Walsh Theatrical Troupe, performing musical numbers and melodramas with equal aplomb—until the show hit Abilene. That was where her first husband, Raymond P. Walsh, abandoned her and the show and ran off with a dance hall girl, taking with him all the costumes, sets, wagons, and horses. Quinn had met Serena shortly after that, when she'd gone to work managing an Abilene saloon. She'd been bitter and angry toward men, but at the same time, was as feisty and lusty a woman as he'd ever known, and they'd spent more than a few satisfying nights together before he'd moved on. Then some months later he'd run into her again, down in Texas. She'd gotten herself married to the owner of the Yellow Rose Saloon, and she sang and danced onstage twice a week—until her second husband got himself shot dead during a saloon brawl. Not many days later she discovered that the place was mortgaged to the hilt, and after the funeral expenses were paid and the cost of repairs taken into consideration, there was nothing left to pay the mortgage and she was forced to turn over the deed.

So she'd gone to work as a prostitute for Madam Lola's brothel—and Quinn, after having spent a pleasant few days and nights in her company following his round-up of the notorious Stark gang, lost touch with her until he'd hit Hope a couple of years ago to scout out his newly acquired property and found her the owner of her very own boardinghouse.

Fate had seemed to throw them together time and time again, and Quinn had thought once or twice that if ever he were to settle down, it would have to be with Serena or someone like her, someone who had known nearly as rough a life as he had, someone who understood that some people weren't meant to put down roots, that nothing good ever lasted, that you should only rely on yourself.

Someone who didn't trust, didn't need, didn't want anyone else—except as a useful and pleasant distraction when the night was cold and the urge for human companionship got the better of your good judgment.

"Why, Quinn, honey, don't be silly. I don't want anything from you—I just want to say that you surprise me. You've been in Hope for quite a spell now and not once—not *once,* mind you—have you come calling at my door. Down south where I come from, folks know that's no way for an old friend to behave."

He recognized the teasing tone, the luscious, red-mouthed smile that was pure invitation. Once, he would have taken her up on that invitation without a second thought, but tonight he just wished she hadn't waylaid him. His mind, for some reason, was fixed on Maura.

He hadn't been able to stop thinking how downright scrumptious she looked in that soft yellow dress. Had she really not known how good she looked? She was just lucky he'd let her keep all those pins in her hair, the ones holding it off her face. He'd been tempted to slide them out one by one and watch the curls come tumbling down.

The gown would have fallen to the floor directly after—and then they might have missed the whole damn party.

He knew how much going to this party meant to her—and now he hadn't even been able to see if she was enjoying it, because Serena had taken it into her head to corral him.

"I'm a married man now, Serena," he said coolly. "It wouldn't be fitting for me to come calling."

"Quinn Lassiter—don't tell me you give a fig about respectability! Or appearances!" Her laugh echoed through the leaves. "I don't believe it."

"It's not what anyone else thinks I give a fig—or a damn—about." He leaned against a tree and watched her from beneath the brim of his hat. He knew most men would be enticed by the swell of her bosom and the way the low-cut violet dress hugged her curves, and once he would have been, too, but tonight all he could think was that he'd been tied up by Serena long enough—and he wanted to get back to Maura.

"Right is right. And calling on you just wouldn't be right."

"I suppose not, honey, seeing as you've gotten yourself married and there's a baby on the way. But tell me, Quinn, is that why you married her? Because you had to?'' Serena inched closer, lifting her face slyly to his. ''It is, isn't it?''

''None of your business, Serena.''

''But you and that skinny red-haired girl don't suit. She's just like those other boring, uppity women in that Hope Sewing Circle. Too snooty and respectable for the likes of us.'' She gave a sharp laugh that somehow rang hollow. ''Do you know they asked her to join when she'd only been in town a few weeks—and *I've* been running my boardinghouse for two damn years? I stuck like glue to this town through all the trouble, and I'm *still* not good enough for them!''

''That's not exactly Maura's fault.'' Quinn spoke curtly. ''If you've got a beef with the womenfolk of Hope, take it up with them, but leave Maura out of it.'' He started to move away. ''I have to find my wife.''

She grabbed his arm. ''But Quinn, honey, why? Why would you of all men want to get married—least of all to her! You can never be happy with her. I know you. You like to ride off at the drop of a hat, go where the wind blows you. Try as I might, I can't picture you with a bawling infant on your knee and—''

She broke off suddenly and drew in a deep breath. ''Unless you're in love with her?'' She gaped at him. He *appeared* as nonchalant and in control as always, but a faint flush darkened his skin in the moonlight. ''Oh, Lord, Quinn, no! *Are* you?''

''You know me better than that.'' His tone couldn't have sounded more dismissive. And yet . . .

''I surely thought I did. But—'' A terrible uncertainty

assailed her. Here she'd thought Quinn was as doomed as she to a life as a loner, an outcast, always on the edge, and now . . .

Was he truly becoming this upstanding family man, devoted to one woman, a woman who—in Serena's opinion—was as ordinary as spit? Oh, she was pretty enough, in her simple, refined way, and she did have a quiet manner about her, which she supposed might be appealing to certain men . . . but to Quinn?

"Reckon it's time we went in," Quinn muttered.

"Lord have mercy on me, I never would have thought I'd see the day that Quinn Lassiter would fall in love. You are, aren't you, Quinn? Gracious, what kind of a spell did that girl cast on you?" She chortled out loud, trying to sound amused and mildly contemptuous, but it came out bitter instead.

And it died away completely under the blistering stare he gave her.

"Well, Quinn, honey, you don't have to look so—so put out," she blustered. "I didn't mean anything—"

But she was speaking to the darkness. Quinn had stalked away without another word.

Maura felt ill. It was not due to her pregnancy—those symptoms had eased in the past day or two, as had the light-headedness. Nevertheless she had to push down the nausea that rose in her throat as she gripped the railing so tightly, her knuckles gleamed ivory in the moonlight.

From beneath the canopy of trees, Quinn's and Serena's voices drifted indistinctly to her, like fog swirling over a night-shadowed street. Then the front door burst open and Nell Hicks flounced out. "I *hate* him!" she muttered to no one in particular.

Catching sight of Maura, the black-haired girl rushed forward. "I wish your husband would fire Lucky Johnson and he'd move on to some other town!" she declared.

Sick at heart, Maura tried to focus her attention on Nell. The girl's cheeks were flushed an even brighter pink than her gown, and there was the glimmer of tears in her eyes.

"Oh, Nell, I'm sorry." She swallowed. "What has Lucky done now?"

Nell threw herself disconsolately into one of the porch chairs. "He danced with you. He danced with Orchid. He danced with Willa Carmichael and with Serena Walsh. He bumped into me while I was dancing with Cutter Miles and had the nerve to laugh when he begged my pardon. Not ten minutes later he walked right up to me as if he was planning to ask me to dance, and then he asked Miss Ellis—who was standing right behind me—instead. He did it on purpose. He was trying to humiliate me!"

"No, I'm sure he wouldn't do anything like that."

"Like *hell* he wouldn't!" Nell blushed even as she said the words, but her expression remained thunderous. "Well, if he thinks for one minute that I would even *consider* dancing with him, he can think again. I'd spit in his face if he asked me. I'd laugh myself silly. I'd sooner dance with a rattlesnake. Oh . . . Tex!" She beamed as the tall, towheaded cowhand strode out onto the porch.

"You're just the man I was looking for."

Maura noticed that just behind Tex, Lucky and Orchid were stepping onto the porch. Obviously, Nell had seen them too. They were arm in arm and looked as if they'd intended to slip off into the darkness together.

"I believe I lost my handkerchief when I was out strolling with Slim a little while ago," Nell plunged blithely on. Her blue eyes positively glowed into Tex's twinkling brown ones.

"Would you mind helping me search for it? Somewhere over there . . ." She waved a hand to her left, where Alice Tyler's vegetable garden gave way to a belt of graceful willow trees.

"Sure as shootin', Nell. Can't think of a single thing I'd like better than lending a helping hand to a pretty lady." Gallantly, Tex tucked her arm in the crook of his and led her toward the knot of trees.

Lucky's gaze followed them, his mouth twisting into a disgusted scowl as Nell's laughter drifted back to those on the porch.

"Come on, Orchid." But he sounded glum as he tugged her in the opposite direction, toward the trees that flanked the other side of the porch.

Suddenly Maura couldn't bear to be outside another moment, knowing that Quinn and Serena were still huddled beneath the trees. Perhaps they were waiting for Orchid and Lucky to pass by before returning to the house—or perhaps they were too engrossed in each other to notice if anyone else was around.

She spun about and rushed back inside, fighting the churning in her stomach, trying to push away all the ugly, unsettling thoughts. This did her no good—it did the baby no good. And being angry with Quinn would do no good. He couldn't help it if he felt more of a kinship with Serena than with her, if their past relationship and their feelings for one another formed a deeper bond than he was able to form with his practically shotgun bride—

"Grady!" She nearly ran into the lanky, gold-haired ranch hand standing beside the dance floor. She clutched his arm, then took a deep breath and offered her most dazzling smile. "Dance with me? I . . . I feel a sudden urge to waltz."

"My pleasure, Miz Lassiter." His sea-green eyes beamed into hers. "But don't tell Mr. Lassiter, you hear?" he added with a grin. He clutched at his heart. "Ma'am, I'm too young to die."

He led her into the throng of dancers. Maura scarcely heard the music, or his light, gallant compliments as they entered into the dance. Her heart was heavy as she pasted a smile on her face and responded mechanically to all of his pleasantries. If only he knew that Quinn would scarcely care if she danced with every man in the room. No doubt he wouldn't even notice!

Well, she *would* dance with every man in the room, she decided desperately, tossing her head. She flashed Grady what she hoped was a tantalizing smile, and fluttered her eyelashes as he swept her across the floor. She'd dance till her feet fell off before she'd let Quinn Lassiter see that she cared a button about his going off into the night with Serena Walsh . . .

"Reckon I'd like a dance with my wife." Quinn's cold gray eyes pinioned Grady, even as his hand descended hard on the ranch hand's shoulder, halting him in midstep upon the dance floor.

Grady took one look at that hard face and began to nod. "S-sure. I mean, yes, *sir,* Mr. Lassiter."

He threw Maura a nervous smile, his hand dropping

from her waist. But she wasn't looking at him. She was gazing at her husband and her face had gone pale.

"Much obliged for the pleasure, Miz Lassiter, ma'am," he gulped, and loped off to find the nearest bottle of whiskey.

"May I?" Quinn didn't wait for an answer, but stepped closer, his face purposeful in the bright glow of lamplight. Suddenly, as he grasped her hand, Maura couldn't breathe.

A short time ago she would have been overjoyed to see him gazing at her this way, with that intense light in his eyes. She'd have flown into his arms with her heart soaring, but now all the magic had drained out of the night and out of her heart.

"If you wish," she murmured coolly, and saw his eyes darken.

"You've danced with half the men here." He swept her abruptly into his arms and drew her close and tight as the music wove around them. "Like it or not, angel, now it's my turn."

Chapter 27

 IT WAS A WALTZ.

The musicians were slightly off-key, but they straightened themselves out as the dance progressed. At any other time, merely the pressure of Quinn's strong hand at her waist, her own fingers clasped within his, their bodies so close, she could feel the heat of him and the beat of his heart, would have filled her with a pure dazzling pleasure. But tonight it filled her with an almost unbearable ache. She ached for the one thing she could not have. His love.

She was a fool. She never should have allowed herself to fall in love with him. Allowed? She hadn't been able to help it. It had been as natural and inevitable as water spilling over the lip of a mountain in a gushing, unstoppable rush. Head over heels, she had tumbled, and there was no stopping it now.

"Care to explain?" His deep voice cut through the despair swirling through her. To her amazement, his face was a taut, angry mask. What did *he* have to be angry about? Maura wondered, choking back the urge to hysterical laughter.

"Explain what, Quinn? I have no idea what you mean."

His grip on her hand tightened, yet he took care not to crush her fingers. "Why you've danced with damn near every man here and not once with me."

"They all asked me. You didn't."

"That's not the point." He scowled down at her as they swept together across the floor. "You're my wife. How do you think it looks—"

"Since when do you care about how things look?" she countered, her eyes flashing. "And how do you think it will look when you leave me to go gallivanting around, hiring out your gun, disappearing for months."

"That's different."

She gave a high, tight laugh. "I don't see how. You can do what you please, but I cannot? *You* didn't ask me to dance, but I should be expected to sit around and wait while you sneak into the bushes with Serena Walsh . . ."

"Sneak?" His eyes narrowed and a dangerous gleam entered them. "Into the *bushes?* Like hell. We didn't sneak anywhere. We just—"

"No, don't tell me. I'm sure I don't care."

"We straightened a few things out. That's all."

She was gazing across the dance floor, her gaze fixed resolutely on the musicians. "You needn't explain anything to me, Quinn."

"I only want you to know—"

"Don't trouble yourself." She struggled to keep her tone cool. Distant. "I understand—perfectly."

"Oh, yeah? Exactly what is it that you understand?" He glowered down at her, wishing he could see more of her than the top of her head, the tilt of that stubborn little chin.

"Everything."

"What the hell does that mean?"

Maura felt her composure falling apart. The ache in her heart threatened to explode right through her chest, and she took a deep, steadying breath before lifting her gaze to meet his eyes again.

"You and Serena are old friends. Old friends like to spend time together. You hardly owe me any explanations—especially considering the way things are between us—"

"And just how are things between us, Maura?" he interrupted sharply.

"Just as we both want them to be." Somehow she managed to hide her misery beneath an indifferent facade. Yet it cost her dearly. "Friendly, agreeable. That's all. For the sake of the baby."

"Right, but . . . I reckon I thought . . ." Unwittingly, he tightened his grip on her hand and didn't realize it until he felt her wince. Then he loosened his grasp, gritted his teeth, and damn near stepped on her foot.

"Sorry."

"You missed me. But I guess you would have owed me that one," she said tightly. She angled her head up at him, trying to muster a normal, natural smile even though her face felt as if it were about to crack. "I hope you've noticed that I haven't stepped on your feet once so far. Are you suitably impressed?"

"Maura, everything about you impresses me. But you're changing the subject."

Swiftly, she searched those enigmatic silver eyes. "Go on," she said quietly.

"You know what you said about the way things are between us?" Quinn plunged ahead. "It seems to me that things aren't always as simple as they appear. Or as we want them to be."

Now what did that mean? But before she could ask him, the music ground to a halt and Quinn slowly ended the dance. Yet their bodies remained close together, their hands stayed clasped in the pose of the waltz.

Watching them, a glass of brandy clutched in her fingers, Serena Walsh frowned. Even from this distance she could see what perhaps the two of them could not.

Maura saw only the dark intensity of Quinn's face. Their eyes were locked upon one another, their hearts beat together, and in her mind his last words repeated themselves.

Things aren't always as simple as they appear.

"What . . . do you mean, Quinn?" she whispered, her heart in her throat, but before he could answer, Edna Weaver's voice crackled in her ear.

"Maura, honey, supper will be served directly, but Alice needs a hand setting out the pies. Want to pitch in?"

"Yes, I'd love to, Edna, but . . . in a moment . . ."

Edna chuckled and tucked her arm through the younger woman's as if she hadn't heard. "I'll just borrow her for a short spell," she promised Quinn as she drew Maura away.

Maura glanced back, studying Quinn wordlessly as Edna led her across the floor.

He stood in the middle of the dance floor, amidst the throng of men and women, his gray gaze nailed upon her.

A feast had been arrayed for the guests on creamy linen draped over long tables set outdoors. More colored lanterns festooned the surrounding trees and the back porch, and numerous chairs and smaller tables had been moved from inside to out and the latter adorned with bright red cloths and vases of flowers. The night smelled of wildflowers and perfume and damp earth, mingling with the even more pungent and delicious aromas of cooked venison and barbecued steak, fried chicken, platters of mashed potatoes and brown gravy, fresh-baked rolls, corn bread, and assorted cookies, pies, and cakes.

Maura scarcely noticed any of the tantalizing scents, or the charm of the setting. As she set a platter of lemon cookies beside a rhubarb pie, she couldn't stop thinking of Quinn, wondering what he'd been about to say. Yet to her frustration, her thoughts were interrupted by Grace and Carolyn speaking to each other as they carried pitchers of lemonade to several small round tables near the garden.

"I say we take a vote never to admit Serena Walsh!" Carolyn exclaimed. "That woman thinks she can run around bold as brass and behave like some kind of saloon lightskirt and we'll accept her into Hope society because she owns a dozen books!"

"She told me she'd be happy to show us her library if we cared to hold our next meeting of the Hope Sewing Circle at her boardinghouse." Grace sighed. "It's clear she's angling to be on the library committee."

"Well, I wouldn't blame Maura Lassiter one bit if she dropped out were we even to consider stepping foot inside the Walsh boardinghouse, much less admitting that woman to our circle—''

"Pardon me, but I couldn't help overhearing.'' Maura had approached them soundlessly and neither woman had noticed her presence until she spoke. They both whirled around to stare at her, their gowns rustling. Both Grace and Carolyn turned the same shade of red as the table-cloths.

From the corner of the front porch, where she'd been standing unseen, smoking one of the little cigarillos her newest boarder had given her, Serena Walsh went very still.

"It seems there is some misunderstanding,'' Maura said quietly. "I have nothing against Serena Walsh. If we wish to hold a meeting at her boardinghouse, I'd be perfectly willing to attend.''

"You would?'' Carolyn gaped at her, and plucked nervously at her russet gown. "But . . . my dear Maura . . .''

"Why not?'' Maura glanced from one woman to the other. She might not care for Serena Walsh, she might wish Quinn didn't have this connection with her, but she knew too well what it felt like to be on the outside looking in to want the woman shunned on her account.

"The dress she's wearing tonight is stunning. Does anyone know if it was store-bought or if she made it herself?''

"She made it herself.'' Grace smoothed the skirt of her own dark navy gown. "She makes nearly all of her clothes herself. I do believe she's trying to prove to us that she's worthy to join our circle.''

"As if skill alone is enough!" Carolyn broke in waspishly.

"Why is it, exactly, that you feel she's unsuitable?" Maura asked.

"Well, she . . . she smokes cigars. She socializes with the men who stay at her establishment, and . . . she conducts herself in a questionable manner and appears by all accounts to be a loose woman! Only look at the way she traipsed around in the darkness tonight with your husband—" Carolyn gasped and clasped a hand to her throat, encased in russet lace. "Oh, dear . . ."

"Carolyn!" Grace moaned, and turned distressed eyes to Maura.

Somehow Maura managed a careless shrug. "If you mean that private little talk they had, please don't think badly of her for *that*." She forced herself to speak with offhand calm. "Quinn and Serena are old friends, and Serena . . . needed his advice about a problem. I certainly didn't mind their going off together to discuss it. He's scarcely seen her since we moved to Hope, what with getting Sage Creek Ranch up and running and chasing after the Campbells and trying to build another room onto the cabin."

"So you . . . you like Serena Walsh?" Grace asked.

Maura turned and began casually surveying the tables. "I wouldn't want her—or anyone—shut out from the sewing circle on my account. That's all I'm . . ."

Before she could finish the sentence a piercing scream shattered the night.

For one awful moment all three women froze, and then another scream came—a shriek of terror echoing from deep within the knot of willows to the left of the porch, a shriek so earsplitting that shivers pricked like needles across the back of Maura's neck.

"My Lord!" Grace gasped.

Maura started to run, past the vegetable garden, toward the trees.

"Wait!" Carolyn screeched after her. "Maura, good gracious, don't go out there, it could be—"

But she was already racing into the deeper dimness of the willows, along the same path that Nell and Tex had taken.

That scream had sounded like it belonged to Nell Hicks.

She wasn't thinking of anything except that Nell must need help. If it was the Campbells again—she couldn't bear the thought of them dragging that girl off, of her fear and panic. Others must have had the same idea, for she heard the sounds of people running behind her, but Maura never slowed, darting through the darkness, stumbling over rocks and tree roots, straining to see ahead of her through the leaf-shrouded dimness even as more screams rang out, echoing through the night.

Her breath lodged in her throat as she at last glimpsed two figures standing close together, still as stone, ahead of her.

Her footsteps slowed. Nell and Tex were staring up, up, up at the overhanging limb of a pine tree. As Maura watched, Tex began trying to tug Nell away, but the girl was planted there in shock, screaming, unable to stop.

Maura peered up—and the world dimmed to a misty gray. Her hands flew to her throat and she closed her eyes, willing the grisly sight away.

"Oh . . . my . . . God."

Two men hung upside down from the tree limb, bound by their ankles, their arms roped at their sides. Beneath them, puddles of blood flowed through the dark grass, shining black in the moonlight. Their faces . . .

She closed her eyes again, swaying as Nell's continued screams rang in her ears. She'd never forget their faces. Their throats had been slit. They were dead . . . dead . . . dead . . .

"Maura!"

Quinn's arms wrapped around her, yanking her away as her own legs gave out beneath her.

She leaned into him, closing her eyes, fighting the nausea, trying to block the horrible images from her mind.

Judd and Homer would never bully anyone again.

Chapter 28

MAURA DIDN'T SPEAK A WORD DURING THE ENTIRE drive home. Nor did she so much as murmur when Quinn carried her into the bedroom, helped her out of her clothes, and eased her down upon the mattress.

"Try not to think about it, any of it. You hear me, sweetheart?" He knelt down beside the bed and carefully removed the few remaining pins from her hair, letting the bright curls spill freely around her pale cheeks. Her skin was almost as white as her nightgown, and when he stroked her cheek with his fingers, it felt ice-cold to the touch.

Pain tore at him as he studied her stunned face. He hated seeing her like this, silent, agonized, paralyzed with shock and horror. But it was too soon, he knew, for her to do more than absorb what she'd seen. The best thing would be for her to rest, stay quiet, and let the blow sink in.

"Get some sleep, Maura. That's all you need to do now. Sleep. There's plenty of time to think about it tomorrow."

She nodded, clutched his hand, and stared at him with those wide, frightened eyes. That's when he climbed into the bed beside her and pulled her close, just holding her until her tense body grew slack alongside his and he felt her drifting at last into the blessed escape of sleep.

Hours later, Quinn bolted up in the bed. He knew he was alone even before he glanced around the bedroom and saw that Maura was nowhere to be found.

"Maura!"

Panic tightened his chest, but he kept it at bay. The Campbells could hardly have invaded the cabin and dragged her off without a sound. He was amazed that she'd even been able to slip away without his noticing— light sleeping was one of the things that had kept him alive all these years.

And why had she slipped away? That was the question. The night might be warm and fragrant with spring grass and flowers, but it held danger as surely as a grizzly's jaws.

Judd and Homer Duncan could attest to that.

His footsteps made no sound in the darkness as he left the empty cabin, circled the bunkhouse and barn, checked the shed, the corrals, and then on a hunch doubled back through the trees toward the creek.

He stopped, sucking in his breath as he saw her on the bank, near the exact spot where they'd first met Lucky Johnson the day they'd arrived at the cabin.

She was sitting with her back against a tree, staring out at the softly gurgling water.

"What the hell are you doing out here?" Fear for her thickened his voice with anger.

The startled half gasp, half scream she gave did nothing to dissipate it. What if it had been the Campbells who'd happened on her there? Or whoever had butchered her brothers?

"You should . . . never . . . sneak up on a woman who's expecting a child!" she gasped, her eyes glassy in the night.

She wore only her nightgown and her ragged old shawl. Despite the odd combination, he thought she'd never looked more alluring. He wanted to pull the shawl slowly away from her shoulders, slip the nightgown off, and make love to her on the sweet-scented grass, but instead he hunkered down beside her and spoke with curt command.

"Come on. I'm taking you back to the cabin."

"I can't go back there."

"Want to bet?"

Misery shimmered from the depths of her eyes. "I can't breathe in there, Quinn, much less sleep. I keep thinking about it . . . about them. . . ."

"Then don't. Leave it till morning."

She shook her head. "Perhaps you can turn off your thoughts the way one extinguishes a lamp, but I can't. I see it all every time I close my eyes. I see their faces, the tree, the blood—"

He sat alongside her and drew her into his arms. There was no way of knowing if her shivering was caused by the nip in the night air or by the horrors racing through her mind, but he knew it felt good to hold her, and that he wanted to soothe her hurts, ease her fears, banish the cloud of desolation that filmed those hauntingly lovely eyes.

"Who would have done this, Quinn?" she whispered

desperately against his shoulder. "Not the Campbells. They had nothing against Judd and Homer—and besides, they'd have simply shot them, wouldn't they?"

"Seems likely. Did the Duncan boys have any enemies?"

"Many, I'm sure." She drew in a shaky breath. "But they were feared by everyone they terrorized—I don't know who would have had the courage to go up against both of them. And here—in Wyoming? Their enemies would have been much closer to home."

A shudder ran through her.

"You're cold," Quinn said sharply. "We've got to go back—"

"No!" She lifted pain-filled eyes to his. "I need the open sky, the stars. Air. Don't you know what I mean?"

He nodded. The wildness and beauty of the open night soothed. Better than whiskey, better than fighting with gun or fists, better even than a long, punishing ride—or a heady tumble with a woman. The night cleared the brain and eased the soul.

But a woman in the night, Quinn thought, stroking Maura's soft, fragrant curls, a woman in the wild night could cure a man of anything that ailed him.

As if reading his mind, Maura inched closer. Her hands lifted to rest softly upon his chest. The warmth of her fingers sent a shock roiling through him.

"Make love to me, Quinn," she breathed. "Make me forget everything."

He knew he should take her back to the cabin. He knew he should set her down before a log fire and make her drink some tea. Wrap a blanket around her shoulders and let her settle in her own good time.

"Please." The word slid through him like a knife thrust. "I need to forget. And," she said softly, desperately, "to remember."

And in that instant he knew she was recalling the raw passion and unexplainable tenderness of their first night together in the Duncan Hotel.

Their eyes met, held. Then it was as if a dark, hot current jolted between them and she was in his arms, in his blood, and there was no stopping what was happening between them. A bond of something beyond their control fused them in fire, and when Quinn lowered her to the cool, soft grass and heard her cry out his name, the world became a blur of heat and need and dark sensation.

"Damned if I can refuse you anything, angel," he muttered thickly. He couldn't see her dainty freckles in the sheen of the moonlight, but he kissed each one where he remembered it to be, his lips trailing like match flames down her throat, and when he slid the shawl and gown from her body, his own response was fierce and immediate as he drank in the sight of her pale satin skin glimmering in the moonlight, her eyes soft and shining with desire.

Maura was too desperate to think beyond the moment. As she threaded her hands through the thick silk of his hair, she knew only that she loved him with all her heart, that there was too much grief and sadness and cruelty in the world, and that love should be embraced, celebrated, and cherished.

She wanted to tell him she loved him, but the words died in her throat. So she told him with deep, slow kisses that sought to devour the distance between them. She pressed close against him, needy and giving all at once, and when Quinn's hands slid around her breasts, when his teeth began to tug gently at her nipple, she responded with a half-crazed moan and her own hands explored his taut body with ever-growing urgency. They skimmed over iron-hard thighs and found his swollen manhood.

How magnificent he was—this gunfighter with the silver eyes and the body like weathered rock and the strong mouth capable of such hot, tender kisses. His sharply indrawn breath at her touches made her ever bolder—the knowledge that she was driving him as mad as he was driving her sent a flood of delicious power and stunning need through her.

The storm built between them, wild and driving, and together they began to writhe as tender touches gave way to fierce, clinging, seeking thrusts. As Quinn's weight covered every inch of her and his hands brought even the most hidden, sensitive places vibrantly to life, Maura's senses tumbled and whirled. She wanted him, all of him, more than she had ever wanted anything before—she wanted him and the wild cold night and the sweet scent of grass mingling with their sweat and with their desire.

Far above Quinn's broad shoulders, stars whirled through the ebony sky like diamonds scattered across a midnight sea. The wind lifted her hair, cooled her hot skin, and when Quinn thrust deep inside her, his eyes blazing into hers, she knew only a single-minded love that drove everything else on earth into oblivion.

"Quinn—I . . . I . . ."

I love you, she yearned to say, but she caught the words back on a sob as he plunged into her, powerful, sublime thrusts that touched the core of her being again and again and again. "I need you," she gasped, dizzy with the sweet agonizing tension that locked her body in its merciless grip. "I need you so," she cried as wild sensation after sensation swamped her.

His hands were tangled in her hair, his breath rough and hot on her face. "I need you, too, Maura. Damn it, I don't want to . . . I've never needed any woman . . . not like this."

Aching hope and wonder filled her. "Quinn, really? Truly?"

"You make me want to promise things I never thought I would," he groaned. He rained kisses on her, their bodies moving desperately together. "Oh, hell, what are you doing to me, Maura Jane? My sweet, beautiful Maura Jane."

"It's nothing, Quinn, compared to what . . . you're doing to me." He caught her mouth in a bruising kiss and Maura gave herself up to the joy licking through her. She felt his strength and his need crushing down upon her as together they rolled and wrestled and rocked upon the grass, locked in a fierce frenzy that built to a peak so intense, it left them both shuddering. Breathless and gasping, they held on to each other for dear life and toppled over the crest of a mountain so high, it skimmed the stars.

Flying, soaring, Maura clung to him, wordless cries tumbling from her lips, the taste of him on her mouth, the strength of him clenched within her. *Glorious,* she thought as they raced together into hot, biting flames and gave themselves up to the fire.

When the flames flickered down and the smoke cleared like fairy mist and the mountain retreated to a dizzying blur, they lay enfolded and spent in each other's arms. Caught in the grip of sated bliss, they rested, entwined, beneath the silent moon and held on to each fragile moment of togetherness. Silently, each dreaded the breaking of the spell.

It came, of course, all too soon when a hawk wheeled overhead, dipped, circled, and flapped away. Somehow as it crossed the sky, the magic ebbed and reality flowed back. They felt the hard ground beneath them, the cold air seeping over their naked bodies. The sensation of being exposed and vulnerable not only to the beauty of the night, but to human danger, descended upon them, and heaven fled.

Maura stirred first and sat up. Quinn moved faster though. He came to his feet in a smooth uncoiling movement, tossed her the nightgown and shawl, and reached for his pants.

They dressed in silence, all too aware of each other, with memories vibrating between them. But when Maura turned from the creekbank and began to walk back, Quinn stopped her. He scooped her into his arms and without a word carried her through the trees and across the dark, fragrant grass to the cabin.

Chapter 29

 THE NEXT WEEK PASSED QUIETLY. THE IMAGE OF
her murdered brothers haunted Maura from
time to time as she cooked and tended to her
chores, but she was saddened to discover that she felt no
real grief. She hadn't loved Judd and Homer—they'd
never been kind or decent enough to endear themselves to
her or to anyone, perhaps not even to Ma Duncan—but
she mourned the brutality of their deaths and the suffering they must have known.

And like everyone else who had been at the Tyler party
that evening, and everyone who heard what had happened, she wondered just who had committed those brutal
murders—and why.

John Hicks had sent a telegram to the federal marshal
in Laramie notifying him of the crime. He'd also de-
scribed the rampages of the Campbell gang and made a
plea that a lawman be sent to Hope at the earliest opportunity to reassure the citizens and restore law and order.

Days had passed and there had been no reply.

But Quinn took no chances. He left standing orders
that when he was gone from the ranch, at least two ranch

hands remain within shouting distance of the cabin at all times.

Maura tried to tell him that whoever had borne a grudge against Judd and Homer could hardly have one against her as well—and certainly wouldn't know how to find her if they did—but she might as well have been speaking to the meadowlark that sang every morning outside the cabin window for all the good it did her.

And even when she reminded him that the Campbells appeared to have left the vicinity—no one had spotted them in weeks—Quinn just went on cleaning his gun or saddling his horse or chopping wood, as if she hadn't spoken at all.

One bright May morning when the sky gleamed like a sapphire and puffy white clouds danced a slow ballet, they prepared to drive into Hope for supplies.

Just before she went out to the wagon, while she was tying the strings of her bonnet, Lucky Johnson knocked on the cabin door.

When she let him in, she was startled by the grim expression on his youthful face as he tugged off his hat and nearly crushed it in his hands.

"Lucky—what is it? What's happened now?"

"Nothing." He stomped inside, glared around the cabin at nothing in particular, then shrugged.

"You look like someone shot your best friend."

"I do?" He scowled. "Well, nothing's wrong. Everything's dandy. Everything's just as dandy as can be."

"Then why are you here?" Maura asked, torn between amusement and concern. "Do you need something from town?"

"I surely do," he muttered, half to himself, then

glanced at her and flushed at her puzzled expression. He reached into his pocket and dug out a folded scrap of paper. "I'd be obliged if you'd give this to Nell Hicks for me."

Maura stared at the folded paper, then at Lucky's brick-red countenance. "Why, of course."

He started toward the door, but Maura couldn't resist asking a question. "Have you seen Nell since that night when she found . . . you know . . ."

"I rode into town once and tried to see her, but her pa said she was too upset to work downstairs in the store. And he wouldn't go up and get her." He scowled. "But Tex walked in just then and . . . Oh, never mind."

"What do you mean, Lucky? What did Tex have to do with anything?"

"Well, he was with her that night when she saw those two bodies hanging from that tree and I guess he's been coming to call on her ever since then. He had a handful of posies for her, gave them to Mr. Hicks right in front of me." The scowl deepened. "Hicks said: 'What, another bunch of 'em?' and he looked mighty pleased about it. Promised to bring them straight up to her."

"I see." Maura did see. Tex's attentions to Nell, and the fact that he himself had not been able to see her, were obviously not sitting well with Lucky Johnson.

"Perhaps you should take another ride into town yourself. I'm sure that by now Nell is back working in the store."

"The boss has other ideas. I've got cattle to round up in the north pasture. And tomorrow we're doing some building here at the cabin—me, Orville, and the boss. I won't be getting to town anytime soon."

He looked so glum that Maura reached out impulsively and patted his arm. "Oh, Lucky, don't you worry. I'll give Nell the note. She'll be glad to know you're thinking of her."

"I feel bad, that's all," he mumbled. "She's had a rough time of it—first with those Campbells, and then with what she saw. Ladies shouldn't see things like that, you know?"

"I know." Maura couldn't suppress a shudder.

"And I treated her bad. Rude-like. I don't know why, because I'm not usually like that with girls, but I just couldn't seem to help it."

Suddenly he straightened his shoulders and assumed a cocky stance. "But it doesn't matter none. I just thought that since you're going into town, you could give it to her—but on second thought"—he reached for the note Maura still held, his color deepening even further— "maybe it's not such a good idea."

"Lucky Johnson!" Maura exclaimed, thrusting the note behind her back before he could grab it. "You just go on out there and get to work. I'll take care of this note. Now scoot."

"But . . ." Doubtfully, he stared at her, as if contemplating the wisdom of reaching behind her and trying to take the note back.

"Scoot, I said!"

He scooted. Maura dropped the note into the pocket of her gingham gown, gave the spotless kitchen one final critical glance, and sailed out to the wagon.

Few words passed between her and Quinn as they drove into town. She commented on the beautiful, mild spring weather. He said that from the looks of the clouds in the distance, a storm would blow in within the next day. She mentioned that she'd like a chicken coop, and perhaps a pen to keep a pig or two, and he replied that he'd give the matter some thought.

"I've been thinking of something else," she said shortly before they began to climb the gentle rise just beyond the fringe of town. "Names."

Startled, he shifted his glance from the road to look at her.

"We need to decide upon a name for our baby," she explained patiently.

He swallowed. "Yeah, sure. I hadn't thought about . . . a name."

"Most people do have them," she pointed out gravely.

"Most," he concurred, a grin angling at the corner of his mouth. Then he shrugged. "Whatever name you pick is fine with me. But don't you want to wait and see if it's a boy or a girl?"

"Actually, I've been thinking of names for both a boy and a girl. It's always good to be prepared."

"I reckon it is, but there's plenty of time." He glanced at her belly. Beneath the gentle folds of the worn dress it was still nearly impossible to tell that she was carrying a child—aside from a slight rounded thickness around her middle, Maura didn't look much different than she had a month ago.

"There isn't as much time as you might think. When I saw Doc Perkins a few weeks back he said the baby would most likely be here sometime in October. Or early November, at the latest."

November. Quinn felt as if she'd dealt him a blow to the stomach. By November they'd be sharing the cabin with an infant. There would be crying, squalling, tiny clothes, booties. He tried to imagine it and felt only an uneasy tightening in his gut.

"Besides," Maura when on, when it became apparent he wasn't going to offer any further comment, "I love thinking about the baby. Edna has a hand-made crib that she used when her daughters were small and she said we can have it. Isn't that sweet? The sewing circle is working on a quilt and I'm going to start on some baby clothes," she rushed on happily. "And Quinn, I keep trying to imagine what he or she will be like—and look like."

Quinn felt sweat beading on his forehead. Honor had driven him to take responsibility for the child Maura would bear, but he'd be damned if he could get the least bit excited about it. More ties. More things to worry about. It was bad enough he thought about Maura night and day, that she had somehow started sneaking into his thoughts no matter where he was or what he was doing— herding cattle, fixing a fence post, or playing poker in the saloon.

Her face came to him at the oddest moments, her voice whispered in his ear. Making love to her was different than it was with any woman he'd ever known. Hotter, sweeter, more intense.

And afterward, he found himself enjoying those moments of holding her in his arms, inhaling the flower scent of her hair, her skin. Feeling her heart beating against his.

Whoa.

Things were getting out of hand. And he wasn't sure what to do about it. Ever since that night when they'd made love in the grass he'd kept his distance. He wanted her too much. That wasn't good. Wasn't right. Spending too much time with her, getting too comfortable in the damned cabin she kept fixing up and making brighter and cozier, what with needlework pillows, and flowered china cups all matching, and new curtains and thick rugs.

She brought out feelings in him, yearnings—and fears—he'd never known before. And what if the baby did the same?

It was a relief when Hope came into view. He forced his attention toward the look and mood of the town, alert to any sign of trouble. Horses tied to fence posts, rows of stores and shops, people striding up and down the street. Since the Campbells had been chased off the last time, folks seemed to feel more confident. The place was slowly coming to life again.

But Quinn didn't trust the quiet. He knew Lee and Ned and especially Luke too well. He hadn't outlived all his enemies by underestimating them. He'd have to see the Campbells six feet under before he'd even think about letting his guard down again.

"Reckon I'll stop by the mill and get more lumber. I'll come fetch you here at Hicks's when I'm done," he told Maura as he helped her alight before the general store.

"Quinn." She gazed up at him, and the wistfulness in her eyes seemed to stab right through him.

"Yeah?"

"You never asked me which names I'm thinking about for the baby. Don't you even want to know?"

A man shouldered past him, then a woman holding a small boy and girl each by the hand skirted around Maura. The horses snorted in the glowing sun. Quinn stared into his wife's exquisite eyes, feeling that part of him was sinking helplessly into their gold-flecked depths.

"Later," he managed to say gruffly, then stalked to the wagon and left her without looking back.

Maura gazed after him, a knot of sorrow burrowing deep inside her heart.

Why did she keep trying? It was no use.

Quinn was doing his duty and no more. When the baby came, she could only pray he would feel something for it, but as for loving her, or yearning to be a family the way she did . . .

It was time to stop dreaming. Some things were possible in this world, and some were not.

From the window high above the general store, a man watched the woman standing alone in the street. A slow smile lit his face. His palm had itched to pull his gun when he saw Quinn Lassiter driving that wagon, but time in prison had taught him patience and so he held off. He knew that sometimes it was better to wait.

He could have killed the woman and Lassiter from where he watched behind the curtain, but that would be too quick, too easy. Lassiter had to suffer—and suffer slow.

The woman went into the store.

He liked the way she moved, with a feminine sway to her hips that was at once graceful and alluring. He liked the way she looked. All that fine bright hair.

He hadn't seen much of her figure, but that would be remedied real soon.

Stroking his dirty straw-colored mustache, he turned from the window and nodded at his two cousins. They waited impatiently, watching his face, eagerness and bloodlust shining from their eyes. Ignoring the trussed-up storekeeper hog-tied to the chair against the wall, Luke Campbell addressed Lee.

"Get down there with the Hicks girl pronto. Lassiter's woman is on her way in."

Chapter 30

THE LITTLE BELL TINKLED OVERHEAD AS MAURA pushed open the shop door, but she halted on the threshold when she saw Serena Walsh inside, setting a basket of eggs over one arm.

Both Serena and Nell Hicks glanced over at her as soon as the bell tinkled, so she had no choice but to go on in.

"Good day, Nell," she began, then broke off. The girl looked dreadful. Her eyes were swollen and red as if she'd been crying, and there were huge dark circles beneath them.

Moreover, though she was tightly gripping the counter-top, as she looked at Maura her hands and arms began to shake, all the way up to her elbows.

"Good heavens, you haven't gotten over the shock yet," Maura exclaimed, rushing forward. "You poor child—"

"Mrs. Lassiter." Serena Walsh stepped forward, blocking her path. Maura was forced to stop and meet her gaze.

"I was wondering if I might have a few moments of

your time. I'd like to talk with you. When you're finished with your purchases, of course.''

Maura was still studying Nell and anxiety for the girl furrowed her brow. ''I don't have very much time,'' she said distractedly, ''but, yes, if you'd like. We could go to the hotel and have some tea when I'm done here. Then I could watch for my husband from the window. He's coming back for me.''

''I have a better idea. Why don't we have tea at my boardinghouse? I baked some almond butter cookies this morning. The sitting room overlooks the street so you can watch for Quinn.''

''Lovely.'' Maura was sure she did *not* want to hear anything Serena Walsh had to say, but there was no way out of it now. She sidestepped the woman and hurried to Nell, reaching for the girl's trembling hands to cradle them in her own. But suddenly the door to the back room burst open and two men charged out.

''Howdy, ladies,'' the taller of the two said with a snicker.

Maura's stomach clenched at the sight of them. Dirty gold stubble shadowed their faces—she guessed the men were brothers because they both had scraggly wheat-colored hair that fell in tangles past their narrow shoulders, and the same lidless olive eyes, beaked noses, and weak chins. The same pock-marked skin showing beneath weathered tans. The taller one had a jagged scar beneath his right eye and wore a gray hat with holes shot through it. The other man's Adam's apple stuck out like a rock.

Behind her Serena Walsh had gone very still. Nell was staring at the men in mute fear.

"Nell, what's going on? Who are these men?" Maura asked quickly.

The girl tore her gaze from them and stared at Maura, both misery and terror shimmering in her lime-green eyes. "Oh, Lord forgive me, I'm sorry, Mrs. Lassiter. So terribly sorry," she choked, "but they've got my pop tied up upstairs and they said that if I didn't do what they told me—"

"That's about enough out of you, girlie."

The taller brother with the gray hat lunged forward and wagged his finger under Nell's nose. "Not another word," he warned.

"Who are you?" Maura demanded, but inside she was going numb with terror. She already knew.

"Well, we might be this little lady's country cousins—Jimbo and John," the one with the protruding Adam's apple sneered. "Only we ain't."

"They're the Campbell brothers—Lee and Ned. The only ones left," Serena murmured behind Maura.

The taller one peered at her and snickered. "Right you are, ma'am. I'm Lee and this here is Ned. Real glad to make your acquaintance."

Suddenly they had guns in their hands. And they were pointing them at Maura.

"Let's go, little lady."

"What do you mean?" Maura stepped back. Instinctively her hand had swept toward her belly, as if to somehow protect the baby within, but she forced herself to lower her trembling fingers to her side. "What do you want with me?"

"Oh, you'll find out soon enough. Come on, we got us a long ride ahead."

"Forgive me," Nell sobbed, tears streaming down her cheeks. "I wanted to warn you but they said the other one would kill my pop!"

"Shut up!" Ned Campbell spun on her and knocked her backward. Then he stalked into the back room and shouted up the stairs. "Luke! We got 'er! Let's ride!"

Maura felt as if the world were spinning crazily around her. She thought of trying to run for the door, but she knew she wouldn't make it. She also knew the Campbells wouldn't hesitate to shoot her if she tried to get away. Hadn't they nearly run Alice Tyler down in the street—and tried to drag Nell off with them against her will?

They were ruthless men—and her husband's enemies.

She swallowed hard and tried to think.

"Look, boys, you don't want to rile Quinn Lassiter any more than you already have," she heard Serena saying in her soft drawl behind her. "If you take his wife—"

"He'll come after us. And we'll have him right where we want him," Lee crowed, grinning at her. "You want to come along, honey bun?"

Serena said nothing.

"Hey. Answer me!"

"No." Serena had barely breathed the word before Luke Campbell sauntered from the back stairway.

"Well, well, well." Insolently, he surveyed Maura, taking his time. "If it ain't Lassiter's purty little bride."

"He'll kill you," Maura whispered. "If you hurt me, he'll kill you. I'm carrying his child."

Suddenly a slender, frantic hope sparked inside her. "You wouldn't want to hurt a baby, would you?" she asked quickly, desperately, glancing from one cruel face to another.

Luke's hair was thinner and lighter than his cousins', a pale dirty mop that looked like it hadn't seen a washing since he was old enough to shave. He was leaner yet more muscular than the others and, if possible, even meaner-looking with his thin blistered lips and heavy brows. He'd been in prison, Maura remembered, her heart sinking. Quinn had put him there.

"If it's Lassiter's baby, it'll be a downright pleasure to hurt it."

Luke stepped closer and his smile would have chilled the sun. "And you, too, Mrs. Lassiter, ma'am. But mostly, I'm going to enjoy hurting your husband. I'm going to hurt him real bad—before I kill him."

"No!" The word burst from her in an agony of despair. But all it got her was three vile smiles of satisfaction.

"Let's go," Luke ordered his cousins.

"Wait," Nell cried. "My pop—is he all right? You promised . . ."

"Girlie, don't you *ever* shut up?" Lee grabbed Nell by the arm and dragged her out from behind the counter as Luke drew his gun and aimed it at Maura. "You're coming along too," he told Nell. "Last time you got lucky, but your luck just ran out."

Nell began to struggle, but Lee snaked an arm around her throat and dragged her along with him. Serena moved quickly as Luke shoved Maura toward the door. She reached out as if to steady the other woman, but Maura felt something thunk inside her pocket. For one brief instant her wide brown eyes met Serena's before Luke seized her elbow and pulled her past.

"Ned! Tie up our southern belle and gag her. And

you,'' he flung over his shoulder at Serena. ''When they find you, tell Lassiter that if he ever wants to see his little wife alive again, he'll come to Skull Rock at sunset tonight. Alone. If there's anyone with him, we'll put a bullet in her belly. Got that?''

Serena had gone as pale as Nell, as pale, Maura realized, as she must be herself. When Ned seized her roughly and yanked her arms behind her back, the blond-haired woman answered Luke stonily.

''I'll tell him, since you're too much of a coward to wait around and tell him yourself.''

Then Maura felt Luke's bony hand squeezing around her waist, dragging her close. The stench of sweat and unwashed flesh coming off him nearly made her dizzy.

''Let's go, darlin','' he rasped in her ear. His chuckle was as low and rough as bark scraped down a blackboard. ''We got us a ways to ride before the sun goes down.''

Chapter 31

 THE CLOUDS HAD DROPPED LOWER AND DARKENED to a dusky gray by the time Quinn finished stacking lumber in the wagon and walked over to the livery to appraise the new horses Jethro had to sell. He'd said he'd think it over, and had headed back toward the general store, restless for some reason he couldn't fathom.

Some instinct warned him something was off. The weather? The day had been so clear just a short while ago, but though the sun still shone, the storm seemed to be swooping in faster than he'd expected. It could be here by morning, maybe late tonight. Was it that—or something else?

He didn't know what was twisting at his gut—he only knew that he'd learned to trust his instincts years ago and it had always served him well.

By the time he reached the mercantile and saw Edna Weaver and Doc Perkins's wife, Mary, muttering to one another and pushing at the door, every muscle in his body had turned to lead.

"What's going on?" he demanded, striding up to them.

Edna whirled toward him, her face puckered with worry. "Hicks's is never closed this time of day. Grace was here just this morning, and said something about Nell being all riled up—still unsettled after finding those two dead men the other night. So I came over to see if I could comfort the girl, and found Mary here—unable to get in. The closed sign is hanging right there in the window—in the middle of the afternoon!"

"John Hicks! Nell!" Mary Perkins called loudly as she banged with her fist upon the door. "Open up now, will you?"

"Stand back."

The women scattered at the harshness of his tone. Quinn put a shoulder to the door and shoved it in. His chest was so tight, it hurt as he burst in and saw Serena bound and gagged on the floor in the corner beside the flour barrels.

He felt no surprise. The moment he'd seen the two women trying to get in the door, he'd known.

"It was the Campbells," Serena told him when he stripped the greasy yellow bandanna from her mouth. He worked at her bonds while she talked and the other women gasped and exclaimed.

"They took Maura and Nell."

"Where?" Waves of icy fear washed over Quinn as he waited for Serena to answer him.

"Skull Rock."

He sucked in his breath. Silence filled the store. They all knew the place. A lone high rock overlooking a barren canyon of scrub and sagebrush. No approach from any direction without being seen.

He spun about and was halfway to the door by the time Serena could call out to him in a hoarse voice.

"Wait, Quinn, that's not all!" She pushed herself to her feet and glanced at Edna. "John Hicks is upstairs. I don't know if they killed him or not, but someone should go up there and see."

"Serena." Quinn paid no heed as Edna Weaver and Mary Perkins gasped and started toward the back stairs. His marble-gray eyes, glinting with a merciless intensity, were fixed only on Serena's face. Never, in all her years, had she seen eyes so ruthless. Or heard a voice that sounded so cold, as cold as bitter, irrefutable death.

"Tell me exactly what the Campbells said."

"They said you're to come to Skull Rock at sunset. Alone. They said that if you brought anyone with you, they'd kill Maura. They mean it, Quinn," she added quickly. "I've never seen men so determined before, and believe me, I've seen all kinds. But it's a trap—you know it's a trap! If you go there, they'll kill all of you!"

"How many were they? How much head start did they have?"

"There were three of them—Luke, Ned, and Lee. They left me here maybe half an hour ago."

He swore, a string of epithets half under his breath, and started to swing away.

"Wait, Quinn." She reached out a shaky hand to clasp his arm. "You should know. I gave Maura my derringer just before they dragged her out. I dropped it into her pocket—maybe it will help."

"I'm obliged to you." His tone was soft, but so grim,

so filled with deadly fury lashed under a violent control, that Serena actually trembled and dropped her hand. For a moment she almost felt sorry for the Campbells—until she remembered that they had Quinn outnumbered, that from Skull Rock they could see his approach for miles, they could pick him off at any time, and he would be virtually helpless to fight back.

"What are you going to do?" she breathed.

His eyes narrowed to slits. "That's not fit for a lady to know."

He was out the door in three strides, cursing the fact that Thunder was back at the ranch and he'd have to take the piebald from the team. He'd reached the wagon, and was unhitching Nutmeg when he heard Edna Weaver rush up behind him.

"Hold on there, Mr. Lassiter. Please."

"No time." He led Nutmeg away from the rig as the sorrel, Pepper, nodded in the sun. "If this is about Hicks—"

"It isn't. But he's alive, thanks be to God. Those monsters didn't shoot him before they dragged off his daughter and your wife."

"Glad to hear it," he said between clenched teeth. Terror for Maura and their baby racked every muscle, throbbed through every inch of his tall, wide-shouldered frame. He could barely see straight as the knife blade of dread and rage and despair tore at him, but he knew as surely as he knew his name that this was not the time to panic—only cool, calm control and clear thinking could save the life of the woman he loved.

Loved. Emotion swamped him, making his palms sweat. Why had he never told her he loved her? *Why?*

Because he'd never even dared admit it to himself.

And now it might be too late—for both of them. No, he amended in agony, thinking of the child growing within Maura, the tiny life that belonged to them both. *It might be too late for them all.*

With desperate urgency pounding through him, he swung up onto the piebald, intending to stop at the livery for a saddle on his way out of town, but Edna wouldn't step out of the way.

"You can't go yet, Mr. Lassiter! This is important. It's about Skull Rock."

"What about it?"

"If you ride through the canyon you'll be killed. It's a trap—you know that, don't you?"

With the last thin shred of his patience, Quinn stared down at her, frantic to be off.

"I know it's a trap," he snarled. "It doesn't matter."

"What if I told you . . . there might be another way in?"

He went still. "In to Skull Rock?"

She nodded.

"There isn't," he said flatly. "When we were hunting for the Campbells, the posse and I covered every inch of that canyon and the ridges behind it. We saw every rock, every trail. There's no other way in."

"My husband knows one. And so do I. It was years ago—it was buried in a rockslide, but . . ." She moistened her lips. "It would take some work to get to it."

She tilted her head up at him and her bonnet skewed to one side of her gray head.

"Won't you come to the bank and talk to Seth? I do believe he can help."

Help. He'd never asked anyone for help with anything. It wasn't his way. He'd learned young that you couldn't count on anyone except yourself.

But calculating the odds, picturing Maura the prisoner of the Campbells, imagining what they might do to her, he suddenly couldn't dismiss Edna Weaver's offer out of hand.

Help.

Cold beads of sweat formed along his brow, sheened across his face as he looked into the woman's earnest eyes. He may never have asked anyone for help before, but this just might be a damned good time to start.

He swung off the piebald and tethered it quickly to the post.

Even as he did so, he heard the town start to stir and rumble as word of what had happened at Hicks's filtered down the street.

Time was slipping away. Quinn ran toward the bank, with Edna scurrying after him, clutching onto her bonnet.

"I think this might work," she gasped behind him. "It will take shovels, men, ropes—but maybe together we can save Maura and Nell . . ."

Quinn shoved the door of the bank open and stood aside for her to rush in ahead of him. "Get your husband out here pronto. Let's hear what he has to say."

Serena climbed her porch steps and ignored the calico cat that sauntered out from under the rocker to rub against her skirts. She managed to stumble wearily inside the door before collapsing on the maroon velvet settee in the hall.

For a moment she took several deep breaths, willing

herself to find the strength to get to the kitchen, fix herself a cup of coffee and lace it with some of the good brandy from the sideboard.

She'd been in some tight spots before and seen her share of ornery men, but never had she seen such black-hearted evil as had shown itself today in the faces of those Campbells.

She shuddered in sympathy for Maura Lassiter and Nell Hicks and thanked her lucky stars the outlaws hadn't taken her along too. She was immediately ashamed of her cowardice and selfishness, but shrugged it off. It was the truth. That was how she felt—but it didn't mean she wasn't worried about them, and didn't want them to get out of this alive. Hadn't she given Maura Lassiter her derringer? If they'd caught her doing it, no telling what they would have done.

Her head ached, especially at the temples. Like an anvil beating against her skull. She was just about to get up from the settee to fetch the coffee and the brandy when her newest boarder came strolling down the stairs.

"Something wrong, dear lady?" Mr. Ellers surveyed her with concern.

Roy Ellers was a gambler by profession. With his charming smile and enigmatic eyes, he had fascinated Serena from the day he first took a room several weeks ago. But she knew gamblers—men of that ilk liked to keep to themselves, and this Ellers was no different. She seldom saw him, except at mealtimes, and the only exceptions had been when he'd smoked an occasional cigar with her on the porch. He *had* participated in two or three of her nightly card games—and he'd always won. The rest of his time he seemed to spend in the saloon—gambling. And winning there as well, from the scraps she'd heard.

But she'd watched him whenever she had the chance. A slender, debonair man with a voice like honeyed tonic, he was particular about his appearance, his food, the view from his window. She had no idea where he'd come from or where he was headed, but she liked the way every single strand of his silky dark hair was always combed immaculately into place, the way every button on his gray fashionable coat and fancy embroidered vest shone, the way his boots sparkled like polished onyx.

And he always paid on time.

But now she had no strength to do anything beyond meet his raised brows and polite, curious gaze with a weary shrug. "There was some trouble at the general store. The Campbell gang came back to town."

"Oh? How unfortunate. Anyone hurt?" He didn't really appear all that interested, but he did stretch out a hand to help her as she rose, and she was grateful for the strength in those slender, beautiful fingers as they closed around her arm.

"Not yet, but they took two women as prisoners and rode off with them—and they left me tied to a barrel on the floor," she finished ruefully. "I'm in need of a drink."

"Indeed, I should think so." He gallantly gestured her ahead of him through the hall, then followed her into the kitchen.

"Who were the unfortunate women, may I ask?"

"Poor little Nell Hicks whose father owns the mercantile," she said, putting coffee on to brew. "And Maura Lassiter."

"You don't say."

He was silent as she related the story. But he poured the coffee for both of them and added a good dollop of brandy to her cup, though none to his own.

"Skull Rock?" He pursed his lips. "Hmmm, sounds like mighty poor odds for the ladies."

"You don't know Quinn Lassiter." Thankfully, Serena clasped both hands around her cup and drank down the bracing liquid. The brandy swirled hot and potent down her throat. "If anyone can get them out of that place alive, he can."

"Let's hope you're right." Ellers pulled something from his pocket and smiled at her. "I have a little gift for you. You've been such an accommodating landlady, and now you've gone through such an unpleasant ordeal. Perhaps you'd accept this as a token of my good-will."

She stared down at the small enamel box he put into her hands.

"It's a jewel box," he said softly. "Or I suppose you could use it to keep buttons," he added with a smile.

"Oh. How pretty. Thank you." After everything she'd gone through today, Serena had never expected to receive a gift, and such a nice one at that. Surprise and pleasure washed over her. "You've very kind, Mr. Ellers."

"It's nothing. I wish it were more," he said gently, his smile widening, showing beautiful even white teeth. "I wish that box was filled with diamonds. Perhaps one day soon, Mrs. Walsh, it will be."

Serena couldn't contain a snort of laughter. "I wouldn't bet on that, Mr. Ellers."

"Wouldn't you?" He took her hand. "Obviously, my dear, despite all your charms and ravishing attributes, you are not a gambler."

With his eyes twinkling like miniature blue stars, he kissed her hand.

Chapter 32

 "PLEASE. I NEED WATER."

Maura's whispered words were flung into the rising wind. For a moment she thought Luke Campbell, riding behind her in the saddle, couldn't hear her, but then she heard his voice rasp in her ear.

"Shut up, lady. You'll have to wait till we get there."

"Couldn't we just stop for a moment—"

"So Lassiter can catch us? We ain't stupid!"

"Please—"

"Shut up!" Shifting the reins to one hand as his horse pounded over the hard, rutted trail, Campbell grabbed Maura's hair and viciously yanked her head back against his shoulder. At her anguished cry, he shouted, "Keep your damned trap shut or you'll get worse than that!"

Tears sprang from her eyes as he released her with a grunt. With her hands tied to the pommel, she couldn't even wipe them from her cheeks. They streamed down her face as the outlaw whipped his horse to a furious gallop and they passed Lee, with Nell before him in the saddle—her hands tied to the pommel as well. Maura saw that the girl's green eyes were glazed with fear.

Rage for what they were doing to that young girl, as well as to herself, trembled through her. Helpless tears gathered in the corners of her eyes as the wind tore at her hair and flung dust into her face. She had no idea how long they'd been riding, but her entire body ached from jolting over rough trails, up and down hills and narrow twisting passes. Her wrists were chafed and bloody from the rope that bound them to the pommel. But she tried not to think of any of that. She tried to think only of Quinn.

Quinn would come after her. She knew that as surely as she knew that the sun would set, the moon would rise, and the mountains would tower over the prairie.

And when Quinn came—to help her, to save her—the Campbells would kill him.

Horror knifed through her heart. Her fear for him rose in her like a screaming storm tide. She fought it, fought the despair in her soul and tried to stay calm, but the thundering ride through this wild, merciless country went on forever and she knew that at the end of it there would be a trap, that pain and grief and death awaited them.

And what of her baby? Quinn's baby?

These men would not hesitate to slaughter either her or Nell—or the baby. They would stamp out their lives with no more care than they would give to stepping on an ant.

But she was stronger, tougher than they thought, Maura told herself as silent tears streamed down her cheeks. Love for her child and for Quinn swelled inside her.

Love is stronger than fear, she told herself fiercely. *Stronger than hate. Stronger than despair.*

If there was one thing she knew for certain, it was that Quinn wasn't giving up. He would never give up.

And neither will I, Maura vowed silently as the horse beneath her tore ever faster toward the lone mountain in the distance. *I'll fight them and Quinn will fight them— with everything we have.*

Lucky Johnson was driving two stray calves away from a ravine and toward the safety of a hillside where a dozen other cows grazed, when he heard the rumble of hooves. He twisted in the saddle and saw Slim riding hard right toward him, waving his hat over his head.

"Yahoo! Lucky! Trouble!"

The calves forgotten, he spurred Peaches forward.

"What now?"

"The boss sent word from town. It's the Campbells. They got Miz Lassiter—and Nell Hicks!"

Lucky nearly fell out of his saddle. The world around him went dark as he stared into the cowhand's flushed, sweat-streaked face. All of the Wyoming sunshine seemed to have been eaten up, then it returned in a flash, but dimmer, harsher than before.

"Where'd they take them?"

"Skull Rock—but wait!" Slim grabbed Lucky's arm as he started to swing his horse around in that direction. "Don't go riding off doing no fool thing. The boss has a plan—he sent me to find you and Orville and said we should meet him at Cougar Pass. Orville's already on his way, so come on, let's ride!"

Lucky couldn't move. Stunned, he stared after Slim, seeing not the lowering clouds in the sky, the dark, gritty puffs of dust, or Slim's narrow hunched shoulders as he crouched low in the saddle. All he could see was Nell's face—her hurt, stunned expression at that damned dance when he'd walked right past her and asked Orchid to dance with him instead.

He'd done it to spite her, to show her. And he'd never had the chance to dance with her that night, though that's all he'd really wanted to do. Now he might never get the chance at all.

His insides churned. The thought of that saucy green-eyed girl scared and helpless and at the mercy of those bastards made him sick with rage. And they had Miz Lassiter too. He felt something start to scald inside him, felt desperation heat to boiling fury.

With a bloodcurdling yell, he spurred Peaches forward and rode like hell for the pass.

Shortly after the Campbell gang and their prisoners reached the towering gray mountain called Skull Rock, a small army of men began digging frantically half a mile away at the blocked-up entrance to an ancient cave.

"Weaver, you sure this was the one?"

Quinn, his hands tearing, straining at the massive boulder atop piles of other massive boulders, flung a glance over his shoulder at the thick, sweating face of Seth Weaver.

"Not a doubt in my mind. Edna and I were newly married, honeymooners. I was working at the shooting gallery in those days." Seth Weaver brushed a sleeve across his dripping brow and squinted at the barricade of rocks, the jutting gray boulders that hid what used to be the mouth of a cave. "We came here on a picnic, but it started to rain. We sought shelter in the cave."

Quinn and Jim Tyler hauled at the boulder, moved it one precious inch. All around them other men strained at the rocks that clogged the opening. Lucky got a handhold on a sharp-edged rock and rolled it sideways, causing others to shift. Men grabbed, pulled, hefted. They worked in frantic, furious unison and in silence, those men of Hope. Determination shone upon their faces.

"When the rockslide started, we tried to get out but we were trapped. Thought we'd die in there. No way out through the entrance, but the cave went on—and on. Nothing to do but follow it. Sure enough, it was a tunnel. Led us out on the underside of Skull Rock. That opening was covered with brush, but Edna and I, we hacked our way through."

"How many years ago was this?" Quinn's hands were slippery with sweat as he pulled at the rock with all his might. It gave another few inches and a small slide of stones suddenly rolled down from above, nearly striking Jim Tyler, but the rancher jumped aside in time.

"Thirty years ago come September."

John Hicks, pale as death, one eye blackened from Ned Campbell's fist, kicked in frustration at the rock Lucky had been trying to shift.

"Thirty years." His voice was raw. "And how do we know the other side hasn't been blocked off in all this time? Coulda been a rockslide on *that* end—we may not be able to get out beneath Skull Rock from here at all!"

"Easy, John." Jim Tyler stared up at the pile of boulders and rocks that still wedged the cave opening tight as a drum. "If we have to dig our way out the other side, we'll do that too."

Quinn blocked out their voices and set his mind and his strength to dismantling the barrier before him. In his mind's eye, all he could see was Maura.

Dancing with him in the cabin, her auburn hair flying softly in her face. Chatting with him this morning about names for the baby, glancing at him sideways in the wagon, her skin glowing in the sunlight.

Sewing curtains for the cabin, sweeping it, planting that garden of hers. Working in her quiet way, smiling with the corners of her mouth lifting, her eyes warm and golden and alive.

All he wanted at that moment was to ride away from Skull Rock with her and bring her safely home.

Home.

When had the cabin become home? Somehow, it had. It was more than a collection of logs and odd furniture, a shelter from wind and rain. It was the place where he and Maura had shared meals, worked side by side, made love. It was the place where their child would be born and grow up. A place where they could be together, safe and happy . . .

Happy? Since when had he ever been happy?

Since Maura walked into that saloon in Whisper Valley and commandeered his life, that's when. Since the first time he'd noticed the gentleness of her touch—the kindness of her smile. Perhaps since the moment she'd set their first simple meal on the table of the cabin on Sage Creek and worried herself over Lucky Johnson.

He wanted to take her home, dance with her, love her, spend the rest of his life with her.

And raise their child with her.

He thought of all the days and nights he'd wasted, yearning for freedom, for what lay beyond the next rise, the next valley, the next sunrise. When all he wanted or needed had been right under the cabin's sloping roof all along.

When he thought of her up there on Skull Rock with Luke, Ned, and Lee, he couldn't bear it. So he thought instead of what he would do to get her free. To bring her home. To hold her safe in his arms again.

He pictured Luke, Ned, and Lee Campbell as he tore at the rocks. And knew that no matter what else happened, the Campbells had touched her, hurt her, scared her, and they weren't getting out of the canyon alive.

Minutes ticked by and the men of Hope worked side by side, quietly, fiercely, frantically.

Quinn Lassiter, who had never asked anyone for anything, who had never lent himself to being part of any team, or worked any way but alone, struggled and sweated and swore right alongside them.

And every second that he did, with each rock lifted, rolled, pushed, or hauled aside, he did something else that he was not known to do.

He prayed.

Chapter 33

WITH LUMINOUS SPLENDOR, THE SUN WAS SINKING behind Skull Rock. Plumes of pale pink and violet blazed across the sky like delicate muted ribbons laced with gold.

The Campbells made their camp on a tiny gray ledge at the mountain's peak. A half-dozen trees and some scrub brush dotted the bleak clearing. A solitary snake slithered over the rough ground and disappeared behind a rock, but there was no other sign of life.

Beyond the lip of the ledge, the long, shallow canyon glowed purple in the dying sunlight.

There was a campfire, and it was several feet beyond the flames that Maura and Nell huddled together, as far as they could get from where the Campbells were dishing out beans and jerky from a rusted pot.

From where they sat, they could see the rim of the ledge and the vast canyon stretching out for miles in every direction—as well as every trail winding through it.

The trails were all empty.

No sign of a rider, of any human movement. Just a pair of rabbits skittering here, an elk poised there on a high rock in solitary majesty before darting into thick brush. A grizzly showed itself once on a trail high along a red crevice, then it lumbered away down a winding path that led away from Skull Rock.

It was so quiet, Maura could hear her own breath catching in her throat. Nell's muted whimpers mingled softly with the wind sighing through the tall rocks.

"Nell. Nell, listen to me." It was hard to turn, with her hands tied behind her back, as were Nell's, but Maura shifted her body so that she could look into the other girl's pale, terrified face. "It's going to be all right."

She spoke in a whisper, praying the outlaws wouldn't hear. The last thing she wanted to do was draw their attention.

Glancing over her shoulder, she saw that they were still shoveling down their beans and jerky. Ned drank thirstily from a flask, then handed it to Luke, while Lee scraped the last of the beans from the pan onto his metal plate.

"How can you say that it's going to be all right?" Nell gasped. "We're going to die up here. Or worse."

A shudder shook the girl's shoulders and made her lips twitch. "The whole time we were riding here, that animal kept telling me what he was going to do to me once Quinn Lassiter was taken care of."

"Well, he's not going to get the chance. Quinn will take care of *him*—or we will!"

Maura prayed she sounded more confident than she felt. The helplessness of her position, her hunger, thirst, and weakness were gnawing away at the vestiges of hope she'd been clinging to all through the ordeal. As the day ebbed and there was no sign of Quinn, her spirits sank along with the glowing sun.

"We must try to stay calm and think clearly no matter what happens," she whispered to Nell. "If we get any kind of a chance, we'll have to act on it quickly."

"Chance? What kind of a chance will we get?"

"Feel around the ground and try to find a stone. I did. I'm scraping it against this damn rope. If we could get free—"

"They'll catch us," Nell gasped, looking too terrified even to think about escaping. "They'll kill us like they killed my father—"

"You don't know that they killed your father. I didn't hear any gunshots before we left, did you?"

Dazedly, Nell shook her head. Maura saw a thin light of hope struggle within her eyes.

"Quinn is going to appear at the canyon's edge any moment now and I'm *not* going to sit here and let them pick him off." Maura was speaking so softly, Nell had to lean sideways to hear her, but her words were forceful nevertheless.

"I'm going to get free."

She bit her lip as the stone scraped her flesh once more, as it had a dozen times since she'd begun working at the rope. Resolutely she continued chafing it back and forth. She thought the bonds were beginning to fray, that the rope was giving slightly as she struggled against it. But it wasn't weakened enough yet . . .

The flicker of hope grew stronger in Nell's eyes. She swallowed hard and squared her shoulders, and Maura saw her body shift as the girl began exploring the earth behind her in search of a stone. "I'd like to at least hurt Lee and Ned Campbell and hurt them bad before they . . . they . . ." She broke off. "Found one."

For several moments they worked in silence, concentrating on the thick bonds cutting into their flesh, driving the sharp edge of the stones again and again across the rope.

Maura kept scanning the canyon, searching out every trail, every nook and cranny.

Still no sign of Quinn.

The Campbells finished their meal, licked their fingers, drank coffee. Luke Campbell tossed the dregs of his cup onto the ground and stood up. To Maura's dismay, he turned and looked at her, then started forward across the ledge.

" 'Pears your husband's a yellow-bellied coward, ma'am. If you were *my* woman, a sweet, pretty little thing like you, I'd come after you no matter what the odds, honey lamb.''

"Quinn is going to kill you," Maura said quietly, meeting his gaze. She hoped he couldn't hear the wild thudding of her heart. "You must know that. If you're smart, you'll head out of here now and leave us be. That might be the only way you keep on living."

"You talk too much." He reached down, grabbed her arm and yanked her up so roughly, Maura yelped. The stone dropped from her aching fingers and she heard it tumble to the ground. She also felt the little derringer Serena had given her bump against her thigh as Luke pulled her close. She held her breath and prayed he couldn't feel the gun against him. To distract him, she kept on talking.

"I mean it. If you go now, you just might have a chance—"

"Maybe that's why Lassiter doesn't care if we rape

you and kill you. 'Cuz you talk his damned ear off." He spun her around, dragged her to the very edge of Skull Rock, so close that her toes brushed the empty air at the rim.

"You see him? Anywhere?" His laughter rang cruelly in her ears, even as his fingers dug into her flesh. "He don't care what the hell we do to you, lady. Or he's too chicken to try to stop us."

"Don't hurt her." Nell spoke up in a breathless little voice. She was trying to struggle to her knees despite her bound hands. "She's carrying a child!"

"Yeah—Lassiter's child," the outlaw snarled. "Well, we'll just see about that."

Icy terror bubbled in Maura's throat as she scanned the silent, empty canyon with its ridges and sagebrush, its bowed trees and stark rocks. She turned her head slowly, blearily, and stared into Campbell's eyes.

"What . . . did my husband do to you that you hate him so?" she managed to ask between dry lips. If she could keep him talking, it would give them time.

Time? For what? Quinn wasn't even in view at the farthest edge of the canyon. He could never get here before the sun went down. She'd lost the stone, the bonds were still clamped in place, and the hopelessness of the situation descended upon her even as the shadows drifted down over the canyon in shades of lavender and amethyst.

"He turned me in to the law, that's what he did! No one ever tracked me down before—or had the guts to try to bring me in. I killed some people, you see." Luke smiled then, a cold, pale smile that made him look like a straw-haired devil. "A homesteading family that took me in one night during a storm. They had money, gold, some silver. Guess I didn't have to kill 'em, but I had some liquor in me and got carried away. Spent five years in prison for it. Five years! You know what that's like, Mrs. Lassiter? Any idea what that does to a man?''

"N-no. But now that you're out, I'd think you'd want to stick to the straight and narrow and not risk—''

"I escaped, lady!'' he barked. "Killed me two guards doing it. Every lawman in the country is gunning for me now. You know how much the bounty is? Five hundred dollars. Someone's gonna grab me, somewhere. But I made myself a promise. Before they do, I'm gonna make Lassiter pay. Yessir, because he did this to me.''

"You did it to yourself.'' Maura could keep quiet no longer. Her chin lifted and revulsion shone from her eyes. "You deserve everything that's happened to you. And worse. You deserve to hang!''

"Shut up, you damned back-talking bitch!''

Eyes narrowed, he struck her and sent her spinning to the ground.

"Maura!'' Nell gaped at her in horror. "Are you all right?''

But before Maura could even clear her head, Luke Campbell reached down and dragged her back to her feet.

"It's time for me to have a little taste of Lassiter's woman,'' he said with a sneer. "Boys, help yourself to the other one while we have ourselves a little fun. Guess Lassiter didn't have the guts to join the party.''

He lugged her away from the precipice and closer to the campfire. Bracing a hand to each side of her head, Luke dragged her close and clamped his wet, greedy mouth over hers.

Maura reacted on sheer instinct. She brought her knee

up with a lunge and kicked him with all her might. He grunted and fell back, pain half closing his startled eyes.

Ned and Lee sprang forward, yelling, but suddenly a hail of bullets sprayed the dirt at their feet and they froze.

So did Maura.

Behind her, Nell screamed.

Quinn stood at the rear of the clearing. He seemed to have emerged from within the sheer rock that rose at the back of the ledge. Both of his big Colts were drawn and at the ready—one each leveled at Ned and Lee.

"Maura, get over by Nell!" he commanded. The icy deadliness of his tone sent a shock wave through her.

She moved to obey, but Luke moved faster.

He grabbed her, pain still suffusing his face. Before she could try to tear away he had her before him as a shield.

"Drop your gun, Lassiter, or she dies right now!"

Through a haze of fear, Maura felt the six-shooter pressed against her head.

She met Quinn's eyes, saw the fear flash across them. Never before had she seen him look afraid. Of anything.

He's afraid for you. Afraid of losing you.

She twisted at her bonds, and felt them giving way. She worked them frantically, sliding her wrists back and forth, painfully, again and again. The knot was loosening, she could feel it.

Quinn's low voice resounded across the clearing.

"Let her go, Luke. If you harm one hair on her head, you'll suffer in ways you never dreamed of in your worst nightmares."

"I'm gonna harm more than the hair on her head," Luke shouted.

At that moment, the rope gave way. Maura's hands flew up, free, and she shoved against Luke with all her might. Caught off guard, he tumbled sideways toward the campfire and stumbled over it, barely missing being snagged by the flames.

"Get down, Maura!" Quinn yelled, and then Luke aimed the six-shooter at him. But Quinn was already diving forward. He fired from the ground and Luke Campbell went down screaming.

At the same moment Lee and Ned both sprinted for cover behind the trees. Guns at the ready, they took aim at Quinn, but before they could fire, two more shots rang out.

Lucky Johnson, crouched by the wall of rock at the rear of the ledge, fired and fired again. And then so did Maura. Even as Lucky felled Lee Campbell with two clean shots, she aimed Serena's derringer at Ned and squeezed the trigger.

She hit him in the shoulder. Grunting, he spun around and, with an oath, leveled his gun at her.

He died before his finger could pull the trigger. Quinn killed him with a bullet between the eyes.

Then everything happened at once. Suddenly the ledge swarmed with men. *Where had they all come from?* Maura wondered, blinking in confusion. *How had they crossed the canyon unseen?*

Through the commotion, she saw that Luke was still alive, writhing on the ground. But he was surrounded now and no longer a danger to anyone. Dazedly she turned and saw Lucky kneeling down beside Nell, reaching for the rope that bound her. The girl's dark head drooped forward against his shoulder as he worked to set her free and Maura saw her chest heaving with sobs.

Then all she saw was Quinn.

He sprinted toward her, his face the same ashen gray as the rocks.

"Did they hurt you?"

Never had she heard that hoarse, desperate note in his voice before, never had she seen such naked fear in his eyes.

"No. No, Quinn, I'm fine." He drew her into his arms with a gentleness that stole her breath and she felt shock, terror, and confusion sliding away. His arms were tight around her.

Safe. She was safe.

"Quinn." She clung to him, reveling in his solid strength, the warmth and energy that flowed from him as he locked her in his arms.

"How did you cross . . . the canyon?" she whispered. "There was no sign of you—of anyone . . ."

"Seth Weaver knew a back way in. We came through a cave that led us right out to the rear of Skull Rock. Climbed up a few ledges, trying like hell not to make any noise, and we were here. Nearly too late," he added grimly, holding her closer, burying his hands in the riotous softness of her hair.

"I was so afraid."

"I'm sorry." He cupped her chin. "I wish I could have spared you that."

"I was afraid for *you*. They would have killed you the moment you came close enough. I thought there was no way out—"

"Shh, Maura, don't," he said as she trembled like a

feather in his arms. She threw her arms around him and buried her face in his shoulder.

"The baby." He held her tight, rocked her, and wondered how he had ever lived before she came into his life. "Are you sure you're all right?"

"I think so. I'm tougher than I look, and the baby is too. After all, he or she is half *yours*."

"I've been thinking," he said slowly, stroking her hair, finding blessed peace just in the feel of her pressed against him. "About names. For the baby."

"You have? Since when did you have time to think about that?"

"While we were digging out the opening in the cave. What do you think of Maureen, if it's a girl? Named after you."

"Well, *I* was thinking of Kate—Katharine, after your mother."

Through the gloom of impending dusk, he smiled. "Kate," he repeated. "Kate. Katharine Maureen Lassiter."

"And if it's a boy?" Maura began to prompt, fascinated and amazed that he was thinking about the baby at a time like this, but finding a marvelous peace in it, for she'd much rather snuggle in his arms and think of baby names than have to face this bloodied ledge littered with bodies.

"If it's a boy," Quinn began, and his big hand stroked tenderly down her dirt-streaked cheek, "I was thinking of—"

"Quinn!" John Hicks's voice interrupted.

Maura started out of Quinn's arms. "Oh, Mr. Hicks—thank God they didn't kill you!" she exclaimed.

"No, ma'am, but Luke Campbell's about to croak. He's a goner," he told Quinn with satisfaction as Quinn glanced over at the fallen outlaw.

"Wait here," Quinn told Maura, and stalked over to where several men stood over Luke Campbell, who lay in an ever widening pool of blood.

Shadows now shrouded the rocks and the last rays of light had vanished. Cool, mysterious darkness cloaked Skull Rock, but the outline of grim-faced men and the stench of gunpowder and death remained.

Maura turned away from it all. She walked wearily toward Nell, then stopped short. Nell was nestled within the circle of Lucky's arms.

They glanced up and saw her, and she smiled through the thin gray darkness.

"Are you all right, Nell?" she asked softly.

"I am now." Despite her pallor, Nell's young face shone like a delicate moon. A glow of pure happiness radiated from her eyes.

"Lucky gave me a note for you today. I never had a chance to deliver it."

"I delivered the message in person," Lucky said. "At least part of it. There's more." He gazed down at Nell, who lifted her face to his, and she seemed to melt even closer against him. "Much more," he vowed in a low, intense tone.

Maura tactfully retreated as Nell stretched up to touch her lips to those of the young cowhand.

Turning back, she saw Quinn standing over Luke, and even through the deepening darkness she could discern the chilling, ruthless expression in his eyes. She wanted to go to him, draw him away, bring back the loving man she had only begun to discover. But she held back.

He had something to finish first.

"Damn you . . . Lassiter," the outlaw gasped. His voice was no longer boastful and loud, it was weak, yet still filled with hatred. "How'd you . . . get up here? You son of a bitch . . ."

"Save your breath for your last prayers, Campbell. That's more than your cousins had time to do. More than you deserve."

"Prayers . . . you're the one who oughta . . ."

"You're the one who's dying. And going straight to hell."

"I'll see you there . . . one day."

"Maybe. Maybe not." Quinn glanced toward Maura, watching him with silent understanding and love in her eyes. Maybe that beautiful woman carrying their beautiful child would be his redemption. And his salvation.

He glanced back down as a shudder shook the outlaw's chest and writhed through his entire body. Luke opened his mouth, but no words came out. He blinked rapidly and then another spasm gripped him. His eyes widened, then stayed open, staring emptily up at the purple sky.

Quinn felt the icy whiff of death brush his flesh.

Hicks knelt down beside the still figure of the outlaw. "He's gone."

Quinn looked around the ledge. Death. Blood. Darkness. Shadows and ghosts.

He turned back toward the pale, lovely woman with the tumbling auburn curls, the woman who carried his child, the woman who held his heart in her eyes.

She was everything he wanted. Everything he needed. Love, peace, hope, life.

Most of all, life.

Men swarmed around Skull Rock, but he walked to Maura in silence and drew her into his arms. She felt right there. It was, after all, where she belonged.

He spoke quietly against the silk of her hair. "Let's go home."

Chapter 34

 IN THE END, IT WAS LUCKY AND SLIM WHO brought her home. Quinn found himself obliged to help deal with the carnage on Skull Rock and to assist in getting poor Seth Weaver back to town and into the care of Doc Perkins. While going through the cave, Seth had suffered a fall, and it seemed likely that his leg was broken. He'd been helped out of the cave safely, but it wasn't until the women were safe that anyone remembered him, waiting alone on the ledge among the rocks and boulders that had been so hastily removed. While John Hicks and Jim Tyler rigged a litter for him, Quinn helped Maura mount the banker's horse.

"Weaver really came through for me—for us," Quinn told her. "I owe it to him to get him back to town and see that Doc Perkins fixes him up right."

"It looks like the whole town came through for us." Maura glanced gratefully around at the men who'd aided in the rescue. "I don't even want to think about what would have happened if not for that hidden way through the canyon."

Quinn nodded, the tight muscles in his neck relaxing

somewhat as he remembered how all the men of Hope had pitched in together as a team. "I reckon it's not always a bad thing to have friends and neighbors," he said gruffly. Then he rounded on Lucky and ordered him to get Maura home safe and sound.

After pumping water for a quick bath and changing into a clean, soft ivory nightgown, Maura set yesterday's soup on to boil, and placed biscuits left over from the morning into the oven to warm. It wasn't much of a supper, but it would tide them over until breakfast. She knew Quinn must be hungry, and though she wasn't, she did feel weak and figured it would be good for the baby if she had something to eat.

She didn't want to think about the fact that she had shot a man tonight. That man had been on the verge of shooting her husband. She'd done what any woman would have done, what any human being would have done to save someone they loved, just as Quinn had been forced to kill tonight to protect her.

The shock of the violence was still with her, but the cozy confines of her home were comforting, and she wrapped herself in that, forcing herself to think not of the cruelty and killing and bloodshed that had taken place, but of the expression on Quinn's face when he'd come to her and taken her into his arms.

Did he love her?

She thought she'd seen love in his eyes. But perhaps it was only relief. After all, it wasn't as if he didn't feel fond of her. *Fond.* What a weak little word, she thought on a sigh. Then she remembered how he'd looked when he'd begun speaking of names for the baby . . .

The sound came to her as she was setting out bowls

and plates and a dish of butter on the table. A soft *whoosh* was all she heard, all she had time to hear, before she felt a hand snap over her mouth, another swoop around her body and pin her arms to her side.

The shriek gurgled helplessly in her throat.

A silken, clever voice came from behind her. "If you scream and bring those ranch hands running, I'll have to kill them. Is that what you want?"

Helplessly, her heart thundering, she shook her head.

The Campbells were all dead on Skull Rock—who was this man holding her so ruthlessly, frightening the wits out of her?

His voice didn't sound familiar. She wracked her brain trying to think who would attack her here—and wondering just what he wanted.

Then just as suddenly as he had grabbed her, he let her go. He gave her a shove that sent her reeling toward the hot stove, but she caught herself in time and spun around to confront him.

A slim, good-looking man in a fine black suit and well-cut brocade vest stood before her, the lamplight illuminating his smooth-shaven smiling face, neatly combed dark hair, and beautiful white teeth.

She'd never seen him before in her life.

"Who are you?" she managed to choke out. "What do you want?"

"There isn't much time to spare, Mrs. Lassiter, but I suppose some introductions are in order," he said thoughtfully. "I'm Roy Ellers. And *you* are the lady I've been searching for over a quite lengthy period of time."

Maura could only stare at him, as fear swept through her.

"I can't say that the chase hasn't been enjoyable—especially with all its incumbent risks—but the time, alas, has come for it to end." He tilted his head and smiled at her.

"You've been searching for me?" Maura hated the tremor in her voice and fought to steady it. "Wh-why? I don't know you—we've never met. What could you possibly want with me?"

"Prevarication is useless, Mrs. Lassiter. You already know the answer to that question." His glittering blue eyes were fixed on her face, scorching her with their intensity. "I want the diamonds."

"D-diamonds?" Maura's eyes widened. Now she knew he was crazy. "You think I have diamonds?"

He made an impatient gesture and she saw the flash of violence in his eyes, then, just as quickly, she saw him clamp down upon it.

"I'm a patient man, Mrs. Lassiter, but my patience has run out. First I had to track those brothers of yours as *they* tried to find you. Then I had to wait for an opportunity to get you alone, when your formidable husband wasn't around to guard you—or hadn't set one of those tedious ranch hands to do it. And finally, after the Duncan brothers came here to the cabin in my stead and took the box from you, I thought my mission had come to an end. But, alas"—he shook his head regretfully—"I met with disappointment."

Horror swept through her. "Do you mean . . . the *jewel* box? You killed Judd and Homer for the *jewel* box?" she exclaimed, her knees going limp. She clutched at the countertop for support as the soup simmered on the stove beside her.

"Not for the box. For the *diamonds*. But they weren't there. Before your brothers died, they told me that you must have removed them already. They'd found that the false bottom which hid the secret compartment in the box had been ripped—and the diamonds were missing. At that moment, I don't believe they were lying to me," Ellers said with a smile. Then he gave a neat little shrug.

"Not that killing them wasn't a welcome diversion," he added. "I would have killed them anyway, if they'd turned the diamonds over to me or not—because they had no business stealing them in the first place. They took what was mine, and they had to die. No one crosses Roy Ellers and lives," he said softly. "Only ask Justine. She was the first to die."

"I don't understand," Maura managed between dry lips.

She wondered how much longer she had until Quinn came back. She'd thought she was safe, that they were both safe, but now this madman had come out of nowhere with his talk of diamonds. A madman who had killed Judd and Homer, who looked as if he was just waiting for the right moment to kill her. She didn't at all like the small muscle that was twitching in his jaw, and the fact that for all his calm talk, his eyes held an eerie, unsettling sheen.

He wore a gun in his holster, but hadn't drawn it. She thought of the rifle in the corner. What had she done with Serena's derringer? Vaguely, she remembered dropping it on Skull Rock. What had become of it?

"What does all this have to do with me?" she asked, hoping to stall for time. "I knew nothing about the diamonds until you told me about them. I don't see how they came to be in the jewel box.''

His smile became dreamy, indulgent. ''It all began in Hatchett, dear lady. The night of the poker tournament. It was January, and it was snowing. It snowed for days.''

''I remember.''

Good Lord, the night Quinn had come to the hotel. The night they'd made their baby.

''The luck was running against me that night. I folded early and was eliminated from the tournament. And then I came upon Justine, my mistress, upstairs in one of the saloon's sumptuous bedrooms. She was with another man,'' he murmured, his eyes shining like hot little blue flames. ''She was naked—completely naked—in his bed. The only thing she wore was the diamond necklace which *I* had given to her.''

The muscle in his jaw began to twitch even faster. Maura held her breath.

''I didn't let on that I'd seen them, of course. I slipped out as quietly as I had slipped in. And waited for the right opportunity.''

Maura waited, too, waited for him to continue his terrible tale. And all the while her brain whirled frantically. A false bottom in the enamel box. Diamonds—and death. Death had been stalking her ever since she'd left the Duncan Hotel and inadvertently taken the diamonds with her.

''There was a gunfight in the street a short time later. I'm obliged to your husband for initiating it. But when he killed that one-eyed man—I was there in the shadows. Because Justine had come downstairs just before and wandered outside. I followed her. I saw my opportunity the moment I realized that Quinn Lassiter and Black Jack Gannon were about to fire at one another in the street. Guns are not my weapon of choice,'' he explained with a smile, "but in this case, it was too perfect to resist. I shot Justine from the shadows at the same moment that the other men fired. No doubt your husband thought that either his bullet or Gannon's struck her.''

He chuckled and the madness shone clearly in his eyes. Little pinpricks of light leapt and danced in them.

"Lassiter went to her straightaway,'' he mused. "Bent down, stood up, walked away. She still wore the necklace when he left her—I could see it glittering in the snow. But then I heard the law coming down the street barely before the echo of the gunfire had died away, and I knew I had to clear out of there. I figured I could reclaim the necklace later. Everyone knew she was my woman—and that diamond trinket had cost me a fortune. I had every right to take it back and no one would have questioned me.''

Ellers took a step closer and Maura felt her skin prickle. Terror kept her frozen, her eyes glued in horror to his face.

"But someone got to her before the law did. Sometime after Lassiter went to her, and before the law got there and took over, someone came and lifted the necklace from her throat. It took me weeks of asking questions and checking on everyone's whereabouts before I found someone who could tell me what happened—some sniveling weaselly drunk who'd been vomiting his guts in the alley and had seen the gunfight and had seen two men steal the necklace from a dead woman lying in the street. He didn't know their names''—Ellers sighed—''but he thought he'd heard earlier that they were brothers. So I had to find out who they were and where they were from. It took me some time. But I did it."

His face tightened suddenly with rage. "Only to get to Knotsville and find out that the fools had cut the diamonds from the necklace, put them in a damned box, and lost them!" he snarled.

"I don't have them." Maura fought waves of ice-cold panic as he riveted those terrifying glassy eyes upon her. "I didn't know about the diamonds when I took the box—it was a keepsake, that's all. It held some b-buttons. I never saw any diamonds."

"When it comes to diamonds," the gambler said softly, "people lie. No one likes to give up diamonds. Your brothers didn't want to. But by the time I finished with them, they would have told me anything. They didn't have them. So you must. And you'll tell me too by the time I'm done."

His hand flashed down and Maura for one heart-stopping moment thought he was going for his gun. But it was a knife that glittered in his hand.

"Tell me where the diamonds are," he said quite pleasantly, and then lunged at her.

Maura jumped aside, her scream rising high into the rafters of the cabin. There was no time to think, only to react, and she did the only thing she could do—she grabbed the soup pot and hurled the simmering contents in his face.

She ran for the door, his howl filling her ears. When she yanked the door open, it was her turn to shriek again. A man blocked the doorway, and only in the next paralyzing instant did she realize that it was Quinn.

Then everything happened in a blur. Quinn drew his gun and fired over her shoulder. An instant later the knife thwacked into the frame of the door, vibrating against the wood with a low, murderous hum only a scant five inches from Maura's head.

"What the *hell?*" Quinn yanked her outside even as she instinctively peered back over her shoulder. All she had time to see was Ellers thudding against the floor before Quinn pushed her away from the door of the cabin.

"Wait here."

She clung to the wall, trembling, knowing she couldn't have moved if she'd wanted to. It seemed an eternity as all of Ellers's words tumbled again through her head, but actually it was only a matter of seconds before Quinn returned. He pulled her against him and wrapped strong arms around her shuddering body.

"He's dead. Whoever the hell he is," he muttered grimly. With a sigh, he studied her. "Are you hurt?"

"N-no. But he killed Judd and Homer. And that woman in Hatchett." She saw his gaze sharpen, his glance flick toward the cabin and back. "It wasn't you, Quinn. It wasn't your fault. He shot her. He's after diamonds from her necklace. But I don't have them—I never saw them, I swear—"

"Maura. Shhh. Take it easy." He ran a soothing hand down her back, and then cupped her chin between his fingers. He didn't understand what the hell she was talking about, but he saw she was on the verge of hysteria or collapse.

"It's all right, sweetheart." Gently, he brushed a kiss across her forehead.

Maura felt her tension ease the moment his lips

touched her skin. A huge shudder escaped her and she dug her fingers into the reassuring solidness of his shoulders. In the darkness he looked so tall, so calm and wonderfully reassuring, that her breathing began to slow and the thickness in her throat eased.

But then her eyes clouded over again. "Oh, Quinn, I threw the *soup*." A sob racked her. "It was your d-dinner. After all you did today, I knew you'd be s-starving and I threw it in his f-face!"

"Smart going, Mrs. Lassiter." He stroked a hand along her cheek. "I wasn't hungry anyway."

"You're just saying that to make me feel better!"

"Well, yes, I figure that's my job as your husband," he conceded slowly. He was gazing so deeply into her eyes that Maura's heart did several somersaults and her brain went completely blank for a moment.

"And then there's the d-diamonds," she gurgled when she recovered and panic over a new topic raced through her. "I swear I don't know anything about them—I never saw—"

"Shhh. Do you think I give a damn about the diamonds? About anything, except the fact that you're safe?"

His words penetrated the mire of panic into which she'd fallen. She drew in a deep, slow breath and searched his face.

Tenderness and concern lit his normally cool gray eyes. His powerful arms held her so close, she could feel the pounding of his heart as it beat in steady rhythm with hers.

Somewhere in the back of her mind she knew that

there was a dead man in her kitchen, but it didn't matter anymore now than a speck on the moon.

"You and the baby. You're all that matter to me," Quinn told her hoarsely.

"*You're* all that matters to me—to *us,*" she heard herself whispering before she could stop the raw, honest words.

"I don't know why the hell it took me this long to realize something so plain." Quinn touched her hair, slid his fingers through the wild curls with a gentleness that made Maura shiver. "Or maybe I did realize it," he went on roughly, "but just couldn't admit it—even to myself. But when I almost lost you today, when the Campbells had you up on Skull Rock—" The words broke from him fiercely. "I love you, Maura Jane Lassiter. I love you more than anything, more than life itself."

"More than . . . freedom?" she asked in a voice that shook. She dreaded the answer at the same time that she needed it. "More than the open sky . . . the open road?"

"I'm going to spend the rest of my life showing you just how much more," he said.

"And if someone offers you . . . a gunfighting job?" Maura held her breath. "What will you say?"

"Not interested." He traced her lips with a gentle finger. "There's no place else on earth I'd rather be than right here with you," he vowed before his mouth swept down on hers with a fierce, commanding possessiveness that swept every doubt from her soul.

Joy and incredulity surged through Maura. *Love. Quinn's love.*

The one thing she'd thought she'd never have.

"Say it again," she breathed. "Oh, please, Quinn, say it again."

"I love you, Maura. I'll always love you. And if you think you're ever getting rid of me, forget it. Our business agreement is canceled. Like it or not, you're stuck with me on Sage Creek for good."

With a cry of happiness, she threw her arms tight around his neck.

"I'm going to hold you to that, Quinn Lassiter," she promised. Joy rose like a bird in her heart, flying, flying. "For the rest of our lives."

Chapter 35

IT WAS ONLY OCTOBER, BUT THE WYOMING AIR held a hint of snow the day that Maura Lassiter gave birth to her first child. It was a crisp, gorgeous morning and the land surrounding Sage Creek Ranch was aflame with autumn's colors. Birds warbled outside the window when Maura first sank in realization upon her bed, and by the time Quinn was sent for—and Doc Perkins was fetched from Hope—the sun was glinting off the creek, sailing toward a cool, glorious afternoon.

After that, word spread quickly, and by the time Maura's pains became more and more intense, and beads of sweat poured down her pallid face, the cabin was abuzz with friends and neighbors stopping in, offering help, and just plain curious to see the legendary gunfighter Quinn Lassiter pacing the floors in a state of thunderous panic.

"Here. Drink this." Jim Tyler, who had ridden over from his north pasture, pushed a glass of whiskey into Quinn's hand. He watched with amusement as the renowned gunfighter downed it in one gulp and then rubbed his hands blearily over his face.

A muffled scream from behind the closed door of the bedroom had Quinn spinning toward the sound. He started forward, but Jim and Lucky Johnson each grabbed an arm and held him back.

"Don't go in there no matter what happens," Jim warned. "Women are *not* in a mood to be civil to their menfolk at a time like this. Trust me on this."

Quinn felt sweat sheening his face, beading on his neck beneath his plaid woolen work shirt. "Well, what the hell am I supposed to do?"

"Finish working on that there porch you started. It's almost finished, isn't it?" Jim glanced over toward the doorway, where a long, graceful porch extended from one end of the cabin to the other, with three wide steps leading down to the yard. Only the railing had yet to be completed—it ran halfway across.

"The hammering will drown out Maura's screams. By the time you're done, the whole thing will be over."

Over. Quinn reached for one more glass of whiskey. "I can't wait for it to be over," he muttered thickly, and the other men in the room all chuckled.

He saw nothing funny about it. Maura was in there, in pain—in a hell of a lot of pain, from what he could tell—and there wasn't a damned thing he could do about it. He was responsible for what she was going through, and he couldn't even help her, much less put an end to it.

Helplessness made his head pound. He hadn't felt so out of control since he was a boy and . . .

But he blocked those thoughts, those memories of his mother's suffering. That had been man-made, man-inflicted suffering—for cruel reasons—and it had ended in death. He reminded himself that what Maura was experiencing now was natural and life-giving, and would end in a beautiful new life.

A child. A wondrous child born of his flesh, his blood—and hers. A child who would share this home and this ranch and this wide, glorious land with them and who would make their happiness complete.

He couldn't wait to see him—or her—and to see Maura, to know she was all right.

"How much longer?" He blocked Serena Walsh's path as she hurried toward the bedroom with an armload of clean linen.

"Doc Perkins thinks it could be within the next hour or two. He says—"

She broke off at the stunned expression on his ashen face. "Now, now, Quinn, take it easy," she soothed, though her eyes were bright with amusement. "I've seen you face down cold-blooded killers with a smile, and here you are ready to drop at my feet. You do love her to pieces, Quinn, don't you?" she said softly.

"She's everything to me," he said simply.

Serena read the emotion in the eyes of this man who had seen so much of life's roughness, violence, and ugliness, who for all the time she had known him had shut himself off from feelings, from involvement with any other human being, and survived it. And she marveled that someone who had been so scarred, who had wrapped himself in such a hard and impenetrable shell, could feel so much and so deeply.

A tinge of envy crept over her. Maybe one day, if she was lucky, she too would find what Quinn had. She swallowed past the lump in her throat and nodded at him. "She'll be fine."

"Is that what the doc says?"

A shadow of worry flickered over her face and she replied, trying to sound casual: "The doc is a bit concerned about her being so small and narrow-hipped, of course, but he says she ought to do just fine. She's strong, you know. And she has a will of iron. She tamed you, didn't she?"

"I've got to see her." Desperately he headed for the bedroom, and not one of the people gathered in the cabin dared stand in his way.

Maura cried out, squeezing her eyes shut in agony as pain ripped through her.

"Almost over, honey, you just keep on going," Edna Weaver said briskly, placing a cool cloth on the girl's sweating brow.

Doc Perkins, at the foot of the bed, turned as the door burst open. "Mr. Lassiter," he began, "this is not a very good idea—"

But the gunfighter had already reached his wife's bedside. Maura looked tiny and vulnerable as a child in the big oak bed he'd had shipped all the way from St. Louis. He touched her cheek, and she winced.

"Quinn—are you all right? You look terrible . . . ahhh . . ."

"Maura!" Good Lord. Quinn's chest was so tight, he was sure it would explode. As Maura's scream echoed through the sunny bedroom where golden light poured in between puffs of airy white curtains, icy sweat broke out on his brow.

"Isn't there something you can do for her?" he demanded of the doctor, and at that moment, pudgy little Doc Perkins didn't know who appeared in worse condition—his patient or her gray-faced husband, who looked as if someone was tearing up *his* insides.

But before he could reply, Edna Weaver tapped the gunfighter smartly on the shoulder. "Yes, sir, there is."

Briskly, Edna took Quinn by the arm and began steering him toward the door. "You can leave her be."

Alice Tyler spoke from the bureau, where she was calmly laying out towels beside a pot of steaming water. "Maura doesn't want to have to worry about you at a time like this, Quinn," she put in gently. "And if you faint dead away, which I don't mind telling you is what Jim did with our firstborn, you're going to be more in the way than helpful."

"True enough." Edna yanked open the door. "Let the poor girl attend to her own business. Run along and get drunk like Seth did when our three children were born. Go on now."

"Her business? What do you mean 'her business'? It's my business too!" he argued frantically, but as he glanced back over his shoulder at the pain contorting Maura's face, his courage crumpled.

"I n-need to work on the porch," he said between clenched teeth.

Serena, who had followed him in, gave him a push through the door. "Good idea, Quinn, honey. You work on the porch."

"I love you, Maura," he flung over his shoulder, but she was already squeezing her eyes shut yet again and bracing herself for another scream, and he fled before it could pierce his ears and his heart.

He heard it, however, as the door banged closed behind him.

Quinn rushed to find his hammer.

Maura sank back against the pillows, barely hearing the soothing words of Alice Tyler or the bracing ones of both Serena and Edna. She readied herself for the next volley of pain, and reminded herself that this torture would all be worthwhile when she held her baby in her arms. That moment would be a miracle, and she awaited it eagerly, clinging to her goal with all that she had left of strength and of hope.

But she was vaguely aware, even as she drew each ragged breath, that there was another miracle taking place right in this room besides the birth of her child. The bond of friendship that had drawn these three women—Serena, Edna, and Alice—to her side throughout all this, that was a miracle too.

So much had happened since those terrible spring days when violence had touched all the citizens of Hope. Hope itself had flourished—with the threat from the Campbells gone, the town was growing bigger, bolder, and more prosperous than ever. Several new families, including relatives or friends of those already residing there, had come to settle, and new businesses had been added by the month. There was actually a new mill now, and a bakery and a freight company. There was a shooting gallery, as well—and Serena had opened a tearoom in the parlor of her boardinghouse.

But not only the town had flourished.

The Hope Sewing Circle was more lively and industrious than ever. After Edna and Alice learned that Serena had given Maura her derringer, they had reconsidered their opinion of her and decided to invite her to join the circle.

"I know it's because of what you said to them at the May Day dance," Serena told Maura afterward. She had driven out to the ranch to return the jewel box Ellers had given her. The federal marshal had finally arrived to take charge, and had informed her that the box had been stolen from Maura Lassiter.

"I heard you speak up for me with those prissies. And I appreciate it. You're what I call a true lady," she drawled. "Quinn—"

She'd broken off, then squared her shoulders. "Quinn is a damn lucky man. And don't you think he doesn't know it."

"So are you going to join?" Maura had wanted to know. "I do hope you will," she'd added, and meant it.

"Maybe I will and maybe I won't." Serena had hunched a taffeta-gowned shoulder. "But if they think I'm going to give up smoking cigars in my parlor with my gentlemen boarders, they've got another think coming!"

As it happened, she had joined the circle and she hadn't given up cigars. But no one censured her for it— the other women even seemed impressed with Serena's outrageousness. She often said and did things they could only imagine doing. At any rate, they followed Maura's lead and accepted her for what she was—a hardworking woman who had made her own way in a challenging world—and a fine seamstress to boot.

In the days right before her time came, Maura had worked feverishly on baby clothes and blankets, and Quinn had not only carved a handsome cradle but had begun building the porch she'd dreamed of the very first time she saw the cabin. There was no end to his energy, even as hers had seemed to wilt a bit each day.

But mostly they'd laughed and talked and planned and made love. An aura of happiness shone through the cabin that had once seemed so plain and barren. Now every nook and cranny seemed to glow with the love of the family living within its sturdy walls.

A sudden pain more intense than any of the others tore through her and Maura gave a stifled shriek. Doc Perkins turned to the women gathered in the room.

"I believe it's nearly time," he announced.

It better be, Maura thought. "I'm not sure how much more of this . . . I can stand," she gasped aloud.

Alice took her taut, shaking hand and clasped it in her own. "It will all be over soon. And you'll have a beautiful baby to show for it."

A beautiful baby. A beautiful baby. Maura held the thought close as she writhed and gasped and endured.

Soon she would be holding Quinn's baby.

"Well, look at that," she heard Serena say from the window. "That Nell Hicks waltzed in earlier and said she wanted to help. I set her to serving pie and coffee to everyone out there waiting. And where is she? Spooning by the creekbank with Lucky Johnson!"

Even in the midst of her agony, Maura gave out a weak laugh. "Love is more important than coffee, Serena," she gasped.

Edna placed another cool cloth upon her head and grimaced. "Maybe. But it's sure not more important than pie."

* * *

"You let me go right this very minute."

Nell found it quite difficult to pull her lips away from Lucky's hot and confusing kisses, but she did so at last, and pushed hard against his chest. "I'm going back inside to see if I can help."

"Seems to me Miz Lassiter has to have that baby all by her lonesome and all those folks are just in the way," he retorted, grinning as he pinioned her wrists and yanked her even closer against him. "You and me—we're being more helpful just staying out of the way."

"But I promised I'd serve coffee and Mrs. Weaver's blueberry pie. So you just stop making cow's eyes at me, Lucky Johnson, and let me go right now!"

"I reckon I'll think about it." Then his mouth closed over hers again, and his hands began roving over her back and downward to cup her bottom.

"Don't think about it . . . um . . . um . . . do it . . ." Nell insisted, but her tone was soft and breathless, and her hands were wound in his thick, sunlit hair.

"Do what?"

Lucky deepened the kiss and heat lightning seemed to blaze red-hot through both of them. When at last he lifted his head, Nell's green eyes were dazed and unfocused, her cheeks flushed seashell pink.

"Do what, did you say?" Lucky murmured, tilting her head up so that she gazed directly into his warm, gleaming eyes.

"L-let me go . . ." It was an unconvincing whisper, made all the more unconvincing when her arms locked tightly around his neck. "You really must . . . let me go . . ."

"That's what you want?" He began nibbling at the

corners of her mouth, grinning as he felt the delicate shudder run through her.

"Ummmm. I reckon I'll . . . think about it," Nell murmured, and pulled his head down for just one more of those deep, intoxicating, Lucky Johnson specialty kisses.

Lucky was only too glad to oblige. For the past few months, since that bloody night on Skull Rock, he hadn't been able to think about anything else except how much fun it was kissing Nell.

"After we're married, you're not going to ever tell me again what to do," he said, pulling her down with him on the crisp autumn grass and brushing a stray lock of dusky hair from her eyes.

"After we're . . . what?"

"You heard me. Married."

"Who says I'm going to marry you, Lucky Johnson? I never gave you the slightest reason to believe that I . . . ummmm . . ."

Her voice trailed off as he pushed her down into a patch of fading wildflowers and covered her body with his, and they lost themselves to dizzying sensation after sensation.

"Well, come to think of it," Nell whispered eventually, gazing up into his eyes, which were now just as glazed as hers had become, "I reckon I'll think on that too."

Maura twisted and writhed soundlessly in a world of pain, dazzling sunlight, blurred figures, and dim voices. Through it all she clung to an image in her mind of Quinn holding their baby. She held tight to the image through every torturous second and finally with one shuddering, bone-wrenching *push* it was over—and she heard Doc Perkins's soft triumphant snort—and Edna's voice trumpet merrily through the room.

"It's a girl, Maura Lassiter! And a right fine little beauty she is, too!"

Small cries filled the room as the baby let loose its indignation at being plucked from its warm dark cocoon and thrust into a strange, bright new world. Alice hurried to draw the curtains as the doctor tended to cutting the string.

"Please, let me hold her." Maura reached out her arms, scarcely able to contain her excitement. She couldn't tear her eyes off the tiny child as Alice wrapped the infant in a fluffy yellow blanket.

When the precious bundle was laid against her breast, Maura thought her heart would burst.

"Oh, my darling," she murmured over and over against a fluff of jet-black hair. "My precious, beautiful darling." Then she glanced up, her eyes alight. "Will someone please tell my husband that his daughter would like to meet him?"

At that moment, the door opened a crack and a crimson-cheeked Nell slipped in. "I just wanted to see how . . . oh! The baby! You had the baby!" the girl squealed.

Edna pursed her lips. "If you want to do something useful, find us some ribbon before that young lady's father comes in here. Land sakes, that baby has more hair than most one-year-olds. Won't Quinn get a kick out of seeing her with ribbons in her hair and her only a minute old?"

"Oh, yes, quickly," Maura exclaimed with delight as

she cuddled the baby closer. So tiny. But with such big, wondering eyes—and little curling fingers. "Look over there in the sewing basket, Nell," Maura directed as she tucked the warm little bundle against her, examining tiny fingers and tiny toes with careful eyes. "There should be some pink ribbon in there somewhere . . ."

"I don't seem to see any," Nell fretted, riffling through scraps of fabric, yarn, knitting needles, thread, and sharp-edged sewing scissors. "Are you sure—"

"Oh, just bring it here," Serena ordered impatiently, loath to leave the bedside for even a moment. Like the other women, she couldn't seem to tear her gaze from the beautiful black-haired baby who was staring at the world through marveling eyes.

Nell set the basket near the foot of the bed and turned it upside down, dumping the contents out. "Here's a scrap of gray ribbon, but surely there must be some pink, or white even . . . why, what's this?"

She held up a rough, dirty brown pouch, not much bigger than her thumb.

"What *is* that?" Maura studied the pouch in surprise. "I've never seen that before."

Nell tossed it aside. "Well, it isn't a pink ribbon, that's for sure . . . ohhh!"

As she'd grabbed at the basket again, the pouch had tumbled off the bed and onto the floor with a thud and then a clattering sound. Both Nell and Maura glanced down as six tiny glittering stones tumbled out and rolled across the bedroom floor.

Only they weren't stones, Maura saw, as her eyes widened in shock. They were diamonds.

Nell bent and began gathering them up. "Diamonds," she gasped. "Six of them."

There was silence in the room.

"I put the jewel box in the sewing basket when I was working on my dress for the dance," Maura said slowly as the baby began to nuzzle hungrily at her breast. "The false bottom must have caught on the scissors or the needles or something and somehow the pouch fell out." Suddenly she remembered how she'd danced with Quinn—and tripped over the basket. Perhaps then . . .

"I never saw the pouch," she murmured. "It must have gotten mixed in with the fabric and the thread—"

"It doesn't matter now," Edna said. "Except you'll be able to make yourself a real pretty bauble, or order some mighty fancy store-bought baby clothes for this little lady, or buy her the biggest, prettiest pony in the world—if you've a mind to."

Maura didn't want diamonds that had belonged to a dead woman. Diamonds that had led to Judd's and Homer's murders—and nearly her own.

She shuddered and peered down at her daughter, feeling peace steal over her again. "Will someone bring Quinn in here please?" she asked softly as Nell dropped the diamonds back into the pouch and set it on the bureau.

Doc Perkins started toward the door, but at that moment it burst open.

"There you are." Maura smiled mistily from the bed. "Just the man we've been waiting to see."

Quinn was pale in the dim light. His silver eyes swung from Maura to the baby at her breast, and for a moment he didn't move or speak.

"You're both . . . all right?"

"Couldn't be better. Come meet your daughter." Pride and love filled her smile as her husband approached with slow, almost reverent steps.

"Ahem, I think we'll leave the proud parents alone," Doc Perkins said, clearing his throat. The women all swept out behind him and closed the door.

Quinn's legs felt rubbery, but he gripped the edge of the bed as he kissed Maura's sweat-glistened brow, and then gazed down at his daughter's soft, puckered cheek.

Awe filled him. And a joy more potent than a dozen bottles of red-eye whiskey.

"She's beautiful," he said hoarsely. "*You're* beautiful."

"You must be drunk." Maura's soft laughter was like silk against his wire-taut nerves.

"Drunk? Like hell. I've been working on that porch while you've been lollygagging around here." Grinning, Quinn knelt beside the bed. He stroked one finger along her cheek, then gently touched the baby's cheek.

"The railing's finished now. Whenever you're ready, Mrs. Lassiter—and you too, Miss Lassiter—you can sit out on your porch in a rocker together and look at the stars."

"That sounds wonderful." She smiled into his eyes. "If you're there to enjoy it with us."

"Just try to keep me away."

Touched that he'd remembered her long-ago wish, amazed at how far they'd come, how much had changed, Maura could only gaze with wonder into his eyes. She was holding her baby daughter, watching joy soften and warm the face of the man she loved, surrounded by friends and neighbors in her own cozy, precious home.

It was all she had ever wished for.

"I know what we should name her," Quinn said suddenly, and reached out to touch the rose-shaped cameo at Maura's throat. "Rose. Rose Katharine Lassiter. How does that sound?"

"It sounds perfect," Maura whispered as Quinn leaned in close and kissed her.

In that moment, with his lips warm and sure and strong upon her own, Maura knew she had everything that could ever matter to her in the world.

There would be time later to tell him about the diamonds, time to decide what to do with them, time to get on with the normal business of life. For now, she wanted only to savor this perfect kiss, this perfect man, this perfect moment, so she could hold them in her heart—forever.

Epilogue

THE TOWN OF HOPE THRIVED DURING THE FOL-
lowing years and Sage Creek Ranch prospered
right along with it. Eventually nearly a thousand head of cattle bore the Sage Creek brand, dotting the
lush grazing land that bordered both sides of the creek.

Maura Lassiter sold the stolen diamonds and donated
the proceeds to the town of Hope's community fund,
which used the money to help erect a library directly
across the street from Serena Walsh's boardinghouse. Serena Walsh and Edna Weaver—co-chairwomen of the
building committee—christened the building together on
the Fourth of July.

One year later, Lucky Johnson became one of the
West's youngest but most dedicated sheriffs, and he married Nell Hicks on a brilliant June morning with the
whole town in attendance.

Nearly two-year-old Rose Katharine Lassiter was their
flower girl and toddled giggling down the aisle of the
church tossing rose petals all about her.

Maura, who'd just the day before received a letter from
Emma Garrettson with the news that she was expecting

another child, had watched her husband Quinn's face beaming with pride at their daughter's performance. She waited until that evening to tell him that they, too, would be welcoming another child into their lives by the time the winter snows came to the little cabin on Sage Creek.

But the little cabin wasn't so little anymore. Quinn had added on steadily and now the original structure was only the centerpiece of a long, rambling log house with a big kitchen, a dining room that boasted a red and gold Turkey carpet, two parlors, three bedrooms overlooking the creek—and even a sewing room for Maura.

And, of course, the porch. On soft summer evenings, it was not unusual for the ranch hands to come now and then to stand at the doorway of the bunkhouse and peer through the starlight at the two figures on the porch often found dancing to music only they could hear. Maura and Quinn paid no heed. They were lost in each other, in the life they had built—two strangers who had come together, who had found love, nourished joy, discovered hopes and dreams they could only fulfill together.

And that is what they did. Together day after day, night after night, year after year, they celebrated their home, their love, their land, their children.

And a day never went by that Quinn Lassiter didn't say a prayer of thanks for having learned the truth at last— that love was not a prison, a fence, an ending . . . it was a wondrous beginning. It brought healing, joy, and a boundless vista of dreams for the future.

Love—and Maura—had set him free.